THE ONE

Brian Porzak

Copy & Concepts, Ltd.

Published in the United States by Copy & Concepts, Ltd.

Library of Congress Registration Number TXu 227 299

Porzak, Brian, 1943–

THE ONE

I. Title

ISBN 0-937 98300-4

Cover Design by Geoffrey Stevens

Manufactured in the United States of America

Copy & Concepts, Ltd.
22 Grove Street
New York, New York 10014

Limited First Edition

Limited First Edition Hologram by American Bank Note
Translation of Ogam on hologram base: "Hidden place"

The author gratefully acknowledges Marta Weigle's BROTHERS OF LIGHT, BROTHERS OF BLOOD (University of New Mexico Press 1976) for background information on the true Penitente, Edward F. Anderson's PEYOTE—THE DIVINE CACTUS (University of Arizona Press 1980) for background information on peyote ceremonies and Marc Simmons's WITCHCRAFT IN THE SOUTHWEST (University of Nebraska Press 1980) for information on Indian religious beliefs.

Perdona Tu Pueblo, Señor, old Spanish hymn.

TO

My ONE and only

With special thanks to Tom De Poto, Geoffrey Stevens, Suze Chelsea, Mary Schultz Wood, Dr. Herbert Holt and you, the reader.

A cocoon can seem a prison,
If you don't know what it's for.
But, sometimes, you don't know . . .
You just don't know.

The Karmic Butterfly

Prologue

Black, raven-like eyes watched the dark tempest that was enveloping most of Eastern Europe. A blood spot above the left pupil—there since birth—seemed to gain in intensity from the electric night, pulsing with every lightning bolt. The man known simply as THE ONE was pleased with the chaos shattering the tumultuous sky. It signalled his greatest triumph was at hand.

Exactly 666 miles west of THE ONE's stone tower overlooking the Romanian River Olt, a hologram shattered into a thousand pieces.

A fierce gust of wind had slammed the loosened window shutter against the abbey's outside wall. The suddenness startled Father Vittorio, and the glass plate slipped from his grasp.

It had been an interesting piece; a reflection hologram, in which the light of an ordinary bulb turned the seemingly blank glass into a three-dimensional image. This particular hologram had been of a dove and a raven, perched on opposite ends of a rod. The fulcrum was off-center, as if to give the supposedly lighter dove a fighting chance at maintaining equilibrium. Off in the distance, however, there were vague shapes of other birds approaching . . . or was one a plane? Allies? Of the raven or the dove?

When the light hit the glass at the correct angle, the heads of the principal birds seemed to project from the surface . . . and one could swear the rod was teetering one way or the other, just by shifting the point of view. The piece was called Balance.

Having never before held a hologram, Father Vittorio had been sitting mesmerized for nearly half an hour, moving it back and forth in the light. He had, in fact, become oblivious to the storm.

With the abrupt crash, the aging cleric felt his heart pounding and was both surprised and embarrassed by his jumpiness. He brushed his thick, graying eyebrows with the back of his hand and bent down to pick up a shard. A moment ago, it had held the image of a raven. Yet now . . . and to him this was the incredible thing about holograms . . . each of the hundreds of pieces before him held the complete image that had existed in the unbroken plate.

The phenomenon returned him to the trance he had been enjoying and Vittorio's mind struggled for focus within a collage of thoughts; the relationship of each person to the whole of humanity, the relationship of good and evil within himself . . .

The thought sequence broke as he noticed a thin, red stream of blood running over the piece of glass. The sharp edge had cut a finger on his right hand.

"*Accidenti!*" he cursed under his breath.

The priest dropped the fragment and, with his left hand, reached under his white cassock for a kerchief.

His mind had returned to the surface, and the reality of the raucous night.

The flapping of the curtains, coupled with the penetrating

draft, took Vittorio to the window. He gazed over the rainswept Alban hills. Flashes of lightning illuminated the darkness over Rome, bringing dimension to the inky sky. It was a beautifully powerful sight, swells of gray clouds cascading over the crested horizon in the intermittent brightness. The contrast flickered the memory of the hologram's image.

A wind sweeping out of the western valley filled his nostrils, forcing the prelate to take a deep, calming breath. There was a scent of spring's freshness in the air. It took Vittorio back to the morning's ceremonies at St. Peter's. Palm Sunday had always been one of his favorite celebrations since his youth in Florence. Each year he had gone with his family to the Duomo, the city's cathedral, to participate in this special feast. Young Vittorio had, especially, loved the sound made when the entire congregation waved palm branches. He imagined himself transported to a tropical paradise where palm trees grew like fields of wheat.

Another flash, and the following darkness seemed even blacker. The wind moaned funereally and Vittorio felt a sense of foreboding.

It didn't take a "sensitive" to note the underlying scent fighting spring's sweetness. Like the whirling wind, the odor of decay had been welling up for many months now. Winter's cold had not smothered its fume. Instead, it had seemed to make it thrive. The essence he had detected was not, however, of rotting leaves or fallen fruit. It was the stench of Evil.

Like the gathering storm clouds, the forces of darkness had been amassing since at least last autumn. Yet no fury had been unleashed. It had begun to frustrate Vittorio. Nothing was happening. Nothing he knew of. And it was the white-robed Capuchin monk's job to know all.

Father Vittorio was the Guardian of The Light, a small, clandestine group, consisting primarily of cardinals and bishops who had banded together after World War II, as other such groups had seen fit to do from time to time throughout the ages, to cleanse the Church of "infection." As Guardian, Vittorio was the one charged with uncovering and rooting out any cancerous growths infesting The Bride of the Lamb . . . as he referred to The Church . . . By any means necessary.

Having no official sanction and being woefully financed with monies "borrowed" from various Church funds, it was, at best, a difficult task. But that's why the gaunt, thoughtful man had been selected.

As a "sensitive," one with the unexplained ability to perceive . . . a psychic, the secular world would mistakenly term him . . . it was felt Vittorio could work without a lot of sophisticated, i.e., expensive, equipment and the need for possibly turncoat intelligence sources.

Vittorio, himself, wasn't sure where the boundary between "sensitivity" and a high level of intuition existed . . . or perhaps he was just a good guesser . . . but he liked the challenge of the assignment. If people thought he had some special gift, so be it.

Oh, yes . . . It was also felt a sensitive would be the least corruptible . . . "If they only knew . . ."

But the founders had chosen a conscientious man. And Vittorio, in turn, tried to choose his people well. The "employees" of The Light were a motley crew consisting of priests, monks, brothers, a few nuns and some lay people . . . mostly male.

It had not been easy for Vittorio to learn to deal with women, although they were now of increasing importance to the organization. It was not so much chauvinism on his part, however, as it was latent lust. This sensitive was, bottom line, vulnerable and it was all too easy. . .

There was another streak of lightning followed by a thunderclap. It sounded like a cannon report. The priest's mind wandered back to wondering when the looming battle with Evil's forces would take place? Where? With whom . . . ? Who would be Evil's representative this time?

The Guardian unwrapped his finger from his bloodstained kerchief. The bleeding had stopped. He turned from the window and went back to sweep up the remains of the hologram. As he did so, Vittorio recalled bits of a thought that had started to crystallize before. What was it?

Eight time zones west of Rome, an Indian woman sat on a windswept plateau in northern New Mexico. Cloaked in a Navajo blanket of Wide Ruin design, she seemed in a waking trance as she stared in Vittorio's direction. The grayness of the ebbing storm clouding the eastern sky before her belied the fact it was nearly midday.

The woman was of indeterminate age. "Ancient" would apply . . . and yet the light in her clear, amber eyes bespoke youth.

She was known as The Bruja, The Witch, by both Indians and Spanish Americans throughout the area; this, because of her supposed powers in the art of healing and "other matters."

Like her fellow sensitive in Rome, she, too, had smelled the scent of Evil in the air. But, unlike Father Vittorio, she believed in her special abilities and knew when the battle with Evil would be fought . . . where . . . and with whom.

The Bruja closed her eyes as she tried to recapture the muddied fragments of the vision she had had at twilight . . . the image of a man divided in half, and the riddle concerning him —"the one who is not the one, yet may be the one." She attempted to understand whether he was to be the enemy's envoy or an ally. But the answer eluded her.

She was certain, however, his arrival was imminent . . . and it would herald the beginning of the deadly conflict. For the battleground between Good and Evil was to be here. And the enemy had a bloodstained eye.

1

DOMINGO DE RAMOS

"You're a phony, a goddamn schizoid phony . . . "

Ian Stone was dumbfounded. What the hell had brought this on; the love of his life standing there, shouting at him . . . her blue eyes radiating anger?

"You don't remember what you say or do from one day to the next. I never know how you're going to act. One day, you're gentle, the next . . ."

Dressed only in a red bathrobe, Meredith Carey was shaking, not as a result of the shower she had just left, but with the fear of resolution.

"I don't want . . . ," she sniffed and tossed her still wet, blond mane, unmasking a facial bruise for a brief instant. ". . . I don't think we should see . . . I don't want to see you anymore."

Ian felt the thud of a heavy door shutting. This couldn't be happening. Not now. Not after he had finally given in to loving her. And why? What was the reason?

"I don't understand . . ."

"Of course you don't," she snapped. "That's why it won't work."

"But why? What did I do?"

Her crystal blues iced over, "You've made me despise you."

Ian was seared . . . seared right through to his agnostic soul.

"But I love you . . ." came whispering forth like a dying breath.

It might have been uttered to the void. Meredith had already turned and bolted. In a flash, she was gone.

* * *

Suddenly, there was a roll of drums and Ian Stone squirmed in the reclined seat. His normally hazel, but now bloodshot, eyes opened and he realized he had been dozing again. The westbound TWA flight was still cruising along at 36,000 feet over a dome of dark clouds toward Albuquerque, but the music from his headset didn't sound the same.

As he tried to clear the stale taste from his mouth, Ian remembered the piece had started in triumph, trumpets heralding an adventure. But soon the pace had slowed. A mournful flute, sad strains of violins had resonated through the earphones, lulling him to sleep.

More sadness is what Ian had wanted to avoid.

Now, however, timpani swells caused the awakening passenger to tremble and tug nervously at a lock of his dark, wavy hair, with the vague awareness he had again relived the terrifying last scene with Meredith.

Ian's semi-conscious perception was, in fact, correct. What had been Berlioz' "Don Juan" was now Wagner's "The Flying Dutchman."

Ian swallowed to clear the phlegm from his throat, and simultaneously the music elevated once more. Perhaps there would be triumph after all.

In all his 36 years, the man's taste in music had never before been classical. At least, not that he could remember. But since his breakup with Meredith, "things were changing."

Of course nothing had really changed. Ian Stone was simply back in fantasy again. The only difference appeared in his doing what he had always done best . . . *ex*changing one fantasy for another.

But this time it hadn't been so easy. For the past four weeks reality had struck some pretty hard blows.

Once again there was a swirl of violins and Ian felt himself plummeting into a musical vortex. He closed his eyes and was swept along. Lost in sound.

Giving in to the music allowed Ian to give in to some deeper feelings as well. Meredith had, of course, been right. He was a phony. There was a reason why he always focused on the future, was nervous in the present . . . never talked about the past. Ian Stone had none. At least none he could remember.

As far as he could recall, he was "born" in a Saigon army hospital 16 years ago. The memory flashed through his mind like dank air from an attic opened after many years.

He had awakened from his coma a war hero, but couldn't remember what he had done. They said he had escaped from a Cambodian prison camp. The wounded man didn't dispute the fact, just went along with the program. He wanted out and figured, if he told them he couldn't remember anything, they'd keep him there.

When they sent him home, he learned his mother had died of grief, thinking him dead. But he couldn't grieve because he couldn't remember her. There was no other family he could find; there were no pieces to pick up. So after futile attempts to recapture any prior memories, Ian just made everything up, changing identities like some people change their socks. For awhile it was all based on what he thought people wanted to hear. Later, he just said nothing.

It never bothered Ian when acquaintances . . . come to think of it, until Meredith he had no one he would call a friend . . . referred to him as "The Enigma Shrouded in a Myth." He had always parried questions about parents, siblings and places with the greatest of ease. Ian was master of the non-answer.

His "birth" drifted out as quickly as it had drifted in, for he had another in his recent series of self-realization flashes; it dawned on Ian why his relationships before Meredith had been such whirlwind affairs. As long as he kept moving . . . never stopped . . . he could always keep the focus ahead.

Ian knew that was why a lot of women were attracted to him in the first place. Life with him could be fantastic. Most would admit to that. But he never before understood why no one could sustain his pace. Sooner or later, they wanted off the merry-go-round. It was as if they got vertigo or something. He would even chide them for being too chained to realism, not free enough to achieve his level of romance. When he'd really get bitter about it, he'd accuse them of not being able to face up to a single orgasm, much less his constant one.

The truth was, neither could he. After all, up until a few days ago what was he, when not playing Casanova? A marketing consultant to a score of Fortune's 500. Some romance.

Something was out of balance. Had always been. He.

Ian now wondered whether his women had all been practical enough to recognize his avoidance. Maybe he had even chosen them to compensate for his impulsiveness.

With this realization, a feeling of having come to terms . . . having made peace . . . swept over him. But as usual, this new self-honesty was becoming exhausting. Ian had to come up for air. Next fantasy, please!

There must have been some romantic strings playing now, although Ian was no longer conscious of sound. Thoughts of HER swept over his mind and once again it was, as it had been for almost every waking minute of the last four weeks, "Meredith Time."

Ian re-remembered being attracted to Meredith from the very beginning . . . the lilting poetry of her walk, the way she tossed her blond hair, the impish gleam in her azure eyes. Meredith was not at all conventional, yet she certainly seemed more mature than her 27 years. She didn't play the games Ian felt most women played.

Nor did she allow him to play them, either.

So this time, Ian had held off. Instead of the usual week, it had taken six months for him to fall in love with her. That is, "absolutely" in love.

It *had* been different from his other relationships. He was sure of it. Ian felt he had actually seen glimpses of the real Meredith through what he had come to understand from her as being "the veil of your own projections." He even allowed her to be herself, didn't he? What more could a woman want? Who had a more positive relationship?

So, why did she leave?

It was the same question over and over again for the past month. But still no answer. Just the ultimate reality. She, who Ian thought he had known . . . the one he had, finally, found to stand beside him . . . the one woman, supposedly, as much a romantic as he . . . Gone.

The doors to the past were still closed. There was that familiar feeling of the present being too unbearable. And as Ian had come to believe these past weeks, there wasn't any future either. He was back where he had been since the beginning of this ordeal . . . at a standstill. It was the first such experience since he had lain in that Saigon hospital, waiting for his knees to mend.

And with the month-long standstill had come all sorts of regressions. Ian felt he had shrunk from his normal 5′10″ to 5′6″ as he lumbered around stoop-shouldered, holding his left hand to his chest. It didn't matter whether he was in public or in private; the jilted lover felt there was a gaping wound in his heart, and he didn't want anyone to see the blood. It embarrassed him.

When the equinox came and went, Ian's depression had progressed to the point where he didn't think there would be a spring for him this year. April would be a cruel month. It, he had decided, would be the month of his death.

Suicide had been on his mind almost as much as Meredith the past few weeks. It didn't just have to do with her. As Ian saw it, everything had gone against him. He had tried out various identities and none of them had worked for him. He wasn't satisfied with anything. He couldn't satisfy anyone.

He had even lost the reservations for the trip to Aspen he

and Meredith were supposed to have taken together. No good explanation. Like Meredith, they, too, were just gone.

It might have seemed trivial to someone else, but to Ian it was the last round. He no longer felt any control of his life; felt he never had any. He was aimless. A loser. Life was worthless. It needed an end. So . . . suicide.

But it was just another flirtation. The resolution to self-destruct wasn't quite there yet. There were no real guts behind the decision. Commitment was still being flooded out by self-pity. No wonder, then, the materialization of this opening at Taos Ski Valley had changed Ian's focus so quickly. It was a glimmer of hope his luck could change . . . had changed.

Ian had heard of the St. Bernard Lodge. The reputation was that one had to book a year in advance. But perhaps it was because this was the last week of the season and someone . . . his travel agent? . . . felt guilty about the Aspen fiasco. Anyway, why look a gift horse . . . ?

When he told his office he was leaving, it had been, "Look, we have a client emergency. You can't abandon us now."

Office emergencies. Always "emergencies," never just, "important." Ian had been amazed. They didn't understand what this was all about. It wasn't just a vacation. This was bye-bye.

"We know you've had some personal problems," Gabe, his boss, pushed, "but business is business and it's time you got back to the real world."

The "real world" . . . Who knew his real world? Not even he. It was the last straw. Ian quit right then. *That* commitment had been forced upon him.

As the headphone music turned to Strauss, Ian regained consciousness enough to take the blanket from the empty center seat, wrap it over his Pendleton plaid shirt and snuggle into his own cushions to keep warm.

It all seemed so safe and peaceful up here above the clouds, streaking along in the 727. Ian was feeling the first bit of calm in 29 days. He closed his eyes and wondered if he would find some inner strength or actually end it all. And if he did decide on the latter, could he really do it . . . kill himself?

It really didn't matter what the answer was. Ian felt he could no longer tell how much of his thought and feeling was honest and sincere. Maybe he bullshitted himself as much as he did everyone else.

So what? He no longer had Meredith . . . So, nothing mattered.

Well, almost nothing. There was a budding fantasy that had started when the plane left New York . . . Ian Stone, Superskier.

There had been steadily increasing improvement over the past few ski seasons. Ian had, gradually, overcome the fear for his once shattered knees. Now he would go all out, even if it . . . well . . . killed him. Under the current circumstances, it didn't matter if this trip was his swan song.

The Strauss over the headphones was subdued, causing Ian to relax even more. He glanced out at the thick cloud cover below, and then felt himself sink deeper into his seat as the plane lifted to a slightly higher altitude. The rise also seemed to create a greater depth for him to fathom within his own mind. Ian drifted down, down . . . riding the violin strains, looking for reasons, trying to find where he had gone wrong this time and every time before . . . trying to work up the courage to attempt once again to delve into the parts of himself hidden away so long ago. Only then, he was sure, would he have a chance at a true identity.

"My apologies for interrupting your music, Mr. Stone, but I must talk with you."

The calm broke. The daydream shattered . . .

It was a gruff-sounding voice. And it wasn't out there . . . there, where everyone could hear it . . . but directly in his ears, over the headphones!

2

Ian's eyes flashed open as he shot forward in his seat. The nerves in his groin were buzzing as if he'd seen an open wound. Sweat beads swam across his brow. His hands oozed moisture. Then his brain triggered a breath of air and a charge of adrenaline rose as Ian fell back against his seat. What was going on?

There was another passenger who noticed, also wondered what was going on, and took immediate action. The figure moved quickly up the aisle from the rear of the plane.

"Please don't remove the earphones, Mr. Stone . . . "

There was a note of sarcasm in the pronunciation of his name, as if the speaker, too, knew he were a phony.

". . . Listen carefully to what I have to say."

Ian's mind was scrambling, trying to focus. He didn't recognize the voice. Who knew him? He wiped the beading sweat from his eyes. Was he dreaming? Was this some practical joke? Candid Camera?

The figure moving up the aisle swept past, barely taking note of Ian. It was a man dressed in khaki Sportif pants and a brown turtleneck, his head completely wrapped in bandages. The white skull pivoted right to left searching for the cause of Ian's discomfort.

There, two rows ahead of Ian and to the left of the aisle, by the window, he found the source . . . the man with the graying beard, "dictating letters."

Grabbing the headrest of the row's empty aisle seat as if for balance, the figure quickly inserted a small pin-like microphone. Without breaking stride, he kept moving toward the magazine rack near the galley.

"CIA," he thought to himself. "Clever, but overly dramatic."

"Inside your copy of the airline magazine," the voice continued in Ian's ears, "you'll find my credentials."

Ian fumbled with his tray to search the seat pocket for the magazine. He did not notice the legs of the mysterious figure as he again moved past him toward the rear.

The issue opened to the page where a plastic I.D. card had been taped. Ian wondered why he had not seen it before? Simple. He never looked.

Ian felt foolish as he stared at the card. It identified the speaker as Allen Hamel, CIA. Name, photo, security clearance . . . it looked genuine.

"I'm going to stand to get something from the overhead bin and you can verify."

Hamel stood. He was tall . . . about 6′2″. The shock of seeing him pop up so close increased Ian's pulse rate, almost causing him to forget to look at the man's face.

He had flaxen hair with streaks of gray and hard, cold eyes . . . the kind that almost get lost in the upper lid and show a lot of white underneath. He was dressed in a pale blue shirt with muted red stripes and wore a navy blue and red club tie loosened at the neck. There were sweat stains under his armpits. The face matched the photo, to be sure.

By the time Hamel sat down, another pair of ears was listening over a headset tuned to the pin mike planted next to the agent.

"Obviously, I wouldn't allow you to have something as important as my I.D. if I didn't hold something important of yours. For starters, your photo."

While Ian wondered what the hell he was driving at, the eavesdropper took note of Hamel's nervousness. He recalled now the man had taken at least three trips to the bathroom since the flight started. No doubt he was wired on coke.

Meanwhile, Ian had blurted out, "Wait a . . . ," before he realized communication was only one way. The Hispanic woman sitting in the window seat stirred in her sleep at the sound.

"We want you to be a double agent for The Company," Hamel continued. "My Control realizes this is not the usual type of assignment for an assassin of your caliber, but you have the entrée, and the information we need is vital."

The guy *was* nervous. To the listener at the rear, this sounded like a canned speech.

"Your business with the Penitente is not our concern," Hamel went on. "What we need by Friday of this week is a verification of the source and the extent of their finances.

"You'll receive your usual fee, plus a bonus, if you can furnish us with the exact location of their holdings.

"That's about it . . . If you refuse . . . well, now that we know what you look like, we'll publish your picture and an account of your prior dealings with your cult friends. I assume that would make you an embarrassment to them, as well as prey to certain interested factions.

"You *may* be under observation by your associates. You *will* be by us.

"I don't think that there is any need for dialogue now. We will establish a pipeline when it is safe.

"Please leave my I.D. in the magazine.

"It's a pleasure to deal with The One. I've admired your work."

Mozart. "Concerto Number 16." Communication was over.

What the hell was this? What was the Penitente? Double agent?! Assassin?! How could someone mistake him . . . ? Suddenly Ian felt threatened by imminent death. He couldn't swallow. He couldn't move a muscle.

Another mind clicked more analytically. The CIA knew an "Ian Stone" was on that plane and had linked him both to the assassin known as The One and the "John Paul Affair." Only two men could have given them that information, and one of them had invited him to Taos. The leak had to be in the Vatican.

Anyone who had dealt with the world's master assassin knew he worked only with principals and only on the highest-level assignments. That's why he was known as The One. They also knew a violation of confidence meant the violator's own death. Obviously the Agency had no regard for its informant, despite the fact he was a Prince of the Church. And where did they get off sending this flunky, Hamel, to threaten him? He was not to be treated this way. He accepted no authority . . . NO dictation of his work.

The thinker's hand played with the headset he had just removed. The One had correctly guessed this scenario would be fraught with players. He had been wise to set up a pawn to smoke them all out.

Meanwhile, his pawn sat, numbly, as if staring into the inner surface of his own cornea. A bell rang. It sounded like the end of a round, but it was just the twenty minute warning to fasten seat belts before landing. Ian snapped back into consciousness. The gaiety of the current piece of music was in counterpoint to his fading spirit. He removed the headphones and resolved to see Hamel; tell him there was some error . . . that he had been talking to the wrong man.

As Ian started to rise, the firm hand of a passing figure landed on his shoulder, pushing him back down as the man continued past. Was it an accident? He couldn't see who it was as his view of the figure was blocked by the stewardess moving forward in pursuit.

Ian heard her say, "You'll have to return to your seat, sir. We're starting our descent."

"Could you please get me a glass of water?" was the response. "I'm feeling a bit nauseous. I'll wait here."

As the stewardess walked forward to the galley, the man disappeared. Ian surmised he must have sat down somewhere near Hamel.

Within seconds, the pin mike was removed and another pin was inserted; this one into Hamel's hand. Hamel moved from his drugged state to death's oblivion in an instant. His wrist camera and "dictaphone" were quickly removed and the figure stood to meet the returning stewardess, "Thanks so much."

The man moved to the rear of the plane, followed by the stewardess. But Ian wasn't paying attention anymore. He barely noticed the pairs of legs.

"Fasten your seat belt, sir," the stewardess directed.

Ian looked down and, with trembling hands, tried to strap himself in.

3

A cold, light rain was falling on Albuquerque as the plane touched down. To Ian the city seemed barren; stranded on an empty plain with its few skyscrapers looking more like paper-weights trying to keep the town from blowing away.

A good wind could have blown Ian away, if his legs hadn't turned to lead when he gazed down at Hamel. With his head resting against the window, the agent looked asleep. But Ian knew better. He knew intuitively the man was dead.

The exodus of passengers pushed him on before he could confirm his suspicion. It wasn't until Ian was about to step onto the exit ramp that a woman's scream ricocheted through the cabin, telling him he was right. Ian's knees began to buckle and he would have gone down had not a strong hand . . . hadn't he felt the same firmness on his shoulder a half hour before? . . . grabbed him under his left armpit.

"Steady."

It was almost a command. Ian regained his footing and looked at his rescuer. The bandaged head was a shock to him. And, before Ian could focus his gaze at the eyeholes, the man moved on.

The encounter allowed Ian to recover his composure, and the white head provided a focal point as he followed it into the terminal.

Once inside, Ian felt like running to escape. Why, he thought? What had he done? Ian looked nervously at the other passengers and continued on at a more rapid pace, his footsteps seeming to him to echo louder than others'.

A few ground attendants ran toward the plane as Ian continued his journey to the airport lobby; and two more, carrying a stretcher, went past him as he reached it.

The terminal was fashioned after an adobe structure with beams and turquoise accents. As he rode down the escalator to the baggage claim area, Ian looked through the glass windows of the coffee shop. His stomach felt empty, yet the thought of food nauseated him.

Someone inside the restaurant was looking through the windows at the arriving passengers. Ian thought the eyes must be searching for him, but there appeared to be no recognition before he descended from sight. Ian finally allowed himself to relax.

As he stared down at the escalator's steel grooves, Ian felt the exhilaration of escape. He took a deep breath. Now that he was away from it, he could look back on the event as an adventure.

Hamel did not die of natural causes. Ian was sure no one in the CIA died of natural causes. But who? The Penitente? Maybe someone else listening to the classical music channel could have overheard Hamel. Maybe . . . A lot of maybe's; most of them ridiculous. But, that there were eyes on him in the baggage claim area, Ian was certain. Whoever did it, he felt, had to know *him* as well.

Ian put on his blue Gerry ski jacket more as a shield than anything else. As he did, his eyes darted about the area trying to pick out his observer. But no one betrayed himself.

Mercifully the baggage came quickly, the ground crew obviously oblivious to the drama overhead. The passengers, however, were buzzing with news of the tragedy.

"Heart attack," the older travelers murmured.

"Probably o.d.'d," reasoned the younger set.

Ian picked up his black ski bag and his blue duffle and carried the gear outside where a bus for Taos Ski Valley was already boarding passengers from his and other flights.

Ian was relieved to be away from the din of the terminal. A different sort of chill now went through him as he joined the file of skiers in the gusty drizzle. It felt more natural than those he'd been having over the last hour. Was it only an hour ago his euphoria had been snapped?

As Ian stowed his gear in the bus's baggage compartment, he realized he had not thought of Meredith during all that time. It was his longest streak in four weeks. A smirk crossed his face as he stepped on board. But all those eyes quickly wiped it away.

Ian moved nervously through the aisle. Toward the middle of the bus there were two empty seats. One was on an aisle next to a woman. He could tell she was attractive, despite her silvered sunglasses, knit cap and tightly zipped white Bogner jacket, its collar pulled up around her face. The other was a window seat next to a young boy, sitting across from a couple Ian assumed were his parents.

Ian took the window seat. Did he note surprise on the part of the woman?

A bear-like man with wavy gray hair, wearing a bulky green parka and black beret followed after and sat beside her. The man introduced himself in an overly loud voice and then started up a conversation at the same decibel level. This was not going to be a quiet ride.

The loudmouth commented as the man with the bandaged face stepped onto the bus and moved toward the rear, "Smart fella. Had his accident before he came."

His laugh was, thankfully, obliterated by the starting of the motor. Ian relaxed. He had escaped again.

The boy sitting next to Ian was docile, so the latter was able to turn his attention fully to the rain, without and within.

Ian remembered a drizzly day in New York the past summer. He had rented a car to take Meredith up to New England for the weekend and double-parked in front of her West Side apartment to load their gear. There was enough space for cars to get by; indeed, some had. However, as Meredith was putting a basket of food in the back seat, a cab came speeding along, the driver making no attempt at all to slow down. The vehicle hit the corner of their rear door, missing Meredith by inches; then bounced off the car parked across from them as well as the van in front of it.

Ian recalled dropping his package and vaulting over the hood of the car at the curb. He rushed to the cab, whose engine had stalled, and reached into the window, grabbing the driver by the shirt with his right hand. His left connected with the cabby's face.

It had all taken place in what seemed an instant. Without thought. The cab driver put on the gas and left him holding part of a t-shirt.

Ian knew he could act when the need arose. Why had he been so afraid today? After all, he was ready to toss in the towel anyway. Wasn't he?

Yes, he told himself. He had nothing more to lose. Next time, he promised himself, he'd react more assertively.

4

It began as a soft whine. But as the noise increased, Ian could discern it was a siren.

Suddenly, his veins ran cold. "They" were pursuing.

The bus continued cruising along at the same leisurely pace, while the sirens kept getting closer. Ian looked around. No one else seemed concerned. But why should they? They were coming for him, not them.

His mind raced over other options; a fire, emergency ahead. . . . No, no . . . they were coming for him!

Ian felt his heart pumping as he pulled himself to his feet and started walking up the aisle. Everyone seemed to be involved in conversation and no one noticed. He moved faster toward the driver.

"Get out of there. I'm taking over," he yelled.

The driver looked at him aghast. Then, Ian pulled him out of the seat with such force, the man toppled into the entrance stairwell and was knocked unconscious.

Without losing a beat, Ian got behind the wheel of the moving vehicle and gunned the motor. He looked in the side mirror and saw the revolving red lights in the distance. As he raced ahead, the pursuers no longer seemed to be gaining, but Ian continued to increase his speed.

The passengers were now aware of what was happening, but were too shocked to move. What was taking place did not seem to sink in until the bus started to shimmy.

Ian checked the side mirror again. The red lights were fading. Now, however, it was the passengers who posed a threat. Some of them started to come forward. Ian glanced at the inside rear view mirror and saw them approach. He turned toward them and yelled . . .

"Get back."

They immediately recoiled in horror. A few women began screaming. Ian didn't understand as he turned to face the road again.

There was a thud followed by more commotion. Someone had fainted. Ian raised himself in his seat to check the mirror and caught a glimpse of his own reflection. The glass reflected no face. It was a blank. He was seeing it, but there was nothing there. Nothing.

Ian screamed and started to beat on the mirror with his fist.

* * *

Ian's forehead bounced lightly, but steadily against the window. It wasn't the rhythm, but the coldness of the glass that awakened him.

Another damn dream. Another in the series of frightening dreams.

Ian shivered, then yawned and rubbed his eyes. The boy next to him was asleep, but the others around him were talking and laughing.

The bus was at a higher elevation now. The rain had turned to snow and the large flakes made it seem they were riding into a fairyland.

Off to the right, Ian could see a white-capped mountain range and felt a swell of anticipation in his breast. Just as he had blocked out his past, the memory of the afternoon's events had already been hidden away. Even the memory of the dream quickly became lost in the merriment of the passengers around him. The expectation of a fabulous week of skiing could be felt without hearing the specifics of conversation. Ian was ready to join in. He wanted to be part of the group.

As the bus rolled north past Santa Fe, there wasn't much merriment in the halls of Langley, Virginia, however. The report of Hamel's death had filtered through the ranks of the CIA headquarters, confusing nearly everyone. Hamel was supposed to be on his way to Venezuela, not New Mexico. His immediate Control, Randolph Neri, was furious . . . as much that a Sunday afternoon with his mistress was interrupted as by the news.

The only one not confused was the man who had sent Hamel on the mission. Kevin Braden was outraged. Whatever anyone else might think or whatever an autopsy might show, he knew Hamel had been murdered.

Braden's gray tie . . . he always wore gray ties and, usually, like today, a gray suit . . . was wrinkled from his squeezing it. Attempts to calm himself worked only sporadically. The twitch in his upper lip, which Braden had taken so long to overcome, was going again at record pace. He had, therefore, ordered he not be disturbed.

"The son of a bitch . . . "

He was referring, of course, to The One, and again pounded the leather pad on the top of his desk. It was not often anymore that "Ice," as he was called by some of his subordinates, displayed such an outburst . . . certainly not in the past two years anyway. Braden had worked hard to keep his temper in check. He preferred to express his ruthlessness as if there were no passion behind it. That, he felt, was more sophisticated.

It had been this reputation for cool cunning that had brought Kevin Braden to the "underground" position of Control for worldwide covert operations . . . the real power in The Company; that quality and a healthy dose of nepotism.

Up until his death a little over two years ago, Braden's father had been one of the prime movers in the Organization almost from its beginning. When The Company had been given back its balls by Congress in the latter part of the '70s, the senior Braden had instigated the move to place the real authority underground. The old man wanted to be ready in case the tide ever turned in favor of those weak sisters who, he felt, were responsible for crippling the intelligence community. Although only 40 at the time, his son had gotten the job.

As one of the dissenting members in The Company's upper echelon put it in confidence to an aide, "It's a case of sleaze over smarts; but that's the tenor of the times." The man wasn't merely speaking of the younger Braden's appearance . . . the matted birdnest of graying brown hair, the dirty gray eyes that looked more vacant than alive . . . it was more a matter of disposition, of style. Or better, the lack of it.

As a case in point, the commenting member was soon moved out, having been betrayed by his aide.

It was true Braden's weakness lay in not having enough smart people around him. But smart people intimidated him. They were too questioning. And his mode of operation was, as one of the secretaries put it, "ruling with a heavy-handed whim." Braden's immediate team was therefore composed of obedient soldiers like Hamel.

As he considered his next move, Braden's fingers unconsciously rubbed the circular amulet hanging from a neck chain under his Egyptian cotton shirt. His instinct had told him something like this might happen. That's why he had tested the water with Hamel instead of Neri. Hamel was more expendable. His cocaine habit was, in fact, becoming an embarrassment to The Company.

Braden looked at the picture of his father across his desk. How would he have handled this? He stared down at the Assassin File lying before him. "The One." He smirked at the arrogance behind the alias and opened the folder for the umpteenth time:

CODE NAME: The One
aka Joshua/Enigma/Succoth/Ursus

Now "Stone," Braden thought as he closed his eyes. Suddenly they snapped open. "J.E.S.U.S." The bastard has a sick sense of humor. Either that or he's some sort of religious fanatic.

Braden made a note to run a check on the assassinations attributed to The One in an effort to establish any "religious" pattern. Perhaps the Assassin *was* on some sort of self-styled mission. Braden was desperate for any clues to The One's character.

DESCRIPTION: Nothing accurate. Believed dark-complected.
BACKGROUND: Believed to be English speaking. Reputed to also speak Russian, French, Spanish, Italian, Farsi, German, Mandarin and Nepalese.
FIRST KNOWN ACTIVITY: Paris, 1968.
MODUS OPERANDI: Operates with extreme secrecy. Contact established through an ad in the *International Herald Tribune.* Uses elaborate maze for negotiation and payment. Will not play unless he feels principals are involved. Promises death for violation of negotiations or confidentiality. Has made good on this threat with at least two sources for this file. Specialist in "accidental" or simulated natural cause assassinations. Often sets up innocent third parties to take blame for direct hits. Offers impeccable service. Master of disguise.
COMPANY ACTIVITY: None.
EVALUATION: Best in the business, although quite temperamental and extremely expensive. To be considered for highest priority assignments only.

Braden knew the file was incorrect. The One *had* worked for The Company once in 1973 . . . Operation Songbird it was called. His father had proposed his use, but negotiations went through the senior Braden's Control. It had been a beautiful double-cross.

Operation Songbird was a tongue-in-cheek reference to the other "birds" in the family. It was felt the former President was mellowing too much in his old age and might expose some very embarrassing information in his memoirs. Certain parties wanted to avoid that at all cost.

The senior Braden used the opportunity to try to turn up some details on The One. As it was, they were unable to get even a valid fingerprint. And, as a warning not to attempt to break his cover, the Assassin set up the Control with unprovable suspicions of dastardly deeds surrounding the former President's death. Many on the inside said that's when the The Company had its legs knocked out from under it. True enough, but the senior Braden knew it would be short-lived and, with Control out of the picture, he would eventually end up on top. That's exactly what had happened. Unfortunately for the old man, however, he was short-lived, too.

His father had confided in and used the younger Braden during the whole affair, so Junior couldn't claim he wasn't aware of the Assassin's volatile behavior. The truth was, Hamel hadn't been well enough prepared. Braden pounded the arm of his chair once more. What a waste, he thought. He hadn't even gotten a photo of the Assassin in the bargain; nothing to make the "expense" worthwhile. Now he *would* have to use Neri. But it would be important The One think Neri was the Control. Braden didn't want to lose another man if he didn't have to, especially since he himself didn't understand what this was all about.

To give Neri the necessary input, he would need more intelligence. For that, it would be necessary to contact the man who had ordered this assignment, the man upon whom he had looked as a father the past two years, the man who had made his life so much easier and richer . . . , the man known as THE ONE. THE authentic ONE.

Braden knew he had delayed long enough. Soon it would be midnight in Romania.

He began to sweat nervously. As he left the walnut-paneled office for Communications, Braden was aware of the true source of his anger and frustration. This would be the first time he would have to report failure to his mentor. And he could think of nothing more distasteful than that.

Communications was, usually, fairly empty on a Sunday evening. He had hoped it would be. Braden did not want any prying eyes or unwanted ears while he set up a channel to Porumbacu de Jos.

5

Taos Ski Valley looked to Ian like an alpine oasis . . . a bit of the Tyrol transplanted in America. Unlike most U.S. ski resorts, growth seemed to have been kept to a minimum and charm had been taken to the maximum. Swiss-style chalets dotted the slopes adjacent to the ski area and a goodly percentage of the instructors and staff he had noted on the way up to the rustic St. Bernard Lodge seemed to be European.

The people didn't seem to be interested in showing off the latest winter fashion. It was obvious they had come to ski.

The mountain had the reputation of being for experts only and the seemingly vertical Al's Run, trailing underneath the main chairlift, appeared to bear this out. A sign invited the newcomers not to panic, but the mindset was established nonetheless. Ian suspected that was the way the regulars to the Valley preferred it.

The St. Bernard delighted Ian. Owned by a French family boasting a few Olympic champions, the Lodge was decorated in a very simple, but warm and cozy style. The comfort almost made Ian forget the events of the early afternoon.

The new guest was put in Number 18, an A-frame chalet adjacent to the main lodge. It was just at the foot of the slopes, and a few steps away from the spa. Large, with a loft, there was enough room for five people. Ian couldn't believe it. It was beyond anything he had expected.

The temperature was much colder here at the 9,000 foot level. The falling snow lay as a dry powder. Since the road conditions had delayed the bus, Ian had to unpack somewhat hurriedly to get ready for dinner. His haste did not, however, dampen his orderliness. It was his way of trying to cope with the episode on the plane . . . that and an unshakable trepidation, lingering in spite of his best efforts to block it.

Ian filled the oak dresser; sweaters and shirts in one drawer, underclothes in another . . . with socks and incidentals in the two smaller top drawers. Everything else was hung in the closet. Next, the items from his toilet kit were neatly arranged on the bathroom counter. As he did so, Ian noticed there was a good supply of towels. He liked that.

His new boots and skis . . . Lange Nordicas and Pre 1200s . . . were put with his poles alongside the window flanking the right side of the door. His lift pass the young man hung over the lamp next to the easy chair by the double bed.

After everything was arranged, Ian washed the upper part of his body, smiling at himself in the bathroom mirror all the while. Being there was beginning to totally absorb him. But a chill passed through him as a memory of Hamel's face swept across his mind.

Ian put on a pair of dark brown corduroys, a green woolen turtleneck and his hiking boots. Then before descending for dinner, he went out on his terrace to look at the slopes.

It was a beautiful sight. The still falling snowflakes caught the light from the Lodge and reflected it like twinkling stars as they descended to the softly illuminated landscape. So peaceful.

Ian's thoughts turned to Meredith. Why? Why wasn't she here with him?

His last vacation had been with her. It had been his best . . . the two of them in the south of France.

He could picture her surveying the Mediterranean from the terrace of the Eden Roc Club at Cap d'Antibes. In her red, one-piece maillot, Meredith had stood out even from those women who were topless. It was her first trip to Europe and her eyes were as wide and as sparkling as the sea before her. Her smile engulfed wave after wave after wave. His gamine.

As Ian entered the Lodge dining room, he felt a ripple of silence cross the room. Again, his mind flashed back to France, to the dining room at the Inn in Noves, when they had entered together. His Gigi had been transformed into a goddess. There had been one common intake of breath and no other sound as the room sat transfixed. Her simple black dress, a gold chain at her throat, her blond hair swept back; the *Auberge* had its third star.

There was a difference in this hush, however. Ian felt it and became conscious of a presence over his shoulder. He glanced back and was struck with a dizziness that seemed to spiral down into the pit of his stomach. The man with the bandaged face had entered the room behind him. It was he, not Ian and the imaginary Meredith, who had drawn the attention.

"Pardon me . . . ," and the man moved by to join a table. There was something mysterious, frightening . . . perhaps both . . . about the man. And it wasn't just the bandages. Maybe it was the voice. It sounded ominously familiar. Had he spoken to him on the plane? Yes, Ian remembered that . . . but there was something else that eluded him.

Ian stood motionless while the other man found a place against the wall on the opposite side of the room. Then he took a breath to calm himself and surveyed the dining area.

Near the center of the room was a huge, circular stone firepit with a conical copper hood that went up through the ceiling. Surrounding the fireplace were curved benches. An inviting mesquite blaze crackled within.

To Ian's left was a rough-hewn bar with an old-fashioned brass cash register and a long wine rack above it.

Ian felt he needed a drink.

The rest of the room was on two levels; the outer one near the windows only slightly raised to conform to the grade of the mountain slope. Wooden latticework separated the two sections but did not make them seem totally apart.

Both areas were filled with long rectangular tables, most seating twelve people on curved-back chairs or benches. Over each table, lantern-like chandeliers hung from the ceiling, their orange glass hurricanes providing a warm glow in which to dine.

Most of the tables were already filled with the Lodge's guests and those of the Edelweiss, which was owned by the same family and shared the dining facilities. The limited remaining space was available to outsiders. However, there was usually quite a long waiting list, for those who dined at the St. Bernard ate not just well, but fabulously well. Claude, the chef, had once been a *sous-chef* at Maxim's in Paris and brought the best of France's culinary arts to the Ski Valley.

Ian looked around for a place to sit.

"Hey, we've got an extra seat here. Sit down and join us. I can tell . . . You're from New York, right?"

It was the loudmouth from the bus, his blue eyes beaming mischievously. And, before he could protest, Ian was sitting between him and the couple with the young boy who had sat next to Ian on the bus.

Dan, Ellen and their son, Chris, were from Chicago. Ian wondered why that was normally the first thing people from the Windy City said to identify themselves, sometimes even before their names. He thought it was all right to be proud of where one came from, but, having been to Chicago often, he couldn't understand what all the fuss was about. In any case, the Cosgroves were a pleasant family, all smiley and cheerful in their Wranglers and colorful ski sweaters.

At the head of the table next to Loudmouth, whose real name, Ian learned, was Eli Weiss, sat a latin type named Antonio

Troni. He was a smooth, urbane-looking man, obviously from wealth. Troni wore a very fine chamois shirt, designer jeans and lizard skin boots. Antonio and his wife, Cecilia, who sat across from Loudmouth, were originally from Chile and now lived in Mexico.

Cecilia also looked like she was from wealth, with a strong, jutting chin and jet black hair that hung down to the silver Indian belt she wore with her turquoise skirt. A lovely shape lay beneath her salmon-colored hand knit sweater. The couple's room, Ian learned, was directly beneath his.

At the other end of the table was a man named Geoffrey Hull. He and his wife, Elizabeth, were English, but now lived in L.A.

The couple were both in their mid to upper fifties. She was a bit larger than he, at least so it appeared as they sat. Elizabeth attempted to hide her rather large chest with a white frock. Geoffrey was on the portly side, too, his girth accentuated by a knit fisherman's sweater. The Englishman had a bit of the cleric about him. Ian wondered if he might not be a minister.

Next to Elizabeth were Roger and Melissa Duquesne, a couple from Birmingham, Alabama. Roger was a burly man with baggy jeans and a red flannel shirt. He was, apparently, involved in billboard advertising because he was telling the Hulls a related story when Ian was being introduced. Roger was also very funny, his biggest fan being his wife—petite, pert and giggly in her pink jumpsuit.

Ian hoped the southerner would give Loudmouth a run for his money.

The remaining empty seat was directly across from Ian. He had just finished his introductions to the group when *she* came over to it.

"May I?"

It was a silly question, at least to the men. She looked like someone Ian had always wanted to meet; it didn't register he could have sat next to her on the bus that afternoon. Her penetrating gray eyes met his and she smiled. Yet for some strange reason Ian's initial reaction was to go on automatic defense.

"Diana Bastian," she announced to the table.

She had the trace of an accent he couldn't place. Ian exhaled forcefully, disappointed in his first response. Then, as he took in a deep breath, his maleness rose and Ian's gaze went on the offensive. Unfortunately, she had already passed on to the right side of the table.

When the introductions finally came around to him, Ian peered down the hallways behind her eyes only to find himself feeling stranded. He had penetrated to his limit, but it seemed there was still quite an enormous distance to go. And even if he were able to go farther, something told him he should beware of a trap; as open as the passage seemed, somewhere ahead was "no man's land." Diana passed on to Loudmouth and the other end of the table.

Ian remarked Diana's nose was faintly aquiline like Meredith's. Her hair was longer; auburn, not blond . . . and even more luscious, more beautiful than his former lover's. She was also a bit taller, perhaps 5′7″. Looking at her made Ian realize the incredible emptiness he had been feeling. For the last month, any welling up of spirit had fallen back with the dull rattle of a lead coin hitting bottom in a dry, dank shaft. Now, a fresh rain had broken the dankness. Life stirred.

Jean, the Lodge's owner, came over with the first course, a large crock of French onion soup. Jean looked like a Gallic leprechaun; about 5′5″ with warm, brown eyes and a cherub smile. Yet one could see that under his blue cotton turtleneck there was a taut physique.

"*Bonsoir. Soyez les bienvenus.*"

He knew the English couple; "So happy to see you again." And he meant it.

Another crock was brought to the other end of the table and Geoffrey and Cecilia did the honors, filling the bowls for their respective ends.

Everyone was hungry. That the soup was perfectly prepared made it seem heavenly.

They were next treated to a smoked salmon and watercress salad.

"No *charolitas* here," Cecilia commented.

"Excuse me?" Ian thought she had been talking to him. Besides the food . . . this being the first meal he had actually tasted in quite awhile . . . his concentration had been on Diana.

"*Charolitas* are local lenten dishes," Antonio interjected. "Not that we came here expecting such fare, to be sure. But I think my wife would feel less guilty if they serve some *panocha* for breakfast."

"That's a sweet lenten porridge," she clarified. "You see, we didn't come just for the skiing. Since this is the *desagravias* season, we were hoping to observe some of the ceremonies."

"*Desagravias*?" Diana questioned.

"I'm sorry . . . how do you say? . . . the lashing season. Today is *domingo de ramos,* the Sunday of Palms . . . the start of *semana santa,* the Holy Week. There is a religious sect around here dating back to the Middle Ages we are told. They practice ancient rites such as flagellation . . . ," she stumbled over the word, " . . . and crucifixion."

Melissa jumped into the conversation from down the table, "We went to the Millicent Rogers Museum on the way up from Taos . . . you should all really go . . . It's real neat. Anyways, they had an exhibit of this sect's meetin' room . . . What did they call it, Roger? *Mortada*? No, *morada.* And they're the Penitente, right?"

Ian swallowed down the wrong pipe.

"Some people don't like to discuss 'sects' at dinner," Loudmouth bellowed while Ian tried to recover.

The Penitente. Hamel. The meal had masked it, but now, it all came back.

The Penitente was some kind of religious group. Why would the CIA be interested in them? They weren't supposed to be involved in domestic activities, were they? So what else was new?

"You mean they still do that?" Diana queried.

"So we understand." Antonio spoke to Geoffrey at the other end of the table, "You have been here before, I take it. Have you heard about this?"

"Well, we come primarily for the skiing, you understand. This is our fourth time at the St. Bernard. We've seen the Pueblo in Taos . . . over 500 years, I believe, and still inhabited. I recommend it highly. And, of course, D.H. Lawrence's home and the galleries. But I'm not familiar with this group you mentioned. Are you, my dear?"

"I think I remember hearing something about them, though I assumed it was all in the past," said his wife.

Jean arrived with a platter of Beef Wellington.

"By Jove, I think we should all take a lash at that, however," Geoffrey concluded the discussion.

After the main course, they went on to Baked Alaska. Ian's apprehensions, for the most part, had subsided. Thoughts of Hamel and Meredith weren't forthcoming. They were overwhelmed by the food and by Diana.

Ian marveled at how well Diana parried questions about herself into getting others to talk about themselves. It had been a tactic of his for so long now, he was impressed that someone else could still show him some pointers. But why was she so evasive?

She lived "occasionally" in both London and New York and traveled extensively . . . something to do with fashion consulting. She was there to ski, but was also interested in the native culture and might accompany Antonio and Cecilia to see some of the local religious ceremonies. Ian knew where he'd like her to accompany him.

Did she feel the same? Perhaps he would invite her for a drink after dinner and find out.

They were having their coffee when Ian noticed Diana looking past him toward the entrance at the other end of the dining room. He glanced back over his shoulder and saw a young policeman talking with Carol, the Lodge manager. Diana's eyes kept darting back and forth from the table conversation to the one at the entrance. Finally, however, she focused entirely on the discussion around her.

Ian was quite off guard then, when Carol came over and tapped him on the shoulder.

"Excuse me, Mr. Stone . . . There's a police officer from Albuquerque here. He's questioning passengers who were on your plane today and would like to have a word with you after dinner."

Ian thanked her and turned back to the group. He could feel the sweat start to roll from his armpits.

"What's the matter? You didn't pay your parking ticket?" Loudmouth asked.

Ian took a deep breath and smiled, "A passenger died on my flight out here . . . heart attack, I think. For some reason they want to talk to the other passengers."

"Maybe it was the airline food," jested Eli. "I'll tell you a secret: you don't have to be Jewish to order kosher. It's not only better, it's a lot safer."

Ian laughed. It was the first time that evening . . . in quite awhile for that matter. It, not the jesting, seemed to bring a smile to Diana's face as well. Or so he thought.

Ian felt as if his insides had been awakened. He wanted to show off for this woman. He was ready to play the game, whatever it might be, with this cop or anyone else. It felt to Ian his mind was, finally, churning its way out of the lethargy in which he had wallowed this past month. There would be no more retreating. After all, the trooper hadn't stormed in. And he was willing to wait. It was probably just routine.

"I might as well find out what he wants. Are you all going over to the bar?" he asked.

"We'll save you a seat," Diana said. Ian's elation made him feel he could go through a brick wall.

As he walked to the tiny reception room by the Lodge entrance, Ian reflected on what the officer might have to link him to Hamel. The man in the bandage mask did also.

If anything, Ian thought, the tie would have to be the I.D. card. He should have taken it. But that wasn't the deal. Hamel was expected to retrieve it.

If that *was* it, however, what would be his explanation? He could plead ignorance; say he never opened his magazine. No, damn it, he had left it on the seat.

Maybe he could say *he* was an agent. But, where was *his* I.D.?

Ian's burst of spirit was starting to wane. Then another thought . . . perhaps he didn't have to admit to anything.

The young police officer stood up as Ian entered the reception area. He had a boyish face one did not want to take seriously. The young man obviously knew it and over-compensated in most every way. He was one of those wiry pain-in-the-ass types.

"Mr. Stone?"

"Yes . . . ?"

"Officer Wilcox, Albuquerque P.D."

Ian was relieved the young man wasn't a tough guy and relaxed somewhat. "What can I do for you, Officer?"

"I'm here investigatin' the death of a passenger on that flight from New York you came in on today," Wilcox stated.

"Yes, I heard about it when I was getting my baggage. Heart attack, wasn't it?" Ian asked innocently.

"We don't know for sure yet, sir, but I'm questioning some of the passengers about it. The deceased's name was Hamel. Did you know him?" the officer asked.

"No, I didn't," Ian smiled pleasantly.

"Well, I was wonderin' if you mightn't have spoken to him. Did you speak to Mr. Hamel, sir?" he persisted.

Ian swallowed, "No, I kept pretty much to myself; in fact, entirely to myself. I just listened to music mostly."

As soon as he said it, Ian knew he shouldn't have. There was probably some kind of special receiver in his earphones that Wilcox found. The officer didn't seem to be aware of the I.D.

"He didn't speak to you?" It sounded intimidating.

Ian went for broke, "No, I don't think I was that close to him. As I said, I just listened to music."

Ian remembered now that the earphones were collected before landing. His courage swelled, "Is anything wrong?"

"I'm not at liberty to say, sir. They don't even know . . . ," the officer stopped short.

He was fishing. Ian was sure of it. It figured that the CIA would try to hush up this matter, investigate on their own. Wilcox must have stumbled onto the earphones and was trying to show them how smart he was. He was probably looking for a job. Yet the point remained, no matter how much he would have liked to forget it . . . there was a Hamel and it was quite probable he did not die of natural causes. And someone else . . . the person who killed him . . . could have removed the I.D. What's more, that person could be there right now, watching him talk to the officer. What would *he* or *she* do to Ian, if he didn't maintain his cool?

"Perhaps it was a suicide," Ian offered.

"Sir?"

"Well, if it wasn't a heart attack, maybe he committed suicide," Ian clarified.

"I didn't say it wasn't . . . ," Wilcox stammered.

Outside, in the parking area, the *person* who had removed the I.D. was making a few disrepairs on Officer Wilcox's car before his own interrogation.

Meanwhile, Wilcox went on to his next interview, leaving Ian totally renewed. He had pulled it off! And yet, he felt a bit sorry for Wilcox. He was a smart young man who moved quickly. But Ian sensed the CIA wouldn't want him. He was too independent. Ian felt that about himself as well. It was probably why the corporate world had bored him so.

There was nothing to bore him here, however. He was up to his eyeballs in something he didn't understand. Someone was probably using him to shield himself; someone called The One, if Ian remembered Hamel's one-sided conversation correctly.

What happened to the photo, Ian suddenly thought? He remembered Hamel mentioning having his picture . . . "now." That meant no one had it before. But it was *his* picture. So it didn't necessarily mean he looked like The One. Anyone there could be him. Anyone. What if they found the photo? No, the killer would have taken Hamel's camera. Wouldn't he? Ian was starting to get a headache. What else would be expected of him? Was he to be the killer's fall guy?

As Ian walked back to the bar area, he resolved to learn more about the Penitente. If he ran the danger of being implicated in something, he wanted to know what the hell it was all about.

A Blue Grass band was setting up on a small stage across from the bar. The tables were filling in anticipation. Diana had saved Ian a seat and waved him over with a smile as he entered. His interest in her had been more than piqued. But as he walked over, Ian couldn't help wondering what Meredith was doing. Had that picture of him come off her bedroom wall?

Diana sat near the windows with the Dusquesnes and the Hulls. A waitress met Ian on the way over to the table and he ordered a hot buttered rum. As she went off to get it, he saw Loudmouth approaching Diane's table and quickened his pace lest he lose his seat.

The table conversation was of Blue Grass, but as he arrived, Ian sensed an air of wonder.

"You were right . . . ," he said to Eli as the latter came up to them, " . . . Should have paid my parking ticket." Ian laughed. It sounded even heartier than he hoped it would.

He sat down and shrugged, "I suspect there may have been more to it than a heart attack, but the officer's not saying. He's just interested in finding out if anyone talked to him."

Ian looked to see if any of the faces registered something out of the ordinary.

"Maybe the conversation bored him to death," Loudmouth guffawed obnoxiously.

"Come to think of it, he did say something about wanting to talk to you," Ian winked to the others.

"But I came in on the Chicago flight . . . Ohhh . . . ho, ho . . . ," he waved a finger at Ian. "All right. I can see I'm the odd man out here. I'll make myself scarce. I don't like Blue Grass anyway. It's too loud." He bellowed again and was off.

There was a sigh of relief around the table, but Ian had noted a warmth in the older man that hadn't been there before. He was almost sorry he didn't stay. Ian also noted something about himself, too. In the past, he wouldn't have been as sensitive to someone like Eli.

"Oh, look at that!" Melissa exclaimed.

"What?" Roger turned to the window.

"It looked like there was a ball of fire out there. It just whizzed by."

"You're kidding," said her husband.

"Perhaps it was a reflection from the fireplace in the dining room," Diana offered.

"Or, maybe, it was a witch," Elizabeth Hull spoke softly.

"What?!" the young Alabamian was wide-eyed.

Elizabeth went on, "I once heard the Indians around here believe in witchcraft. I think when we visited the Pueblo someone told us witches travel around as balls of fire on the wind. Gave me quite a stir. I never forgot it."

"But surely not on Palm Sunday," Roger retorted.

"Why not?" Elizabeth asked.

"Now, I was afraid you were going to ask that question. Let's order us another round and maybe I can come up with a clever answer," he chuckled.

They all laughed, although Melissa not as heartily as the rest. She *had* seen something and it had frightened her.

The waitress came over with Ian's drink and another round was ordered while the band cranked into gear.

Ian kept glancing at Diana as they listened to the music. There was definitely something inscrutable about her; something beyond the mere mystery of being a new woman to him. After downing his drink, Ian couldn't focus on it, however. He began to feel drowsy. Then a lid dropped.

"It must be the altitude. I'm wiped," he admitted, swallowing down a yawn at the first break. "I'm afraid I'll have to call it a night."

"It's best to rest. If you're not used to it, you can get quite a headache," Roger offered.

Ian got up and smiled at Diana, "Goodnight. It was very nice meeting you."

"Perhaps I'll see you in ski class," Diana smiled back.

"That would be great," he beamed.

It made his night.

But Ian had a premonition the night was far from over.

6

The lamplight illuminated Cecilia Troni. She was seated in the chair by Ian's bed, reading.

"It's good you didn't make it a long night, Mr. Stone. You have a bit of a ride. My husband waits for you behind the Edelweiss."

"The Penitente . . . ?" he blurted.

"I had hoped my speaking of them would alert you," she responded.

He smiled in acknowledgement, at the same time wondering how she had gotten in. The entrance was locked . . . Then he noticed the trap door on the other side of the bed. There was a passage from the Tronis' room to his. Why couldn't it have been Diana's room?

"Convenient, yes?" she said, noting his gaze.

Without answering, Ian grabbed his ski parka and gloves, turned off the light and left her sitting in the dark. He felt that was the right thing to do. It was.

As Ian walked down the hill behind the A-frames toward

the Edelweiss, his tiredness was replaced by a spirit of recklessness. If he could play out this role, whatever it was, perhaps he would have another shot at adventure. What did he have to lose? It made his blood pump. It wasn't as frightening as suicide . . . yet.

Ian got into the waiting car and, without a word, they were off.

It had stopped snowing and the plows had been through, but a thin layer of blown powder covered the road. Ian glanced occasionally at his driver, but Troni kept his eyes ahead.

Nearly ten minutes later, as they rounded a curve, Ian saw the skid marks made by the police car. Their headlights caught a glimpse of it lying on its roof in the gully alongside the road.

Antonio cast a knowing glance his way. At first Ian thought it meant he was being looked out for, but then he realized Troni had assumed he had taken care of the matter himself. Obviously, he hadn't. Obviously, the ex-patriot Chilean wasn't The One. Then who? Or perhaps it was just an accident . . . another accident. But Ian knew there was no avoiding the reality. Officer Wilcox was out there, probably lying dead . . . the second murder of the day. People who talked to him were dying. He was involved very deeply in something over which he had no control. Once again, he had no control. Where the hell was he being taken?

The mountain air was more powerful than his nervousness. Ian decided it was best to rest in order to prepare for what might lie ahead. Soon he drifted off . . .

* * *

He was on a dimly lit street with Meredith. They were both laughing about something. Suddenly, it grew darker and he had a sense of foreboding. He tried to get her to move away with him, but instead she faded. He heard loud footsteps on cobblestones behind him and became apprehensive. Then he started running. Soon he was moving faster than his feet could go and fell to the ground.

* * *

Ian awakened. He could feel the sweat under his shirt. He wiped his brow with his hand and looked ahead. They were on an unpaved road now and Troni had slowed his speed considerably. Still, the car slipped as they descended. The road finally became too steep and they stopped. From out of the darkness the lights of a jeep flashed.

"This is as far as I go, Mr. Stone," Antonio said. "Enjoy the performance."

Ian hadn't the slightest idea what he meant, nor what the hell he was doing there. What was Meredith doing now? He shook his head. This was supposed to make him forget about all that. Diana flashed into his mind. He thought it would be nice to take a jeep ride with her.

As he got out of the car, Ian realized it was about ten degrees warmer than up in the Ski Valley. The snow was wet, not crisp, and only a few inches deep. An owl hooted. Ian accepted this would be an appropriate place for an owl to be hanging around.

He walked slowly, but steadily toward the lights, trying not to slip. As he approached, the motor started. He now saw two men in dark, hooded robes standing beside the vehicle.

Ian stopped in front of them and one of the men extended a similar robe to him. "*Bienvenido, mano,*" was the only thing he said. Ian donned the robe and got into the jeep.

Meanwhile, a figure dressed completely in black had slipped from the cab of another jeep parked off the road above their position. As Troni's car and the jeep holding Ian left in opposite directions, the mysterious figure pulled out a pair of cross country skis and poles. He quickly moved down the road and, by the light of a lamp attached to his headband, followed the tracks of the other vehicle.

The jeep slowly wound its way down into a valley. Soon there was no road, but Ian could make out the tracks of other vehicles in the snow. Shortly, they came to a gully cut between two steep hills. They drove up the ancient riverbed less than a mile until it seemed to dead end. The jeep's motor was shut down and they waited in silence. Only the chattering of insects broke the night air . . . and that owl. Was it following?

Four black-hooded figures appeared and moved aside the brush that blocked the way. The jeep restarted and spurted ahead through the natural opening cut in the side of the hill. It emerged into an area where the headlights caught many parked jeeps as well as vans, old cars and pickup trucks.

The vehicle stopped and Ian got out between his two guides. He continued to follow the hooded pair through a narrow pass. In the distance could be heard the sound of flutes and drums. Ian thought back to the music on the plane that afternoon. Had it only been this afternoon?!

In a few moments, the trio emerged into a natural amphitheatre about half the size of a football field. The area was lit by huge bonfires and what Ian guessed were a thousand or more candles held by black-robed figures, some with white and others with dark hoods, clustered around the open "stage" area. The only sounds were the flute and the drum. Then the music stopped and there was only the wind.

It was an eerie sight, but not half as strange as the procession that began moving slowly past him into the amphitheatre.

Led by an acolyte holding a single candle, a dozen men, hooded, but bare to the waist, walked two abreast. As they marched to the beat of a new sound of wooden claquers, or *matracas,* they were whipping themselves with long, knotted cords barbed with what looked to be pieces of cactus. Whatever they were, drew blood.

But the flagellants were not nearly as bloody as the man who followed. Unmasked and wearing only a loincloth, he dragged a large wooden cross. Two men, with red kerchiefs knotted on top of their heads to represent Roman helmets, followed after, scourging the cross-bearer with even more brutal-looking whips.

"Holy Christ!" Ian thought, suddenly realizing he was watching a Passion Play. But this was no Oberammergau. The blood was real. Ian could smell it as they passed. He had smelled the blood of agony before.

Where?

His mind tried to drift back. He saw a vision of soldiers with torn limbs screaming, "Medic! . . . Medic! . . ."

The vision was shattered by a still more startling sight. Two men, wearing only red rags over their faces and mid-calf white trousers, entered the amphitheatre pulling a wooden cart about half the size of a bathtub. It must have been as heavy as a tub as well, since the cart was full of rocks and the wheels did not turn. Perched on top of the weighty carriage was one of the more hideous things Ian had ever seen . . . the skeleton of some deformed human. Could it have been real? The large, grinning skull with scraggly hair was perched atop a small body with huge hands. In the hands was a drawn bow with an arrow set into place.

The frightful thing rocked in a macabre dance as the cart was dragged along by the horsehair ropes which cut into the shoulders of the two men pulling it.

As the cart passed Ian, it slipped over a large stone and jolted. The grotesque skeleton's hand was shaken and the arrow let loose from the bow, striking the ground at Ian's feet.

Ian was so stunned, the snap of his head sent his hood slipping back. But, it seemed his honor guard was even more surprised. He heard distinct expressions of shock. In fact, the shockwave seemed to ripple throughout the amphitheatre. It was followed by an instant of suspended silence . . . a lost beat of the *matracas.* Then the arrow was retrieved and the procession continued. As Ian replaced his hood, he was sure everyone there was now aware of his presence.

Of all those thousands of eyes, none followed the new arrival more closely, however, than those of another *anglo,* who was quite conscious of keeping well hidden within his own hood. As Ian was seated nearby, the observer studied him, surprised not only by there being another *gringo* at the ceremonies, but more so by the indication he was an honored guest.

Ian was mesmerized. Yet nothing that had transpired up until then was as remarkable as the unfolding of the Passion Play.

With various Penitente men taking the roles, the traditional 14 Stations of the Cross were celebrated: the Christ figure falling three times, being helped by the Simon of Cyrene character, meeting his mother, having his face wiped by Veronica . . . all this with prayers from the crowd at each station.

Ian found himself mumbling along through automatic memory. Had he done this before? Shadows from the past swept through his mind, although none took focus. Then quite unbelievably, the Christ figure was nailed to the cross, and there was no going beyond the present.

Ian was not alone in his surprise; a good portion of the crowd in the amphitheatre seemed to join in his gasp. And despite the fact he was at some distance, Ian had to avert his eyes by the third stroke of the hammer. As he did so, he caught sight of the equally astonished eyes of the man who had been observing him. Those eyes, immediately, shrank back into the folds of the hood, which had momentarily slipped back and unmasked them.

A new, harder pair of eyes had also joined the proceedings. The now black-hooded figure had slipped into the amphitheatre without notice and, as the cross was raised, caught the glazed eyes of the *Cristo* through a small pair of binoculars. It was not chemical drugs the man was on . . . he knew that look. The man was on something stronger. His was the gaze of fanaticism.

In what was a pitiable fading of strength, the crucified man exclaimed Christ's last seven phrases before he fainted. At least, that's what Ian hoped had happened. The One knew better, and there was no doubt to anyone once a spear opened up a wound in the *Cristo's* side. The man was dead.

The master Assassin knew this pageant had been staged to impress him. More than a thousand staunch Penitente had gathered in a show of force, willing to sacrifice one of their own so he would believe in their sincerity and join them in some "noble" cause.

The One surmised he had been invited by the Penitente to be offered the position of enforcer for some new moral order. They had already paid him for the death of a pope. Perhaps he wasn't the first. But what exactly their current plan was, he had not enough information to even speculate. That's why he had brought his pawn, Ian Stone.

7

Randolph Neri was a "face man" . . . a smooth-talking, chiseled-featured front who could smile prettily and cajole senators, the military . . . the Washington community in general; in short, anyone from whom Braden wished to keep himself hidden . . . which was, basically, everyone. On top of that, Neri was a killer. One of the best The Company had. He was methodical, thorough, precise. He also liked it. Neri was the kind of lieutenant any commander would want; a man who would carry out his orders without question. Normally. But as his special charter flew on toward Albuquerque that night, Neri was both confused and frightened.

Earlier he had just been pissed, the report of Hamel's death having ruined his afternoon with Darlene, the one member of his staff who, quite literally, worked under him.

Darlene looked like the Breck Girl gone bad, and the very thought of her was enough to get Neri hard. This lust had dulled Neri's other senses and it never dawned on the self-styled Lothario that Braden kept tabs on him through her.

Now, however, it would take a lot more than Darlene to bring the curly-haired agent around. Neri stared vacantly out the plane window, grinding his teeth and rubbing his sweaty palms back and forth over his thighs. An untouched drink was beside him. And Neri was never one to leave a glass lonely.

This was a setup and he was the pigeon. Neri could feel it. Not that this hadn't been the case before; that was the nature of Company business. But *was* this Company business?

The incredible file before him had been thrown together in an obviously hasty manner. That, in itself, confirmed the nervousness Neri had noted in his meeting with Braden; the latter constantly rubbing the bridge of his nose and covering his mouth. The twitch was back. "Ice" had cracked. And the things that normally would not have been betrayed were unmistakeable . . . like the original sheet stuck to one of the xeroxed copies. True, the ink may not have reproduced well, but Hamel sure as hell didn't work with the original. And, its message being virtually repeated in his assignment sheet, Neri was sure it wasn't intended to be there.

The paper and the feminine handwriting were European, and Eastern European at that. Neri fancied himself an expert in such things. In the assignment sheet, it came across as Braden's tone. But it obviously wasn't his order. Neri revived from his daydream state, and beginning with the original, plunged for the second time through the file as he had reshuffled it. He knew his life would depend on close attention to details.

> "The assassin known as The One will be traveling to Albuquerque, New Mexico, under the alias Ian Stone, according to the attached itinerary. He is to meet near Taos with the Penitente leader known as El Conciliador.
>
> "Contact and commission The One to verify the extent and, if possible, the source of Penitente finances. If necessary, use the threat of exposing his prior dealings with the Penitente and the dissemination of his photo, which must be taken.
>
> "Information is needed by Friday of this coming week. Relay immediately and await instructions as to disposition of The One. This is a priority."

Who, Neri wondered, outside of a small handful of people in *this* country, could make such a demand on Kevin Braden? And who was able to pinpoint the itinerary and alias of someone as elusive as The One?

Neri thought back to Operation Songbird as his eyes rested on the copies from the Assassin File. It had been his baptism of fire. He remembered how excited he had been to be made a member of the "inner club." At the time, it didn't matter he was the "go for" in trying to uncover information on The One. It wasn't until later he realized he could easily have taken the fall, if The One had not wanted to teach Control a personal lesson.

Now, as then, Braden was using his lieutenant to protect himself. "You must make him believe you are the Control," Braden had stressed earlier in the evening. Neri had made a career of saving his boss's ass. And it was a great career. The question now was, was it worth saving Braden one more time?

As he reread the dossier on The One, however, Neri realized the real question was, *could* he do it one more time?

Even if he could convince The One he was the Control, the contact protocol had not been used; there had been no ad in the *Herald*. Obviously, The One didn't like that.

"Hamel was a fool . . . He was either too stupid or too heavy-handed," Braden had said. "Treat him with respect and it will go all right . . ." Fine. But how would he be treated? The One had somehow been unmasked and demands were being placed on him. Weird demands. What the hell was this really all about?

Neri turned to the next set of papers:

"The Penitente"

"A North American religious sect with origins tracing back to the Third Order of St. Francis and the *disciplinati* of the Dark Ages.

"*Disciplinati* were characterized by the practice of self-flagellation to atone for the sinfulness believed to have brought about the plagues.

"In the 16th century, their tradition was carried from Spain to the New World with the conquistadors.

"The sect grew northward from the Yucatan into modern day New Mexico . . ."

The Spanish probably having much to atone for, Neri surmised from what he remembered concerning their treatment of the native cultures.

"As a group, the Penitente first grew in religious importance when Mexico became independent of Spain in the 1820s. The Spanish monks were forced out and, there being few native priests, the Penitente took over many religious duties. From there it was a short step to political power, which they accumulated until the arrival of the French missionaries, who attempted to dilute the importance of the Penitente by condemning their practices as excessive. Eventually, the French had them excommunicated.

"This tactic, however, simply drove the Penitente underground and further ingrained their communal pride and separatist spirit.

"Never more than ten or twenty thousand in number, the Penitente dwindled in size during the early 1900s and were all but obscure by the start of World War II.

"It was remarkable, then, not only to witness their resurgence after the War, but also to see the Church reinstate them in 1947 as members in good stead.

"Today, there are estimated to be five thousand or more Penitente scattered about northern New Mexico and southern Colorado. Their fervor is reputed to be at a peak.

"Note: From its beginnings, Penitentism had always been one of those rare organizations to which poor, uneducated natives might belong. It was they who ran the show, and the head brother was never a higher up in social status.

"Now, however, there are indications of a deference being paid them by members of the Roman Curia and, further, that appointments of extremely conservative Church officials have been made at their insistence in Spanish-speaking countries. Although this has not been substantiated, it is recommended that an investigation be instituted to . . . "

The report had been written in 1950 by the FBI.

There followed some investigatory accounts from the early '50s indicating that little of importance was uncovered besides the fact that,

> "in thanksgiving for their reinstatement to the Church, a Nativity Scene of life-sized *bultos,* or carved wooden statues, was sent to the Vatican . . . "

and

> " . . . the leader of the sect goes by the name of El Conciliador."

Whether this title was passed on or stood for a particular individual did not appear to have been determined.

One of the accounts stated that someone contacted for information had been killed in a car crash shortly after being interviewed, but there was no evidence that it was in any way linked to his speaking to the Bureau. The entire investigation was dropped shortly thereafter.

It was the next item that had started to make sense out of this whole thing. And it was a real shocker; a message decoded by Braden himself. Neri had the feeling it had come in recently . . . that is, since Hamel's death. The handwriting evidenced the same nervousness he had witnessed in his boss just a few hours ago.

> "The liberalism of Pope John XXIII was too distressing to a conservative faction within the Church. Contrary to public knowledge, therefore, the Pope did not die of natural causes, but was slowly assassinated by a member of the Curia.
>
> "Pope John Paul I was, also, killed; he, by the assassin known as The One.
>
> "Both assassinations were done at the behest of the Penitente leader. Check 1957 Romewatch file on Church finances. See also *Il Populo*, September 23, 24, 25, 30 and October 7, 8, 14 and 16, 1947."

It had crossed Neri's mind at the time someone might have realized the election of John Paul was a mistake and wanted to nip it in the bud. Of course, it was just second nature for him to consider the possibility. There had not even been a hint such was the case. But the kindly old man he remembered from when he was still a teen . . . astonishing!

The last portion of the file contained the '57 Romewatch report plus blowups of the *Il Populo* articles. Neri could imagine Braden working furiously to pull it all together in time for their meeting.

The Romewatch report read:

> "Through some documents of questionable authenticity found earlier this year in Munich, fuel was added to a long-lived rumor of a conspiracy within the highest echelons of the Church to support the Nazi cause during World War II.
>
> "The documents hint Vatican art treasures were sold and vast amounts of cash and gold were handed over to members of the German high command. However, no proof as to these allegations is offered.
>
> "The supposed Vatican/Nazi tie stems from rumors of credit problems reputed to have existed from '44 through '46 when the Church was somewhat standoffish with some Allied financiers.
>
> "However, by the middle of '47, the Vatican appeared to be more open with creditors and any suspicions or fears with regard to possible holes in the Vatican vaults were allayed."

The report went on to say, if the rumors of Nazi collusion had been correct, the Church treasury could only have been replenished with the fabled Nazi gold which had never been recovered, but was reputed to be somewhere in South America; either that or some independent source of extraordinary proportions.

Both possibilities were rejected as being absurd by the report and the Munich documents were labeled a hoax.

The first *Il Populo* article was datelined Basel, Switzerland, and covered an aborted robbery attempt on the estate of one of Switzerland's most important banking families. Neri's knowledge of Italian wasn't all that good, but he understood one of the major items held in police custody was a cross of pure gold that had belonged to one of the popes and was supposed to be in the Vatican.

The next day's article reported there were errors in the original police report about the items recovered and specifically mentioned that no golden cross had been involved, nor was any such item in police custody.

On the following day, there appeared a photograph of the golden cross displayed in the Vatican Museum. The photo was purportedly taken the previous evening.

The other dates included news stories or obituaries on the deaths of people mentioned in the first two articles . . . the Swiss banker and his wife, the investigating officers, the robbers, etc. There was no mention of any coincidence.

Neri leaned his head back and sighed deeply. Putting it all together, the insinuation was the Munich documents were correct and it was the Penitente who bailed out the Church in return for influence in running the show, or a fair part of it, from the sidelines. They were able to operate at such a high level and with such secrecy popes could be assassinated and no one would know. But someone had figured it out and that "someone" controlled his boss.

For awhile now, Neri had questioned Braden's behavior. Ever since his father's death he had acted strangely. For all the devotion he had shown him . . . and Neri knew it was genuine . . . there was not the kind of grief he would have expected. It was almost as if the old man hadn't died or . . . a new thought hit him now . . . *someone* took his place. And, although this file illustrated whoever it was knew the inner workings and intelligence of The Company, Neri would bet anything he or she wasn't part of it.

The agent's heart started to pound. He realized there was no fall-back position for him. He had to succeed completely. Braden had told him to treat The One with respect, but added, "be prepared to take *any* necessary action." That was a direct countermand to the handwritten note stipulating orders on the disposition of The One were to be awaited.

If he were forced to eliminate The One, someone very powerful would, no doubt, be upset enough to have him eliminated. But if he disobeyed his superior, Braden would probably eliminate him. And if The One didn't believe he was the principal in this affair, he would do the job.

Succeed or not, Neri had had it. This would be his last mission.

He felt a cramp, then waves of nausea swept through him. Neri did more than burn papers in the plane's bathroom.

8

LUNES SANTO

It was almost pitch black as Ian trudged through the six-inch snow. The cloudcover had temporarily blocked the moon and he had to guide himself toward the eastern hills by instinct. All he wanted was a place to lie down and rest.

Then he heard it: the crunching of the snow behind him. He was being pursued.

Ian increased his gait, but the rapidity of the movement in back of him increased as well.

He slipped behind a pine as the moon peeked out, and looking back, could make out three dark-robed figures; two with white hoods led by a lone figure all in black.

The pursued felt he had no choice. He darted toward the hills, knowing the sound of his feet would be heard.

Ian crossed the flats quickly and began moving up the side of a steep incline. The snow became deeper and more slippery, slowing his flight considerably.

The pursuers could now be heard rapidly approaching, so Ian began using his hands as well as his feet to climb. Suddenly he struck a slick patch and began sliding backwards. Ian grabbed at an exposed root and twisted over onto his back as he came to a stop.

An arrow struck the spot he had vacated, missing him by inches.

The hooded figures were now within 25 yards. Ian was quite visible, an easy target. Or did they want to take him alive?

Ian rolled over and began moving up again, using every ounce of strength in his body. The cold air did not prevent him from breaking out in a sweat. If only he could make the top . . .

Now, even the breathing of his pursuers could be heard. They were on him. But with one last superhuman effort Ian dove over the crest . . .

* * *

. . . and awakened with a pillow tucked into his gut.

It was bright daylight. Ian was lying in his bed, sweating and breathing hard, trying to orient himself. He could hear the sound of his travel alarm ticking nearby. Outside, he could hear the sound of the lift motor and skiers laughing and yelling. He turned over and through the window over the doorway he could see people streaming down the slope. He could also see the time. It was just past noon.

Ian shot up like a bolt, "Goddamn it!"

He had missed the first morning of skiing. He had missed his class. But, how? . . .

He could only recall a hideous skull and an arrow falling at his feet. But wasn't that in his dream?

And where was Meredith, Ian suddenly wondered? What time was it in New York? She'd probably be getting back from lunch about now. No, Monday was the day she ate in.

She was probably reading another psychology book. It was incredible how she digested them so quickly. He had asked her once if it were possible to get an overweight mind. "Perhaps just intellectual indigestion," she had replied. The truth was, he had been envious of her learning capacity, her curiosity.

No, it wasn't a dream. He had been there all right . . . the Passion Play to end all Passion Plays, especially for the leading man. My God, who the hell were these people?

Ian yawned. He was thankful to be safely back in his room. For the life of him, he couldn't remember how he had gotten back. Oh, yes . . . It was Troni. He drove him back.

As Ian reflected on the previous night, a disheveled-looking skier walked out of the Abominable Snowmansion. The small lodge was in Arroyo Seco, a little town about 10 miles from Taos Ski Valley. Most importantly, it was near the *morada* to which The One had tracked Ian's greeting party after the Passion Play.

He knew none of them would be El Conciliador, the man who had sent for him. They were only lieutenants. But they represented a level which had to pass on Ian Stone. El Conciliador either believed in involving his commanders or had only a tenuous hold on them.

On the assumption the *morada* might be a possible meeting ground, The One waited until everyone had left, and then broke in and set his bug. By that time, even the master Assassin was exhausted and had to sleep. The Snowmansion wasn't the St. Bernard, but it was there. And it made a perfect listening post.

The room had been rented for the rest of the week.

Meanwhile, Ian dressed with a vengeance, hoping to be out on the slopes before any more mystery guests showed up. He started to shave and suddenly wondered why. A fragment of his dream crept into his consciousness and he spun around, expecting to see a hooded figure about to shoot an arrow at him. Ian dropped his razor and grabbed his equipment.

He hopped down the steps leading from his terrace and stepped into his skis. The Geze bindings snapped shut. Ian grabbed his poles and began to climb the hill leading to the lifts.

The slopes were crowded with people coming back from

classes and their morning runs. Ian recognized Roger Duquesne in one of the groups.

He wanted to avoid being seen by anyone, but the lifts suddenly shut down temporarily and his, "Oh, shit!" caught the class's attention.

"What's the trouble, old fella?" Roger asked as he came over.

"I overslept," Ian admitted dejectedly.

"Guess you didn't do as I told you. Too much partyin', I'll bet," Roger scolded.

"It's the altitude. It will do that to you, if you're not used to it."

The diminutive ski instructress spoke with an accent; Germanic, he thought, though her dark eyes and hair made her look native to the West.

"This is our teacher, Theresa Kittinger. She's just fantastic," said Melissa.

"Thank you, Melissa. And you are? . . . " Theresa asked.

"Ian Stone."

"So, Mr. Stone, I take it you did not have a chance to ski Taos yet, or have you been here before?"

"No, this is my first time," Ian replied.

"Well, you seem to have the right equipment. I like the Pre skis," she complimented. "You need such expensive bindings?"

"I've spent a long time trying to strengthen a pair of torn knees. I can't afford a break," Ian informed her.

"So, it's good to have the best, yes? Okay, then, if you like, I show you the mountain after lunch. I have no lesson 'til three o'clock. We'll see what class you should be in," she offered.

"Thank you, that's very kind," he said, astonished by her generosity.

She was very gracious. Ian felt her genuine warmth.

"Why don't you join us for lunch?" Ian invited in return.

"Oh, thank you. I never turn down a chance for Claude's cooking," she admitted.

Roger locked all their skis together and they went into the St. Bernard.

The bar was crowded with boisterous day skiers, eating sandwiches and drinking beer. Meanwhile, the inn crowd was filling up the dining room.

"Terrible about that policeman, isn't it?" Roger commented as they entered.

"What policeman?" Ian had tried to block it out.

"The one who questioned you last night," Roger said. "Died in an accident on his way down the mountain, I hear. You'd think the natives could handle these roads."

"My God!" Ian sounded convincing as the confirmation of his fears brought back the picture of the car in the gully. He suddenly wondered what was in store for him today. Perhaps it was over. Hopefully, The One didn't need him anymore. But that thought conjured up even more ominous possibilities.

Ian couldn't decide whether he was hungry, but when Claude's cream of leek soup arrived, the decision was obvious. He downed three bowls full.

Theresa Kittinger was an interesting woman. Her father was Austrian . . . came over when the Nazis were gaining power and ended up marrying a Zuni Indian. After the War, the family moved back to Austria and Theresa grew up on skis.

Her parents were friends of the Ski Valley's founder. In fact, it was her mother who suggested he look for a mountain in northern New Mexico for his resort. A run had been named after her . . . Whitefeather.

When her father died in the mid '60s, Theresa came back with her mother and set herself up in Taos to paint and to ski. Now she lived with a guy named Max and seemed to have it all together.

It relaxed Ian to be with her. It felt like being on vacation.

From across the room, their table was being observed by Randolph Neri. He wasn't sure whether it was a case of jet lag from traveling all night or what, but he was disconcerted. This was The One . . . the magic man, who put even the legendary Carlos to shame? Neri had known a lot of killers, men who could slip from one identity to another at the snap of a finger, but the seeming naivety of the man he was watching was not to be believed.

Frustrated expectations, Neri laughed to himself. Then he quickly soured. The One knew he had been unmasked . . . that someone would be coming. Yet he had the balls to sit there in the open, calmly eating lunch.

The agent felt his teeth clench. He wanted to wipe the smile off the Assassin's face. He resolved to act fast. And to succeed. All the while, the newcomer himself was under observation. In his new, weathered skier guise, The One had monopolized the phone booth between the bar and the dining room and had spotted Neri from his vantage. He did not need to wait to check the microfile back in his room. He remembered the agent from Operation Songbird. He was also aware of the agent's reputation since then.

What bothered him, however, was Neri's visibility. Principals were usually more discreet. The One wondered if he were fronting for someone else. It was time to place a pin mike on his pawn.

Diana was also wondering . . . wondering how to get around a frustrating set of circumstances. Her femininity had been working against her all morning. And she, of all women, hated that type of situation.

Her curiosity had been stirred with regard to the Penitente and she had wanted to learn more about them. However it was already obvious to her the sect was extremely male dominated, and as a woman it would be difficult to go beyond what was written in books . . . to really get close to them.

She had gone to the Millicent Rogers Museum, a beautifully converted white hacienda on the outskirts of Taos, to get some literature and see the reproduction of the Penitente *morada* Melissa had mentioned.

Diana had found it bizarre; the altar, the whips, the statue of a bleeding St. Francis crowned with thorns and, most of all, the grinning skeleton, *Doña Sebastiana.* But it was also fascinating. It had reminded her of the catacombs in Rome.

The guide, a sweet Indian girl named Guadalupe, had been very informative. Since the museum had been fairly empty, Diana was able to ask a lot of questions.

The girl eventually admitted her family was Penitente, but had denied any excesses in their practice. Diana feigned ignorance of what she was talking about and brought up her own search for people with deep fervor, lamenting how hard it was to find nowadays, even in Rome.

Guadalupe relaxed after that and went on about her father and her brother, their religious conviction despite their poverty . . . how, even as Indians, they were the *real* Penitente.

What had she meant, *real?* Was there some other kind of Penitente? Guadalupe grew silent. She had said too much.

"Anyone who has strong faith is a Penitente," she finally offered . . . and then excused herself to get ready for another tour. Diana could tell the girl was afraid; it was not for a woman to speak or to know.

Seated inside her car outside the Museum, Diana now pored over the books she had purchased. In one of them, she found something about the distinction between active Penitente members and a group called the *secretos,* who joined for political reasons and wished not to be publicly associated with the society. Perhaps that's what Guadalupe had been referring to. But why were these to be feared?

Diana wondered why she was reading books and worrying about all this instead of enjoying herself. She was supposed to be on liberty, wasn't she? "Watchful liberty," the Guardian had put it.

Diana tried to recall what had so intrigued her about coming to Taos? Was it a sensitivity or a feeling? She still had trouble distinguishing between the two, the subtleties between mental and emotional response.

There had been a time in her life when Diana believed only in "feeling." Life was to be lived on the ragged edge of raw emotion. *That* was the only reality. It was the only way to struggle against the suffering and pain that was the true condition of humankind.

However, as the ragged edge does, the longer it's sat upon, the deeper it cuts; and finally, in Diana's case, the emotions, being too much for her to handle, were severed away. "Feeling" became an intellectual concept instead of a lived reality.

The split had coincided with an event . . . the attempted rape of Diana by a hillsman in Corfu . . . her taking of his life . . . her escape from the island.

It was then Diana realized she could deal with what she most hated in life . . . her father, or more precisely, the memory of the father who had deserted her . . . and, by extension, all men.

In her bitterness, Diana resolved to treat men as if they were strictly "business"; as, in fact, she perceived they treated her. Soon, life was a business, and, believing she learned she could do it without remorse, she attempted to make the "necessary" taking of life *her* business.

"Necessity" . . . the mother of invention. Diana's necessity was the venting of anger against the injustice done when her father shipped her off to an orphanage. Since her revenge could not be taken out on him directly, however, it would be transferred to those who had supposedly done injustice to others. The good, the meek, the weak; they all needed protection by the strong. And Diana was ready to steel herself to this mission. It had taken her three years of therapy to understand these underlying motivations.

Fortunately, before she could begin the trade of The One, a better opportunity for true achievement, for true self-realization was opened to her. Diana was recruited to help the institution that had made her suffer most, the institution she felt most confined her when she needed to vent her anger, the institution that somehow most represented her father . . . all fathers of all women in that hateful orphanage that had been her world . . . the institution that, ironically, was most in need of her special fervor—the One, True, Holy Catholic Church.

It had taken 30 years for The Light to get around to hiring women. It had been repugnant enough to its pious members to think they often had to resort to their adversaries' tactics in order to keep the Church Christian, but to have women involved? . . . Incomprehensible!

Nonetheless, the combined factions of politics, business and the clergy . . . all gnawing at the soul of Christ's Representative on Earth . . . had finally made it necessary for the Guardian to integrate his "secret police."

There were now more than a few like Diana. She didn't know Father Vittorio thought of them as his Vestal Virgins . . . that he had to in order to keep his distance.

Why would Diana work for the very institution that was the object of so much of her anger? The reason was, for better or worse, it represented the only father she knew. And, *this* "father" needed her.

Intuitively, the Guardian realized what those, like Diana, supposedly did out of hate was, in reality, done out of the need to be loved. But despite his age, it would have shocked Diana how much control Vittorio had to exert to hold back from giving her that love in a most carnal way.

Diana had trained hard under her patron. As a result, her own sensitivity had increased. Or was it that her humanity had been reawakened? Whatever the case, Diana was grateful she had never been called upon to harm anyone in a physical way. She would have been surprised to learn the Guardian had anyone do such a thing. She realized her work was now being done out of love for the Church, out of love for . . .

It had become apparent to her she more than idolized her mentor. She knew it was some kind of psychological transference. She had also experienced it with her psychotherapist. Still, there it was. And it was time to get away before it got out of hand.

Like most members of The Light, Diana, too, had been able to perceive the recent signs of impending evil. So more than anyone, with the possible exception of the Guardian himself, Diana felt relieved when Vittorio dispatched the members of his team on this "watchful liberty" to wherever their sensitivities directed them.

Diana hadn't remembered hearing of the Penitente or seeing

them on any list of groups on which The Light kept tabs. Given their extreme practices, she now felt it a bit odd.

But the real reason for her picking Taos had been to see the western United States. It had been as simple as that. Hadn't it?

Diana closed her books and turned the ignition key. She smiled to herself as she looked at her reflection in the rear-view mirror. Then she reflected on the haunting eyes of Ian Stone. Would he be a part of her enjoying this vacation?

Diana headed back to the Ski Valley . . . followed by the car that had been shadowing her all morning.

As she passed the site of the previous evening's "accident," an elderly police inspector from Albuquerque stood alongside the wreck of his prize young officer's car, arguing with the sheriff of Taos.

"Look, Sam," said the inspector, "I'm telling you to forget what you read. You shouldn't have gone through his report anyways. Now, this was an accident, and that other incident we've got orders to stay clear of."

Sam Redding spat on the ground, "*You've* got orders to stay clear of it."

With one hand, the barrel-bellied Sheriff pulled up his pants by a silver belt buckle. With the other, he smoothed his thinning hair and replaced his hat in a cocked position. Sam Redding meant business.

"Look, you want to make trouble for yourself? Make trouble for yourself. This . . . ," the inspector pointed to the battered car . . . , "is what happens when people go off half-cocked. Wilcox was a good boy. Good boy. Keep your nose out of this, Sam."

The inspector shook his head and walked off toward his car. Redding spat again. A dead government agent and a dead cop . . .

The officer's afternoon report had indicated feelings of suspicion about the former's death. The Sheriff was suspicious about *this* fatality. Too many accidents.

Redding looked up toward the Ski Valley. He had copied the list of people Wilcox had interviewed before the inspector had arrived. The Valley would be his next stop.

"Okay, take it away," he ordered.

The tow truck started cranking and the police car was pulled from the gully even as Ian was being pulled up the chair-lift.

Lunch had been great and so was Theresa. As the two of them drifted above the mountain's surface, she pointed out the trails, telling him their names and degrees of difficulty.

Theresa assured Ian he did not have to be one of those adventuresome experts trying to navigate the sometimes treacherous run beneath them.

This had been a good season, she told him. The year before had not been, with barely half the base the Valley usually received.

They got onto the native population somehow and Theresa went on about her feelings for the Pueblo Indians, "You must visit the Pueblo in Taos . . . And later this week, they will come and dance at the St. Bernard.

"But, I talk too much," she said. "Tell me about you."

Ian frowned. He didn't want to talk about himself. Most of all, he didn't want to lie to her. She was too genuine.

Theresa sensed his withdrawal, "Ah, your story will have to wait. I hate interruptions and here we are near the top."

They weren't quite there, but Ian appreciated her considerateness. Suddenly he wanted to tell her all about himself, discuss things he didn't even dare discuss with himself. It was the first such desire he had had in the past 16 years.

When the boards hit the snow, it was an immediate high. The Pre skis had a glide Ian hadn't experienced before. The pack was perfect and he sped on following Theresa's trail.

Ian's mood had altogether changed for the better. The breeze on his cheeks was crisp and he was in control. Past and present concerns slipped by for the moment. He was primed for enjoyment.

They skied over to the second lift and started toward the top.

"You move well," Theresa said.

"Thank you. It's my first outing this year," he confessed.

"You wait until the end of the season to ski?"

"I've been busy. Too busy," he said.

"What do you do?" Theresa asked.

"What did I *did,* is the question," he joked. "I'm retired now," he laughed. "Actually, I was a marketing consultant. I would tell big companies how to sell their products."

"Oh, I hire you to sell my paintings," she joked.

"Why not?" Ian laughed again.

"You want to ski some special trail?" she inquired.

"I don't know the mountain at all. Why don't you pick a good intermediate trail to start," he told her, feeling he would, quite literally, follow her anywhere.

"Okay, we take Honeysuckle to Lift 3 and then we go to Kachina Basin."

"Sounds good."

By the time they reached the top of Lift 3, Ian was relaxed enough to be aware of everything around him. But that awareness now included the feeling they were being watched. Whether it was by someone on the lift or someone already on top, he wasn't sure . . . only that there was someone. Perhaps the Penitente were looking out for him. Or The One. He seemed to have no dirth of protectors. So what's to worry? he asked himself.

Then they hit him—the questions he had been avoiding. What *was* that all about last night? And why was he playing along with this charade? He was here to ski, not play games. But it was just so natural for him to fall into games. Besides, what did he have to lose? Had he forgotten? This was his last play, his negative side reiterated. And he might as well go out doing something exciting.

Theresa spent nearly an hour with Ian, giving him pointers and critiquing. Then it was time for her to go and teach her lesson.

"Listen, I want you to consider this a lesson," Ian said. "I . . ."

"No, no. This was my invitation. You can take private lessons later in the week." She was adamant.

"Can I be in your morning class?" he asked politely.

"If you don't oversleep," she jested.

She was gone like a sprite.

No sooner was she out of sight than the feeling of being watched came over Ian again; that and a feeling of emptiness in the pit of his stomach. Vacation was over.

Then, he saw him. He was sure of it. A lone skier in a black parka standing by the lift. As Ian turned away, he caught the beginning of movement. The man was coming toward him.

Ian started to skate across the slope . . . slowly, rhythmically . . . then began to pole as he picked up a little speed.

Down or across? He had a choice.

Spotting a lone track to his right, he followed it.

Ian saw the marker for Hunziker Bowl and disregarded the "Closed" sign, keeping his momentum and skiing to the sloping terrain that led up to the Bowl.

As he sidestepped the incline, Ian looked back to see if he were still being pursued. The man in black could not be seen.

The Bowl was a wonderland of pure powder. Ian had to lean back as he slid along, following the tracks along the rim. When he got to the far side and was about to descend, he saw the yellow jacket at the entrance to the slope. Ski Patrol. A waving hand warned him not to descend. No chance, Ian resolved, and started down.

The descent was one rush after another, but Ian could see the Ski Patroller traversing to intersect his path. He banked toward a knoll up which the other would have to sidestep if he wanted to reach him. It was the least he could make him do in exchange for the reprimand he was going to get. Unfortunately, it didn't seem to cause the other skier much effort or pain. He was there in a flash.

Ian had readied himself for a lecture, but not for the grenade the man held in his hand. It was obvious an easing of the man's finger muscles would detonate it.

"Mr. Stone?"

"Yes," he was Stone.

"Randolph Neri. CIA. I'm in need of your services. And we don't want to hurt each other, do we?"

Ian said nothing. What the hell could he say? He was paralyzed with fear.

"I don't know what, if anything, my man Hamel did to offend you. All I know is the information I asked for is necessary. There are no pictures. There will be no pictures. And I never saw you. I'm offering immunity, plus your normal fee for what I want."

"And that is?" Ian had found a voice. It didn't sound like him, but who the hell else was there?

No one physically, but via the pin mike there was someone listening to their conversation from the trees across the slope. The One also viewed them through the scope on his custom-built rifle. Underneath his bandages and white knit mask, his nostrils flared. Something did not sit right with him. Sure, Neri looked the part, but he sounded as full of shit as Hamel. Maybe it was time to dispense with Ian Stone and handle his dealings with the Penitente in the usual obtuse way . . . or at least test his pawn's mettle to see if he could go the distance.

"I'm sorry. I thought that was communicated to you," Neri responded. "The Penitente wealth . . . Does it exist? What is it? Where is it?"

"Why is it important?" Ian asked.

"Because . . . ," Neri seemed to be making a dramatic pause. But, in reality, he was interrupted by the bullet The One had just put into his back.

The hand with the grenade began to rise and Ian's eyes bugged out. So did Neri's. Blood trickled out of his mouth and he began to pitch forward, his fingers slowly loosening their grip. Strangely, it almost appeared the look on his face was one of relief. But Ian wasn't looking at the man's face.

Ian heard himself scream and the noise awakened his reflexes. He crouched for some leverage against his poles and pitched himself over the top of the knoll. The drop was only 20 feet but, having never jumped before, it was the Olympics to Ian. He tried to stretch out in the interminable half second he was in the air. There was a moment of calmness as he waited for the explosion of the grenade, the snap of a limb.

And sure enough, just as Ian's head fell below the level of the precipice, the explosion came. He could hear the rush of fragments above him as he hit the ground and somersaulted. Ian righted himself with one ski on and the other just under his foot. He stamped his foot back into the binding and was off in a fury.

As the explosion echoed through the Valley, Ian himself began to explode with sweat. Avalanche. The thought swept through his mind and he pressed the skis to their limit.

Step. Pole. Step. Faster. A faint rumble could be heard behind him. He was sure of it.

Press. Harder. His breath came while panting. He could see a trail out of the Bowl, but the snow was too deep and he couldn't make the turn for it. Ian was in the trees.

He pounded to a stop with his shoulder against a pine. The "bug" The One had placed on his jacket shattered under the impact and fell to the ground. But the pain cleared his mind.

Ian looked back. The trail was behind and above. Too much work. He had to find a path.

The rumbling was still only faint. In fact, it seemed to be subsiding. Perhaps he could take it easy. In reality he didn't have a choice. His strength was sapped.

When he came out of the trees onto the open slope, Ian looked up and saw skiers stopped above. Some had edged over toward the Bowl and were trying to peer through the trees. A few members of the Ski Patrol could be seen moving through the crowd into the woods.

Ian tried to catch his breath.

"M..Mr. Stone . . ."

It wasn't possible. The man in the black parka. Neri's killer?

"That was a n..narrow escape," the skier said, nervously. "I saw who did it. Come. We must talk."

Ian looked at the kindly face. The man had a well-manicured gray beard and soft brown eyes. Ian realized he had seen those eyes . . . recently. Before he could place where, the man turned down the hill. Ian followed automatically.

As they descended, Ian's lungs felt cold. He realized he was breathing through his mouth and swallowed, trying to switch back to his nose.

The other man was moving quickly, putting distance between them. Despite his exhaustion, Ian increased his speed, not wanting to be left behind.

Suddenly he remembered when he had seen those eyes before. It was the previous night, peering at him, and then slipping back under a hood . . . the other *gringo* at the Passion Play. A Penitente? Hopefully, at least, a man with a few answers.

9

Once they reached the bottom of the mountain, the man in the black parka skied over to the condominiums on the side of the beginners' slope opposite the lodges.

Ian's guide stopped at one of the nicer complexes, built and decorated in typical chalet style. The man removed his skis and, without questioning, Ian followed suit. He carried his equipment up a flight of stairs toward one of the units the other man indicated.

"Th..That was a workout for me," the man stuttered, breathing heavily as he reached under the doormat for a key.

Ian had already noticed the man was using rented equipment. On entering the apartment, it was obvious he had not been there long enough to unpack his belongings. Ian also took note of the bottle of dark rum on the kitchenette counter. That, more than anything else, he thought, was going to make his stay worthwhile.

"Make yourself at home," his host said. Then, noticing Ian eye the bottle, he asked, "Would you like a drink?"

The man's voice was a bit raspy, but had a gentle quality to it. He also wheezed slightly before starting a sentence.

"I'd love some of your rum," Ian responded. "Hot, if possible."

"Hot it shall be, then. The bathroom's down the hall if you wish to use it," he added.

He had read Ian's mind. The younger man had burned off a lot of nervous energy and needed to relieve himself.

As he whizzed, Ian felt he was in his own space for a moment. He also felt more comfortable. He was with some sort of ally, maybe. And he could get some answers as to what was going on, perhaps.

Ian looked down and saw his hand was shaking. He was spraying the rim of the bowl.

He had just come very close to death. And as much as he thought he was ready for it . . . even welcomed it . . . the prospect had scared the hell out of him. He was now sure he had no desire to die. Where was that drink?

Ian returned to the living room where the other man was just putting a few mugs of hot buttered rum on a coffee table.

The man had taken off his parka and hat, so Ian finally had a chance to get a good look at him.

He guessed his host was about ten years older than he, perhaps 46. Without the ski boots, he was also a few inches shorter than Ian . . . about 5′8″. The man's sandy hair was graying, though not as much as his beard. And he had only the slightest hint of a paunch.

"I found a stick of butter . . . or perhaps it's margarine . . . and some sugar the former tenants must have left. I..It won't be the best you've had, but . . . "

"Right now, anything would be fine," Ian said, gratefully.

He sat in the chair to which his host gestured and picked up one of the mugs. Through the window on the opposite side of the room, he could see people riding the chairlift to the top of the beginners' hill.

"My name's Dashwood," the man said as he picked up the

other mug, "Alex Dashwood. I'm an archaeologist, historian . . . now treasure seeker as well. Cheers." He lifted his mug in a toast and they both drank.

It tasted great and Ian felt himself begin to relax. He had a name to his new "friend."

"I don't know *who* you are, Mr. Stone, but I dare say you're at least in over your head and, at worst, in quite a lot of danger. Perhaps we could be of use to each other."

"You saw me at the Passion Play last night," Ian said, taking another swig of his drink.

"F..Fascinating, wasn't it?" Dashwood commented. "I've been to Oberammergau, The Black Hills and elsewhere for such performances, but they were nothing like that. The man truly d..died, you know."

"How did you find me here?" Ian was anxious to learn; and just as anxious not to remember last night.

"After the ceremony, I followed your jeep until they transferred you to that other car. I noticed a rental sticker on the bumper and it headed toward the Ski Valley. I couldn't follow then because most all the other vehicles were headed away from here and I didn't want to arouse any suspicions. So I came back this morning, got this place and started looking. Found you at lunch. Couldn't keep up with you on the slopes, however. You're pretty fair."

Ian smiled. Today he had been, indeed.

"You say you saw the man who shot the CIA agent," Ian said.

"C..CIA! CIA!," Dashwood began to ponder. "Tell me about that, if you will."

Ian had let too much slip.

"You're going to have to tell me why you're here first," he stipulated.

Dashwood looked into Ian's eyes. He noted the unusual brown and green tints. In the recesses he saw an honesty that was overlayed with a fear of its admission. He liked the younger man. He had already decided he wanted to trust him.

"As you will. What do you know about myth, Mr. Stone?"

"Myth?" Ian was perplexed.

"The ancient legends that shape man's thoughts and dreams, that offer answers about his origins and destiny . . . "

Ian was not sure what to say. Instead of saying anything, he just stared at Dashwood openmouthed.

Alex saw he had obviously taken the younger man unawares.

"Perhaps I should start at the beginning," Dashwood said. "I came over from England as a lad during the War."

"*The* War?" Ian's eyes widened. He had been way off on Alex's age.

"I don't look it, so they say, but I am 56. My work keeps me fit, you see," he said, and then coughed. "Well, fairly fit.

"Anyway, I enrolled in a college and went down to Mexico for a summer dig as part of my work. I had always been interested in the Aztecs. Do you know anything about them?"

"No, nothing," Ian admitted.

"Pity. But, no matter. They were one of the many people of Asiatic ancestry who migrated to this hemisphere from one of the core areas."

"Core areas?" Ian asked, puzzled.

"I'm sorry. The places where civilization began . . . Mesopotamia, Nepal, Tibet . . . where people first learned magic and the consequences of its misuse; where the spirit of the quest and the penalty of banishment first arose. It's my own theory, but the common links are all too obvious. You've heard of the sacred Incan mountain of Machu Pichu, haven't you?" Dashwood didn't wait for an acknowledgement. "In Nepal the sacred mountain is Machu Puchare."

He winked as if Ian should understand.

"I visited a tribe in the Nepalese jungle, the Tharus, who were virtually cut off from the outside world until this century because of the malaria all around them. Through natural selection the tribal members had built up an immunity, you see. Well, my friend, I was witness to their native dances. And I tell you, they were the same as the dances I saw the Pueblos from Taos do last year at the St. Bernard. Even their jewelry designs are the same.

"But I digress. Forgive me," he coughed and wheezed slightly, then took time to down some of his rum.

Ian found himself being both irritated and fascinated at the same time. What in heavens name was this guy talking about? He also found himself wondering whether his father had ever told him stories. No matter, he was going to sit back and enjoy this one.

"The Aztecs were a very warlike tribe," Dashwood continued. "Their religion, like that of the Penitente who were obviously influenced by them, required pain. In fact, at the dedication of their sacred temple, they sacrificed over 20,000 victims.

"Most all of their neighbors they subjugated. And they amassed fortunes in gold, jade, what have you . . . until, as you know, they met up with," his brows raised, "*Señor* Hernando Cortez.

"The Aztec emperor, Montezuma, had been warned about him, but he wanted to believe that Cortez was the second coming of Quetzalcoatl, a white god of legend whom the Aztecs worshipped in the form of a plumed serpent.

"Of course, Cortez was much more the devil than the god," Alex lectured, and then lowered his voice as if telling a secret in a crowd. "On July 1, 1520, he and his men tried to clean out Montezuma's treasury and escape across the narrow causeway that led out of Tenochtitlan, or what is now Mexico City. But, alarms were sounded and they were lucky to get away with their lives much less a small part of the treasure. They claimed it was a third to keep some face, but I estimate it was far less. Far less.

"Anyway, within a month they reattacked the city and by mid-August had reconquered it. Only thing was, they found no gold, no treasure. It had all quite mysteriously disappeared," Dashwood laughed.

"Of course, legends abound as to what happened to it. Obviously, Cuauhtenoc, Montezuma's successor, had it hidden. But where? Cortez, to be sure, tortured him, but never found out."

Dashwood stopped to cough and take a sip of rum.

"You know, some legends put the Aztec treasure in the mountains east of Santa Fe . . . but," he winked, ". . . I know it's near Taos."

Alex took another swallow while Ian sat staring at him, wondering if the old man were for real.

"Yes, yes, it's all quite real, to answer the question you're no doubt asking yourself," he responded to Ian's silent expression.

"You see, my dear Stone, while working on a dig north of Mexico City in '46, I happened to stumble across what turned out to be the equivalent of the Rosetta stone that unlocked the secret of Egyptian hieroglyphics . . . perhaps even more amazing. It may be the key not only to finding the Aztec treasure, but more importantly for me, to understanding who this god, Quetzalcoatl, was. And by extension, the origin of 'gods' in general."

Dashwood was, obviously, excited. Ian, however, could not help wondering whether the man was playing with a full deck. On the other hand, he found himself wanting to see where this bizarre tale was going.

"It's a metal disc," Dashwood continued, "not much more than a foot across . . . probably an ancient shield. I smuggled my find out of Mexico in the door panel of a '42 Chrysler and I've spent almost 35 years trying to decipher it."

"Why are you telling me all this?" Ian wanted to know.

"Because, my dear boy, I need an ally. You see, I don't particularly care about the treasure . . . Oh, sure, a bauble or two would be nice . . . But my interest is in deciphering myth, uncovering the origins of legend. And the Penitente are the key to solving this mystery. I'm sure of it."

"I don't understand. How so?" Ian was beginning to see where he might fit into this. Dashwood needed a tie to the Penitente. But what was *their* tie to the Aztec treasure?

"About six years ago," Dashwood continued, "I took a teaching position at the University in Albuquerque. Since then, I've gotten to know the people and the area as well as any *anglo* can. And I've put a few facts together . . .

"The Penitente had been outlawed by the Roman Church for over 100 years. They were virtually nonexistent before the War. Then, suddenly, the Church readmits them and they're treated with unusual respect," Alex said excitedly. "I found out from a priest in Santa Fe that a member of the Curia, the body of cardinals that runs the Church, has been coming here every year, supposedly for vacations, for quite some time. And membership, as we saw last night, is booming. That takes organization. And organization t..takes cash," he said, pausing to light a pipe.

"I just have a feeling they found it; either they or their leader, some mysterious bloke known as El Conciliador. There are a lot of holes and things I don't know, but you seem to be important to them and, well . . . that's why I'm here," he finished.

"Alex, are you on the level?" Ian questioned.

"What do you mean?" the older man asked naively.

"Look," Ian said, "all I know is that, ever since the plane yesterday, a lot of people are thinking that I'm somebody I'm not. Now you're telling me some crazy story about Aztec treasure. It's all too unreal."

"I assure you, Ian, if I may call you that . . . it is real. All legends are based in reality. But the best ones are meant to confound so only the few, who are meant to, can unravel them.

"I will show you a drawing of the disc I found and explain the story as I have unraveled it thus far. But first, it's your turn to put something into the pot. After a refill, of course," Alex said, extending the bottle to Ian.

They began drinking their rum straight as Ian related what had been happening to him since the flight out.

For all his questions about Alex's eccentricity, Ian genuinely liked the man and it was a relief to have someone share his burden.

"Then you see," Dashwood broke in, "it has to be true. If

the CIA is aware of the possibility the Penitente have some source of wealth, while to all appearances they're as poor as church mice, they must have found it!"

Alex did not need to hear anymore. He felt confident in going on. He had watched Ian's eyes as the latter spoke and his trust had grown. Besides, he was too excited to consider he might be wrong about the young man.

"Here, l..let me show you."

Dashwood went to one of his bags and took out some rolled cloth.

"I've made tracings of the disc which will be more clear to you," he said. "One side, the more elaborate one, relates the journey northward to this area. The other side tells of the return."

He unrolled the two pieces. At the top of the "journey side" were characters in the form of pictures.

"This type of writing is called rebus. Allow me to translate. You see," he pointed to some figures, "Cortez and his men have departed in this direction . . . Montezuma, here, is dead . . . The treasure is collected from the waters into which it fell during Cortez' flight as well as from some huge cache the Spanish, presumably, didn't know about . . . From what I can make of it, Montezuma was going to make it a surprise gift to them.

"The stupidity of greed," Dashwood said, shaking his head.

"Anyway, here the caravan starts off due north using the Spanish horses that were left behind. Remember, they hadn't invented the wheel, so everything had to be carried by man or beast.

"Now this symbol," he pointed to something resembling a zodiac, "I'm sure means they were to walk until the equinox, at which time they would be shown a sign as to where to hide the treasure. That would give them about 80 days."

Ian looked quizzically, although he was becoming more and more intrigued by the story.

"Well, I'm sure it looks like Chinese to you," Dashwood again read his mind. "After all, it took me years to crack the code.

You see, all these little marks were so confusing because I thought they were part of it . . . and indeed they are, but they're not Aztec."

"That looks like a cross, there," Ian interrupted without having understood Alex's meaning.

"And indeed it is, my boy, but not a Christian cross. It was also the symbol of Tlaloc, the Aztec rain god. Apparently the lads ran into rains that lasted until close to the equinox and they feared they would see no sign. Then they met up with a tribe of Zuni Indians, who, apparently, thought the treasure was a gift from white gods of their own legend.

"Now, the Aztecs were a tricky lot. They played along with them and, see here? . . . they attempted one last subterfuge in case they were being followed. A false caravan was sent out to the mountains east of Santa Fe while they brought the treasure north along the Rio Grande.

"And here's the amazing thing . . . ," he indicated another rebus. "The Indians did a dance to their sun god and the weather cleared. So, on the dawn of the equinox, they arrived upon the secret spot to which the Indians had led them, and there, saw an incredible sight . . . an eagle perched on a rock, eating a serpent . . . the same sight that, according to Aztec legend, determined the spot where Tenochtitlan, their capital, was built.

"And the place to which the Indians had led them," Dashwood said, wide-eyed, "was itself a hidden temple!"

Alex was rolling now.

"Wait a minute," Ian was incredulous. "How can you tell all that from this?"

"Well you may ask, Mr. Stone. Not from the Aztec, certainly. As I started to say before when you interrupted, from these."

Dashwood pointed to the scratch marks.

"The scratches?" Ian asked, befuddled.

"Yes, those scratches," Dashwood beamed. "They'd confused me for years until, by happenstance, I visited a Celtic temple when I was back in Britain six years ago. It was there that I saw the Celtic symbol for Bel, the sun god, and realized I had seen that same symbol on the disc . . . See, here . . . And all the scratches were not scratches after all, but Ogam, Celtic writing! That's when the disk really began to make sense. Anything I could not decipher from the Aztec became clear in the Ogam, and vice versa. Hence, my Rosetta stone."

"But what was a Celtic temple doing here in New Mexico?" Ian asked.

"Ah, *that* is the question," Alex responded. "You see, there have been many findings of Celtic temples and Ogam writing along the East Coast of America. Farmers used the stones from what they thought were old storage sheds to build houses and barns. After all, these temples were usually not very big, and the writing was mistaken for plow scratches. It's ironic, but these stones with their pagan writing are found holding up Christian churches throughout New England," Alex wheezed a laugh.

"A few of these temples have even been found in Oklahoma. But nothing this far south . . . until now."

"Assuming you find it," Ian interjected.

Dashwood looked exasperated, "Right.

"Now, going to the other side of the disc for a moment, where it's almost entirely Ogam . . . a white magician had come from the south centuries before, bearing treasure and a powerful potion. A Celtic settlement already existed around here and they took him in as he was ill and dying.

"After his death, he was buried in their secret temple because they had come to revere him. Then many of the Celts departed for the south, in search of more treasure, I presume. The rest either died off or intermarried with the Indians. In any case, the Indians thought the Aztecs were emissaries from the long departed white men.

"My guess is the 'magician' was Quetzalcoatl," he said, looking up at Ian. "From other studies I've done, I have a feeling his popularity may have stemmed from the fact he taught the use of some drugs; for one, the potion given the Aztec sacrificial victims to numb them before they were murdered.

"In view of the fact he didn't have to fight the Celts, I have the notion he probably taught them a few things, too.

"All in all, this Quetzalcoatl was undoubtedly a very peaceable gent. He probably left the south because he couldn't take the killing. That's only supposition, of course," Alex admitted.

"Amazing." Ian was totally absorbed now.

"It gets even more so," Dashwood went on. "Going back to the first side again, the Indians recounted the story of the white man who was buried there and opened the tomb during a big celebration the night of the equinox. It was a shock to the Aztecs. They could not accept their god had died of natural causes and assumed he had been slain by the ancestors of the Indians. So in the middle of the night, the Aztecs took their revenge, slaying all except a few who were connected with the temple . . . obviously descendants of the original Celts. They might have even thought they were Quetzalcoatl's descendants.

"Anyway, one of them was the writer of the Ogam and, I'm assuming, creator of the entire disc . . . no doubt at the behest of his captors.

"That was one of the things that had always bothered me before I understood what the Ogam was," Dashwood explained. "The disc was not like any known Aztec piece. It was metal work they did not do . . . probably a shield carried by either the Celts or even Quetzalcoatl himself!

"The Ogam Writer was, undoubtedly, put to work in conjunction with one of the more artistic Aztecs and used the opportunity to tell his side of the story, perhaps without their even realizing it.

"In any case, the treasure was sealed up in the tomb, quote, ' . . . never to be found until Quetzalcoatl's plume will rise and his thunder shakes it loose,' " he translated.

"The bodies of the Indians and all traces of the Aztecs having been in the 'hidden place' were removed. The caravan, then, returned to Santa Fe to intercept the bogus party that had gone into the Sangre de Cristos. Unfortunately for them, a Zuni awake was a lot more difficult to defeat than a Zuni asleep, and although victorious, the Aztecs suffered heavy losses. They ended up killing all the hostages except the Ogam writer because they feared not being able to handle them.

"The other side of the disc became the writer's diary of the return trip with a few Aztec symbols added, no doubt, to keep his captors happy," Dashwood conjectured.

"Only a handful ever made it back. But, of course, there was no Tenochtitlan to come back to. The Aztec empire had been destroyed.

"The story was never completed. It ends something about, ' . . . if the *blank blank* disk is lost, the secret is on the skull.' I don't know what that means. The writer probably died or was killed," Dashwood sighed. "As for the rest of the band, who knows? Their leader might have killed them, they may all have committed suicide or, perhaps, just dispersed. But someone lived to spread the legends. Someone had to lose the disc."

Alex puffed his pipe, "There are still parts I can't decipher completely, but that is the gist of the story.

"The early Celts, obviously, never found their way as far south as Tenochtitlan and Quetzalcoatl is either still resting in his grave or on El Conciliador's mantelpiece. Where the poetic justice lies, I'm not quite sure," Alex concluded.

"Anyway," he puffed again, "whatever free time I've had these past six years, I've mainly devoted to exploring around these parts . . . s..so far, with no success.

"Of late, I've gotten into the Indian lore in a big way. It probably was a mistake not to have done so sooner, but it's difficult to get close to them. I haven't learned much of help taking that course," he confessed, "but this past year I finally have been able to put two and two together about the Penitente. And that's where I am."

Dashwood leaned back in his chair and took a small pouch on the lamp table next to him to refill his pipe.

"So, what do you say, Mr. Stone? Shall we unravel a bit of legend together? I do realize that you are in danger if you proceed . . . but do you have the option to turn back?" he asked.

"Two CIA agents and a policeman killed by someone obviously watching you . . . ," he shook his head. "The Penitente? Or this assassin?"

"Who was he?" Ian had almost forgotten his initial question.

"The man I saw fire? You know, it was quite by accident I saw him," Dashwood said, relighting his pipe. "I thought I would meet you at the exit trail from the Bowl. Then I caught a glimpse of what I thought might be you in the trees. I couldn't stop fast enough, however . . . which probably saved my life. As I started to edge up, I saw the man fire. He was all in white with a white ski mask. The only other thing I remember is that he seemed odd-sized or out of proportion somehow."

"What do you mean?" Ian asked.

"I'm not sure. I ducked into the trees as fast as I could and, within seconds, he moved past me down the hill. He knows his skiing, I'll say."

A crash from outside interrupted their conversation.

"What's that?" Ian jumped.

"Snow sliding off the roof," Alex shrugged.

"Are you sure?" Ian asked nervously.

"No . . . But, p..probably," Dashwood responded.

The approaching evening and the downed bottle of rum had increased Ian's paranoia.

"I better leave," he said.

Ian put on his blue parka and walked over to his skis.

"These babies saved my life," Ian said, stroking the edges like old friends. He turned back to Dashwood, "And you've answered a lot of questions."

"My dear lad, there are so many more. I hope we can get to the bottom of them together."

"I hope so, too," Ian declared.

"Then you'll persist?" Dashwood sat up.

"As you said, I probably don't have much of a choice. I'll think about it. See you later?"

"I'll be around," Alex said, smiling. "As close as I can be."

Ian started to leave. The older man interrupted him.

"Stone . . . ?"

"Yes?"

"They think you are a killer," Alex said, wide-eyed. "The Penitente have hired a killer. Why?"

Ian had no answer. He was both puzzled and elated as he left. He now knew he did not really want to die, but would rather unravel the secret to his locked-away past. Perhaps then he could forge an identity he would be proud of. But what would be *his* Rosetta stone?

10

Theresa Kittinger was relieved and gratified as she left the main Pueblo building and looked up into the starry night. She had always been proud of her Indian heritage. She had studied Indian ways, attended open functions and extended kindnesses. Because of that, though only half Indian, she was more than half trusted by them. Yet today was the first time she had ever felt truly accepted.

Theresa had been summoned to see the Cacique, the head of the Pueblo. It was an honor rarely granted to an outsider. But tonight she had not felt herself treated as such. The Cacique had been most kind to her . . . had even called her "sister." But when he had asked the questions about Ian Stone, Theresa feared there would be a price to pay for this kindness . . . the possibility she might be asked to do Stone some harm. How eased she had then felt when, instead, she had been asked to watch over him along with the four young Indian men who followed her from the Pueblo; to report to them should any harm threaten Stone.

Theresa liked the young man. It was no chore, but rather a pleasure to be of service in this request. And, yes, of course, she would keep this meeting secret.

"Would you like a ride?" she asked the young braves as she reached her car. Theresa turned to them and noticed their ankle boots were now tied to their belts and the four stood barefoot in the wet snow.

They were gaunt, handsome young men, all with long hair which three of them let hang and the fourth, the tallest of them, braided over his left shoulder.

"No, thanks," the tall one said. "My brother and I are going up to the Valley. And my cousins are going past Espanola."

"Well, I can take them as far as town," she again offered.

"It's a nice night for going on foot," the brave smiled. "Be sure to stop for gray wolves." They all laughed as she got into her car.

Theresa had heard stories of strange Indian cults and wondered if the four young men were part of one, like the shape-shifters about whom she knew little and understood less. Of one thing she was sure, these men weren't Pueblo.

As she drove off, Theresa looked into her rearview mirror. In the receding illumination of her taillights she saw the young men take some skins from their backpacks and begin to remove their clothes. Theresa focused her eyes rigidly ahead, not wanting to see more.

The dinner conversation at the St. Bernard was all about the unidentified ski instructor blown apart on the mountain. Everyone speculated on the ski tracks leading away from what was assumed to be a crime.

"Can ski tracks be identified?" Ian heard some young woman ask as he entered the dining room. Although tired and aching, he had, until then, been feeling fairly calm. Now, however, it crossed Ian's mind he could possibly become a suspect.

"Probably not. Maybe the pole pattern, though," was the response.

"Yeah," another chimed in, "if the the poles had an unusual basket. Or maybe the combination of both."

"We'll all have to be ski-printed," the first laughed.

"Frank, it's not funny. A man's been killed," the young woman scolded.

Ian thought about his poles. Were they kidding or not? His poles were the only thing he hadn't bought new this year. They were a very old pair, different from the ones being sold now. Would they leave a distinct mark?

Then Ian noticed the robust police officer standing by Jean at the far end of the dining room. The Lodge's owner was setting up a microphone as the two of them talked.

"*Attention, mes amis.* A bit of quiet, please," Jean began.

The room settled down as everyone took a seat at his or her table.

"You all know there was a tragedy on the mountain today," Jean went on. "We don't know exactly what happened, but a man was killed. It may have been suicide or an accident or something else. This we don't know. We are not even sure who it was who died, although, thankfully, it was not one of our guests or staff.

"This is Sheriff Redding from Taos. He'd like to say a few words to you."

The big man swaggered to the microphone and looked as if he were going to spit, but suddenly remembered where he was. "I'm sorry to disturb your dinner, ladies and gents, but this is an extraordinary occurrence for us out here and we would appreciate any help you all might be able to give us.

"I'd like everyone who was up near Kachina Basin at the time of the incident . . . that was about 2:55 . . . to come over to the Thunderbird at eight o'clock," the burly man said. "Please do now. Thanks kindly. Enjoy your dinner."

He talked like a country bumpkin, this Sheriff Redding, but Ian knew the man was no fool.

He started to pore over the events before and after the meeting with Neri. Theresa knew he was there. And they had been very visible. Perhaps he was even seen entering or exiting the Bowl. Ian looked around, expecting to see recognition in someone's . . . everyone's . . . eyes. Seeing Diana's warm grays startled him.

"Ian, how are you?" she asked with animation.

He was beginning not to be well.

Ian realized he was being too quiet at dinner and occasionally tried to join in. Each time he did, it seemed to him his voice rang false. He would then grow quiet again. At the other end of the table, Cecilia and Antonio got into a conversation with Diana about the Penitente. Ian wondered if that was supposed to be another signal to him. A smile crossed his lips. If they only knew what he knew.

Alex had not shown up, but then it was difficult for a non-guest to get a reservation.

As they ate, Ian's eyes kept drifting to Diana's and hers, he thought, to him.

A few tables away Ian noticed the English couple sitting with Loudmouth Eli, whose voice was, as always, very much in evidence. The man with the bandaged head sat with them. It was odd, but Ian felt, despite the man's back being to him, he was somehow watching him. It was his most accurate perception of the evening.

During dessert, the woman alongside Ian excused herself and Diana came over to take her place. It was an unexpected surprise.

"Why so sullen?" Diana asked.

She wished she had the power to lift his spirits and wondered if it were a maternal instinct or something else. Whatever it was, it felt nice.

Ian really wanted to tell her what was bothering him, but couldn't . . . "Still unwinding. It's been a hell of a year."

"You have such interesting eyes, Mr. Stone. They tell far much more than your lips," she commented.

Ian started to tilt his head back, assuming an attitude the way he had often done in singles bars.

"No, don't slip into a role on me," she admonished, aware of what he was doing. "Just talk to me . . . *if* you feel like it."

Ian swallowed, and again smiled weakly, thinking, "Checkmate."

"It's difficult to talk to a beautiful woman you don't know without slipping into a role," he confessed and took a deep breath. "Well, that's better than I might have said it," he beamed more vigorously.

"Then there's hope for you," she smiled.

Their eyes met in a crystal toast to a newfound friendship. She raised her glass in confirmation. Then they both laughed heartily.

Their conversation became fluid . . . pleasant. Not deep, just pleasant. Ian had the impression Diana was trying hard to block out everything except the moment; really trying. The more she talked, the more the furrows in her forehead dissipated and the corners of her mouth turned up. She was very pretty, with a strangely innocent sex appeal.

They both danced around their pasts and stuck to current events until a few minutes to eight, when many of the guests started to leave for the Thunderbird.

"Are you going over?" Diana inquired.

Why did he suddenly feel this had all been a setup? "No, I had already descended before it happened," Ian sniffed. "And it's a bit too grizzly for me. How about you?" he asked, downing his drink.

"I wasn't around, but I thought it might be interesting anyway," Diana shrugged. "Sure you wouldn't care to join me?"

"I was planning on turning in early tonight," Ian replied, feeling more and more wary. "I'm feeling drained. But how about tomorrow? I'd like very much to ski with you."

"Then it's a date," Diana confirmed. "On one condition."

"What's that?" he asked, more relaxed.

"That our conversation gets a little more depth to it," she said with a sparkle in her eyes. "You know what I mean?"

Diana was off without waiting for his answer. As he watched her leave, Ian remarked how lithe her hips appeared in the black leather slacks she wore. He wondered, too, why he wasn't more turned on. As far as hips went, hers were his ideal. Maybe it was because he felt he couldn't really trust her. Maybe because he knew he couldn't trust himself.

Desperation suddenly began to move over Ian in waves. He wanted to get back to his room quickly. And as he stumbled through the bar, thoughts of Meredith again poured through his head. But now they seemed at a distance, like dying embers across a cold room.

As Ian neared the steps to his terrace, his gait became more and more plodding. He made it up with difficulty, then entered his room and slumped into a chair. There he sat quietly in the dark. The courage felt in daylight had fled into the night.

A crawling chill came over Ian, and then sweat beads burst like water balloons in an arcade. He started to shake, first lightly, then uncontrollably. He began to freeze. Ian grabbed the covers off the bed and pulled them over his shoulders as he struggled to get on top of the shakes. He began breathing forcefully through his mouth as he desperately tried to calm himself.

What was he doing with his life? Who was he, really? Surely not the man he had been living with the past 16 years. But what was the alternative? He didn't know who he had been. Even if he did, would that allow him to "be himself?" Would he know who that self was if he ever came face to face with him? Ian was totally confused. He didn't know whether he was losing his senses or starting to gain them.

"Mr. Stone . . . ," Cecilia's voice seemed to rise from hell as she poked her head through the trap door. It seemed hours later. It was.

Ian got up and went out. The car was where it had been the night before. They were off again.

Arroyo Seco was very quiet when they arrived, only the night chatter of insects trying to keep warm. It seemed as if the rest of the town was asleep; but there was not a townsman in bed tonight.

The car pulled off the main road and went down a dirt lane with the headlights extinguished. In another moment, Ian stood before the carved wooden doorway of the *morada* to which The One had followed Ian's escorts of the previous night.

Standing there, Ian felt like running for the first time; not for fear of his escort or of any of those who might be within, but from *what* might be within.

One of the two large, hooded bodyguards by the door knocked with a loud rap.

"*¿Quién toca en las puertas de esta morada?*" came a voice of authority from within.

The knocker responded, "*Non son las puertas de la morada. Sola las puertas de su conciencia.*"

Ian did not understand much Spanish, but he had the feeling the response was prophetic. The doorway was an entrance to something he might see within himself, and the thought panicked him.

But when the door swung open, Ian was suddenly at home. Why, he knew not. The things that seemed familiar were the things not even there. A feeling . . . a sense of the past. But the reality was far removed from any place he had been. Or was it?

The chamber into which he was ushered was lighted entirely by candles, hundreds of them. Ian's nostrils immediately curled from the heavy smell of incense. He had been familiar with that smell at one time. He had once been an altarboy! The memory hit him like a battering ram. But there was another smell, also . . . something heavier, the one being covered. He felt familiar with that as well. It was the smell of blood.

"*Bienvenido, mano,*" came the coarse voice from across the room.

Ian looked around at the hooded congregation kneeling on the earthen floor. Then he focused on the man in the white robe, standing at some ten paces in front of a small altar. Blending against the white walls of the small chamber, the bare hands of the robed figure seemed to be floating in the flickering candlelight as he moved them in a blessing. His hovering eyes seemed to be floating, too. They were eyes into which Ian wished not to look, yet from which he could not look away.

Another figure came up to him carrying a black robe across his forearms. Ian broke his trance to look at the robe and its bearer. His eyes now swept the room, taking in the white lace curtains drawn across the shuttered windows. On the altar there was a large wooden statue of Jesus, bound and bleeding, with a crown of thorns on His head. A hand-hewn cross hung on the back wall. And all along the white walls there were red specks, the source of the heavier smell . . . dried blood.

The figure at the altar spoke, "Descendant of Fasani, you are offered the opportunity to fulfill your heritage. It is a rare honor for an *anglo*, but it is the wish of El Conciliador and your ancestry validates his request.

"By accepting this robe, you will signify your desire to become an *Hermano de Tinieblas,* to pledge dedication to this fraternity and to its rules, to be devoted to the Blood of Christ.

"Do not act lightly," the figure continued. "Joining us will require a confrontation with your own failings in order to return to the light, to be reborn an *Hermano de Luz.* Donning the hood, you will go through a transformation; you will become aware of God's potential within yourself, witness within what you saw last night . . . Christ's suffering and death . . . and only then can you truly reconsider the world and your place in it. Only then can you experience resurrection."

Ian did not have to be asked again. He took the black robe, put it on and fell to his knees.

The white-hooded celebrant turned to the altar and raised his arms, "*¿Quién en esta casa de luz?*"

The others chanted, "*Jesús.*"

"*¿Quién la llena de alegría?*" he continued.

"*María,*" they responded.

"*¿Quién la conserva en la fe?*"

"*José,*" was the response.

"*Miserere nobis . . .*"

Ian found himself mouthing the Christian song of sorrow as if he had just regained his speech. He realized the song had once been familiar to him. But concentration on this fact was broken as the members of the brotherhood let their robes fall to the cords at their waists and began striking their own exposed backs with whips of loosely plaited yucca fiber.

Only a small group to the left of the altar remained robed and motionless.

Ian knelt as if he were in a hypnotic trance. The long-forgotten words to the chant now came forth softly from his lips. He remained suspended, caught between the present and a long-hidden past.

Members of the group to the left of the altar nodded to each other with white glints of teeth showing in the candlelight. They were satisfied with their guest's pious demeanor.

Within the *morada's* inner chamber another *hermano* watched the proceedings through an opening in the wall. He, too, was satisfied. El Conciliador could sense the air of acceptance and knew his plan was working.

And in the small lodge less than a half mile away, The One listened in satisfaction. He had underestimated how far Ian would play along with this charade and was happy his pawn had survived the grenade blast. There was much to learn and Ian Stone would be useful still.

Of what importance was it to the Penitente leader to have the man he paid to assassinate Pope John Paul I become a member of his organization? And why was the most clandestine part of the CIA structure involved? Was the source of the Penitente wealth so awesome as to make these peasants a threat to America? What's more, who was Fasani? Who was this ancestor who made an *anglo* acceptable to such a chauvinistic group?

While the eavesdropper pondered, Alex Dashwood sat downstairs by the lodge fire enjoying the hot toddy with which he toasted himself. He was sure he had finally found a link to the hidden temple for which he searched.

Only one man was unhappy that Monday night.

Neri had already missed two check-ins. If he missed a third within the next five minutes, Kevin Braden would have to presume his agent was dead.

What kind of man was this "Stone"? How was he able to see through and dispose of his best so easily? Had he realized it was not the U.S. Government who was interested in the Penitente? It must be so. No one, not even the old KGB, had had such casual regard for his organization. Could the Assassin then know of Metamorphosis? How could it be possible? And if so, how could he dare interfere?

There was, however, another, more personal consideration that had been plaguing Braden. Why had *he* not gone in the first place? He knew the Assassin's modus operandi. And he had purposely disregarded it.

Braden began to sweat. He knew he would have to face the truth or lose it all . . . The fact was he was afraid of being bettered. He had made this foe into something unreal, a phantom. And he had become frightened by him. "Think straight, man," he told himself. The Assassin couldn't have taken the title, The One, in mockery. No one who knew the power to be confronted would do that. It had to be a coincidence. Only the members of Metamorphosis knew of THE ONE.

11

Ian walked into the Thunderbird Lodge and took off his jacket. He had noticed the sheriff from Taos slip into the kitchen as he entered. It was going to be a setup, but Ian wasn't afraid anymore. He had gotten out of enough scrapes lately to have some confidence in himself. It was time to have some fun.

Ian went over to the bar and ordered himself a hot buttered rum. From out of nowhere, Diana came up to him. But he expected that, too.

"You missed it," she said, her gray eyes beaming.

"Oh yeah?" he smiled back affably.

"It was quite interesting," Diana went on.

"I'll bet."

"A few people said they saw someone enter Hunziker Bowl about 2:45." Her eyes were probing.

"Really . . . ?" Ian attempted to be uninterested.

"I met your ski instructress. She says you're quite good."

She was fishing for some reaction. Ian was sure of it.

"She wore me out," he complained. "I could hardly keep up with her after our session."

"She said she was already at Lift 3 when the explosion occurred." She was baiting him.

"I know. I stopped a bit above her to catch my breath. When I heard that bang, I got going, though. You never know about avalanches."

Ian met her gaze head-on as he reached for his drink. Suddenly a firm hand grabbed him by the wrist. Ian spun around, only to be yanked up against the bar and have the wind knocked out of him. As his eyes focused, he found himself staring into the sheriff's paunchy face. Redding was smiling as he held up a needle. Fluid spit into the air. And before Ian could recover, the sheriff plunged the needle into his arm.

"Now, let's find out who you really are," the big man said.

"No! . . ." Ian shouted as he awakened.

* * *

MÁRTES SANTO

Diana was seated on Ian's bed. His shout made her let go his wrist.

"I didn't mean to startle you," she said, "but I thought we had a date."

Ian cleared his eyes and spoke to the apparition before him, "Oh, God, I was just dreaming about you."

"Sounds like I was too much for you," Diana smiled coyly.

"You were being bad," Ian managed a weak smile in return.

"Images . . ."

He didn't understand . . . "What?"

"To your subconscious I represent some dark aspect of yourself," Diana pontificated.

"Why not? You're a woman of mystery," Ian countered, now more fully awake.

"How so?" Diana demanded to know.

"You never really talk about your past . . . ," Ian spoke seriously, ". . . what you do."

"You're the one to say," she laughed. "I'm just more interested in the present, that's all. Besides, I'm on holiday. I'm here to have fun. And I wanted very much to ski with you this morning."

She looked very beautiful to Ian. He felt she really did want to be with him. The dream had been a lie.

"Well, give me a few minutes and I'll be ready," he said. "What time is it?"

"The morning's over," she frowned.

Ian whipped around to glare at the clock. It was almost noon. The sun was shining through the windows. It was a clear day.

"Shit. Not again . . . ," he said dejectedly, falling back against the pillow.

"Your nocturnal cavorts seem to be exhausting. I'm envious."

"Yeah, you would have loved it," he said sarcastically. "Shit . . . "

"You said that," Diana responded cooly and stood. "Go ahead, and then we can ski all afternoon."

Ian couldn't shake his disappointment.

"Sure," he said angrily.

"Well, excuse me," she said, starting to turn for the door. "I'm not used to stirring such excitement."

Ian leaned over and grabbed her arm, "Wait . . . I'm sorry. I . . . I had a rough night's sleep. Please . . . stay."

Ian didn't want to be alone. He also didn't want to be without her. Diana felt his sincerity and was relaxed by it.

Ian realized he was still wearing the shirt he had worn at the *morada.* It reeked from a combination of sweat and incense.

"I'll be all right once I shower," he laughed.

Diana liked the sound. It was genuine and that excited her. So did his smell. Her voice slipped an octave, "What's your hurry, Mr. Stone? We've missed the morning and lunch isn't for half an hour."

There was total silence as Ian braked to a standstill. Her eyes bore into his. A slight quiver ran across Diana's lips. Her own honesty had made her vulnerable and his pulse quickened.

"Oh God, what is the matter with me?" he muttered.

"I hope it's nothing serious," Diana said as she sat on the bed and began to unbutton his shirt.

Ian awakened all over as he watched her chest heave. He hadn't been with a woman in a month . . . hadn't even felt like masturbating during that time. And neither the desire nor prospect of meeting someone on this trip had ever crossed his mind. Meredith had been too much a part of his thoughts. But she had deserted him. He owed her nothing. Absolved, Ian began to reciprocate in disrobing Diana.

As he pulled her sweater over her head, his breathing came in short, rapid bursts. Instead of pulling the sweater off her arms, he pulled her arms down and slipped it to her elbows, locking them behind her . . . putting her at his mercy.

Ian's mind raced back to his last time with Meredith. He had had a premonition he was losing her and, out of desperation, had pulled her terrycloth robe down to lock her arms in the very same way. It had been an attempt for an advantage he had not really needed; the anger he had felt inside himself was not met. She had been willing. So why had he felt it necessary to force himself on her? Did some part of him know it would be their last time?

He had the same feeling now. The first time might be the last, and Ian wanted desperately to savor it.

He tried to tell himself there was no need to be angry now. This wasn't Meredith. But, WHY WASN'T IT?! Who was it? Could she replace her? He really didn't know.

A swell of emotion erupted through his chest cavity and Ian freed Diana's arms from the pullover. Their eyes met and his questions dissolved, giving way to reality and the desire now engulfing him. Ian cradled her head gently and drew his lips to hers. His fingers ran down each side of her spine until they unhooked her burgundy-colored bra.

His palms continued to sweep around her rib cage, coming forward to rest on her breasts.

Ian was struck by Diana's musculature. Her body was hard like a trained athlete's, her breasts incredibly firm with large, dark nipples. He closed his eyes as Diana's hands, now free, ran all over his back and sides, almost as if searching . . .

Ian began to wonder why she was there. Why was she attracted to him? He slackened and Diana felt it. Her fingers reached low around his buttocks and under, pressing into his perineum, and Ian firmed immediately. Her other hand ran along the underside of his penis as she stood to remove her skipants. As she squirmed from her outer layer, powder blue panties came part way down, revealing the auburn tufts covering her mound. Her fingers slid them over her thighs and they dropped to her ankles. She stood ready before him.

Ian was now like a rock and Diana knelt before him, taking his member and stroking it, making it swell and throb all the more. Then, without letting go, she straddled his hips, guiding him to the oozing entrance to her pleasure.

As she parted her fur, Ian could see the inner labia extended beyond the outer lips. He had never seen that before and his throbbing became almost unbearable. He could feel those lips grab him as he entered and she pushed him to the hilt. But it wasn't enough. He pushed harder, wanting to go farther, deeper . . . and pushed and pushed.

Ian opened his eyes to finds hers wide and staring, almost flashing. His flashed back. He had overcome his month-long agony.

The thrill pulsing through him could not be contained. Ian felt himself losing all control. He could hold back no longer. As he exploded, Diana's eyes rolled shut. Ian continued thrusting again and again and again, putting every drop of himself into her . . . and then again, when there was no more. Finally, slowly, she stretched her body over his, letting him take her weight.

When he opened his eyes, she was still staring.

"What can I do to please you?" he asked.

"What makes you think you haven't?" she smiled.

Ian smiled back and gently moved her off of him. Then he started to laugh and slid to a sitting position on the floor.

"What's so funny?" she asked.

"Life . . . is just too bizarre."

Ian crawled back onto the bed and kissed her tenderly. Then he rolled his tongue down along her chest and belly until it came to rest within his own juices. Diana started to protest, but he spread her thighs apart and rolled his tongue around the extended labia and, finally, in between. Ian probed and sucked and licked and swirled while Diana's back arched and fell with ever-increasing rhythm. She grabbed at his ears, but he would not relent and her arms fell away and clawed at her own thighs until, finally, she arched high and fell back with a short, throaty cry.

While they showered, an old man, tending a few young goats, walked his small herd through a gully a few miles from his hacienda. To anyone noticing his middaily ritual . . . and it was only, from time to time, a few children . . . he appeared a peasant-type with his gimpy right leg, tattered, khaki bib pants and straw hat. None of his neighbors knew or suspected the old man was *Señor* Ramon Mortez, known to another level of society as the Research Director of the Interspec Foundation, a half dozen miles to the south. And only his elite guard and those working at the Foundation knew Ramon Mortez was El Conciliador . . . one of the most powerful men in New Mexico and, by the end of this week, if things worked out as Mortez planned, the world.

Tending goats was only a cover. In actuality, Mortez was off to his midday prayers. He had much to pray for . . . that he had foreseen and covered all contingencies . . . much for which to be thankful . . . that his new "general" had arrived and was being well received.

Prayers of supplication and thanksgiving. What of atonement? Yes, perhaps a small token to appease . . . Who? What? It must have been a few decades since he had ceased to believe in God, since he had come to realize, in prayer, he was merely turning within to talk to himself. Still, there was a proper place even for that and, as he had done for more than half a century, the old man moved aside the shrubbery hiding the tunnel in the foothills . . . the entrance to his sanctuary.

The Society of Thieves of New Mexico, the 40 Thieves, had

found this ancient hideaway a century ago. And the last of them, Mortez's grandfather, had taken him through the tunnel on his tenth birthday, the old man knowing he would not live until his grandson's coming of age.

Each day thereafter for a month they had walked his grandfather's 41 paces, "One for each of the thieves, and the last for you." It was still 41 for him, since the adolescent fall down a rock chute that had given him his limp.

And as they had then, Mortez stepped out into the small, circular plain surrounded by steep, natural walls ringing into the mountain.

It had changed little since his first visit. In the center was a raised stone slab that seemed like a primitive altar. And on the far side of the half acre or so of space was the entrance to a cave.

There were no birds about today, although they often came. Mortez could remember once being frightened by three eagles. He had hidden in the tunnel until they left.

Today, however, he felt no fear as he strode across the plain followed by his braying companions. He stood confidently before the natural opening, the entrance to his private chapel . . . the cave of the 40 Thieves.

Mortez looked up at the symbols carved over the opening; the big circle, the scratches he likened to notches in a gunslinger's pistol grip. At sunrise, on certain days of the year, the light illuminated the symbols and seemed to make them dance.

To the left of the entrance were some torches, one of which Mortez ignited. Not that it was altogether necessary. Plenty of light spilled in from the courtyard. But today he wanted absolute clarity.

The cave itself was not large, perhaps some 30 by 40 feet. Mortez had hung some religious paintings and an antique tapestry in front of which was a large crucifix suspended from the 15-foot domed ceiling. Below it he had placed an altar table.

El Conciliador knelt in front of his altar and continued to reflect on his first visit.

His grandfather had never shown this place to his father because he felt his own son was too weak, too pious. He had hoped his grandson would be different, but had no time to wait and find out. The old bandit knew he was dying and had to take the gamble or have the secret die with him.

Had he lived, the old man would have discovered his grandson had inherited his cunning. But what of his guts?

When Pearl Harbor came and all the brave young lads enlisted and made their *promesas,* asking God to let them return, Ramon retreated to his cave. His asthma, not to mention his injured leg, would have disqualified him from service anyway . . . everyone knew that . . . but Ramon would not give them that satisfaction. According to him, they were fighting the wrong side. He was an admirer of Mussolini and did not want this country to side with allies who opposed him. Why he had never gone to fight for his idol, he would not have liked anyone to ask.

Mortez knew he was destined for a greater purpose than serving in a *gringo* army. The secret cave became his refuge, and each day he searched within himself to find his hidden purpose. Piety grew to mask his cowardice and any weakness in others was attacked for want of being able to attack himself. "They," his Spanish-American brothers, were weak. And it was surrender to the *gringo* world that kept them weak.

Mortez had witnessed what, in those days, he considered the dying of faith amongst his contemporaries. They were beguiled by the *gringo* pleasures, no longer came to mass, no longer wished to join the societies of their elders.

His father had been a Penitente, but never used the lash . . . because he was weak. Where was the kind of faith that moved mountains?

The faith he mourned had been put into the atoms of destruction. And on July 16, 1945 that heathen faith did, indeed, move his mountain.

From the Jemez Range to his cave, the earth rumbled and shifted the balance of his world, the balance of his power. The testing of the first atomic bomb disturbed the support of the wall behind his then small altar, causing a fissure to form. And when, with the end of the rumbling, Ramon's fear dissipated and he peered through the opening, it was as if God had spoken back to him. Lo and behold, a treasure so fabulous it could not be imagined. In a frenzy, Mortez broke through to the inner chamber where he spent literally days . . . weeks . . . ruminating amongst the elements of the once pagan treasure, now his.

Ramon had heard the legends of the Aztec treasure, supposedly hidden somewhere near Santa Fe. Who could believe it really existed and was his? His!

And of all the pieces, the one he treasured most was the golden skull now adorning the altar . . . his first convert.

Mortez reasoned it had been the wealth of converted pagans that financed the early Church, so it was only fitting for pagan wealth to save it now. Little did he realize in how much need of saving the War had left the Church.

As the Armistice neared, Mortez's cunning went into action. He plotted the use of his newfound wealth to accumulate power. But in whom would he confide?

Ramon went to the elders of the remaining Penitente. These had been his father's friends. He carefully sounded them out, but they were meek men . . . meaning weak, to him . . . with little desire for power. They would, however, welcome his membership and help in replenishing their ranks.

Mortez was no fool. He humbly accepted the role of recruiter. And as the veterans returned, he sought out the superpatriots among them, the men who could be counted on in his new war.

He brought back the old Penitente traditions of discipline and the harsh initiations to insure loyalty. While he turned away no one, Ramon clearly knew who would be a "regular" member and who would become part of his own brotherhoods within the Brotherhood: the *occultos,* or *secretos,* who joined for more selfish, often political reasons; and his handpicked group, including some imported Basque refugees, which he called the *cryptos.* The former he would finance in their businesses and aspirations, political or religious. The latter was a core of men who had demonstrated their fanatacism for his secret cause . . . the eventual control of the Catholic Church.

All this was done with special care to win and keep the favor of the elders without it ever appearing it was even he who was responsible for the growth. From the very beginning, Mortez had begun to set up layers between himself and any notoriety. The elders were, therefore, not aware of his tactics or of his amassing of influence. So the unsuspecting Brotherhood became Mortez's base of power. And as the elders died off, he replaced them with men of his own choosing.

If there was ever any opposition, he had Vincente Cruz as his enforcer.

Young Vincente Cruz came home planning to atone for the necklace of Japanese ears he had styled for himself in the Pacific. Instead he became Ramon's *Guardia de Concilio* and was shown how to use his brutal talents for the greater glory of . . .

Though Mortez had not entirely realized it then, things were no longer being done for the glory of God. The figure on the crucifix that had looked down on his weakness in the cave, had even seen him masturbating on the floor . . . it had to be rejected. Over time, there was a transference of identity. The figure before him had become his suffering, isolated self . . . eventually in carved actuality as well. So in truth, all things were being done for the greater glory of Ramon Mortez.

Within a year after the War, Mortez had melted a good portion of the treasure into bullion and, through his support of the proper politicians, eventually got a bank charter for a board of men who fronted for him.

Properly based and properly shielded, Mortez was ready to contact Rome.

Unbeknownst to him, it was none too soon.

As the Vatican jet broke through the clouds over Santa Fe, Cardinal Casimero Velenari was reflecting on these same past events.

The plane, a Lear, had been a gift to the Holy See stipulated for Church financial business . . . Velenari's bailiwick. The donor had been Velenari's own dummy corporation; so, in reality, it was a gift to himself. The 75-year-old prelate had been proud of this coup, primarily because he had done it on his own, without El Conciliador. It had marked his independence from his one time savior, an independence that was a long time coming. When they first met, Velenari felt exactly like he did today . . . desperate.

In the late '30s there had been in the Vatican and elsewhere amongst the clergy a body of men who felt much like Mortez had initially felt, i.e., faith had gone soft and the only hope for mankind lay in submission to supreme authority . . . one rule under God. The fascist regimes of Il Duce and Hitler represented the opportunity for that structure.

A plot was, therefore, implemented to make "withdrawals" from the Vatican treasury and vaults in order to sell the contents to aid the fascist cause.

Only a handful of men really knew the vast scope of artworks and precious gems and metals forming the core of the Church's wealth, and most of these were principal players in the scheme.

The corpulent and, then, dark-haired and dark-eyed Velenari . . . "Cochon" to even his associates . . . was perhaps the most ardent.

All was done carefully and all would have gone well, except for one problem . . . the swastika bent the wrong way and the plotters ended up staring into the hairy asses of the War's losers.

By this time, the Vatican treasury was sorely depleted and exposure could have crumbled the financial foundation of the Church.

At the same time Mortez was building his base of power, Velenari and the others were trying to cover their tracks, eliminating any of the weak links to the plot. They had even set up an organization called The Light to help in this effort. Who would suspect its founders of being at the root of evil in the Church's ranks? Not even the organization's "sensitive" Guardian, who reported only to them.

Meanwhile, the embezzlers were also desperately trying to find a source of wealth great enough to replace what had been lost. Cardinal Velenari became the roving ambassador for Catholic Relief . . . his own.

One of Velenari's meccas had been the American oil fields where he searched for the Godfearing among those who feared nothing.

By '46, he had been near despair, vowing if he ever got out of this mess he would never again be caught on the weaker side.

It was as if he were pardoned his transgressions, then, when the Bishop of Santa Fe told him he had been contacted by a pious individual with access to enormous wealth.

Velenari had found his savior, the redeemer of the Church's loans. And believing the end justifies the means, the donor's demands were not so outrageous to him as to be a burden . . . at least not at first.

The donor was to remain anonymous, to Velenari, to everyone. Any attempt to uncover his identity would result in immediate cessation of his generosity. On each of the occasions they met, El Conciliador had remained hooded and inscrutable. And though Velenari had a natural inclination to know with whom he was dealing, he was not about to lose his golden eggs for the knowledge.

The reinstatement of the Penitente to the Church was also easy . . . done, January 28, 1947.

Looking the other way with regard to the practices that initially caused the group's excommunication was again no problem. As far as Velenari was concerned, the discipline was good for them. More people should be so inclined.

When it came to selection of Church hierarchy in the Southwestern U.S., Velenari always agreed on the choices anyway.

After all, his mother had been Spanish and he was as partial to that heritage as he was to his father's.

Even when the "recommendations" increased to all the Spanish-speaking countries and some Vatican positions, Velenari and El Conciliador saw eye to hooded eye.

A bank set up in Milan held and disseminated the bullion that arrived in the carved religious *bultos* sent via diplomatic pouch. A bank in Taos oversaw the entire operation. Unbeknownst to Velenari, it was El Conciliador's bank.

For each, the setup was foolproof.

The Church's major artworks were reacquired almost without incident. And there were never more than vague rumors of problems with Vatican finances.

Each had used the other for his own ends, yet their shared goals made it a perfect partnership. At the time, the Cardinal never realized the extent of his own import to his benefactor, nor the ultimate goal of the mysterious *hermano.* It only mattered that he became as indispensible to the Curia as El Conciliador was indispensible to him.

And his growing power only made him more valuable to El Conciliador, who likewise became indispensible to numerous political and religious factions just because he was able to get results from the Cardinal.

Tension did not erupt for more than a decade, until El Conciliador "asked" to have Pope John XXIII removed from office. Velenari had done much, but killing a pope . . . impossible! Then, when the good pontiff started to look unfavorably on him, Velenari relented . . . on the stipulation that it be done slowly, over time, as had been done in the last century when his great-great-uncle had assisted in the murder of Napoleon.

But Velenari was to pay for his initial reluctance, or was it for showing weakness in relenting? For eight long years after John's death he and El Conciliador did not speak, but only dealt through intermediaries. And the funds were cut substantially.

Velenari turned within to deal with the crime in his own

conscience. Ultimately, the Cardinal lost his faith for fear of having to face the wrath of God.

Velenari never understood the cutting of funds had little to do with punishment. El Conciliador had to be content with his empire as it then was. In reality, he feared the depletion of his fortune. After all, even the Aztec treasure was finite.

But once again, the heavens gave Mortez a sign . . . the removal of the fixed price of gold . . . and his fortune became a mega-fortune. It was El Conciliador's signal to spread his influence over the entire Christian world.

Mortez was back in personal contact with the Cardinal, but his manner was no longer humble . . . it was demanding. And after awhile, it became demeaning.

By the time Velenari reached 70, he was fed up with doing El Conciliador's bidding. He would be forced by Church rules to retire in five years and wanted to live out the rest of his days on his own terms. The Cardinal decided to recontact some of his former Nazi friends in South America and, in doing so, learned they had gained enormous wealth within the drug world. He could, too.

A year later, El Conciliador was complaining Velenari had let his hold on the Church's conservative reins slip by allowing the liberal John Paul I to be elected to the papacy. He wanted him out immediately.

The Cardinal was not yet in a position to refuse, but he wanted no personal hand in the deed. He asked his Bolivian friends who the best man for the job would be. They recommended the assassin known as The One.

Afterwards, El Conciliador had sent his papal puppet a golden cross as a reward for a job well done. But Velenari could not wear such a thing, could not even have it in his possession.

He remembered the incident of the golden cross 30 years earlier. After it had surfaced in the aborted robbery of the Swiss banker who had refused to sell it back, the cross had been returned to the Vatican through a young *mafioso.* The man was now reputed to be the power in the Cosa Nostra.

Had this cross not been recovered, it could have exposed the raid on the Vatican vaults. Yet nothing was ever asked in return for this favor. Velenari thought, even at this late date, it would be a nice gesture to use his unwanted present to repay the kindness. Besides, in his drug dealings he might need the friendship of the Cosa Nostra again someday.

Within six months Velenari's life changed, more radically than ever before, more radically than he could have ever imagined possible. As a result of his gesture, he had been brought to the attention of an organization no one dreamed could exist. He had been introduced to Metamorphosis, the fraternity of THE ONE.

It was Velenari's introduction to real power, power in the ideal form. And in the few years since then, the Cardinal had also come to realize power within himself. At 73 he was having experiences far beyond those of his youth. He had trimmed more than 100 pounds off his 300; dropped 20 years from his appearance. Velenari had felt like a young god.

But the Cardinal's humanity finally reaffirmed itself with the stroke he suffered the previous summer. It had taken him four months to recover from the ordeal . . . recover and rethink.

And that was the reason he was, now, so disturbed, why he wrestled within himself so desperately as the plane touched down.

This meeting THE ONE had instructed him to put together had been giving Velenari nightmares. To be sure it would rank with any of the great meetings of this century, but quite possibly it could bring about the destruction of his life's work within the Church.

True, Velenari no longer had faith in God, but he did believe in the organization he had established. He had, like El Conciliador, worked to control men's minds and to keep Church power in the hands of the Southern Europeans, despite even the election of this Polish pope. The prospect of his organization now becoming the domain of the Devil of the Flesh Incarnate frightened him . . . in fact, revolted him . . . in the same way memories of his own unbridled passion during the past few years now revolted him.

Velenari did not believe THE ONE was coming merely to add to his collection of treasures that once belonged to fallen kings. There had to be more to it. And the Cardinal had a feeling whatever it was would somehow put *his* Church in jeopardy.

That's why, today, despite his feeling toward El Conciliador, he would let the Penitente leader know with whom he was dealing; let him know the visitor coming from Romania was no mere antique collector.

His confession would mean violating an oath far more binding than his vows to the Church. But Velenari hoped he could both appease his conscience and cover his tracks so no matter what the outcome, his worst fear would not be realized . . . he would not end up on the losing side again.

12

"Fasani, Raniero—Umbrian hermit. Organizer of the first society of *disciplinati* in 1260 following a major plague the preceding year."

Ian Stone's ancestor? The One had not gone back so far in his research of the Penitente; obviously a mistake. And the Assassin did not like making mistakes.

Anyone checking into Ian Stone's background would find information only on his mother; and she was from part Italian ancestry. It *was,* therefore, possible she could be Fasani's descendant.

But more important than their tracing the name back over seven centuries was the fact the Penitente had linked The One to Ian Stone in the first place. That had bothered the Assassin for the last five weeks. How? And how much else did they know?

The man with the bandaged face closed the reference book and sat back to think. There was no one else in the Taos Library to bother him. For over 15 years he had had no name, only aliases. He was The One. And he had never before used his real name; would never think of using it unless he were in imminent danger. What's more, neither his fingerprints nor his teeth could be linked back to his true identity. He had even managed to switch his army records. And there was no one who could link him to Ian Stone now that his mother and his aunt were both dead. So what happened?

"No, no . . . It couldn't be," he mumbled as a previously avoided thought hit him. Perhaps there *was* someone else who would know if Stone was related to Fasani. The ancestry did not have to be on his mother's side.

After all these years, had his mother's worst fears been realized; had he been discovered by his father? El Conciliador wasn't his father, was he?

The One thought back to the original communication:

> "Accept this [an old army photo of him] not as a threat, but as a gesture of friendship. You have aided us once through our dear brother in Rome. Now, we ask you to join us as our brother, so that we might serve each other. Come meet with us in Taos during the Holy Week. Together we shall make this world a great place in which to live.
>
> El Conciliador."

It had been addressed to Ian Stone.

The letter had been entrusted to Cardinal Velenari, who obviously knew how to contact him by mail from their first dealings. But the "dear brother in Rome" had, for some reason, decided to betray him to the CIA. It had to have been Velenari. Who else?

He would contact Rome and learn Velenari's whereabouts. The Cardinal would be sent a deadly "gift" from Penitenteland.

What other sources did this El Conciliador have for getting his information? The One was not about to accept the discovery of his father; at least, not readily. He recalled only too well how his mother had lived in fear of being discovered by his father, from whom, he had surmised, she fled . . . to whom she was probably never married. She had refused to relate the entire story. After her death, he tried to retrace the steps of her early life, but his mother had covered her tracks well . . . a trait she passed on.

Before Viet Nam, it was important to know who his father was. After, he had other things on his mind.

Where would El Conciliador get a photo of him? If it were from his father and his father knew who and where he was, why did he never come after his mother?

And, if he had betrayed him, why didn't Velenari give the CIA a copy of the photo? Neri had told Stone there was no photo. Was he lying?

The One didn't have any satisfactory answers and he didn't like the feeling. He decided he would work with what he did know . . .

For one thing, he was now confident this wasn't a trap to get rid of him. His supposed ancestry legitimized Stone to the Penitente. Either the Penitente needed him or the man behind them was forced to make him acceptable to the others because he was needed.

It was, of course, entirely possible there was no relationship to Fasani. It might all be a ruse, nothing in the least diabolical.

On the other hand, it would not be difficult to believe his pawn was Fasani's descendant, certainly not after the way he took to the ceremonies of the last few nights. The Assassin never ceased to be amazed at the actions of his alter ego. Would anything ever shake the block in his mind? Would he ever realize he was not Ian Stone?

The One realized he didn't despise "Ian" so much anymore. "Stone" was doing well what pawns are supposed to do . . . protect the king.

As he left the Taos Library, the man with the bandaged face was more relaxed, despite the questions plaguing him. He had opened himself to more possibilities and that, in itself, was progress.

In the microfile in his room, The One had the name of a

man at the Geneological Society in London. He would cable to see if the Stone heritage could be traced to Fasani. The rest would unfold shortly, for he was certain the main players were about to enter the stage. In this regard, *he* was a "sensitive."

Ian had sublimated his troubles. This was a perfect day. All afternoon he had accepted Diana's wanting to be with him and his wanting to be with her. There had been no daydreams of Meredith. There had been no need. Someone else found him desirable.

If he thought about it, he was more in demand than he had ever been, albeit out of mistaken identity. Ian realized he liked being in demand. He decided to make the most of this new situation.

But what about Diana? She didn't know his real world. Was she impressed with him as he was, or could she have mistaken him for someone else, too?

"Are you all right, Ian?" she asked as they removed their skis.

"Hmm? Oh, sure. My mind was just wandering. You really wore me out today. I think I'll take a nap before dinner."

"Would you like company?" she asked coquettishly.

"Then I wouldn't nap, and I'll need it for tonight."

"Do we have big plans?" she wanted to know.

Ian knew he was tired. He was mouthing off too much.

"Unfortunately, I made arrangements to see an old friend of mine later," he lied. "But I hope you'll share a bottle of wine with me over dinner," he hastily added.

Suddenly Ian started to panic, "Diana, I didn't know this would happen. I didn't dream . . . And tonight's not what you might think."

"It's all right," she consoled him, wondering why he had reacted so apologetically.

She started to walk away.

"Wait a minute," Ian yelled.

A new focus was coming into play. He had no obligations to anyone . . . only to himself. Screw the Aztecs and their treasure. This was supposed to be his trip and his time, and everybody had been usurping his desires as they always had.

"Yes?" she turned.

"I really don't like sleeping alone," he smiled, almost shyly.

Diana saw the genuineness that had attracted her in the first place. She came back. Together, they carried their skis up the stairs to his chalet and went in.

Ian recognized the odor right away. It was the same as last night. Dried blood. He glanced at Diana. She seemed to know it, too.

"I don't think you needed me to not be alone," she whispered.

Strewn across the bed was the body of Cecilia Troni, her throat cut. As they moved forward, they saw the note pinned to her body:

> "You've inconvenienced me. Now, it's your turn . . . until you're ready to cooperate.
>
> "If you want to talk, come to the hot tub. Get in and keep your arms on the rim where they can be seen."

Ian felt himself trembling, "Oh my god!" He turned to the equally astounded Diana, "I don't know how to begin to explain . . . You'd better leave. I don't want you implicated in any . . ."

Ian couldn't say any more. The blood rushed through his system so quickly, he couldn't hear himself think.

"Ian, you're going to have to trust me," Diana responded. "Who did this?"

He looked at her, his eyes wide with incomprehension, "I don't know. I swear to you, I don't know."

She stared at him in disbelief.

"You've got to believe me," he exclaimed. "I don't know what it's all about. All I do know is this lady was an innocent and I don't want you hurt."

He began kicking off his ski boots.

"What are you doing?" Diana asked. "You're not going to meet this killer, are you?"

Ian slipped on some short boots and started for the door, "I've got to get to the bottom of this. Please, go back to your room."

"I think I'm going to be sick," she said. "Go on if you must. I'll leave in a minute."

As Ian descended the stairs in a daze, Diana quickly reexamined the note, and then the room.

From the lining of her jacket she removed a sensor with which she swept the walls and the furniture. She was surprised at what she found . . . two different bugs, both sophisticated; one European and one American.

Diana realized her voice had been heard by both, so she went immediately to the bathroom and pretended to throw up. Not much time had elapsed. It might pass.

She then placed a third bug, not as sophisticated as the other two, but then, neither was her budget.

Diana knew she had stumbled upon something major. Who was this man Stone? And who was so interested in him? She remembered her instructions from the Guardian, "Keep your eyes open, but if you see anything, don't interfere without checking with me first." She would have to do that tonight.

As Ian approached the door to the spa, he suddenly froze. What the hell was he doing? Who would want to kill Cecilia? Who had been "inconvenienced"?

Then it came to him. It had to be the CIA. How stupid to kill her, when she wasn't even involved. Whoever this new jerk was, he was sure to get himself killed as quickly as Hamel and Neri. Ian also realized there was no way he could be implicated in this murder. He had been with Diana all day. Why not just go to the cops?

"Excuse me . . . "

Another skier moved by him into the spa. As the door opened, Ian could see a half dozen people inside. He turned quickly and was heading back toward his room as Diana came down the stairs carrying her skis.

"Come on," he said, pulling her. "What happened?" she wanted to know.

"Nothing. If I go in there, I'll never get my nap. Let's go to your place," he pleaded.

"You're crazy," Diana said. "What about the body? Someone will find her and . . ."

"And what? I'm not involved. I obviously didn't do it. You'd testify to that, I hope," he pleaded, wide-eyed.

"Well, sure . . ."

Diana was perplexed. If this man were a professional, how could he act this way?

"Good. Then let's get a message to the sheriff," he said, his face turning redder, as if he were buzzed up.

He pulled her into the bar to use the phone, but as usual, there was a line.

"Great!" he said with exasperation. "I need a drink. How about you?"

"Ian, I don't believe you're doing this," she said.

"Brandy . . . ," Ian called to the bartender. "Sure you don't want something?"

She shook her head, no.

"Room 18," he said, downing the drink in a flash. Then he pulled her through the dining area and past the reception desk. He was feeling giddy.

"You know what I love about you best?" Ian quizzed.

"No. What?" she responded, not knowing how else to handle him.

"Your nostrils."

Diana had to laugh, "My what? . . ."

"No, really. They are the most beautiful nostrils I have ever seen," he said with absolute seriousness.

"You're a crazy man!"

"Schizoid," he echoed Meredith.

As they left the lodge, a cold blast of wind caught Ian unawares. It was a bit of reality. He didn't like that. It made him wonder again what the hell he was doing? There was a dead woman in his room. Where did he get off joking around when someone lay dead? Was he just performing for Diana . . . or for himself?

He looked at her as they walked in silence. She seemed strong. He took comfort in that. Ian leaned over to kiss her cheek, and instead she gave him her lips.

He became more confused. There was no trace of her having vomited, nor of his mouthwash. Why did she say she might be sick? Perhaps, she just wasn't . . . Who was she, really, Ian started to wonder all over again? No, he couldn't be suspicious of her now. He didn't have the energy. He really needed to rest.

Diana's room was in one of the bungalows behind the Edelweiss. It was quiet and comfortable, with windows on two sides. There was a large bed; the furniture, rustic.

Ian sat on the bed as he removed his clothes.

"You know what?" he stated. "I'm wiped."

With that, he lay back and dozed.

* * *

Ian was in a gym, peddling an exercycle. Every wall of the room was a mirror, making it seem as if he were part of a whole team of cyclists. Suddenly, one of the cyclists stopped peddling, turned toward him and stared.

Ian's knees locked . . .

* * *

. . . and he awakened.

He was naked, with Diana lying along side, stroking the scars on his knees. It was dark both outside and in, save for the flicker of a candle next to the bed. Ian gave a start as he became conscious.

"Easy . . . I'm here," she said. "Bad dream?"

"No, not this time, I don't think. I can't remember. What time is it?"

"Dinner time," she said.

"Why didn't you wake me?"

"You looked like you needed the sleep. Besides, I wouldn't think you'd be in a hurry to face the police . . . which, I believe, is what's ahead for you unless you have a very understanding room maid."

He smiled.

"What?" she asked.

"Come closer," he whispered.

She was already close. The warmth of her body, her skin touching his, made Ian sigh heavily. It was, more than anything, a relief.

Diana looked into his eyes. The gray of her iris was the color of dark storm clouds, her breath like the wind before the tempest.

Her hand went up from his knees and cupped Ian's scrotum, firmly but gently, before rising up the side of his penis. Ian's blood surged and another heavy sigh escaped from his lungs. Suddenly Diana was on top of him, again her hair blinding Ian in a silky moss which she swirled back and forth over his face. Still holding him, she rubbed the head of his swelling member in her juices, then plunged him deep within.

Ian's back arched off the bed in reaction and Diana rose, then fell with him. Her hand cradled his jaw and she darted her tongue between his lips, making slow, languid circles around his own. Ian was trembling with excitement, but relaxed under the hypnotic sensation, abandoning himself to her, willing to follow her lead.

Diana's head rose as she sensed his capitulation. She placed a hand on each of his shoulders, pinning Ian to the mattress. Her hair cleared his eyes and Ian opened them to see the breath swelling her chest, making her breasts appear even larger and more firm. Diana's hips rocked from side to side and her vaginal muscles alternately tightened around him and released their grip. Ian could feel the pulsing of his cock, the warm glide against her walls. His toes curled, he bit his lip and his eyes rolled in delirium.

Diana's teeth clenched and her own eyes shut as she sensed penetrating chambers . . . both physically and emotionally . . . she had never let any man explore. Ambivalence of total surrender to passion made her push down harder against him to demonstrate her power, but it only took him deeper still. Her eyes shot open as she felt herself approach a forbidden zone. She looked down expecting to see an antagonist, but found a face pleading for acceptance. A cry darted from her lips. This was a moment to try and hold onto, a moment she did not want to end. She sucked from her navel, wanting every bit of her to be filled with him. Her palms began to sweat. Diana felt her juices running down her inner thighs, matting his pubic hair. She felt his penis swelling beyond its limit and knew he had to come. Diana wanted desperately to stop, to freeze . . . But fire does not freeze. The end had to come. They had to come. Now. Together.

"Aaahh!" a piercing whimper of a frightened bird. Her arms slid forward and she came down on top of him nuzzling his chin with her mane. Her entire body was shaking and Diana wished she could let herself cry.

This was the first time Diana had ever been able to have an orgasm with a man inside her. She had never before wanted to give a man that satisfaction, that warmth, that release of her control.

And Ian was overjoyed that she had reached her orgasm with him. Meredith never had, nor had she ever been able to come without oral or manual stimulation. It had made Ian feel inadequate, even though he felt it was a psychological rather than an anatomical problem. He believed it almost always was, despite what the unfortunates claimed their analysts said. It merely convinced Ian analysts didn't know any normal women.

Lately, he had come to believe he didn't, either. Ian had even felt he was catching the dreaded "disease." Now all that was in the past. Savoring their self-victories, the two lovers remained speechless, suspended in the silence of their thoughts, still pulsating with the warmth of afterglow.

A world away, a slight tap was heard against the window pane. It was not a threatening sound, but it made them start from their reverie.

"Ian," a low voice wheezed. "I..It's Alex."

"Beautiful."

Ian slid from the bed to the window and eased it open. Instinctively, Diana extinguished the candle.

"How'd you know I was here?" Ian demanded.

"Wh..Who doesn't know you're here? Theresa spotted two other stakeouts."

"Theresa! My ski instructor?"

"The same. No time to explain now. L..Let me in," Alex whispered.

Dashwood entered through the window before Ian could protest, tumbling onto the floor in the effort.

"We're going to have to switch places," the older man said.

Diana slipped on her robe as he got to his feet.

Alex reddened in the darkness, "S..Sorry, I didn't mean to make it sound like that. I'm frightfully unhappy to have to meet you under these circumstances, Miss Bastian. I'm Alex Dashwood."

Diana nodded in amused acknowledgement.

"Look, Alex, I'm out of it," Ian declared.

"What is this all about, Ian?" Diana wanted to know.

"Oh, sorry," Alex wheezed again. "I guess he hasn't brought you up to date. Dear me, I assumed he would. I've forgotten how the new intimacy works."

Ian was losing patience, "What's wrong? Did they find the body?"

"Wh..What body?"

"The one in Ian's room," Diana interjected.

"I have no idea. There wasn't one there when I went to find you. Who was supposed . . . ?" Alex started to ask.

"When was that?" Ian interrupted.

"T..Ten minutes ago. Before Theresa told me you were here," the older man responded.

"Alex, what is she doing keeping tabs on me?" Ian wanted to know.

"I'll give it to you in brief," Dashwood said. "We don't have time.

"Last night Theresa invited me to a command performance at the Pueblo in Taos. Seems we were seen together. They've been keeping their eyes on you. Or was it the reverse? No matter. They're very concerned about . . . well, a lot of things, really, but especially about what's happening with the Penitente. You see, a lot of the Indians are Penitente. Well, the long and the short of it is . . . I told them our story."

"All of it?!" Ian asked, incredulously.

"Well, mostly mine. You see, they are descendants of the Zunis, and even the Aztecs . . . the rightful heirs, as it were. Besides, I thought we'd need allies."

"I'm not at war," Ian corrected. "All I need is . . . all I want is just to be with this woman."

"Ian, my boy, I'm afraid it isn't a game. It's s..serious business and you're seriously involved," Alex admonished.

"Ian, do I get a vote?" Diana asked, looking at him with beseeching eyes. They glowed even in the darkness; eyes he couldn't refuse.

There was an unsteady pause.

"Sure. Why not? It's obvious I can't run my own life," Ian complained.

"Go speak to these people. I'll go with you," she offered.

"Well, I don't know . . . ," Alex interjected.

"You heard her. If she doesn't go, I don't go," Ian stipulated.

Alex was dubious, "All right. But first, she and I will have to lead the others off the scent. Then we'll join you."

Ian and Diana both dressed quickly while Alex gazed into the night. As he watched Diana slip on her slacks, Ian wondered whether he would ever see her beautiful legs again.

Ian put on Alex's ski jacket and hat. The latter had already taken his.

"Goodbye, love," Diana said, kissing him.

Then as she and Dashwood exited, Ian slipped out the window and proceeded in the direction Alex had specified.

No more than ten paces out, an Indian entered Ian's path from the brush, turned and led the way. Ian barely heard the two others who fell in behind as he passed the same spot from which the first appeared.

Suddenly there was a howl like that of a wounded coyote. A pair of hands from behind pushed him on faster. The quartet broke into a full run toward a van hidden in the trees, its motor running. They jumped in and were off without lights until they reached the drive leading away from the lodges. When the lights went on, Ian saw the driver was Theresa.

In the dim light provided by the dashboard and the moon, Ian fixed on the troubled face of the Indian who had shoved him into the van. Something had gone wrong. That howl . . .

The tall young man grabbed some object Ian could not see from a backpack on the floor, opened the van door and leapt out as they neared the main road. Ian was speechless. The others betrayed no emotion.

Braden had been thrown off by the Indian and the two who exited the room disappeared. Now, to the CIA chief's astonishment, the wounded man had disappeared as well; there was just a small pool of blood and a trail that suddenly and eerily vanished. Braden thought of the Transylvanian countryside and wondered why he made the connection. He felt confused.

The only thing of which he was sure was the man who exited Diana Bastian's room with her was not Stone. But who was he? Who was she? And how would he find his quarry?

No one spoke until they were down the mountain. Then Theresa was told to take a left where there was no road. They followed a route across the prairie so as not to be followed. At least, that's what Ian assumed. A few miles later, Theresa was told to turn off the headlights, and they finished their journey by moonlight.

The tiered adobe structures making up the Taos Pueblo were an awesome sight in the moon's near-full illumination. Ian remembered the first night's table talk of how ancient it was. Entering the grounds was like entering another time zone . . . a more peaceful time.

As they got out of the van, Ian looked directly at Theresa. She smiled, but said nothing. Her expression seemed fiercely proud and her eyes were more striking than he had noticed before. Although confused as to what was happening, Ian took strength from her gaze. As he followed the two young Indians toward one of the larger buildings, he started to relax.

Upon entering the adobe structure, Ian found himself in a large domed hall. A log fire burned in the center of the space, its smoke rising through a hole in the ceiling. As in the Penitente *morada,* the floor was earthen.

A group of elderly Indian men sat around the fire in silence. No one looked up when they entered; not until Ian was brought up to the circle.

"Welcome, Ian Stone," said a man with an incredibly strong face. He looked like the land; fissures and rivelets running across his forehead, down his cheeks and neck. And, like the land, his age was timeless. His energy seemed that of a waterfall.

"Come sit with us, Ian Stone," he continued. "Some things are better said with the knees bent."

As Ian sat, one of the others in the group passed a long-stemmed pipe to the man who had spoken. The passer then lit the tobacco as the other puffed. As soon as the pipe was going, he gave it to Ian. Luckily for him, he puffed lightly. It was strong stuff.

Ian started to pass it back, but the Indian indicated with a simple gesture that it should continue around the circle.

"Tonight, we use the ancient customs because we will speak of ancient things. I am George Montoya," the man said to Ian, ". . . Brown Bear, to my people. I am the Cacique, or head of this Pueblo in what you would call a religious sense.

"Mr. Alex Dashwood has told us an amazing tale," he continued dryly, looking into Ian's eyes.

"We have long lived with the Penitente," Brown Bear mused. "Bloodlines have mixed and there are Penitente among us . . . those who believe in the *Cristo.* But since the great war of nations, there have been many changes . . . changes difficult to understand.

"Dashwood's story explains, yet baffles. We have heard of El Conciliador, the mysterious leader, who seeks to bring the Penitente to a position of power and spread their numbers across the land. Many follow him, sounding his praises. Yet many would be appalled at such as you witnessed this Sunday past."

A few elderly women entered the hall from the opposite end, carrying a large kettle. A few more followed with bowls and cups. One held a big coffee pot.

"Ah, food and drink," Brown Bear said, switching focus. "I hope our simple fare will please you."

The women dished out steaming chili and bread slices to all. The coffee was put on a hot stone from the fire. Then they left as quietly as they had come.

The chili was spicy, but delicious. Ian hadn't realized how hungry he was.

As they ate, the Cacique continued speaking, "Mr. Stone, unlike your people, we Indians have no single God who judges good and evil. Ours is a universal spirit that may take many forms. And these spirits give us various powers. I, for instance, am a *curandero,* or healer.

"Also, for us the notions of good and evil are not as defined as your people would have them. To the Navajo, it is simple . . . good is beauty, evil is anti-beauty. To the Hopi, good comes from a tribal cooperation; it is the use of power for the self as opposed to the tribe that is evil. And for us, good and evil are ways of thinking . . . the evil being a negative force lurking in the shadows that exists in all of us. Something that must simply be endured.

"Much of good comes in respect for the spirits of the earth. This land is sacred to us," he said with a sweeping gesture. "It is our trust. A learned man of your people, called Cayce, once wrote of the great energy here. That is why much art is made in this land. The energy stimulates creation.

"We have shared our land with your people. We have," he said with a trace of bitterness, "endured your bombs, your yellow arches and much other foolishness because we have been able to keep a balance.

"But now the signs show the dark powers are growing. An old *bruja* in the ruins confirms this is so. You see, Mr. Stone," Brown Bear said, touching Ian's knee, "when those who think the evil way amass strong power, it takes strong power to break them. Unusual alliances must be formed, as, when the disease is too strong, I must go to the *arbulario,* or witch doctor, for help.

"And so we come to you, Mr. Stone. Your coming was foretold to us in The Bruja's riddle . . . 'The one who is not the one, yet may be the one.' It was not known whether you were on the side of good or evil. But there are those who now say you, yourself, are not evil," the Cacique smiled. "So, with your help, we hope to unravel this riddle."

Ian sat dumbfounded as the old man continued, "We must understand fully who you are thought to be, who is using you and what is wanted from you by all involved. You must have extraordinary courage, for it means you must continue."

Ian knew he should have guessed the payoff.

"But I didn't ask to be part of this," he pined. "It's not my . . ."

" *'De la muerte y de la suerte, nadie se escape'* " Brown Bear quoted. ". . . Death and destiny, no one can avoid, Mr. Stone.

"For centuries we have kept our peaceful vigil, waiting for the times of greater and lesser magnitude when action would be necessary. One such time is at hand, Mr. Stone . . . for us and you. Look within to find that which blocks recognition. Listen to your dreams. They are the key. Then, awaken to your destiny."

They sat in silence a minute. It passed all too quickly.

"And now it is time to go. No doubt you are expected at your *morada* . . . Yes?"

This was it! Ian was panicked. He didn't understand. What was a *bruja*? Why did he have the feeling he should do exactly what they wanted him to do, even though he feared returning to the *morada?* And where was Meredith? Why wasn't she . . . no . . . Diana . . . It was Diana who was supposed to come.

One of the young braves who had brought him entered the hall and, behind him, Ian saw the Indian who had jumped from the van. He was naked, except for an animal skin wrapped around his loins and a belt from which his boots hung, the laces tied together. He moved back into the shadows as the other came over to the Cacique.

How the hell did he get there so quickly, Ian wondered. And why was he dressed like that?

"Your friends will not be coming," Brown Bear said to him. "It is too dangerous. One of the Coyote Clan has been hurt."

He stood and Ian rose after him, wondering why he had to like these people . . . why he felt so comfortable with them?

"Here. Take this," said the Cacique.

He handed Ian a tied cloth bag that had been hanging from his silver-studded belt.

"It's filled with herbs," the Cacique said, " . . . *cachana* and *calabazilla.* And a special stone . . . a *piedra iman.* They will bring protection from without and, hopefully, even from within.

"Examine your dreams. Remember, all the characters in them are aspects of *you*. And expect visions," Brown Bear warned. "Some may be from your god of good and some may be from your god of evil. You must learn to distinguish which. All may depend on it."

One of the Indians in the circle started a chant which was taken up by the others. Ian could not, of course, understand the words, but it seemed uplifting. It added a bounce to the questions racing through his mind.

"You have many questions," the Cacique intuited, "but now is not the time. We shall smoke again."

"I don't understand . . . ," Ian mumbled, shaking his head.

" . . . why it is we face evil or even life in such different ways?" Brown Bear again intuited.

Ian looked at him in awe. It was exactly the question he would have wanted to ask had he been able to find the words.

Brown Bear chuckled, "The Indian religion is to be happy . . . the white man's religion is to be sad. That's why we are two different people."

Then he laughed, "It takes hard work and much power not to make life so serious. Our religion *is* life, and therefore we spend much time on it. But go now."

Ian took great comfort in the Cacique's words. He wondered if they would be his only comfort that evening.

13

Ian stood in the dark before the *morada.* It was very quiet . . . just the sound of the wind whispering through the aspens.

Unlike the previous night, there was only one other car besides the pickup the Indians had given him to use. Ian was surprised he had been able to find his way, but then he always did have a good sense of direction.

Why was it so quiet? Perhaps there was no meeting tonight. Maybe the death of Troni's wife scared them off. His breath froze as Ian wondered if this were a trap. Then why hadn't it been sprung?

Ian took a deep breath and approached the carved wooden door. Only a flicker of light was discernable through a small crack. He knocked.

A voice came from within, "*¿Quién toca en las puertas de esta morada?*"

He responded automatically, "*Non son las puertas de la morada. Sola las puertas de su conciencia,*" not believing he had remembered correctly.

"Venga," the voice invited.

The voice was not familiar to Ian, but it was to The One, who listened from the Abominable Snowmansion. The Assassin moved like lightning.

Ian entered and immediately donned one of the hooded cloaks hanging by the door. In the light of a lantern on the altar, he could see the lone, hooded figure sitting before it.

"Approach, my son." The voice was friendly.

Ian walked eleven of the thirteen paces to the altar, wondering if this was El Conciliador. A hand raised to him from the folds of the robe exposed a red cassock beneath, and Ian knew it was not. He automatically went down on one knee, leaned forward and kissed the ring belonging to a cardinal of the Church.

"It has been awhile, has it not?" spoke Cardinal Velenari in his thick Italian accent.

Ian didn't know what to say. It didn't matter, for the Cardinal continued.

"I would never have supposed you would have had this desire in you. How fortunate for El Conciliador at this time . . . for Holy Mother Church.

"But I must beg your temperance, my son. I do not wish to question your actions, yet I must tell you that the death of the Troni woman could frighten those whose acceptance of you is most important. And there are others whose support could disappear with a scandal."

"I did not kill her," Ian replied hoarsely.

Velenari stopped, as if subconsciously troubled by the response, and then went on.

"I did not think it was so. That is why I have come, hoping you would as well. It demonstrates your innocence for you would have undoubtedly forced tonight's location from the poor woman."

The Cardinal's breath seemed short and he paused to clear his throat before continuing, "Tonight's ceremonies are at a *morada* in Talpa. It's not far.

"Last night you gained the acceptance of the Penitente's inner core. Tonight may be more difficult. You must convince the membership at large of your interest in joining their ranks.

"A time of great power is at hand," the Cardinal said with a forceful gesture. But Ian noticed a shakiness in his voice.

"You will share in that power," Velenari continued, "but to achieve it will require an army. Go now. If all transpires as it should, tomorrow night you will meet El Conciliador himself.

"Take these directions," Velenari said, extending a piece of paper from beneath his robe. "Present them at the door. It will show you learned from me and not the Troni woman."

Two hands locked onto the sheet of paper as the old prelate tried to look into the recesses of the hood with questioning eyes. But with his other hand, Ian took the Cardinal's from the paper and bent again to kiss his ring. Then he turned and left quickly.

Cardinal Velenari sat deep in thought as the pickup's engine revved into gear and faded down the road. Something was amiss. He could feel it. Feel . . .

The old man shot up like a bolt, "Impostor!"

A mischievous laugh echoed through the empty *morada,* "No, Velenari . . . pawn."

The prelate froze as the hooded figure strode into the chamber.

"And a good one . . . as you saw. Although I commend you on your perception. Sit down, your excellency," the voice came threateningly.

Velenari had no choice. He was too old to run.

The figure moved forward and went down on one knee before him. Velenari extended the ring on his trembling hand, but instead of a kiss, his wrist was caught in a vise-like grip.

"You know what my employment stipulation is, don't you?"

"*Certo* . . . ," he said hoarsely. "Of course."

"Complete confidentiality," The One said firmly.

"It has been observed," Velenari winced, his circulation cut off.

"Then how does the CIA know of my involvement with John Paul?" The One asked.

"CIA?! . . ." he echoed, perplexed. "They did not learn from me," he spoke truthfully.

"Only you and your El Conciliador were party to it. Who else knew?"

"No one," Velenari responded as his mind clicked away at the possibilities.

"Why was I invited here?" The One asked.

"Invited? You ask . . . "

The One was getting a picture, "Go on."

"You asked to join the Penitente," the Cardinal said, shakily. "You claimed a legacy."

"To whom was this request made?"

"To El Conciliador directly . . . through the letter delivered to me. But I gave it to him. I never opened it before he did. I swear."

Velenari was also starting to get a picture, "Who . . . who invited you to join?" The old man had guessed what was happening, but he needed confirmation.

"Your El Conciliador . . . through you," The One responded, watching the Cardinal's face carefully.

Velenari broke into a cold sweat as the puzzle came together for him. This scenario had been engineered by THE ONE. Exactly how, and for what reason, he did not know. But the position in which he now found himself was the penalty for betraying his master in his confession to El Conciliador earlier in the evening. Whatever fate was in store for him at the hand of this assassin would be far more merciful than the consequences THE ONE would exact for his transgression. Perhaps . . . No. Now that he knew of the pawn, there was no safe harbor. Velenari knew death was at hand, but he had to try to survive.

The amulet! The prelate put his hand to his neck, hooking his thumb underneath the cord from which his crucifix hung. At the same time, he hooked a second chain from which the amulet hung beneath his cassock. As he ran his thumb down toward the cross, the amulet came forth. It was a circle of gold surrounding a gelatinous circle within. Pretending to kiss his crucifix, Velenari bit into the inner circle, extracting its liquid.

"Please make it quick," he begged.

The One knew it would be useless to torture the old man. His constitution wouldn't take the strain. And he would have gone the limit, because it was obvious there was someone considerably more frightening to the old man than he.

"Mi dispiace, padre."

As the Assassin drew his pistol, a transformation seemed to come over the old Cardinal. His eyes flamed, his lips curled back and his hands flexed like a cat extending its claws. Then a growl ripped from his throat, masking the squirt of the silencer. Velenari's face contorted as the bullet's impact pitched him off the chair.

The bandaged face looked down at the fallen Prince aghast. What had he just witnessed? Nothing like even he had ever seen. But something with which he would not have wanted to tangle. He bent down and yanked the amulet free from Velenari's neck and sniffed the coated gelatin. There was no odor; and all the liquid was gone.

Suddenly, the Assassin began to feel like a pawn himself. It angered him. He was . . . would be no one's pawn.

But speaking of pawns, who else was using his? The girl was a professional. He had found both her and "The Man's" bugs when he removed Cecilia Troni from Ian's room. For whom was Diana Bastian working? And how did the man who disguised himself as Ian fit in? His pawn seemed to be building his own contingent.

Tomorrow, a lot of questions had to find answers. Yet, one was apparently answered tonight. El Conciliador was not his father; whoever engineered his being here . . . perhaps . . .

The Assassin reached down with one hand, took Velenari by the nape of his neck and pulled him toward a wooden casket leaning against the wall. It was to hold the *bulto* of the *Cristo* on Good Friday. The One opened the casket and laid the Cardinal's corpse inside. He removed the silencer from his pistol and put the small gun in the dead man's hand, then closed the lid. It would appear a macabre suicide.

As he removed the traces of the true scenario, he realized a decision had to be made; who would meet El Conciliador? His pawn had proved far more valuable than he had expected. It would be a shame to have to get rid of him now. Was he beginning to feel? . . .

It was too quiet outside. The One pulled the hood back over his head and snuffed the lantern.

The silence broke. West. East. Amateurs. Where was the professional?

With the stealth of a Ninja, he moved toward the front entrance. Overhead was a trapdoor leading to the small bell tower on top of the *morada.* A rope hung through a hole to just within arm's reach. In an instant, The One flipped the trap open and was up inside.

It was cloudy now and the moonlight was fleeting. Still, he could see a vehicle off the road to the east. That one would be safe. His would not be. And he had disabled Velenari's.

"We must speak now, Mr. Stone."

North. He was a good tracker. Very good. He might be The Man. The goons, he knew, were only there to "inconvenience" him. He would have to demonstrate his skill.

A pop was heard as the gas pellet fractured the *morada* window. The Assassin closed the trap and waited.

In a minute, two large locals came out from behind the aspens to the south. Both were wearing gas masks. As they entered the building, the moon slipped behind a cloud and The One vaulted over the side of the tower and dropped to the ground in front. Before the moon reappeared he had taken their former position behind the aspens at the lip of the empty pond.

There were at least five, he figured; so, there was probably more than one vehicle. He would go east. As the flashlights searched the *morada,* he moved.

"He's out," a voice called. "Vargas . . . "

Bastard. He must be using infrared lenses, The One guessed.

Suddenly, a giant of a man rose up from the bushes in front of him. The Assassin went low into a crouch, and then rose up with the tops of his bent wrists slamming into the man's crotch. The upward momentum lifted him into the air and over The One's head. The man crashed behind him with an agonized yelp.

He could hear the two men rushing from the *morada,* the flanker and The Man. The race was on.

A vehicle started to the north. Six. Then the lights flashed from the vehicle toward which he ran. Seven. He closed the distance swiftly, a ghost floating along the dark landscape. The motor in front of him revved, and the pickup started to move.

He angled off toward a cluster of rocks near the road, belying the vehicle was his goal.

When the pickup slowed as the driver tried to judge the terrain, the prey used the moment to reverse and head straight for it. The driver hit the brakes as the cloaked figure leapt onto the hood and then the roof of the cab. The Assassin reached through the window and stuck his other gun into the man's ear before the driver knew what was happening.

"Get out of there," he ordered.

The driver responded immediately, opening the door and diving out. The vehicle was still rolling in gear as The One swung through the open door. Without missing a beat, he hit the gas.

A shoulder slammed into his . . . Eight? Automatic response knocked the attacker against the passenger door. He didn't rebound. It was Antonio Troni; The Man's source. Dead.

The One sped ahead knowing full well what he wanted to use as this race's finish line.

Within seconds he was off the prairie and bouncing onto the road back toward Arroyo Seco. He heard the thud of the other vehicle as it, too, hit the road, less than a half minute behind him. The lead was sufficient for his strategy, if he could maintain it.

The Assassin burned rubber as he swerved around the corner

by the Abominable Snowmansion and headed toward Taos. The '74 Chevy didn't have much to offer, but he banked on the other vehicle being handicapped by a heavy load of personnel, even if it was more powerful.

By the time The One had covered the five miles to the main road, he had not lost ground. But the main road was not his goal. He sped straight across it toward the open plains . . . and the Rio Grande Gorge.

Seven miles west, the Rio Grande ripped its way southward, having opened a crevasse 650 feet below the surface of the highway. It was a spectacular sight at any time, but tonight it would be more so.

The fox wanted another 15 seconds to set up and pressed hard down the straightaway.

Unwanted, the moon peeked through the clouds. The One needed complete darkness for his plan. He tried to calculate the drift. It would be close.

The vehicle shook as the speedometer was hitting 95, and he was starting to lose ground. The other vehicle was bigger and more powerful than he had hoped it would be. It now became a question whether he could even beat it to the bridge. In two minutes, tops, he had to come up with an alternate plan.

With a mile to go his lead was still diminishing. No more than 200 yards filled the gap. Then, finally, cloud cover immersed him in darkness.

Just out of range of the other truck's headlights, he killed the lights on the approach to the bridge. He had made it by an instant.

The Assassin pulled the emergency brake and turned the wheel, putting the truck into a spin . . . 45° . . . 90° . . . 135° . . . fractions of a second. He hit the lights . . . 180° . . . and threw the dead man onto the gas pedal before bailing out, rolling onto the walkway against the rail.

. . . 200° . . . The oncoming vehicle started to swerve, but there was no place to go. Its higher front end rode up onto the hood of the pickup and it launched over the smaller vehicle, shooting across the guard rail. The back wheels grabbed at the steel safety for a desperate instant before taking a section of it along as the truck floated out into space and then dove into the abyss. Half twist . . . full . . . end over end . . . impact. The explosion echoed off the sides of the Gorge and rose up to the bridge where the pickup had continued its spin until the back end slammed against the rail and exploded.

The Assassin caught his breath after he stopped his roll, and then backed down the bridge into the darkness.

The Man, he was sure, was not in the other vehicle. He had picked up another fraction of a second right before the bridge. His antagonist had probably expected a trap and bailed out in time. Most likely he was there, on the other side, nursing the same aches he himself had.

It had been an exercise. Each had demonstrated his machismo; but the Assassin had achieved his objective. His assailant was isolated on a seven-mile stretch of prairie, not even a car to steal between there and the main road.

Of course, the fox had hoped he would have been driving back, but it was just as well. The walk would give him a chance to think. He had to try and figure out the master plan that had brought him there.

El Conciliador was supposed to feel his coming would be to the Penitente's benefit. Why? Was the CIA, perhaps, the prime mover?

Once again, he was glad he still had his decoy . . . his pawn. But for how long?

Ian stood in the doorway of the *morada.* Leathered faces squinted their gaze at him from within dark hoods. The smell of incense seared his nostrils. The shadows created by the flickering candles danced above him.

This *morada* was a newer structure. Instead of the mud and stick ceiling, there were beams with stucco in between. The walls were not blood-spattered. There was no stench to cover over.

Behind the altar there were pictures of the Christ Child, a few *bultos* of saints and a bare cross.

The atmosphere was less threatening than the other night, more like something perhaps from his past . . . a place where he used to go and hide. In any case, it gave Ian comfort . . . except for the judging eyes. But he would not have to look at these. To the astonishment of everyone, he went prostrate, his face to the ground. Ian would play this role with feeling . . . But surprise, surprise to him, he was soon to realize the feeling was real.

Ian hadn't known it when he walked in, but this night marked a dead end for him. He had reached the point of admitting to total darkness before him. Coupled with his closed-off past, there was now nothing ahead of which he was absolutely sure, nothing on which to grab hold, nothing for which to hope. But, perhaps, there *was* the moment. And that might be something in itself.

The last few days had played up the farce of the Meredith tragedy. She was merely an instrument of the destruction he had been wreaking on himself. It wasn't her fault she realized the "disease" she could catch from him . . . she became aware of the decayed image that would crumble into ash with the first breath of air, if the sarcophagus was opened. The moment of truth had arrived despite her absence . . . now all the forces around him were prying that crypt open.

A wail started to ripple up from his chest cavity. But he was conscious of it and that would render it false.

"*Toda o nada* . . . all or nothing." The time for pretense was over. It was not an intellectual decision; it was emotionally felt.

And that's exactly the kind of decision it took. The wail started again, but this time it came from some hollow at the base of Ian's bowels. It almost made him throw up as it cometed through his innards. By the time it ripped through his stomach, his throat and mouth had both rounded into a continuous tunnel. The bleating, blaring sound shot out, shaking the room and icing whatever warmth existed. A universal chill came over the brothers. They could no longer look at the prostrate man. Their eyes were forced within.

The *mano* had come to the dark mansion within the interior castle of his soul. It was that for which the *morada* stood. Whatever this man's sin, they were not going to judge it. They could judge an act, but not the condition of being human.

14

Ian was only vaguely aware of the drone of prayers as he arose and walked to the center of the room. He squeezed his eyes shut to clear the glaze covering them, then opened wide and blinked a few times.

The morada *had seemed so small when he entered, but now the ceiling appeared to rise some 30 feet above him. The room was, in fact, cavernous. Ian wondered where the benches had come from. Tiers of benches rising along the walls . . .*

There was an overpowering hush from all those seated figures shrouded in their hoods . . . From where did the drone emanate?

Ian turned to the altar and saw only an empty platform with a staircase leading from it. His eyes climbed the steps and reached a gallery of hooded figures seated and mumbling amongst themselves as they looked down on him. All were wearing black robes with white hoods, except for the one in the center, who was dressed all in black.

As Ian's eyes reached him, the dark figure rose and extended an accusing finger toward him. As he did, Ian could see the inner folds of the black cloak were red. Blood red.

The creature was about to speak, when Ian could no longer bear the weight of blame he felt being projected by the grim assembly.

"No!" came again from his bowels. "You have no right! You have no right to do this," he screamed, pounding his fist against the air. "I will not be judged."

And they laughed at him. Torrents of laughter rolled down in waves from all three sides. Ian turned around, looking for a way out, but there was only darkness behind. The noise became deafening and he could not think as he turned back to face them. The darkness was frightening, but not nearly so much as the glistening white of teeth caught by the flickering candlelight.

A phrase came back to Ian, something recalled from ages ago, something which seemed to call out to him now . . . "If you want to arrive at that which you know not, you must go by a way you know not" . . . and he turned a face toward night.

It was a choice made because he felt he had no choice. With luck, he hoped he could keep moving until he found daylight.

* * *

MIÉRCOLES SANTO

When Ian awakened, it was daylight. He was huddled on the floor next to his bed. It was 7:00 a.m.

He quickly put on his ski clothes, grabbed his gear and left.

As he went down the stairs from his terrace, Ian decided he would not breakfast at the St. Bernard. Instead, he put on his skis and glided across the beginners' slope to a small restaurant on the other side. He was the first customer and had a hot chocolate and an apple.

As he ate, Ian sat in daydream . . . letting no thought take hold, his brain too exhausted.

As soon as the chairlift began to move, Ian was out and riding up to the slopes. For once he was on time and truly alone.

Diana was still trying to put all the pieces of the puzzle together as she and Alex drove back to the Ski Valley in the midst of the morning ski traffic.

They had spent the night at the Pueblo, having arrived long after Ian left. What Diana learned, she had had to learn from

Alex because the Indians would not admit her to their meeting room. That situation had upset her, but she was in no position to do anything about it. Luckily Dashwood was sufficiently talkative without her having to pry obtrusively. The problem was his interest lay in the incredible story of alleged treasure, while she was more concerned with Ian and the Penitente. Still, Diana felt she had discovered more than she might have imagined possible a day ago.

But what she had learned disturbed her. It was not so much the content of the information as it was a matter of feelings . . . feelings for someone who could be the enemy. Was Ian some kind of victim as Dashwood portrayed, as he, himself, portrayed? Or was he like all the rest of the men who had lied to her? On that she was blocked.

Diana needed advice and would have called the Guardian already had she been able to reach him. She remembered he had left Rome for a few days' retreat and was not due back until tomorrow. He would be pleased to hear her sensitivities had placed her at a very important scene.

The wind had picked up considerably and snow was beginning to fall as Ian reached the top of the third lift. He put on his goggles and made his way over to Hunziker, moving slowly, methodically . . . with a kick like a cross country skier. As the snow fell silently, Ian heard only the sound of his skis. Nothing else. And nothing else concerned him.

By the time he reached the Bowl, the snow was becoming even heavier. But nothing was going to deter him. He had been frustrated the other day, and now Ian had but a single thought: to ski faster than he had ever skied in his life.

Ian approached the lip of the Bowl and hung his tips over. He paused for a moment, breathing the crisp air, and then he was away in a swirl of white.

Ian made short radius turns as he began the descent. As he picked up speed, he picked up courage. A cry gurgled from his throat and pierced the valley as he pointed his Pres straight down the chute.

Soon Ian *was* going faster than he ever had. Within seconds he had reached the first plain of the Bowl and was shooting across the flats, invisible within the whirl of powder around him. His momentum took him airborne over the lip of the lower slope and he sailed in near perfect jump position, landing with the grace of a professional . . . a cut above his virgin jump made out of desperation two days prior.

The wind gusted, causing a whiteout, and Ian continued his descent hoping . . . no, feeling . . . whatever happened, he would survive. And that sort of "feeling" was something new to him.

The snow settled enough so he could see the bend, and then the chairlift. He had made it, and the fact he had done so was trying to trigger a thought just out of reach.

Trying to unravel the thread, Ian had to go back and do it again. And again.

By his third run, the classes had started to reach the Basin area and the noise broke Ian's concentration. Whatever he was trying to put his finger on continued to remain just beyond his reach.

"Well, for once you made it. Better late than never."

It was Theresa Kittinger, smiling as if she hadn't seen him since his lesson. Was all the rest a dream?

Meanwhile, Ramon Mortez was distraught. The mystery of Cardinal Velenari's disappearance had been solved no more than an hour earlier. And Mortez needed answers. This after the death of the Troni woman! And where was her husband? Who was responsible? Why was it happening?

Was it Stone? What would be his purpose? And then to go to the *morada* and win the hearts of the Penitente . . . It didn't make sense.

But someone was trying to sabotage Sunday's meeting. Of that, Mortez was sure. The news about Velenari made Stone all the more important to him, if he could be trusted. He would have to meet him now . . . let the Assassin know his plan . . . persuade him to be of the same mind. Or get rid of him.

In the meantime, Velenari's death would have to be kept quiet. Nothing could stand in the way of Sunday's meeting . . . his chance to come face to face with and, hopefully, best the world's most powerful man.

Mortez punched his intercom, "Bring Stone to me."

* * *

Three bugs . . . three playbacks. Two happy faces—Diana and The One—one sad face, Braden.

It had been a long night for the CIA chief, and now he was crushed. His adversary had gone skiing! The fucking balls!

Today would be different. Braden didn't like being made fool of. He was going to nail this bastard no matter what. No matter what . . .

He thought of his orders. Why was this man so important? Yes, he was the assassin nonpareil with the coincidental audacity to call himself The One. But why was he necessary? Wasn't Velenari involved with these Penitente? Couldn't he have found out what was needed? Or had he been suspected of some betrayal? Was it hoped he would be killed?

Braden had long tried to understand his Master's mind, but to no avail . . . to no goddamn frustrating avail.

But he was sure now this was a contest. Whether this assassin was being considered for admittance to Metamorphosis or not, this was a contest. And he was damn well going to win it. He would let no one else be THE ONE's favorite.

While Braden stewed, the first of those who would never question their Master appeared in the Valley. Most might mistake him for being of Hispanic origin. Under sunglasses, he seemed to have the same features. But, seeing the naked gaze, one would be troubled. It had not the suffering or the honesty of the Spanish countenance. The look was more searing, more pragmatic. It showed no attachment to place . . . to a land. It was the face of a *tsigane* . . . a Gypsy.

To an outsider, these nomads of Eastern Europe are all the

same. A Gypsy is a Gypsy. But within the fold, there are two very distinct groups, each with its own *buli basha,* or leader.

The older is the group whose members roam from land to land eking out their livelihood by whatever means possible, often pretending to the magical powers of the Gypsy Queen whose memory still serves as a focal point of tribal identity.

The members of the other group roam the world with a definite purpose. They are emissaries who may cross any border in the world to pass on their instructions, make deals, carry out orders. They are, as they have been for half a millenium, the personal army of THE ONE.

There are many claims in life for "Best": Best Gunfighter, Best Lover, Best Movie, Best of Show . . . Song . . . Play . . . ; you name it. "Best" is an approbation bestowed on someone or something. And there is always someone else who may come up with another opinion, naming another "Best." Time moves on to another year in which there are new "Bests."

The "ONE" is a claim . . . a claim rarely made; a rarity due to the absolute power and endurance necessary to sustain it—the power of myth . . . myth that overshadows life . . . and the endurance of centuries . . . the shield of time to mask the reality of its beginnings.

In this context, its use by a single assassin, no matter how proficient, is merely an amusement, of the same level as some comic strip character.

There are few legitimate contenders for this status. In religion, there is the ONE True Church . . . in peoples, there is the ONE Chosen Race . . . in His heavens, there is the ONE God . . . and in Porumbacu de Jos, there is THE ONE.

THE ONE . . . the Apex of the global drug trafficking pyramid . . . the Prime Mover . . . the Dealer of Dealers . . . THE ONE to whom the highest of the high in every major underworld organization from the Assassini to the Yakuza pay homage, even as their predecessors had come suppliant to his ancestors for centuries. Only now, there were also powers of state . . . major states . . . who formed part of the coterie. Powers of capitalism and powers of communism . . . Political ideology meant nothing in Metamorphosis, the inner circle of Radu Scotia.

The source of the incredible myth behind Scotia's power over men goes back over 500 years . . . back to a crazed Prince of Wallachia who, even as a mere boy, so frightened even his reputedly cruel father, his parent delivered him into lifelong imprisonment at the hands of their country's enemies. The father's fear was not unfounded; the boy survived not only to escape his Turkish captors, but to avenge the treatment by both the Turks and his old man.

His real name was Vlad Tepes, but as ruler, the young man was so ruthless he was given the nickname, Son of the Dragon, *Draculya* . . . the man behind the modern day legend of Dracula.

Myth can aggrandize or myth can mellow. In Vlad Tepes' case, it mellowed. Far more horrible than any vampire, Tepes was responsible for the deaths of over one hundred thousand of his own people, let alone countless enemies. To him, there was little distinction. All were to be distrusted.

Beginning as a butcher of bodies, he later turned to the business of enslaving souls, and his heirs had followed suit for half a millenium.

While imprisoned in Turkey, Tepes had come across an amazing secret . . . the secret of the poppy. All the wealth and lands he could acquire during his short reigns of power were put into gaining control of the poppy fields in the lands of his enemies. Vlad, more than anyone, knew the power of politics was temporary, so he built an empire of drugs soldiered by Eurasia's wandering tribe, the Gypsies. They became the disseminators of his product and the guardian of his domain. Before his death, Tepes had amassed a control over the market that could not be broken . . . could never be broken while his family maintained the force behind the power . . . the secret that allowed men to "run with the wolves."

Alchemists attempt to turn base metals into gold; drugs attempt to free men from the pain of reality. The height of the drug experience is the total release from the bonds of civilization, a reduction of self to the primitive state.

The agonies of dealing with an evolving mind had often sent primitive man scurrying into the forest to find such release. At a time when men like Raniero Fasani practiced mortification to earn the mercy of a punishing God, others turned away from the Deity and a plagued civilization that seemed near the point of doom, and looked to the Antichrist.

Satanic drug cults spread throughout Europe and elsewhere, all seeking the wonder drug to liberate them from the condition of man . . . to bring them back to the beast. Many began to follow an arcane tradition of tribes close to nature . . . skinwalking, prowling the darkness in the hides of animals. From this, legends of shapeshifting, or "becoming the animal," arose . . . the werewolf or *lobombre* popularized in fiction.

But—as Dashwood would agree—as in most legends, there was a basis in fact. The Gypsies had a potion whose formula was known only to their queen. It produced an animal experience of such ecstasy, no other pleasure in life could match it. Under its influence, one felt as if he could see life through the eyes of a wolf, absorb it through the animal's senses, smell through its nostrils, run like it.

Reality or illusion?

To the one having it, there was no experience more real. To the few observers who claimed to have seen them in light, there was the description of an animal image surrounding the corporeal man. To the many who met them in the dark, there was the same fear, the same tangible result of death and destruction.

The Gypsy queens had kept the secret of their formula for centuries. There was no price high enough to pay for it. Except, finally, one . . . perpetual freedom.

Her name was Leto, like the goddess of old, a raven-haired beauty loved by her tribe. She had visions of the impact of civilization on the future of her people and became enamored of Tepes' power early on in his reign. She knew what she wanted of him, and what she could give in return. Leto became Tepes' mistress and bore him a son. The elixir was his for the price of making their son his heir and for perpetual protection of the Gypsy way of life.

The bargain was made and kept . . . to this very day. The Gypsy still moves freely and Radu Scotia was a direct descendant of Vlad Tepes and the Gypsy Queen.

But, for these past centuries, running with the wolves was reserved only for a small elite group . . . only for those powerful enough and, therefore, of utmost necessity to maintain the family power—the members of Metamorphosis.

To be admitted to Scotia's inner circle was the ultimate honor. Lifelong enemies, holders of opposite ideologies found themselves sitting across from each other at the stone table within the fortress at Porumbacu de Jos in the Transylvanian Alps and soon growling like brother wolves. The price they paid was fealty to THE ONE . . . a price that came easily since it brought not only the ultimate pleasure, but the riches and power that held them in their positions for as long as nature or, in reality, THE ONE allowed them to live.

From first born son to first born son down through the centuries the power had been maintained and strengthened. THE ONE's emissaries spread across the globe since the time of the early explorers to the New World, searching for new sources of drugs and acquiring new land. From Turkey to China to the Golden Triangle to the Pacific Islands to Peru; and whether it be opium, heroin, marijuana, cocaine or lollipop versions of the gypsy elixir such as LSD . . . ultimately, all fell under the rule of THE ONE.

There was no one more outside the law than Radu Scotia. He, more than anyone, knew every philosophical movement, every religion, every political ideology, every social cause was just someone's scam . . . and his was the best.

Scotia had reached 64 the past May 5. White streaks had only recently begun to appear on his jet black mane, but age had not begun to hamper the grace with which he moved the lean yet solid construction of his five-foot, nine-inch frame. He had, in fact, a regal bearing that was only enhanced by his stare. The hawk-like nose, jutting chin and thick Tepes lips were hard to focus on and remember, for an observer was always drawn to his eyes . . . the gaze that held its beholder long enough to cause a chill from groin to neck hairs before forcing the viewing eyes downward in homage and fear. The right eye was as black as a raven's wing; the left had green rays emanating from the core into the surrounding blackness. And just above the pupil was a red blood spot that gave the appearance of a warning light.

Now, however, the blood spot seemed to glow with anticipation as Scotia watched the helicopters being loaded into a cargo plane for the first leg of his premier trip to the New World. There was a deal to be made. Probably the most important of his life.

But it wasn't gold for which he was coming to lay claim . . . nor even priceless artifacts. There was something more . . . something for which his family had long searched, and to which the treasure of the Aztecs might hold the key.

And even that was but half the reason for this journey. It was time to groom an heir.

15

It was nearing noon when all paths began to converge. Morning instruction was over and most everyone was descending the mountain for lunch.

Ian was euphoric. He had had a good lesson and wanted to practice some of the moves Theresa had taught him while they were still fresh in his mind.

From the top of a run called Zagava, Braden recognized the black jacket of the mysterious figure he had seen entering Diana Bastian's room the night before. He schussed down and followed Ian over to Lift 2. They rode toward the summit with the CIA chief a dozen chairs behind his quarry. And half a dozen chairs behind Braden was a skier with a bandaged head.

Braden was beginning to cool down by the time Ian unloaded from the lift . . . And then it happened; a young girl in the next chair got her pole caught as she tried to disembark. The lift ground to a halt. His prey began to move off and Braden's teeth began to grind as well.

Ian took no notice of the stopped line as he approached the traverse trail to Lift 3. His attention was on the ridge of peaks above him. Theresa said she might take him there on Friday . . . *if* she thought he was in good enough shape. If he was still around was more like it.

Ian's peripheral vision noticed two skiers he had previously seen at the top of the trail descending the other side of the mountain. They were now coming back in his direction as he put on his pole straps and began the traverse.

It had stopped snowing about an hour before, and there had been glimmerings of sunlight through the gray. But once again, a heavy cloud cover was rapidly enveloping the Valley.

Ian felt a chill as he took the first bend and began to pick up speed. He wanted to concentrate on shifting his weight, but a sixth sense told him there was something ominous about the three men stopped less than 200 yards away. They were waiting, and it took Ian but another second to feel certain they were waiting for him. A half turn of his head told him the two skiers behind were the other jaw of a vise.

The traverse ran along the rim of a steep bowl whose moguls were obscured by the morning snow. Ian had not skied it yet, for beyond was an expert trail called Walkyries, which he had heard described as "moguls in the trees." It sounded like fun, but with his knees, Ian had not wanted to risk it before. Now he felt he had no choice.

Ian banked to his left and began cascading down the bowl. Within a few turns, he caught an edge and fell on his side.

"Great start," he muttered to himself. "Very impressive to the boys."

Fortunately, his skis stayed on and Ian used his poles to quickly regain his feet. As he did, he noticed all five of the men on the traverse were converging on him. They all looked like good skiers . . . damn good skiers. Do Penitente ski? He doubted it, and certainly didn't feel like waiting around to ask. Ian dug his poles in and pressed forward whispering, "Knees, don't fail me now."

The chairlift jerked and started again with Braden chomping at the bit.

Meanwhile, Ian was working harder than he ever had, trying

to turn at the top of every mogul . . . extending . . . bending . . . extending . . . bending . . . the sweat pouring down his arms and legs. There was no possiblity of looking back to see if he was keeping his lead. He could not afford to break his concentration. It was a matter of doing better than the best he had ever done and hoping like hell it was better than anyone else could do. He needed a miracle.

Two of his pursuers took falls and a third had to reduce his speed to keep from falling. But they weren't the only problem. As Ian started to see a clearer path to the floor of the bowl, he spotted four skiers at the edge of the treeline leading to the Walkyries run. They also looked as if they were waiting for him.

Ian straightened out his skis and shot across the floor of the bowl, directly toward them. One of the four began to raise his hand. Ian did not wait to see if there was a gun in it. He cut to his left, spraying a snowscreen at the group, and plunged into virgin snow among the trees.

Braden reached the traverse just in time to see Ian disappear into the forest. He headed into the bowl followed by the man he thought he was pursuing. The One stopped long enough to get a good view through his binoculars. He now knew the identity of The Man. He remembered Braden from Operation Songbird. He knew his father had been the kingpin then and was aware of the power the son had been accumulating since the old man's death. If he were not the Control, he was close to it. The One remembered something else, too. He didn't like Braden. He was human scum; not because of disadvantage . . . the Assassin never held that against anyone. No, Braden had *all* the advantages . . . he just had no class.

The trees came up fast . . . too fast. If the powder had not slowed him, Ian would already have impaled himself on a branch. He wasn't experienced in deep snow and angled desperately toward cut tracks and some wider space.

Two of the skiers who followed him down the bowl were the first of his pursuers to enter the trees. Ian could hear them some 50 yards behind as his mind raced to keep up with the obstacles popping up in front of him . . . trees, moguls, rocks, a drop-off, his own exhaustion.

Mogul . . . step . . . mogul . . . step . . . tree . . . step . . . mogul . . . step . . . breathe . . . Blink away the sweat. Again . . . again. Shins aching. Shit, how long does this go on? he wondered.

Someone was gaining on him. He could feel it even before he could hear it. Ian hit a flatter and wider section . . . pointed straight and cruised along, mopping his brow and quickly looking back. The closest assailant was only 10 yards behind, another maybe 25 and coming up fast.

Braden was halfway down the bowl when a "Trail Closed" marker was put up on Walkyries. One man was left behind to wave off Braden and any other skier that came by, but the CIA chief determined to go straight through him.

The trail started to rise in front of Ian for a stretch of some 30 yards. He pushed on his poles to keep his distance, but his assailants kept closing. As he reached the crest, the gap narrowed to less than half a dozen yards. Ian hoped there would be people on the other side, as if their appearance would frighten off his pursuers. But there were only more trees . . . and more moguls. Ian barreled ahead while continuing to lose ground.

Soon he could even hear the closest man's breathing. He had to act. But what?

He spotted a narrow opening . . . not more than a body width . . . between two trees. He went for it.

No more than a few pole lengths separated the two skiers as Ian approached the opening. Ian tossed his right pole up so as to grab it in the middle. The strap caught on his thumb and he almost lost it. He had intended to lay it across the opening as he passed through, so as to trip up his chaser. Now it was out in front of him, barring his own way. Ian let go and ducked low as the pole slammed into the two trees about neck high and started to drop. His pursuer automatically veered, but there was no place to go. He smacked into a pine with full force, his skis splintering into pieces just before the bones in his neck. A bit aborted, but it had worked.

"All right," Ian yelped. He was pleased with himself, not realizing the man was dead. This was all still part of a fantasy.

At that same moment, Braden had gone through the trail guard, firing a knockout dart from a wrist gun which dropped the man in his tracks.

The One was impressed as he joined the flight through the Walkyries. Just because the man was scum didn't mean he couldn't be effective.

Ian had already realized he could not let up. Two more men were coming up fast behind. The more he perceived the reality of the situation, the more dire he realized his position was. And trying to navigate with only one pole was bringing reality into focus fast.

A snowmobile moved out of the trees in front of him. Ian saw it too late. He swerved and a branch caught him in the stomach. Another smacked his brow. End of race. Lights out.

The two trailing skiers came up quickly. Another snowmobile came out from behind the trees farther on. The driver yelled at them, "What the hell is going on? You were to escort him, not to chase him."

The driver of the first vehicle examined Ian. "He's only unconscious," he said with a heavy Spanish accent. "Thank the good Lord for the small favors."

"He will be angry when he awakens," said the other driver. "What are you thinkin' of," he yelled at the skiers again. "Can't you do anythin' right?"

A shrill whistle sounded through the trees.

The reprimander looked up, "Someone pursues. Hurry, get him on board."

Three other skiers came on the scene as Ian was put into one of the snowmobiles.

"Miguel does not answer on his radio," the one holding a walkie-talkie yelled.

"Quickly, change jackets with him," ordered the driver of the second snowmobile.

Two more skiers came out of the trees. "Peter is dead," one of them called out. "Bring up one of the snowmobiles."

"There's no time," said the driver in charge.

Ian's equipment was loaded on the other snowmobile along with that of two of the skiers. Each of these two climbed aboard one of the vehicles and they sped off.

"*Vamos,*" said the skier now wearing Ian's jacket. He moved off swiftly with two of the others in mock pursuit. The remaining two pulled guns from their jackets and moved into position among the trees.

Braden became puzzled as he sailed by the dead skier. Something wasn't right. Why hadn't The One shot the man? Could he be without a gun? It was too incredible.

He reached the bend where Ian had fallen in time to see the phony prey disappear, followed by his "pursuers." Braden wasn't fooled. The "pursued" had two ski poles.

Braden cut a wide arc while pulling a short automatic weapon from his jacket. Before one of the hidden skiers could turn around, The Man cut him down. The other moved out of position and was taken out likewise.

Braden's pursuer heard the muffled reports as he passed the skier with the broken neck. He smiled at what he figured was his pawn's handiwork, but worried about his present status.

As he checked out the two bodies, Braden spotted the snowmobile tracks. The One taken by these Penitente henchmen! Extraordinary! Braden saw where Ian had fallen. He noticed blood on the broken piece of branch that had knocked him unconscious. As he stooped to retrieve it, the small sapling behind him shattered from the impact of a bullet. Braden hit the ground as a second bullet blew off the back of his left ski. Sweat and anger poured out of him. He had been duped by a goddamn lousy trick. The One had used a pawn to smoke him out. And it had worked!

But he was not being taken out . . . not today. Braden slid

back down the hill on his belly. When he felt he was out of range of his assailant's weapon, he took off, staying low. A weaker man would have had a stroke when another shot split his right pole. But the humiliated CIA chief pressed on, knowing, despite his miscalculations, the range limit had to be soon.

Braden exited the Walkyries onto the easier Winkelried. Amongst people. He tossed away his other pole and set a record down the Rubezahl chute to the bottom of the mountain. There, he stepped out of what remained of his skis and quickly hurried away in order to get rid of the clothes that now identified him.

But there was no need to hurry. The One had missed his opportunity and would not take the chance of being seen. He had a formidable adversary, one who was now aware of his pawn. It would take some thought to see if he could somehow prevent it from working to his detriment.

In the meantime, the Assassin examined the bodies of Braden's victims. They were not like the inhabitants of the area. One had not at all the look of a Spanish-American. He was either a true Spaniard or a Basque. The One leaned toward the latter; probably part of an elite corp. The Assassin thought of the Mafia chief, Gambino, bringing Sicilians into New York because he felt the home-grown hoods weren't tough enough. The mysterious head of the Penitente had the same cunning.

It made sense for El Conciliador to have invited him for the same reason. But he was now sure that's what someone else had *wanted* him to think. Actually, The One would have felt better if he thought this were all a CIA setup. Yet something told him it wasn't the case.

Perhaps there would be some clues in the details his pawn would learn from El Conciliador. The One was sure Ian was being taken to him. And for the first time, he wasn't worried about Ian Stone being able to pull it off. In fact, The One realized he no longer despised his pawn. Instead, and it was amazing to him, he was feeling a kinship toward him.

It was a very foreign feeling. The Assassin had always been a loner . . . a man apart. Having no father to claim and a mother he had grown to hate, The One had, at an early age, vowed never to be dependent on anyone. To him, a strong man was never dependent. His Viet Nam and Cambodian experiences confirmed it. The only time he had ever depended on his unit, he had been captured.

While in his prison camp he vowed, if he ever got out, he would deal with the world only on his terms, and never again with underlings. Having been put in jeopardy by what he considered the weakness of his government's leaders, he determined to rid the world of people who symbolized that weakness, and be paid very well for his services. No job was more perfect for him than Operation Songbird. He would have done it for free. It demonstrated he was in control.

That was the key . . . the control. The Assassin never wanted to be under anyone's control. And now he was. He had been duped in the same way he had duped The Man. It was hateful to him.

The admission broke his tension. He smiled. The irony was his pawn probably knew more about what was going on than he did. Perhaps, on his return, he would give Ian Stone the shock of his life. Perhaps it was time for Ian Stone to find out who he really was.

16

Ian felt like a cork bobbing on water. There was a pounding noise that matched his rise and fall on the waves. His eyes flickered.

"*Mira,*" he heard someone say.

As his eyes opened, he saw a swarthy Spanish face looking down at him—the face of the less intelligent of the two snowmobile drivers. Ian was apprehensive, but he noted a lot more fear in the other set of eyes.

"*Señor,* please to forgive the men. It was an accident," the big man said. "El Conciliador tells us to escort you to him. We wished not to anger you or cause you . . . but they were nervous . . ." He swallowed, "We are at your service, *Señor.*"

"*Gracias,*" Ian tried to smile as he felt the throb in his head. El Conciliador's soldier drew a sigh of relief. The guy was so big, Ian almost laughed at the incongruity of his apology. Then he was handed a towel wrapped around a chunk of packed snow. Ian put it to his head and looked about.

They were in the rear of a truck . . . the two snowmobiles,

he, the big guy and a smaller man he assumed was one of the skiers who chased him. With each bounce, the rear door jolted. He recognized the source of the pounding noise.

"We will be there soon," the big one offered. "There was someone who followed you. We left men to prevent us to be . . . followed."

"*Bueno.*" Ian was quickly exhausting his Spanish, but he felt it was worth reciprocating.

The truck soon jerked to a halt and, within seconds, the rear door was opened from the outside.

"Are you feeling better, *Señor?*" the soldier asked, wanting some final assurance.

There was a dull throb, but Ian was feeling better and nodded affirmatively. He got to his feet and tried to look impressive as he jumped off the back of the truck. In mid-leap he realized it was the wrong kind of jump to be done while wearing ski boots. As the pain of impact rose up his legs, he decided to lay off trying to impress anyone.

The guest's eyes widened at the new Sikorsky helicopter sitting in the glade awaiting them, "Holy . . . "

The worried one kept trying to ingratiate himself, "You like? It is new. The El Conciliador gets for special guests like you."

Ian just nodded, climbed in and belted himself.

El Conciliador's soldier mopped his brow. The *gringo* did not seem angry with him.

The *gringo* had other things on his mind besides a headache. He knew he had been in a helicopter once before. His knees began throbbing as he tried to remember when and where. Surely, in Viet Nam; but at what point . . . when he was rescued from the prison camp? Did it crash? Was that when his knees were shattered? They seemed to be telling him something.

The liftoff brought Ian back to the present. He was going to see El Conciliador, the head Penitente. The Cardinal had said it would be tonight if all went well. Things must be going very well, he thought, and wondered if the Cardinal would be there, too. Perhaps he'd even get to see the treasure. Now, *that* would be exciting!

The copter headed north and west of the Ski Valley. Ian could see the Rio Grande way out to the left.

Ian found himself looking at the controls. Lots of dials, and somehow it seemed familiar. He shut his eyes tightly and tried to recall why.

The pilot started talking into his helmet phone and Ian looked out the windows again. They were coming up to a plateau. Suddenly the helicopter descended, then came almost straight up very close to the slope.

Must be some sort of clear zone, Ian thought. He looked down and saw a guardpost on the road below. There was a sign, "Interspec Foundation." What did that have to do with the Penitente?

As the helicopter came up over the plateau, Ian saw what he assumed to be the research center. It was a sprawling modern adobe structure topped with a radar scanner and a satellite receiving dish. Very impressive, he thought.

At each end of the building, there were also observatory-like turrets. Ian wondered what they were for . . . telescopes?

The craft landed about 50 yards from the building and two armed security guards came out to meet it.

"*Bienvenido,*" said one with a lean, muscular face. "Welcome to Interspec. May I ask what size shoes you wear? We will get you something more comfortable."

Ian told him he wore a size 9 and the man reported into a small transmitter as they walked toward the building. By the time Ian entered the door, a pair of size 9s were waiting for him.

After changing out of his boots and removing his jacket . . . where had he picked up this one? he suddenly wondered . . . the guard in charge led him down a well-lit corridor. They passed a windowed room housing what looked to be a state-of-the-art computer installation. There were also banks of ticker tapes and TV monitors. A few men in white smocks were in evidence. All of them looked Spanish.

At the end of the corridor they came to a meeting room. It was very well appointed with a large oval table of marble and high-backed wooden chairs that looked as if they were out of a 16th century Catalonian castle, which, indeed, they were. There was a step down at the entrance that gave the room the spatial effect of a high ceiling. This was enhanced on the north side of the room by raised skylights through which the somber daylight now bathed the interior. A colorful Aubusson tapestry of reds, oranges and greens draped the north wall behind the table. Ian noticed a projection unit built into the ceiling on the opposite side of the room. He assumed there was a screen behind the tapestry and was impressed with that as well. His guide took note and smiled proudly.

As they crossed the room to the far side, Ian was puzzled there didn't seem to be a head chair at the table.

A door led them to an antechamber off the meeting room. There were no windows, just a few niches with *bultos* and another door beyond. In contrast to the first, this one was of heavy wood and iron. It looked as if it came from an old vault or prison. The guard inserted an identity card into a slot and the massive door clicked open quite easily. Ian noted, however, the man had to use considerable muscle to swing it.

On the other side of the door was a spiral stone staircase which they began to descend. Up to this point, Ian had a cheery impression of the structure. Now, however, he was feeling a bit claustrophobic . . . as if he were descending into the pit of the damned.

Ian estimated they had gone down some 30 feet by the time they reached the subterranean floor. Electrified antique sconces provided the light. Finally, they arrived at a metal door and the guard knocked. "*Venga,*" came the gruff response within.

The guide swung the door open for Ian, then closed it behind him and returned up the stairs.

In contrast to all but the meeting room chairs above, the room was decorated in a very elegant, classic Spanish style. It was a large chamber, perhaps 40 feet in both length and width with at least a 14-foot ceiling. Shelves of leather-covered books occupied most of the dark stone walls on two sides. Paintings and medieval weapons decorated the fore and back walls. One of the oils looked like an El Greco, another a Tintoretto. Fine reproductions, Ian thought.

"They are real. Those hanging in the Vatican are fakes," a voice rasped from across the room.

Ian's attention was drawn to the huge wooden desk at the far end. He could hear the whirring sound of computer equipment inset within the antique bureau, but no one was visible. Then a balding old man rose from a large oak and leather chair and came around the desk. For some reason, Ian was surprised at his age. Perhaps he expected someone even older. The man wore a dark suit and walked with a limp.

His host paused a moment and Ian got the feeling he was not what was expected either.

"They are quite beautiful," Ian responded.

A smile crossed the old man's face and he extended his arms, "*Mano* . . . come in . . . come in."

The two came together and clasped hands, "I am Ramon Mortez, chairman of the board of this foundation, but my followers know me only as El Conciliador. As you are The One, so I am Brother One."

This was the mystery man; short, wizened, wiry with dead opal eyes. His affable air gave the latter a hint of light, but Ian felt they were probably like dry ice most any other time.

Ian was directed to a sitting area with couches of both tapestry and brocade. Against the wall Ian noted a chair similar to those in the meeting room. It rested on a section of tiles exactly like those in the room above. Ian's eyes rose and he saw tracks running up the wall between the bookshelves to the ceiling, a cable between them. The chair was obviously an elevator by which the meeting room could be entered and exited. Fantastic!

Mortez picked up a decanter and poured two glasses of port.

"If I had had some notice, I might have dressed for the occasion," Ian bantered as he was handed his glass.

"I apologize, but haste was needed. And my men wish you to understand they were not chasing you, only trying to catch up. To our mutual interests."

Mortez raised his glass and drank first to show, Ian felt, the drink was not drugged. He took a sip.

"Sit . . . sit," said his host. "I had thought to wait until after your initiation for our meeting. I confess, it was to be sure of your sincerity. As a man of caution yourself, you appreciate my position.

"But these tragedies . . . the death of the Troni woman . . . Cardinal Velenari . . . "

"The Cardinal? . . . " Ian blurted with convincing surprise.

"Then it was not you . . . ," Mortez sat back more comfortably. "But it could have been. If you'd kill a pope for me, why not a cardinal for yourself? The computers chose that scenario, but I can't always trust them. Forgive me, my son, for doubting you."

Ian's mind had wandered . . . "kill a pope?" The Pope was dead?

The old man noted his distraction, "Have I confused you? . . . Let me explain."

Mortez took another sip from his glass and set it down.

"First, I will tell you that, since you asked to join us, I have analyzed your 'work' . . . such as I could uncover. You operate so well, there are only rumors . . . insinuations. With your willingness to unmask, I have, obviously, been able to find out more.

"I used the computers. The Foundation is a resource as well as a shield for me," Mortez gloated. "We have been able to tap into various government information banks, among other things.

"Do you have experience with computers? Less time between question and decision," Mortez pontificated without waiting for a response.

"In any case, I find a thread of commonality in your victims. They were all politically weak. Cancers of the left. Those who would let the standards fall to the godless . . . to the devil. You are a true descendant of Fasani, the first Penitente. It was only right for you to want to join us . . . your brothers."

The man was rambling. Obviously, Ian thought, he liked to hear himself talk. And for all his talk about the godless, he didn't appear to be very Godfearing himself.

"There is a major task before us now," he went on, " . . . our greatest challenge. And someone seeks to subvert it."

If it weren't for the persistent dull ache in his head, Ian would have felt as if he were in a dream. He couldn't figure out what this madman was talking about. Was this where the Aztec gold was hidden? Was there any? More importantly, was he going to get out of there?

"The CIA has attempted to have me verify your wealth and locate its source," Ian broke his silence, sounding succinct and sure. "Two of them are dead and there is another here now."

"The CIA . . . yes . . . Only Velenari and I knew of your coming and when it would be. Our friend may have been playing a triple-cross. I assume your identity was still hidden from them?"

Ian's blank stare was taken for an affirmative.

"Of course . . . I have tapped their file on you. But now I am confused," Mortez said, waving his hand before his face. "I must tell you the story Velenari told me yesterday. Supposedly, there would have been more details last night. We must decide how much is true."

The opal eyes stared dead ahead as he pondered, "The CIA could have put him up to it, and then gotten rid of him when he fulfilled his purpose. It could be they who are out to sabotage Sunday's meeting."

Mortez thought a second and spoke again, "I will check this scenario later."

He patted Ian on the knee and looked soulfully into his eyes, "I need you, my son.

"Verify and locate, indeed," he laughed. "It goes beyond their comprehension.

"You have chosen to unmask yourself to me," Mortez said, again patting his knee, "and that is why I have unmasked to you. Our success depends on our being open; so I will tell you a story few know."

Without, unfortunately, going into location, Mortez related the finding of the Aztec gold and, in the callowness of his youth, the melting down of all but, to him, the most interesting pieces.

Ian was surprised at how little of the origins and significance of the treasure the old man knew. But then, he didn't have Dashwood's disc.

"I call my inner circle the *cryptos* from the crypt in which the treasure lay," Mortez went on.

"There *was* a body!" Ian could not help exclaiming.

Mortez was confused by his inflection.

"It sounds more Egyptian than Aztec," Ian covered.

"Ah, I see you are a student of history. I did not realize. I, myself, know little of such things. But, yes . . . a golden skull . . . the symbol of the new order, my gilded Adam . . . man free in the way he was meant to be . . . free from the bonds of choice."

He stared through Ian as if talking to someone else, "But choice is freedom, one may say. A delusion. What else does it provide but an endless questing after knowledge, a quest producing nothing but self-anger.

"Under the order we establish," Mortez emphasized, "all necessary knowledge will be supplied as it once was. There will no longer be concern with questions that cannot be answered. That burden will be borne by those of us who lead."

Mortez shook his head, "The people are like children. They must be directed, told what is good for them. Like these simple Penitente . . . like the original *disciplinati* . . . all they need is the surety they are guilty and a formula to follow so they might be saved.

"We have already launched the new order," Mortez assured him. "Velenari was its cornerstone. Through his position and my wealth, we have placed my *cryptos* and *secretos* in key positions throughout the Church. All over the Southwest and most of the Spanish-speaking countries, I have financed politicians and businessmen as well. My dependents. Even Velenari had always been my dependent. Would you believe, in 35 years he never knew my true identity?

"The older I get," Mortez shook his head, "the more I realize how few men really have a mind for power. It is agonizing having to put up with weakness all the time; but even more frustrating is always having to convince these peons what we do is right.

"Sometimes I wish I could operate independently, as you," Mortez moaned. "But it is the duty of the strong to exert the power . . . to establish the authority so the others will not flirt with the devil. Perhaps your own realization of that has brought you here now," he stated without expecting a reply.

"As Fasani's descendant, you have the power to legitimize what is distasteful to these meek souls more than my outlaw ancestry allows. I hope you will join me in protecting what has been built . . . in making it grow. Our hour is at hand," Brother One hissed.

His speech over, Mortez refilled their glasses. Ian had a feeling these had just been the opening remarks. Now they were finally going to get down to it; and whatever *it* was would be equally as interesting as Dashwood's story.

"After our disposal of the Pope . . . "

Ian could hardly surpress a cough. There it was again—The One was a pope-killer.

" . . . I violated my own rule not to expose any of the Aztec artifacts. It was a small gift for Velenari. It looked so much like a Greek cross, I didn't think . . . "

He related Velenari's wartime activity and what the Cardinal had told him of his passing on the cross.

"It was over a year ago when the good Cardinal first told me of this anonymous wealthy collector who would pay dearly for any more artifacts. I, of course, refused, but the offers kept coming until last month the price reached ten million in diamonds just to *see* whatever I had . . . and this as a down payment against a purchase price of one hundred million if I had what he thought I did! Since Velenari never knew the source of my wealth, I could only assume the offer came from a legitimate collector. And someone who could pay such a price, I wanted to meet. After all, even Montezuma's treasure is finite and such a sum could serve as the endowment needed for our final push. In any case, the long-awaited meeting has been set for this Sunday, *Pascua.*

"Then yesterday, Velenari comes to me with a confession. The wealthy collector, he tells me, is someone so mysterious only a few dozen people in the world know he even exists. He is known by these few—and this is why I know I can trust telling you, for I doubt you would have dared your nickname if you knew of him—as THE ONE and, purportedly, he controls all of the drug production and traffic in the world . . . in the world, mind you! . . . as his family, which dates back to the man behind the Dracula legend, has supposedly done for over 500 years. *This,*" he threw up his hands, "is what Velenari tells me. Is it too fantastic?! But the man was serious.

"*And* . . . ," he shot forward, tapping Ian on the knee again, "the real reason for his coming is to make a deal whereby *I* will join his inner circle, composed of some of the world's most powerful men . . . and help *him* become pope."

The old man laughed, "*I* will join *him!*

"I asked Velenari why I would want to join him, even for one hundred million dollars, and how he would come to know such a man anyway?

"To the latter, he confessed he had been trafficking in drugs for about five years in an effort to get out from under my thumb. It seems I was too demeaning to the poor man," Mortez laughed. "Velenari, a kingpin in the drug world! Under my very nose . . . using my people! But now he was worried that what he had spent a lifetime building might be desecrated. What *he* had spent! . . . If he hadn't died last night, I would have commissioned you to kill him. I might have even done it myself."

Mortez's face twitched with anger, then relaxed and was

crossed with a smirk, "As to why I would join THE ONE, he told me there is some potion so powerful, once under its spell, it gives the feeling of becoming like an animal . . . a wolf, to be exact. Nothing in life matters more than their meetings when they apparently run around playing wolfman.

"I told Velenari he was out of his mind, but he insisted it was so . . . only because of his stroke was he able to break the spell. Supposedly, it would kill him if he took the potion again."

"Who are the members of this inner circle?" Ian was curious now that the story had gotten his adrenaline flowing.

"This I did not learn. Poor Casimero was so frightened in the telling . . . Confessing even to the feeding on the blood of children. Can you believe such things exist? Even in what you have seen of life? Perhaps . . . perhaps . . . ," Mortez trailed off into thought for a moment. "Anyway, we were interrupted with the news of the Troni woman, and we decided it would be best for him to speak with you. I had hoped to learn more on his return.

"Well, my son, what do you think of it?" El Conciliador asked. "Was he lying or telling the truth? Has it been a CIA plot all along? What have we done to them? Or is it Velenari's secret police within the Church? He had that, too, you know. The Light, he called them. But why, then, would they kill him?" Mortez shrugged. "Or was it the case my dear brother just had enough and did it himself?

"The computers have been working all night and day, yet find nothing to corroborate the existence of THE ONE. Still, someone comes. I can feel it," he said quietly.

"I think you should act on the supposition Velenari was telling the truth," the marketing man in Ian responded . . . the tactician.

"Precisely," Mortez was reanimated. "When the collector arrives, he is to contact the *morada* in Arroyo Seco to set up the meeting. We will come together, conclude the arrangements . . . I may even offer the papacy before he asks . . . "

Ian could not tell if he was serious or not. How could some little man in New Mexico be tossing around titles like the papacy? Had he really such power as he claimed? Ian hadn't seen any treasure. And could there be a character like THE ONE? He was starting to feel claustrophobic again. The room was reminding him of an underground dungeon.

The old man's cackle brought him out of his wondering, "If he is not for real, then once we secure the diamonds . . . his token of good faith . . . we will show him the thunder of the faith that moves mountains. You will kill him."

Ian went numb as the old man continued, "If he *is* for real, we will work a deal for the hundred million and we can kill him later. The world will be rid of one of its devils and the people will harken to us all the more as defenders of the faith. Then *I* will assume the papacy and together we shall control vast multitudes over all the earth."

Ian began to tune out. He no longer trusted the headache telling him this was really happening. It was far more absurd than any of his dreams.

He was being told to take the opportunity to study the Foundation and develop a strategy for the "hit," assuming the mark could be lured there.

"If this man is who Velenari said he is," Ian could not help interrupting, "he won't come without adequate protection."

"Correct. That is the reason why your initiation must be accelerated . . . so we can mobilize all the Penitente for such an eventuality. Velenari also said THE ONE has a personal bodyguard of enormous strength. So do I."

Mortez pressed a button on the table between them and a door behind Ian opened quickly. He turned to see the entire height and width of the frame filled with a giant of a man, completely bald, except for his drooping, black mustache. Though close to Mortez's age, he had the body of a weightlifter half as old.

"This is Vincente," Mortez explained. "He does not speak. He only acts."

Ian was hoping he wouldn't. "Very impressive."

"As you are, my son," Mortez said as he stood. "I must leave you now. I hope I have not assumed too much. Perhaps you wished to join the Penitente to turn to a life of contemplation. But as you now know, it is not the time for that. Can I rely on your allegiance?"

Ian moved from the couch onto one knee. He took the old man's hand and kissed it. He did it so well Ian was clear on one thing about himself . . . Meredith had been right, he was a true schizophrenic. He had to be . . . for Vincente's sake. And with this realization came another thought; perhaps he *was* an assassin. Maybe he actually *did* the things people thought he did while he thought he was asleep. Maybe he *was* The One. The idea gave him chills.

"You must understand," Mortez apologized, "I am subject to the rules I have created. I cannot dispense with the initiation, only speed it along. Normally, it would take months or even years, but I have let it be known it must take place just after midnight tomorrow.

"So," he slapped his thighs, "is there anything else I can tell you now? I will leave Vincente here at your disposal," Mortez said as he turned.

"Just one thing . . . ," Ian started to ask.

"Of course, my son," Mortez turned back to him.

"The skull . . . the gold one . . . Does it have markings on it?" Ian inquired.

Mortez thought, "Hmmm . . . only scratches. Nothing significant. Why do you ask?"

"Sometimes such things contain messages of significance . . . things one might be lured to see."

Mortez laughed, "I understand . . . The skull will be our bait. You do not cease to amaze me. You will see it Friday night when we meet again as true Penitente brothers. Then we will solidify our plan."

El Conciliador went over to the chair against the wall and sat down, "Do you know we are in a natural cave here? There are many caves and tunnels in this area."

He pressed a button on the chair. Ian expected it to rise into the air, but instead, it began to lower. Mortez descended out of sight . . . to hell, Ian thought. A floor panel moved into place to close the opening. Wonderful.

Ian took a deep breath and surveyed the room with what he hoped would come across as a professional air. He thought of Diana and hot buttered rum. He thought of his race through the Walkyries. It was the best skiing he had ever done. Tomorrow was the Nastar race. Ian hoped he'd live to compete.

A new ache was working on his head. This whole game was getting to be too much to handle.

Ian walked over to the door by which he had entered. Vincente anticipated him, holding it open. Ian nodded to him with pursed lips, feeling sweat break out under his arms. They went up the spiral staircase to what Ian felt was a somewhat more real world.

As they passed into the meeting room, the original guide was there waiting, a plan of the building layed out on the marble table alongside a three-dimensional model.

Ian looked at it casually until he noticed the observatory-like turrets were really anti-aircraft emplacements. Then he studied the plans more attentively.

His courage up, Ian decided he wanted to see the computer room, bemoaning the fact he had little experience with the machinery. He wished he, at least, knew how to get out an S.O.S. message, if he had to. But to whom? He noticed the ticker tape with the day's closing stock prices. He could probably get rich in this business, he mused . . . *if* he was who they thought he was.

17

Ian was taken out the same way he was brought in . . . and brought back to the end of the Walkyries where his, or rather, Dashwood's jacket was returned along with a new pair of poles.

It was near dusk and the lifts had long been closed. Snowcats were grooming the slopes. Only a few skiers and some ski patrollers were still on the mountain.

Ian took his time as he descended. He was tingling all over. He had escaped. He had seen the devil and could hope to tell about it. This was intended as an adventure trip, but it was getting ridiculous. His problem now was finding how to get away before matters got out of his control. It really hadn't sunk in yet he had never been *in* control.

At the intersection of Rubezahl, Theresa was waiting. The gloom in her face brightened as soon as she recognized him, "You're all right? . . . I was so worried."

Ian skied next to her and kissed her on the cheek, "Let's go for it."

They got up some speed, then tucked and went straight out all the way to the bottom.

Only one other person was watching for Ian's return . . . Sam Redding.

The sheriff had spent the last two days going over the deaths of Hamel, Wilcox and the mystery man on the mountain. Today had added what looked to be another half dozen victims from last night's accident at the Gorge. Accident? Redding couldn't help feeling everything was somehow tied in . . . there was some common thread.

Albuquerque hadn't been the slightest bit cooperative on anything. The lid was snapped shut.

The official report on Hamel was he died of a heart attack. The autopsy had backed up the report. But a friend at the airport had told the sheriff the body was flown out on a government plane that had dropped someone else off early Monday morning. Redding knew damn well no autopsy had been performed on Sunday. And who was the passenger . . . the dead man on the mountain? Why else was there no response on the print from the finger found near the blast site? Everyone was on vacation . . . out to lunch. "G-man" was written over the whole deal.

Wilcox's notebook had mentioned a receiver found in a set of earphones on the plane. Then there was the fancy gun and the half pound of cocaine found in Hamel's luggage . . . but no I.D. other than his ticket. It was hard to figure which side he was on. But the whole thing was some kind of drug caper, to be sure. Redding would stake his life on it. And he wasn't going to sit around while his town was being used as a killing ground.

Finally, he felt he had a thread. That afternoon he had busted one very big and very drunk local named Vargas. The man kept raving something about it being better to lose his balls than to go flying in the Gorge. Hopefully, it would become more clear when he sobered. But for now, one thing was clear: Vargas had been driving a jeep rented to someone who had been in the proximate vicinity of at least three of the dead people . . . Ian Stone.

Theresa saw Redding as she and Ian reached the bottom.

"I've been with you all afternoon," she said.

Recognizing Redding, Ian looked at her and shrugged. It could be worse, he thought; at least it wasn't the CIA.

"Mr. Stone . . ."

"Hello there, Chief Redding, isn't it?" Ian took off his glove and extended a hand.

"Sheriff Redding," the big man corrected. "I'd like to have a word with you."

"Now, I suppose?" Ian asked with some irritation.

"You have an objection?" Redding raised a thick, greying eyebrow.

"I think I've tired him out," Theresa interjected.

"It has been a long day," Ian agreed.

"For me, too. But I have a job to do," the sheriff said.

"Well, I don't," Ian said, glaring at him. "Oh well," he softened, "tell you what . . . let's do it over a hot buttered rum. Would you like to join us?" he asked Theresa.

"I have to take my pickup in for servicing," she winked at Ian, signalling she was taking the pickup back to the Pueblo. "It was nice skiing with you. Bye, sheriff."

As she went off, Ian released his bindings, loosened his boot buckles and picked up his equipment, "Just let me slip on some more comfortable boots. I'll be with you in a minute."

Ian carried his skis up the stairs to his terrace where he deposited them and kicked off his boots. He opened the door to his room just enough to extract a pair of after-ski footwear by the door. He had no desire to look inside for fear of what new surprises might be in store. With Redding around, it was not a time for surprises.

The bar was, of course, crowded with aprés-ski activity. Ian ordered his hot buttered rum; Redding, a hot chocolate. They then moved into the dining room, where it was quieter.

"Now, Mr. Stone . . . "

"Cheers," Ian said, lifting and then savoring his drink. One desire fulfilled.

"Right," said the sheriff, raising his mug. Then he continued,

"The other night I asked anyone near the site of the explosion on the mountain to come over to the Thunderbird after dinner. You didn't come. Now, why is that?"

"Because I wasn't skiing there," Ian lied. "I took a trail off to the left . . . Patton, I think it's called."

Redding pulled out a trail map he had in his pocket, "Patton is right next to the Bowl where the incident occurred."

"Let me see that," Ian requested. He looked at the map and pointed, "No, here is where I was. It must be Upper Patton. Anything else?"

"Yes. Could you tell me how the jeep you rented came to be driven by a man named Vargas?" Redding gloated.

Ian started laughing, "No, I could not. Can you?"

"I'd like to know what you think is so funny?" Redding asked, perplexed by Ian's response. "The man was drunk and could have killed someone."

"Well, that is not funny and is not why I am laughing," Ian cleared his throat and tried to be sober. But he couldn't hold it and started laughing again. Just then, Alex and Diana walked in. Ian called to them, "Alex! Diana! . . . Am I happy to see you. Do you know Sheriff Redding?"

"We've met," Alex nodded.

"You're in a good mood," Diana commented to Ian, then turned to Redding. "No, I haven't had the pleasure."

"But you came to the Thunderbird the other night, Miss. I wouldn't easily forget you," Redding complimented.

"I'm flattered, sheriff. Yes, the whole thing intrigued me," Diana said.

"But not your friend here," Redding scowled.

"Ian? I'm afraid all he's interested in is skiing," she winked.

"I was asking him how his jeep came to be driven by a drunk today," Redding went on.

"And as I've said," Ian restated, "I have no idea how anyone could be driving *my* jeep."

"Perhaps it was stolen," Diana offered.

"Then maybe Mr. Stone would like to prefer charges."

"That would be up to the rental company, wouldn't it?" Ian asked.

"Maybe. When did you notice it was missing?" the sheriff demanded.

"I didn't. But then, I haven't used it. I've been skiing all day," Ian said, smirking again.

"Did you use it last night?" Redding countered.

"No, I didn't," Ian said. "These two can vouch for that."

Their faces showed agreement and Redding knew he was getting nowhere. He realized he'd have to wait for Vargas to sober up.

"I think I'll call it a day," he said.

"Then, have a real drink," Ian invited.

The sheriff was surprised at the offer, "Perhaps another time."

"Sheriff, it would be my pleasure. Believe me."

It did sound believable. That's what upset Redding.

"What was that all about?" Alex asked.

"I don't know," Ian said. "I never rented a jeep."

He got up and kissed Diana. She was surprised, but happy.

"What? None for me," joked Dashwood.

"Much better for you. First, take back your jacket. It's too tight in the arms."

Ian chugged his drink and motioned for a waitress to bring them a round.

"It's been a hell of a time since last night," he continued. "And I've got lots of information. But first, I've got a few questions. Ever hear of someone called Fasani?"

"Fasani? Of course," said Alex. "You might say he started the whole discipline thing, with the whips and so on. Back in the 13th century, I believe."

"Well, somehow they think I'm a descendant of his."

"Really? Then that's why you have such an appeal to the Penitente, despite the fact you're a *gringo*."

"The 'appeal' is to El Conciliador," Ian corrected. "He wants to use me to solidify his hold on the Penitente."

"You met him?" Diana blurted. "Who is he?"

"His name is Mortez" Ian whispered. "Ramon Mortez."

"Did you s..see . . . ?" Alex stuttered he was so excited.

"No, I didn't see the treasure, but I heard about it."

Alex was rubbing his hands together with glee, "Don't talk so loudly. S..Start from the beginning."

"At the Pueblo. Or meeting the Cardinal?"

"A cardinal!" Alex exclaimed.

"Velenari, Mortez called him."

"Velenari!" Diana was so startled, she let it slip.

"You know of him?" Ian asked, surprised.

She looked the most vulnerable he had ever seen her. She really liked him. He could feel it. And he liked her, too.

"He's only the most important man in the Catholic Church next to the Pope," she answered as if it were common knowledge.

"*Was.* Apparently, he was killed last night . . . or committed suicide."

"My God!" Alex exclaimed. "Remember, I had told you I heard some important Church official spent time in Santa Fe."

"He was in with El Conciliador. Listen, some of this is very weird," Ian warned, "and I don't know if . . . It's probably very dangerous information to have. I'm not sure if you should get involved, Diana."

"I'm a big lady, Mr. Stone," she answered cooly.

Ian knew he had put his foot in it.

"My boy, we've already been through some hairy situations together," Alex interjected. "Now's not the time to hold back."

"Alex, I've got a feeling that what we've been through is only a picnic to what may be ahead."

The expressions of the other two told Ian he was not going to be able to stop there. Besides, he needed them. Where else . . . to whom could he turn? But, Ian thought, perhaps he had better soften it.

"First of all the treasure exists . . . what's left of it, at least. Where, I don't know. Most of it . . . get ready for this, Alex . . . was melted down and used to bail out the Church's finances which the Cardinal had embezzled to support the Nazis."

The other two had looks of astonishment.

"It gets better," Ian gloated.

Ian told all, from the race through Walkyries to the finding of the treasure by Mortez and of the golden skull with its markings. Alex was beside himself with excitement.

"It's all so incredible," Dashwood responded. "The treasure was sealed off until, as prophesized, 'Quetzalcoatl's plume will rise and his thunder shall shake it loose.' And, the most powerful force created by man is the key!"

Alex tried to follow the string, "Quetzalcoatl existed! But the realization he was a man was, as I told you before, a bitter pill for the Aztecs to swallow. So out of the need to deify, they gilt his skull and our Ogam writer marks it with the 'secret' that I did not understand from the disc . . . a secret obviously contained on a *second* disc the Aztecs had seen . . . ," Alex was rolling, " . . . one done by the Ogam writer, wh..which is perhaps why they kept him alive.

"The secret must be Quetzalcoatl's . . . something he found or brought with him. It seems to be of importance equal to the treasure," Alex's head was bobbing in surety.

"The mystery disc was taken by the Aztecs, so the skull was marked in order to leave a record. Along the way back, the party was split up, or at least the discs were . . . and that's why the Ogam writer added the line about the skull on the disc I found."

"Sounds good. What's it mean?" Ian asked.

"I don't know," Alex shrugged, "but the Cacique might. I think he is going to let me meet the one they call The Bruja . . . The Witch." Alex realized he was talking quite loudly, "I'm s..sorry . . . Go on."

"No, cut in anytime," Ian requested. "*I* sure as hell don't know what to make of it."

The three of them started giggling, punchy from the incredible information they had. Guests started to trickle in for dinner and their privacy began to evaporate.

Ian briefly told them about the meeting set up for Sunday . . . that to see the treasure a wealthy collector was willing to pay ten million dollars as a down payment on a hundred-million dollar purchase price . . . and Mortez planned to use the funds to grab the papacy. Ian didn't have the time or the inclination to get into the mystery man's background. He felt it was too farfetched or, if not that, too dangerous to be spreading around. In reality, Ian couldn't fathom a hundred million dollars much less the amount of intrigue in which he found himself immersed.

"Why were you told all this?" Diana wanted to know. "What is your part in all this?"

"Mortez thinks I'm a killer. Once the mystery man pays his hundred million, I'm supposed to assassinate him," Ian said dryly.

Diana looked very disturbed.

"You see, I knew I shouldn't have said so much," Ian snapped. "This guy Mortez is a crazy man. They're all crazy . . . and I'm in the middle of it. It's all very exciting to be able to be alive talking about it, but at some point El Conciliador's bodyguard is going to tap me on the shoulder, and I'm going to be in big f'ing trouble."

It was Ian's most accurate assessment of his situation to date. He almost had a stroke, then, when another guest tapped him on the shoulder, "Are these seats taken?"

"No, join us," Diana had to answer for him.

A jovial group sat around them, but the three did not join in their levity. Each kept pretty much to his or her own thoughts while the table filled.

Jean was good enough to allow Dashwood to stay. There were two places open since no one had seen the Tronis all day. Antonio had reported his wife was ill, so it was assumed he had taken her to a doctor, or perhaps back to the airport. His things were still in their room. Ian looked at Alex, wondering what deduction the scholar was able to make of it. He did not want to think about it himself.

"Well, well, well. What is this celebration all about?" Eli asked with a twinkle in his eye. "Perhaps you need someone to liven up the party."

He sat down before anyone could protest. The only compensation was the meal.

Claude had outdone himself . . . an asparagus soup . . . canard flambé. Eli bought wine for the table, a not-bad Beaujolais. And there was apple tart for dessert.

During dessert Ian started to get antsy. He felt as if he were at one end of a very long corridor with the table at the opposite end. The dinner conversation was like a muted echo to him. Then he started to sweat profusely.

"Are you okay?"

Someone was peering down the corridor at him. He thought it was Meredith. Why was there this separation? Where was Meredith?

"Ian, are you all right?" Diana asked.

His chair was moving down the corridor toward the table. He blinked and the din of the room came crashing in. Ian looked into Diana's eyes. Most of the others at the table had left.

"I've got to go," he said.

"Go? Go where?" she asked.

"There's another ceremony at the *morada.* I have to go."

She wanted to ask why, to tell him not to go, but knew she couldn't. Diana was struggling deep within. She wanted to be able to trust this man, but she knew there wasn't time enough for it to come naturally. Nor had she been able to reach the Guardian for advice. She was, therefore, trying to leap the hurdles of her mind and get to the end point quickly. But the hurdles were enormously high and the goal seemed to keep moving away.

" . . . I don't know why," Ian muttered softly.

"How will you get there?" she asked him.

"Troni," he said as if in a daze.

"Hasn't been seen," Diana admonished. "Remember?"

He looked into her eyes, "Do you . . . ?"

"Have a car? Yes," she nodded. "Would you like to borrow it?"

Ian shook his head. Diana was beginning to lose patience but realized it was because she cared for him.

"The key's in my room. Do you want to change first?"

Again, he shook his head silently, but seemed hesitant. She smiled, "Don't worry, I won't hang you up. Coming, Professor?" she asked Dashwood.

"Hmm?" Alex was sitting by the fire engrossed in a book on peyote.

"We're going," she said.

"Yes . . . Right," Dashwood said, putting on the jacket Ian had returned to him. "This yours?" he asked. From one of the pockets he withdrew the herb pouch the Cacique had given Ian at the end of their meeting.

"Yes," said Ian, more animated. He had forgotten about it and now wondered whether it had somehow shielded him at the Foundation. He carefully put it into the pocket of his own jacket.

The wind was kicking up again as they left the Lodge, tossing the snow into wispy cones.

They took the long way around toward Diana's room. It was better lit. Just one dark area stretched between the main building and the annex.

Suddenly, Diana slowed, sensing danger.

"What's wrong?" Alex inquired.

"Something's not right," she whispered.

"What?" Ian wanted to know.

"I don't know," she said. "I just feel it."

They moved ahead slowly and turned the corner when a figure popped out of the shadows. It was Eli.

"Jesus Christ!" Ian exclaimed.

"Oy, not quite," Eli retorted, grabbing his chest. "You startled me. I thought I heard you in your room as I passed," he said to Diana. "Must be the maid. Sorry. Say, I was just going to hear the music. You coming back?"

"In awhile," Diana stared at him.

"I'll keep a spot for you," he said as he went off.

Diana shot a glance at the window of her room. It was dark. What had Eli heard? Why was he there?

"Come on," she said, pulling them back in the other direction.

"What?" Ian was confused.

"We're not going," Diana told him. "Someone's there."

"Who?"

"I don't know *who,*" she said with irritation. "Whoever saw us last night."

"How do you know?" Ian persisted.

"Intuition," she said, pushing him on in exasperation.

"What about the keys?" Ian asked.

"Perhaps he should take my pickup," Alex offered.

"Never mind," Diana said. "The door's open. I'll just hot wire it."

They arrived at the car and Diana went to work.

"You really know how to do this?" Ian asked.

"You don't?" She shook her head as if he were trying to be ridiculous.

The air was clearing his head and Ian watched with interest, figuring he was going to have to do it on the way back. It wasn't all that unfamiliar to him. He had seen it done before. Was it television or . . . ? The motor started.

As he drove off, Ian wondered how Diana was able to stay so cool. There was something strange about her, he decided. Who was she, really?

Then his thoughts drifted back . . . to someplace dark. The *morada.* Last night. He had been comfortable. He wanted that feeling again. The car sped on to Talpa.

"*Non son las puertas de la morada,*" Ian heard himself saying. "*Sola las puertas de su conciencia.*"

Tonight, Ian hoped to get past more than doorways to his conscience. It was time for much greater depth.

He entered the *capilla* and there was silence. The *Maestro de Novicios* came forward with a robe. Ian put it on, found a spot and knelt down. The *Razador* continued his reading. And Ian listened . . . hoping to sound the depths of his inner world.

Diana and Alex had, meanwhile, finished a drink at the Hondo Lodge. From the bar, they could look down the hill toward the Edelweiss and her room. The annex was completely dark, yet she knew someone was there, waiting. She could not go back, and yet she knew Alex was anxious to leave. Finally, she made her decision.

"Drop me off at the *morada,*" Diana said.

"The *morada?* Where Ian went? We don't even know where it is, do we? How . . . ?" Alex was confused.

"Don't ask," Diana begged. "Just drive me."

They went to Alex's pickup. The night clouds were drifting overhead, pushed on by a strong northwesterly wind. The moon, now full, glimpsed only occasionally from behind their screen. It seemed incredible, but more snow was on the way.

Alex put the truck into gear and they moved through the parking lot toward the road to Taos.

In the shadows outside the Edelweiss annex, the Gypsy waited. He had almost been caught searching Diana's room and could not risk moving from his position until he felt he would not be noticed.

But he *had* been noticed . . . not only by Eli. From his vantage on the chalet rooftops, Braden had seen the Gypsy enter and leave Diana's room. It was a big surprise to him, for he knew who the man was and what his being there signified. The man was part of THE ONE's elite guard . . . would no longer be, if his sloppiness were reported . . . And he would only be in Taos if THE ONE himself were coming.

Why, Braden wondered, was he getting his men killed and putting himself in danger? What did the Penitente have THE ONE wanted? The answer eluded him. And it only upset the CIA chief more. His father had always kept things from him because, he said, he only had to know his part. That's why Braden now made it his business to know all the parts. He didn't want to feel like a kid again. Like he felt now . . . Whatever was going on or about to happen, he vowed to get to the bottom of it.

Now he had his key. That afternoon he had presented his

credentials at the sheriff's office. Redding wasn't in and the deputy kept falling all over himself, trying to be of service. Braden wired Diana's picture to the central computer and had gotten back her sheet. It had a little notation he himself keyed in a year ago, identifying her as part of The Light, an organization of which the CIA knew nothing; an organization and members of which he alone had knowledge from his deceased brother wolf, Velenari. Diana would be his key to reaching and taking down the Assassin. Braden was glad when he finally saw her drive off with the older man. The cold had been getting to him the last hour and he was in danger of being exposed by the moon. He wondered what part this new character played. From his gait, Braden was sure he was the one who had left Diana's room with her the night before.

Following them was out of the question tonight. Braden was sure the Assassin was lurking in the area, watching for someone to do just that. And he was not about to give himself away again. No, he would wait for The One to make *his* mistake. Besides, Braden had a few surprises he wanted to take care of.

When they neared Arroyo Seco Alex, again, asked how Diana intended to find Ian. It was then she pulled a small tracking device from her bag and switched it on. Alex looked at her, perplexed.

"Don't ask," she warned. "I couldn't tell you the truth anyway. Not yet."

Alex knew she was concerned about Ian. That's all that mattered to him for the moment.

The shadow of the crucifix danced in the flickering candlelight. It took Ian back to Avignon. He and Meredith were there on the autumnal equinox at sunset. The large cross outside the cathedral had sent its shadow speeding up the nave through the open doors until it fell directly upon the altar. An organ recital had dramatically accompanied the biannual event.

At first, Meredith didn't believe it only happened twice a

year. For all her brilliance, she sometimes lacked the most mundane knowledge.

What had been the real attraction? Why this obsession over her? Other women had left him. He had left other women. Why had this been such a cataclysm? Why had his soul been so torn in shreds? Ian had thought about it until, at times, his head ached so much, thought was impossible. Neither was it possible at this moment. Ian had himself to think about now.

He tried to push himself through the wall, but it wasn't coming. Too many years of numbness . . . too much difficulty . . . like cracking through rocks sealing an old tomb.

Ian felt a tear at the corner of his eye. He knew he was pitying himself . . . trying, at least. But there was too much self-anger to allow even that.

A penetrating draft swept through him. But it wasn't from the dampness of the night. It was from a dampness within. Ian slunk back inside himself, cutting away from the outside world. He was going back to the place he had reached the night before. Perhaps from there he could start on a deeper journey. Soon there were only faint drones in the distance. He was, finally, alone . . . isolated.

What next? In which direction should he step? Ian couldn't even see locked doors. Nothing. It was like being stranded on a barren, empty plain. Any direction could be the wrong one . . . so why go anywhere? But he had to. He felt he had to make a choice. And, at last, he was able . . . descending through the crust of the plain. Down lower.

Alex had let Diana off by her car. "Keep him safe" is all he said after Diana insisted she wait alone.

Diana got into the front seat and gazed at the *morada* in the light of the unmasked moon. The building had an eerie glow to it. Was it a heavenly aura, or a flame from the pit? She could not be sure.

As she stared, Diana realized how jealous she was of Ian. He was experiencing whatever was going on in there as a result of mistaken identity. He had lucked-out and gained admittance to the core. But was that the way it really was? Was Ian Stone who he said he was?

The same question was plaguing Ian. He was sweating from the heat again, yet feeling terrible chills at the same time.

* * *

A barrage of images assaulted the walls of his mind from the side he had kept repressed since Viet Nam. The dreamer was standing on a castle parapet away from the edge. He could hear the images crashing, pounding, screaming as they struggled to climb over one another and, thus, formed a pyramid whose apex seemed to be reaching the level of the wall . . . in reality, his consciousness. Ian could see an occasional head, a face, over the top of the wall as the images continued to leap up . . . an old woman . . . a soldier . . . a wolf.

It wasn't these images that made him shake, however, but a feeling. It wasn't a fear the images would climb over . . . into his consciousness. It was, rather, the desire to finally want to face them. Suddenly, it was as if the ground beneath him was rising and the walls he had built to protect himself were lowering until an equilibrium was achieved. And before long, Ian found himself peering at the images gathered before him. There was a silence. It matched the silence of the morada *. . . a pause between prayers. The woman . . . was she his mother? The soldier . . . was it he? The wolf? The Cacique had said they were all parts of himself. Ian had to hold his breath to keep focus . . . to bear to see.*

There was the sound of metal against metal . . . ching . . . ching . . . It was the incense burner being swung by the *Celador General Primero.*

But Ian heard it as the breaking of chains by a lone figure that had been bound to a pillar at the pyramid's base and was now climbing over the other images comprising the structure . . . heading toward the summit. Perhaps recognition would bring the final breakthrough.

"No . . . ," Ian yelled as he shrank back not wanting to see the climber's face.

* * *

The incense wafted through the chamber.

"*Tantum ergo sacramentum* . . . ," voices around him in the outside world began to sing. The abruptness made Ian open his eyes.

He was hyperventilating and nauseous. Mucous dripped from his nose. He had to struggle to rise, for his legs felt like lead. It was too much. He collapsed to his knees again, then gazed around him through the sweat dripping off his brow. Why were they so placid? Why didn't they have to face the images he had to face?

Ian wanted to vomit, but then, a rage crept over him and fought back the urge. He was angry he couldn't break out of his skin and escape into someone else's . . . angry he couldn't get away from this part of himself that was angry at himself . . . angry he really wanted to know the past his mind had been afraid to face. Ian was split, and his head was splitting, too. He was barely able to raise a shaking hand to pull the hood over his brow. Nausea had given way to tears. And they poured forth the rest of the ceremony.

It was almost midnight when the men began to leave the *morada.* Diana did not see them though she sat upright in the driver's seat with her eyes open. She was asleep.

Brothers in cheap leather coats and sheepskin vests departed silently to their pickups and vans to disperse into the night.

Ian said nothing to any of them. He still could not talk. The night air chilled him and Ian began to shiver as he walked to the car, wondering how he would start it. He looked in and saw Diana. He thought she was staring at him until the sound of a motor brought a look of light into her eyes and he realized she had been asleep. It was both bizarre and frightening; it caused him to shiver again as he got in the passenger side.

"What are you doing here? How did you find? . . ." he started to ask.

"I was worried," she said, smiling. "My God, you're soaked. Are you all right?"

"I just need some heat," Ian replied. "Do your magic under the dash and let's get out of here."

By the time they hit the main road, all the cafes and fast food joints were closed. But Ian wasn't thinking about food or drink by then. He was trying to recapture the vision of the figure climbing the pyramid of images. He had felt its presence before. But before, he had been afraid. Damn it, he was still afraid. Now he felt angry at himself for lacking the courage to confront it.

"There's nothing open," he heard Diana say.

"It's okay," he answered. "I'm warmer now. Only tired."

"I don't think we should go back to the Ski Valley," Diana said. "I sense some danger closing in."

"Intuition again?" he asked with a smile.

Diana just gazed ahead and drove. Ian turned to wondering whether his dream-vision was, as the Cacique said he should question, from God or from the devil. And, like the characters in the dream, were both God and the devil, parts of himself?

They turned onto the road to the Ski Valley. The wind was still kicking up, moving the clouds swiftly overhead. The moon was casting shadows in awesome shapes. Ian became mesmerized and started to drift off to sleep. Then he was jolted as the car came to a stop. They were at the Abominable Snowmansion.

"I'll see if they have a room," Diana said, getting out of the car.

They did. And Ian was happy to get out of his wet clothes. He sat on the rickety bed swaddled in his blanket like an old squaw, watching as Diana undressed and put her clothes over the slanted wooden chair.

Her back to him, she unhooked her bra. She was beautiful from any angle. There was no question about it.

"You're beautiful," he said softly.

"What?"

By the time she turned, he was asleep. Diana pulled the sheets and blankets up around him, turned off the light and got into bed next to him. In his sleep, Ian drew her to him and held her tightly.

For awhile, she just lay there, staring through the window across from the bed. Diana had never allowed herself to love before. Yet, at the moment she felt so close to this man. It was a very foreign feeling.

Soon the light left her eyes and they stared vacantly as she joined him in sleep.

Diana had something in common with the man in the next room . . . the master player for whom Ian was a pawn. The One waited until he knew they were both asleep, then lay back to rest himself, knowing now he was still in control of his pawn.

What he did not control was in sleep, his own eyes remained open as well. Had he known, the Assassin would have remembered the words of the monk at the Buddhist monastery where he hid for so many months after his escape from the Khmer Rouge . . . it was an omen of death.

In New Mexico, however, there was another saying, "*Es como los brujos; duerme con los ojos abiertos* . . . He is like the witches; he sleeps with his eyes open."

Which would govern for The One and which for Diana?

18

Ian was walking on a university campus with Meredith and an older woman he could not recognize because of the veil she wore. The trio admired the facades of all the buildings.

A tall man in a gray suit came toward them and Ian excused himself to go talk to him. He greeted the man and together they walked up the steps to the Medical Center.

Once inside the columned facade, it was like being in a bombed-out building. There was rubble everywhere . . . walls blown away and gaping holes in the roof.

Ian showed the man where the computer room was supposed to be set up and asked if anything could be done about the mess. The man didn't answer, just walked into the area and looked around.

Ian shrugged and walked into another part of the building that had not been destroyed. There he stopped to gaze at a display case with samples of meteoric rock. As he did so, two men in white orderly coats walked by talking about some medical students last seen in the research library studying about lycanthropy . . . werewolves. Apparently, they had been missing for some time.

Suddenly there was a commotion down the corridor. Someone yelled, and everybody started running to Room 16, where one of the researchers had been working on a special project.

Ian followed, and when he got there saw the room was all torn apart. The walls were blown out from within. Massive tables were moved as if some giant had just brushed them aside.

The oddest thing to Ian was everyone was trying to put the room back in order as quickly as possible. No one was trying to gather evidence as to what had happened. Ian was confused and wished he had a camera to record the present condition of the room.

Then he looked down and in the dirt on the floor saw a bare footprint. He put his own foot into it and his covered only half the space.

From somewhere he heard a voice say, ". . . and what we are dealing with here is a metamorphosis . . . "

Ian noticed a small recorder under a table and quickly picked it up and put it under his jacket. He looked around to see if anyone else had heard it, but everyone was too involved in trying to make it appear as if nothing had happened.

Ian started walking out of the room, his one thought being to find some place where he could listen in peace and unravel the mystery of the "metamorphosis."

* * *

JUEVES SANTO

Ian awoke feeling euphoric. It was the best rest he could remember. Outside the sky was clear and the air crisp. A great day for skiing, he thought.

He turned to look at Diana. Her hair lay across her face, exposing just her lips. Why was he getting up, Ian wondered? That's what she asked, too.

"I want to get back," Ian told her.

"Back!" she exclaimed.

"The Nastar race is this afternoon. I'm supposed to be in it," he found himself saying. "I know it sounds stupid, but . . ."

Diana was dumbfounded. "Sounds stupid! Oh, please . . . You can't be serious! Do you think you're involved in some kind of game? Important events . . . Events of world consequence are going on, and you want to be . . . you're right, in some 'stupid' ski race! What's wrong with you?"

"Overload . . . Tilt . . . I've had all I can handle for now," Ian shouted angrily. "I don't know what the hell this is all about."

"Keep your voice down," she shouted back.

Ian slumped into the chair across from the bed and spoke more softly, as if he were drained, "You know, I don't understand what this is all about. My life's been all screwed up . . . I came out here to ski and try to get a few things together . . . People are dying all around me . . . Others think I'm some killer . . . Fine. Let them. Let them!" he shouted again. "What the hell do I care? No one is threatening me . . . "

"So far," she cautioned.

He calmed again and looked her in the eyes, "I've got to relax right now. I've got to get away from it."

His hands moved as if he were smoothing out the covers on an imaginary bed.

"I was great yesterday. You should have seen me," he said in a soft voice.

"Fine," she responded. "But answer me this, Skimeister: what are you going to do when Mortez's big bodyguard comes looking for you again and wants you to kill this mystery man who's paying a hundred million dollars for his treasure?"

Ian had no answer.

"Who is this mystery man anyway? Since you're busy, I'd like to meet him," Diana goaded.

"I don't think so," Ian said soberly.

"Why not? Tell me, Ian. I have a right to know what I've gotten into," Diana demanded.

"Well, I suggest you get yourself out of it . . .," Ian jabbed at her. He wanted to tell her all, but felt it wrong to involve her. Why did she have to be so curious? Ian threw up his hands in despair.

Diana thought he was crazy, but he looked as beautiful to her as she did to him. She wanted to have him hold her, but she didn't know how to ask. It could have gone that way, but it didn't. Where men were concerned, she spent too much time thinking instead of acting. Frustration drove her to harshness.

"I don't think you are who you say you are," she rankled at him.

Ian bristled, "Think what you want."

"Either that or you're schizo," she persisted.

A wicked smile crossed his lips, "You think so? What about you?" he challenged. "How did you find me last night? I didn't tell you where the *morada* was. Maybe you're working with all of them," he continued to rant as he dressed. "From what Mortez said, even Velenari had his secret police."

The latter statement stunned her, but her mind was overruled by a feeling of hurt. "Don't be absurd, Ian," she lied. "I'm here on holiday just the way you claim to be."

"Oh, now I *claim* to be?! A lot of trust you give me. Look, stay here. Relax. Enjoy. I'm going."

He slipped on his boots and walked to the door, "The car is yours. I'll hitch." He opened the door and turned back to her, mournfully, "I just want to get away from this for awhile." He started out, then turned back again, "I hope you'll join me later."

Diana smiled a troubled smile as he left. Who was this man? Was he the one they thought he was? If so, why did he let her live?

Meanwhile, The One moved quickly, slipping out his window and down the backstairs to the rented jeep he had steathily retrieved from the sheriff's lot. As he did, his mind raced over the new bits of information he had just learned . . . Mortez, a mystery man, a treasure. Mortez had to be El Conciliador. The treasure the CIA spoke of was real; some archaeological find that tied in Professor Alex Dashwood. And somebody was willing to pay a heavy price for it. Now he needed more facts. He needed his pawn to survive the day. If Ian was going to be foolish, he would have to protect him . . . starting with driving him to the slopes.

The jeep swung around the building onto the road as Ian

clumped away from the lodge. He turned and stuck out his thumb at the sound of the motor. Ian was delighted the jeep slowed to a stop. But his expression soured when he saw the bandaged face within.

"Can I . . . give you . . . a lift?" The One spoke in broken phrases, as if it hurt to talk. Ian, somewhat reluctantly, got in. "Thanks."

He could feel the presence immediately. Normally he might not have, but his senses had keened the last few days. Ian stared at the man as the car started off. It was noticed.

"Fire," the driver said. "Plastic surgery."

Ian nodded as if he were familiar with such cases, "When does it come off?"

"When I . . . get back," was the reply.

"That will be a relief I bet," Ian said unnecessarily. A nod was his response.

As they rode along in silence, Ian grew more and more sure he knew this person . . . somewhere . . . somewhere . . . He had a vision of fire around him, the sound of shells exploding . . . pain . . . The car jolted over a bump and Ian slipped into daydreams of being on the ski slopes, his anticipation increasing with their altitude.

For his part, The One decided it was not the time to unmask yet. It would probably mean he would have to kill Ian, and, for some strange reason, he was reluctant to do that . . . for the moment.

As they entered the Ski Valley parking area, another car departed. Braden was off to check on some fingerprints he had taken from Ian's room. He wanted to know for sure if the pawn was Ian Stone or if Stone might be The One's true identity. He vowed this would not be another day of disappointments. At least, not the rest of the day. So far, it had, at best, been frustrating, waiting in vain for the explosion that would occur as soon as the pawn got into his bed in Room 18. Braden had de-bugged the room and set the explosive device after

Alex and Diana's departure. With the Tronis out of the way, access had been easy through the floor hatch connecting the rooms.

It would appear the gas heater exploded . . . a tragic accident that would, literally, smoke out the man he was after. Patience, he reminded himself as he drove off.

Ian was let off by the main lodge. "Thanks for the lift," he said, relieved the ride was over.

"Be careful," the driver said. It was both a warning and a command. Ian looked back at the man, trying to peer beyond the bandages into the recessed eyes. But to no avail. He closed the door and the car moved on.

"Who was that masked driver?" he muttered to himself.

Ian felt tired as he entered his room. He wanted to flop down on the bed, but the memory of making love there with Diana made him instead take the chair across from it. He gazed for a moment at the memory, then removed his clothes to shower.

Braden second-guessed himself all the way down the mountain. Perhaps the Assassin's pawn already had the information THE ONE needed. It might have been better to force it out of him than to blow him away. But that assumed he could get to Stone without the Assassin getting to him. The CIA chief turned to constructing the story he would feed Diana Bastian. She was smart. Braden knew it would have to hang together. And she could not be allowed to contact Rome for verification.

As he took the curve into Arroyo Seco, Braden started feeling the day would go right for him. There was Diana Bastian walking out of the Abominable Snowmansion. He would have to go with the story as best as he had it.

Braden pulled alongside her car and slipped into his friendliest mode. If nothing else, he was a consummate actor.

"Miss Bastian . . . "

Diana turned, surprised.

"Sorry to startle you. My name is Braden . . . CIA."

He displayed his credentials. Diana first checked his eyes, then the I.D. The former were factual; the latter, genuine.

"What can I do for you, Mr. Braden?" she asked.

"Take a ride . . . mine or yours," he offered. "Here are your keys."

She stared angrily as he extended them to her.

"It wasn't me you sensed last night," he said, perceiving her ire. "I took the liberty of going in later . . . to make sure it was safe."

"Don't do me any favors," she responded indignantly.

"And, of course, to learn more of your motivations," he stated dryly.

"Did you?" she inquired in the same tone.

"Let's take the ride," he said, opening the passenger door.

"Where to?" Diana asked without moving.

"First to the police station. I want to check some fingerprints."

There was something totally unlikable about the man, but Diana sensed she was not in danger. She got into the car and they drove off.

Braden got down to business quickly, "I know you are part of an organization know as The Light. What I'm sure *you* don't know is Cardinal Velenari was the power behind your group and used it to shield his own corruption."

Diana was dumbfounded.

"As far as the Agency," he went on, "I alone know of The Light. You see," he said, looking at her, "it's my job to know everything. And what I need to know now is the reason behind your involvement with someone so dangerous to your Church?"

"Who?" she snapped, not wanting to hear.

"Ian Stone, the world's premier assassin . . . the man known as The One by those who hire his ilk . . . the man who killed, among others, your Pope John Paul I."

"No! . . ." the word rose up from the pit of her stomach. There was almost no breath or sound left as it passed between her lips.

"I'm afraid so," Braden consoled. "I've been trying to unmask him for a long time. Stone's The One."

"No," she argued. "He's being mistaken for someone else. He couldn't . . . "

"My dear woman, you're too smart for that," Braden countered. "These types are schizos. They live two lives . . . sometimes more. I need to know everything he's told you. In return I'll tell you why he's here and how you can be of service to your Church. He's already killed two of my best men. I can use your help," the CIA chief said humbly.

"Schizo," she thought. Hadn't she just called him that?

"But let's wait until after we've been to the police station," he began setting her up. "I want you to see for yourself. I have two fingerprints: the first taken from Stone's room and a second taken from the gun I found with Cardinal Velenari's body . . . "

He looked at her as he spoke. Her reaction was not one of surprise; it was more like caving in. As Braden surmised, it was pure chance Diana met Stone. And one of the Guardian's iron maidens had fallen in love.

"I see you're not surprised about Velenari . . . ," he said.

"Ian . . . Stone said he heard about it from . . . ," but Diana did not want to tell him everything yet.

"No matter," he said. "I'm going to see if they match with those of Ian Stone in the central computer file. If so, I'll assume we'll both be convinced and can talk."

Diana felt as if she were drowning and needed desperately to grab hold of something, "First, you're going to have to tell me why it was necessary to kill that Mrs. Troni . . . and how you know about Velenari."

Braden pulled out onto the road toward Taos, "Fair enough . . . but no need to wait. I didn't kill Mrs. Troni . . . I found the body when I came looking for Stone and removed it," he lied.

"Someone is trying to cut the Penitente out of whatever it is that's coming down. They want Stone to work for them or be out of the picture. I thought it might be you . . . or Velenari.

I'm convinced now it isn't you. Whether it was Velenari or some unknown third party, I'm not absolutely sure yet," Braden shook his head. "In any case, I got Mr. Troni to bring me to the *morada* in Arroyo Seco Tuesday night. Both Velenari and Stone were there . . . Only Stone left. I tried to nab him then, but he got away.

"If you haven't heard about the incident at the Gorge yet, I'm sure the sheriff's office can fill you in. Your Mr. Stone took out Troni and a bunch of locals I had recruited. I barely escaped. And he just vanished. I know it's hard for you to believe," Braden commiserated, "but the man's one of those brilliant psychotics.

"In any case, I made my way back to the *morada* and found Velenari dead, a bullet in his brain. I hadn't heard any shot when Stone was there, so I couldn't say for sure Stone had done it. That's why I went to search his room last night and found a second print."

He looked over at her strained visage, "The rest will have to wait."

The two drove on in silence, Braden proud of himself for the altogether plausible story he had constructed about the *two* prints taken from Stone's room . . . not to mention the part about Troni. There was enough fact blended in with fiction to confuse, if not convince her.

Stone was either Stone or the real name among The One's aliases. Braden was reasonably sure of the former; in which case, he would have Diana in his pocket and learn whatever she knew. He would use her to take out the pawn and the Assassin would have to come forth. Then he would dispose of her.

If, by some chance, the prints weren't the pawn's, there was still the "unknown third party" of which he had spoken. He felt he was on a roll and would find some way to make it work in order to get what he needed from her.

Meanwhile, he let Diana sit and wonder . . . which she did with a vengeance, mulling over the suspicions, the questions

. . . trying to see where his scenario made sense and where it didn't.

As they turned the corner off the main strip toward the sheriff's office, another car crossed the intersection and then stopped.

Redding wasn't there when they walked in and, once again, the deputy tripped all over himself to accommodate the man from Washington. Within a short time, the sheet on Ian Stone was being transmitted over the wire.

It was then Redding arrived and saw them. The glass door to the room with the transmitter was locked and the sheriff wanted to know what the hell was going on. As the deputy explained who Braden was, Diana and he compared the prints on Ian's service record to those the CIA chief had with him:

STONE, Ian. Birthdate: November 16, 1946.

Diana had a thing for birthdates. It was one of the items upon which she made preliminary judgments about people. The onus was on them to show they were exceptions to her rule.

Diana remembered her astrologer friend, Roberta, saying something about that date. It was astrologically one of the worst days of the year for a man to be born. Scorpio. He would be untrustworthy . . . evil. But there was a difference between pre-War and post-War.

Who else did she know with the same birthdate to answer her question? She remembered; it was the closet queen who betrayed the names of some of The Light's agents in Ireland . . . even after they had saved the talentless fellow's life. A very oily man, always with a cold sore on his lips. Unmasking this traitor had been Diana's first assignment. The thought of him gave her the chills. It was post-War. Her Ian was evil.

Eyes: Hazel. Height: 5′10″. Weight: 160.
Hair: Dark Brown. Birthplace: Boston, Massachusetts.

There was his address at the time . . . Hanover, New Hampshire . . . probably where he went to school; his I.D. Number, service record . . . and the photo. The entire substituted file was there, including the prints. Of course, they matched.

Diana felt a stronger chill run through her, icing her veins. Could there be any mistake, she wondered? From a transmitted copy there was no way to see signs of tampering. It was the way it seemed.

Diana had been defiled by the enemy. She had let herself be vulnerable and had been fooled. Diana did not like being used. She would have her revenge.

"Stone is part of a plot to kill off many high-ranking Church officials," Braden interjected. "The Penitente are vying with some other force to take control of the Vatican. But there's a lot we don't know. Who's behind it all? I need to know what you know."

Diana thought she was going to be sick, "Let's get out of here." She moved quickly out the door past Redding. Braden followed, brushing past the sheriff with a cursory, "Thank you."

Redding called after Diana, "Tell your friend he was supposed to sign a release before taking his jeep . . . "

He clenched his teeth as the door banged shut without an acknowledgement. Redding went into the vacated room in frustration and noticed the transmission line was still open. He punched in, "Transmission unclear. Repeat." A duplicate report came through in moments.

Redding sat and stared at it. Stone was his man. But he was obviously the government's, too. The drunk he had picked up yesterday with Stone's vehicle should be sober by now, he thought. He would see what else could be learned about his suspect.

Diana tried to be professional despite her depression. She sat across from Braden in the all but empty Appletree Restaurant and told him what she knew.

Braden had heard a lot of stories in his day, but there was only one to compare to it . . . his Master's family history. To have them both drawn together was simply astounding.

He tried to fathom THE ONE's mind. He had never understood why Velenari had been admitted to Metamorphosis and then why, after his stroke, he had been permitted to live.

THE ONE had an incredible collection of jewels and treasures once belonging to emperors and kings . . . from Alexander to the Tsars . . . but Braden couldn't believe all this had just been a setup to get hold of Montezuma's treasure . . . unless it held something so amazing . . . But what could that be?

This line of thinking was getting him nowhere, so he tried another tack. If THE ONE suspected an attack against him, he would infiltrate the ranks of the Penitente. Velenari was not to be trusted; so he needed someone who had both Velenari's trust and that of the Penitente . . . the Pope's assassin. How would Velenari know whom to hire to kill the Pope in the first place? He would have gone to the people with whom he was in business, and they could have gotten word from THE ONE. Perhaps this Fasani connection was real . . . the more reason this killer would be the logical choice. It was like THE ONE to surreptitiously create a connection, and then use it to infiltrate. As for the Assassin, he obviously didn't trust the Penitente or he wouldn't have brought a pawn. He had been sent for. Yet according to Diana, the Penitente were under the impression he had offered to come. It was THE ONE, all right.

Braden realized Scotia wanted the Assassin to find out what he needed to know and have it passed on through him. Once the information was in hand, his orders were to put The One on ice . . . no doubt so he wouldn't interfere. The Gypsy had been sent in to see how things were progressing. If it looked bad, THE ONE would be a no-show. All very neat. All very much a test as Braden had suspected. *If* that was the scenario. How could he be certain?

The only certainty Braden *did* have was that he now had all the information requested . . . all but the location of the treasure. Perhaps there was a way of using the Assassin's pawn as his own through Friday night . . . if Stone wasn't already blown out of the Valley.

Braden was feeling frustrated again. And more than ever, he wanted to relieve his frustration by getting rid of the mocking Assassin . . . the man who, he felt, might compete for his Master's affection. Only now he didn't have to go against his orders by doing it himself. Diana would be his weapon. He was determined he would succeed. He would prove he was THE ONE's most dependable subject. He had to. It was the only thing Braden really believed in.

"I've got to call Father Vittorio," Diana said. "I should have called him sooner."

"I don't think it would be advisable," Braden warned. "We don't know if we can trust him. Velenari instituted The Light and handpicked The Guardian. I could be wrong, but then, why tip our hand? I'm afraid it's going to have to be me and you. Does that make sense to you?"

He was glad it did.

"Let's think it through," Braden went on. "The men around this El Conciliador are different from the common Penitente, right? This whole effort to have Stone admitted as Fasani's descendant means El Conciliador needs something to solidify his hold on these people. Without Stone, he's just a rich man without an army to do his bidding. Now, would the Penitente be apt to flock to his cause if they knew his henchman were a pope-killer?"

Diana shook her head and asked, "When are these assassinations supposed to take place?"

"Friday night . . . Good Friday," he lied.

"Not much time," she mumbled to herself. "What should I do?"

Braden smiled. He had her in the palm of his hand. "If we try to tell them he's a pope-killer, what proof do we have? None. If we say he killed Cardinal Velenari, what proof do we have? None, without the body. And by now it could have been moved."

"Perhaps not," Diana said. "According to Stone, that *morada* seems to belong to their inner group. El Conciliador could be keeping it there under guard."

"And if it's there and we can get to it, how do we know the gun with the print will still be there?" Braden asked. "In other words, how do we make it believable?"

"Because I'll tell them he told me he did it," Diana said. "And I'm as Penitente as they are."

She turned her head to the right and lifted her hair. There, from the base of her hairline up into her scalp was the brand of a cross. It was impressive to Braden. It would be more so to the Penitente.

"We'll have to find access to the Penitente, as well as locate the body," Braden explained. "You mentioned meeting a guide at the museum. Start with her. I'll go back to the *morada* and see what I can find there."

Braden drove Diana back to her car, then headed to the *morada* to survey the scene. If there were guards, he'd know he'd hit paydirt. If not . . . He hoped he'd hit paydirt.

It was almost noon when Diana got to the museum. "How time flies when you're on vacation," she thought; then wondered how she could think amusing thoughts at a time like this. She simply didn't want to admit how hurt . . . and how much in love she was.

Perhaps, she hoped, Guadalupe could take a break for lunch. Diana honestly felt like pouring out her soul. And that might be exactly what would be necessary to get her to the right people.

She wondered if Dashwood would help. Where the hell was he, anyway? She remembered he was going to see The Bruja . . . whoever or whatever that was. A sob welled up in her chest. It had been years since she cried. The prospect frightened her and Diana fought it back. She had a job to do.

The car that had followed them to the sheriff's office stuck with her until the turnoff for the museum.

There were now two pawns . . . Ian and Diana . . . two players . . . The One and Braden . . . and, including Radu Scotia's Gypsy, two observers.

19

Dashwood was about an hour and more than a few centuries away at a place called Puye Cliff. Once the home of an ancient tribe, both the cliff and the plateau it supported held the ruins of Indian habitats over 1500 years old.

Puye is a Tewa word meaning "where the cottontails assemble." But the cottontails weren't there anymore; hadn't been for years. Today, in their place was an assembly of tribal leaders whose ancestors had seen the Aztecs come through this territory over 500 years ago . . . who had died at the hands of their treachery.

The tribal leaders were there to see the old *bruja* who lived among the ruins . . . a woman whom many of them had, at times, either feared or dismissed as a crazy person . . . when they were younger . . . before the signs of trouble began to appear almost four decades ago. Of course, in the beginning, the signs were few and therefore ignored. It had been a gradual awakening for the majority; for a few skeptics, as late as last year. But no one close to the land could ignore the signs today.

The sound of the gray wolf had been heard at night for over a month, but there had been no gray wolves in the region for years. In fact, only The Bruja herself could remember when they had roamed the area.

Big brown bats had also been flying the night skies in greater abundance. Cattle were dying mysteriously. The air forbode dread happenings. It was an accumulative feeling for even the greatest of disbelievers.

Dashwood had arrived at Puye the night before and had been allowed to attend the *walena* or peyote ceremony. He was still recovering . . . now trying to connect the gaps in the experience. There had been so incredibly much. The sounds . . . colors, the likes of which he had never before seen . . .

But the *piece de resistance* came later when The Bruja led him into a small cave and showed him a round metallic object. Had it been a shield? At the time he couldn't tell. Dashwood was immediately drawn to the markings, the wondrous Ogam markings that danced in his head and stirred the senses of his fingertips as he rubbed them.

It was an ancient story . . . Quetzalcoatl's, he was sure. And equally sure was he the story contained a hidden meaning; perhaps, the key to where the treasure lay. Or had it been something else? Last night it didn't matter; Alex had just floated with the images and opened his mind to let the figures dance where they might.

Now, in the light of day, and with the return of his routine senses, Dashwood labored to read the story and uncover its meaning.

Meanwhile, Ian was exhausted. All morning he had been put through rigorous training for the Nastar slalom event. Theresa Kittinger had seemed surprised to see him show up for class. But when he said he wanted to train hard, she made him work.

She had warned him one morning wasn't going to do much . . . that he should work toward Saturday's race, but he wanted to win the "gold" today.

Now Ian sat at the lunch table unable to move. In fact, he couldn't even eat. He looked around for Diana, Dashwood, Loudmouth Eli . . . anyone. But no one was around. Still, Ian felt certain he was being watched.

Jean came by, "What? Not eating? This is a special soup for Nastar racers. It's just for you. Theresa tells me you worked hard this morning. Go up to the course with me. I'll give you some pointers . . . *if* you eat your soup."

Ian was elated. He ate the soup, but that was it. Even if he had had an appetite, it would have been ruined by that feeling of being watched.

From his seat at the bar the Gypsy kept his vigil; from the other side of the room the man with the bandaged face kept his. The One recognized the Gypsy for what he was, but had no idea what his being there signified.

Ian and Jean rode up the lift together. The younger man couldn't have felt more proud. Jean was a superb skier. He had been in the '56 Olympics and had been the Valley champion for years.

As they skied from the top of Lift 1 over to Lift 2, Ian was able to keep up. That made him feel as high as he had felt in a long time.

On the way up the second lift, Ian lauded Jean on the hotel and the cuisine. He felt very gregarious, but soon wished he hadn't been . . . when he remarked how lucky he was there had been an opening for him.

"It was a sudden illness," Jean said. "Normally, we would have informed someone on our waiting list, but your friend insisted he needed the second room."

"My friend? . . ." Ian started to ask.

"Whatever did he do to his face?" Jean inquired.

"Burns," Ian heard himself mumble.

Jean continued speaking, but Ian wasn't listening. He now knew it had been a setup all along . . . starting, no doubt, with the loss of his Aspen reservations. It was no mistake he had been taken for someone else. He knew, but he had refused to admit it. It was planned. It was all a goddamn plan!

Ian thought back . . . Mr. Good Samaritan this morning . . . just happening along. The man had been on the plane with him. He had killed the CIA agent on the plane! Dashwood's description of "something out of proportion" . . . the bandaged head. He had shot the agent on the mountain! And probably Velenari as well.

He wasn't being mistaken for someone . . . he was being used. He was on point, snaking out the enemy. Son of a bitch. Son of a goddamned bitch!

But why? Why him?

They were at the top and Jean was moving off. "Come on."

The route to Lift 3 was longer . . . faster. Jean was way ahead. Ian used his anger to close the gap.

Why was he picked? When was he picked?

Jean got to the split between Honeysuckle and Japanese Flag. He stopped on a dime to see if Ian was anywhere behind him and was surprised when the latter almost plowed into him.

"Sorry," Ian said, "I didn't know you were going to stop."

Jean smiled. He was pleased.

They went on to the upper Rubezahl and down to the lift. Jean kept shouting out instructions, only half of which Ian heard or understood. Ian finally collapsed into the chair as they rode up to the Basin.

"Very good," said the pro. "Just go for it. You'll do fine."

The course was below them. The event had already begun and they saw the first contestants making their runs through the slalom gates.

Suddenly a racer came around the elbow of the course out of control. He went flying head over heels, skis sailing in two directions.

"See," Jean pointed out, "you've got to begin your next turn as soon as you're at the pole. Change that weight quickly."

Ian started to flush, then sweat. Another fine predicament he was getting himself into.

They reached the top and headed for the course. On their arrival, Jean was warmly greeted and let in before the next racer up.

"What's the time today?" Jean asked.

"26.6 seconds," the starter announced.

"*¡Yamo!*" he yelled, tripping the starting gate, and was off, zipping through the gates at incredible speed. In seconds he had quickly disappeared from sight down the mountain.

The Nastar was an interesting event—a national competition in which there were many medal winners. The top instructors from all over the country met once a year to compete and be ranked. During the season, they would set the pace at their home courses and anyone could run against their time as it related to the supposed time the annual champion would have had if he were there to run the course. Everyone also received a handicap according to age and sex, thus giving a fair opportunity to all. Of course, Nastar supposed the runs were the same on all mountains. Anyone who had skied Taos knew differently. That's why a medal won there meant more.

The starter listened for the report of Jean's run over his headphones and then announced, "26.5."

Everyone was impressed. The next skier went, and blew out at the sixth gate. It was too hard an act to follow.

Ian figured he could do the course in 29 seconds and still win a gold medal. But he had to wait for ten more skiers in front of him. That was unfortunate. The course was being rutted and it gave him too much time to think.

When his turn came, Ian put his skis in the track, placed his poles over the timing rod, flexed back as Theresa had shown him, and then pitched forward, tripping the timer. He was off.

Gate. Turn. Gate. Turn. Rhythm . . . Shift . . . Lean into it . . . Steer . . . Turn . . . Gate . . . Rut . . . . Keep going . . . Gate . . . Turn . . . Gate . . . Turn . . . Control . . . Hang on . . . Gate . . . Gate . . .

From somewhere he heard Theresa's, "Go for it!"

Last gate . . . Tuck . . . He did it!

"35.5," he heard as he skied over to the board.

Ian asked what his time meant. "How old are you?" the timekeeper asked.

"36."

He got a bronze medal . . . one half second off a silver. Shit! How could he do better than that? He had given it everything he had.

Theresa had come over, "So, how did you do?"

"Bronze . . . Just missed a silver," Ian said dejectedly.

"Good. Go run it again," his instructress encouraged. "That was very fine for a first time. Now let's see what you can really do."

Ian descended to the chairlift charged up to prove himself. But by the time his chair passed over the course, he was sure it was all rutted out.

Seeing the course as a metaphor, Ian felt his whole life was rutted out. It was a downhill disaster. He had been satisfied by nothing. The seeming success he had amassed in his career was a facade fronting emptiness. His job had bought him and pressured him to be what it wanted him to be. His woman had probably left him because he was trying to buy her love and pressure her into being what he wanted her to be. If only he had her . . .

"Are you running again?" the starter asked.

"Hmmm? Yes," Ian muttered and got into position.

Ian howled and was off. He moved out faster. The first gates were not bad. The third had a rut. He rode it. Fourth. Fifth, rut . . . Sixth, balance . . . Rut . . . Seventh, rut . . . Rut . . . His life was a rut . . . Too late; he shifted too late! Ian shot over the track, was in the air, smacked a pole and was out of it. End of Nastar. No gold.

One of Ian's skis had come off and he hobbled back for it, then brushed the snow off himself and moved from the course. Suddenly the race had lost its importance. Ian didn't care about anything at that moment except getting back to his previous train of thought . . . Meredith . . . her leaving . . . his leaving . . .

Ian remembered thinking last week, if he were a woman, he would want to look exactly like her.

He realized now she had challenged his way of living; had fought his control; would not be anything but herself . . . and so, left him.

Ian, too, wanted to be himself. He wanted to go back and start all over again. So it was not just a question of looks; he wanted to *be* like her . . . have her abandon. And the realization came over him . . . he *had* left the environment into which he had put himself. He *was* being like her. Yet despite his attempt, he had somehow ended up dancing on someone else's strings again . . . Still not his own man. Ian lay back in the snow. Where was the way out? He wanted to die.

The One had seen Ian leave with Jean. He had to assume the circumstances of Ian's reservation would come up. It had always been a risk. His disguise was, therefore, useless as far as Ian went. He wondered whether he should have talked to him earlier. No matter, he thought. His pawn need only last through the evening. No doubt El Conciliador would have him initiated tonight. Whatever preparations had to be made for their important guest would take time. The only question now was whether Ian would still be inclined to go through with it.

The phone rang. His call to London was ready. The answer to a heritage.

"Of course, Raniero Fasani was your ancestor, Mr. Stone," said the man from the Geneological Society. "We did confirm per your request."

"Confirm? Has anyone made this inquiry before?"

"I don't understand," the man in London sounded confused. "Do you mean other than the verification you wired us to make to that address in . . . ah . . . Arroyo Seco . . . in New Mexico last month?"

"Yes . . . ," The One mumbled, bewildered.

"No, not since the original ordering of your mother's family tree," was the reply.

"Now, I don't understand," the Assassin responded. "When was that exactly?"

"I thought it must have been mislaid . . . the document, that is. All the information was in the original study. It was quite some . . . Ahh, here it is. December, 1946. Other than that, the file is empty."

"Who ordered the original search?" The One asked, his throat going dry.

"Why, your father . . . ," was the response.

The Assassin's heart skipped a beat, "My father?"

"Well, yes, I assume so, Mr. Stone. There are the initials 'R.S.' on the requisition form."

"I'm sorry . . . I never knew my father. Where was the information sent?"

"There's a post office address in Bucharest to which the search was sent. It was a bit before my time, I'm afraid," the man apologized. "Can I be of some further help?"

The One was shaken. Someone was pulling strings on him . . . had been from the beginning . . . *before* the beginning. His father. It had to be. If it were the CIA, why was there that effort to uncover him during the Songbird operation? There would have been no reason if someone had known. No, it was his father.

He closed his eyes and thought of his mother's paranoia of their being found . . . of the painful suffering he endured from the plastic surgery to remove any resemblance of the man she loathed; a pain he suffered more than once. All for nothing. His father knew all along where he was . . . And *he* was the mystery man coming to Taos.

But did the mystery man know about his pawn? The One thought not . . . hoped not. His father knew of Ian Stone and he knew of The One, but he couldn't know they were two people. He musn't . . .

The Assassin was altogether sure his pawn was the only reason he had been able to remain truly free. He was his best disguise of all.

R.S. . . . Bucharest. A place the Assassin had never been. The Gypsy observer now made sense. But there was too much he didn't know and that frustrated him. The vision of Velenari's eyes crossed his mind. He had been trying to avoid the image, but knew it was a mistake. What the hell happened? Why had the Cardinal been so afraid? Again, the answer was his father.

As The One walked out of the Rio Hondo to clear his head, he saw Sheriff Redding's car pull into the upper lot.

What was sustaining this cop's interest? It didn't matter; he couldn't let the meddling local get in his way. Besides, he needed to take his frustration out on someone. It was time to unmask and put Ian Stone in two places at once. The One stepped back into the empty foyer of the Rio Hondo. Within a moment, he emerged maskless. The last minor surgery had worked well. The timing had been perfect. Now, he could not be distinguished from . . .

"Mr. Stone . . . ," Redding shouted to him.

"Yes . . . "

Redding saw the eyes and was taken aback. He had never seen such cat-like fury. It was another instant before he noticed the hand in the jacket pocket.

"Let's take a ride. You drive," said the Assassin.

Redding was furious with himself for letting the other man get the advantage so quickly. They got into his car and drove out of the lot.

A light dusting of snow was in the air. As Redding switched on the windshield wipers, he noticed the silencer being withdrawn from the jacket pocket.

"Why are you here?" the sheriff was asked.

Redding just glared ahead as they took the turns down the mountain road. Without hesitation, The One blew off the sheriff's left knee cap. Redding yelled with pain as the Assassin calmly grabbed the wheel with his right hand, holding the barrel of the gun at the sheriff's neck with his left.

"Tough it out. Tough it out. Keep driving, and answer," he hissed cooly.

Redding was panicky. The pain in his knee was excruciating. It took all he had to keep his other foot on the pedal and try to steer. He was at the mercy of a madman.

"The woman . . . Bastian . . . and a CIA agent came to the station. They had your record sent to my office. They compared some fingerprints," Redding struggled to speak.

The One laughed. Even that sound frightened Redding, giving him chills.

"So, you thought you'd meddle in. You should have left well enough alone, old man," the Assassin said with finality.

Redding felt as if he were nothing. Thirty years of being a tough cop and this man had reduced him to a piece of shit in a matter of minutes.

"I can't drive," he winced.

There was no traffic to speak of as they descended. They were coming up on a boarded cabin with a garage off the road on the left.

"Pull over there," The One dictated.

Redding did as he was told and came to a stop. He grabbed his throbbing knee, but the barrel of the Assassin's gun under his chin made him sit back.

"Tell me about a wealthy man named Mortez who lives around Taos," the sheriff was ordered.

"Mortez is not an unusual name . . . ," he said pained.

"Wealthy. Perhaps very wealthy," The One persisted.

"There's a director at the Interspec Foundation named Mortez. Ramon Mortez. Lives out near the Lawrence Ranch, not far from the Foundation."

"I guess I can use you after all," the Assassin cajoled. "Draw me a map."

He handed Redding a notepad and pen from his pocket. The sheriff relaxed a bit and quickly sketched a map. As he finished, he looked up, smiled weakly and took a bullet between his eyes.

The Assassin got out and picked the lock on the garage door. He then rolled the car inside, closed the door and relocked it.

He put the bandage mask back on, pulled his hat down over it as much as possible and began to hike back up the mountain.

The flurries continued. The only sound to break the silence was the sudden howl of a coyote off to the right. The One was startled and put his hand on his gun. He tried to peer through the trees on the slope. At first, he thought he spotted some movement, but then there was nothing. He increased his gait and tried to shake off the chill which was crawling up his back. The Assassin had other things to think about. He had left his pawn unguarded too long. And there was yet another disguise to prepare.

Ian had made it down the mountain . . . barely. He was too exhausted both physically and emotionally to have to deal with any surprises that might be waiting for him in his room, so he decided to go to Dashwood's instead. The key was under the mat where he had seen Alex retrieve it on their first meeting. Ian made it through the door and passed out on the couch.

Diana was also exhausted . . . exhausted and frustrated. She had spent over two hours in prayer processions with Guadalupe, trying to win her confidence. They walked from *morada* to *morada,* perhaps a hundred people, saying prayers and singing hymns, the hardcore doing it with rice in their shoes. Diana was not to be out done and had suffered with the best of them, but swore she would never eat Chinese again. She did stop short, however, of wearing the cactus band, *cilicio,* under her clothes. Her willingness to suffer had its limits.

Finally, she had a chance to talk with the Indian girl. Diana showed her the brand on her scalp and stressed the importance of the matter. Though, as she and Braden had decided, El Conciliador's name was best kept out of the discussion. There was no knowing her family's loyalty. But once Diana finally won her over, she realized all the woman could do was try and set up a meeting with her father . . . and that not until late in the evening, perhaps even the following morning.

It was one of those times Diana wished she were a man . . . on this occasion, a Spanish man. She gave the girl the number at the Edelweiss and left.

Diana had gone back to the Abominable Snowmansion to leave a message for Braden. There being none for her, she walked outside wondering what to do next. Diana had completed her assignment for now, but she was reluctant to return to the Ski Valley. She didn't want to take the chance of running into Ian or anyone else she knew. She decided, therefore, to go back into Taos and visit some of the art galleries.

Her note to Braden was read and replaced. Diana continued to be followed when she finally got the nerve to go back up the mountain.

20

At first it frightened him. But Ian wasn't sure which aspect caused the feeling . . . that it was what it was or that it was dying.

Ian approached cautiously and then realized it was the latter. He panicked, not knowing what to do . . . how to save it.

On the ground in front of him was a body, but there was no body to be seen . . . merely clothes, the shirt heaving slightly as the breathing of the invisible wearer got weaker and weaker. The clothes were Ian's.

He knelt down and tried to feel for a face, for a mouth. His hands were shaking and he was overcome with emotion. Suddenly, he found the mouth and tears of joy welled up in his eyes as he leaned over and started to blow air into the creature's lungs, again and again and again until the pulsing grew stronger and the breast heaved robustly.

* * *

Ian awakened at 6:30. Dinner had already started. He quickly stripped and showered, then dressed to ski back toward the A-frames.

After killing Redding, The One had returned to his own room and assumed the disguise of Antonio Troni's nephew. He went to the Lodge with bags and skis, saying the sheriff's office in Taos had informed him his uncle and aunt were part of an accident at the Gorge. He had just flown up from Mexico City to identify the remains and was there to retrieve their things. He wondered, however, whether it might be all right to stay a day or so to overcome his grief on the slopes. The St. Bernard was accommodating.

The rest of the afternoon the Assassin had worked out a series of plans for each of the possible scenarios he might have to confront.

The One's main problem was to convince the CIA chief he was ready to comply with his demands. He suspected, whether knowingly or unknowingly, Braden was working for his father. If that was the case, he would have nothing to fear from him. But The Man would be suspicious and would not readily come forth. If only he was out there watching . . . would just walk in . . . perhaps this whole matter could be dealt with quickly. But it was never that easy. So the Assassin had spent a good while studying a map of the mountain and preparing more realistic strategies.

As the afternoon wore on, the possibility grew Braden had taken out his pawn. The One was in a quandry as to whether he should assume his true identity. The prospect of having to go through the Penitente initiation was not at all pleasing to him, but it began to seem possible there would be no other choice.

At times the Assassin's mind had drifted to thinking about his father. He found himself both hating him, and yet yearning to see him.

By dusk he had gotten cabin fever. Still in his nephew disguise, he had gone out for a walk and had seen Diana heading from the parking lot to her room at sunset. For no rational explanation, it had given him hope his pawn was safe.

That euphoria had waned as dusk slipped into the dinner

hour. The Assassin couldn't imagine what had happened. He had even begun to think El Conciliador had taken Ian off the mountain again.

The maid showed up at Ian's room and would soon come to his. The Assassin was just about to leave when he spotted his errant pawn skiing over. He breathed a sigh of relief.

When Ian spotted the maid walking out of his room, he, too, was relieved. He assumed everything must be all right . . . unless she . . . Oh God, he was getting that old feeling of the world being against him again.

Ian put his equipment on the veranda and timidly walked in to change out of his boots. Everything *did* appear to be all right. He relaxed and decided to change completely.

The One waited until his pawn left, then brought his own skis, boots and a pair of shoes up through the trapdoor and began to substitute them for Ian's. By morning he would have to come forth as Ian Stone and knew it might be necessary to have his own things in place. Ian's equipment was put into a ski bag and taken to the Assassin's room at the Edelweiss. Putting on his mask once more, The One headed to the parking lot.

By the time Ian got to the dining room, the guests had already finished their soup and salad. A lamb entrée was being served.

Ian could see that all the seats at his usual table were taken, but there appeared to be some space into which another chair could be squeezed.

Diana was seated at the far end, engaged in polite conversation with the Alabamians, Roger and Melissa. Ian noticed her salad had not been touched. As he approached, she looked up and Ian detected an odd expression of both fear and sadness in her eyes.

Carol, the office manager, came up behind Diana and startled her with a tap on the shoulder. It was not like her to be so jumpy. Carol then whispered something into Diana's ear.

"Does anyone mind if I squeeze in another chair?" Ian asked the group in general.

Eli responded, "No offense, old bean, but I count twelve already and it is . . . what did the waitress say? . . . *jueves, jueves santo* . . . Holy Thursday. Not that it bothers me, you understand . . . but, someone else might be super . . . ummm . . . sensitive. What do we say gang?"

The Loudmouth laughed as Diana got up.

"I have to leave," she said. "You can take my place."

Ian came around the table.

"Sorry to see you go," Eli said boisterously. "Here's rather looking at you," he toasted, spilling the wine all over his sweater. "Whoops . . . I made a boo-boo. Oh, nurse," he called to a waitress, "I think I've been shot."

He got up, "I better soak this. Save my dessert, now. I'll be back."

Most hoped he wouldn't be, as Eli trundled off.

"Where are you going?" Ian asked Diana.

"I was invited to the opening of an art exhibit in Taos," she lied. "You were right about not getting involved. How was your race?"

"Fine," he said weakly. "I . . . "

"I figured you'd be busy tonight. You can take my car," Diana offered. "She's driving . . . the girl who invited me." There *was* sadness in her eyes. "See you later."

She handed him the keys and walked away. Ian knew something was very wrong. It had to be the scene they had in the morning. He wanted to go after her . . . but she had said she'd see him later. Perhaps she wasn't *that* upset.

Ian sat down and ate her salad. He was hungry.

The Gypsy studied his every move, feeling Ian was as much an enigma as his Master.

The One was surprised by Diana's early departure. He had thought this would be an opportune time to search for the transmitter he was sure she had used to track Ian the previous evening. He did not want him tracked tonight.

The Assassin still wasn't clear as to how she fit in. The transmitter he had just found was similar equipment to one of the bugs he had found when he removed the Troni woman's body from Ian's room. It was Swiss . . . inexpensive. He surmised Diana might be part of some Vatican group keeping tabs on the Penitente . . . at least, it made more sense than thinking she, too, was another of his father's puppets.

The One watched as she got into the pickup driven by the Indian girl and wondered whether Ian would follow.

He was again surprised when instead it was Eli who came out of the St. Bernard and watched the pickup drive off. The One looked around to see if he could associate any of the cars with the man. There was nothing obvious. He waited until Eli fixed his direction and then started walking to intersect his path.

Eli's gait was quick and direct. As his goal became apparent, The One waved to him, letting his own car keys fly from his hand. "Shit," he said as he started to grope around the snow.

The Loudmouth chuckled and came over, "Must be a bitch to drive without any peripheral vision."

"Yeah . . . Thanks," the Assassin said.

As Eli retrieved the keys for the bandaged man, The One planted Diana's transmitter on his car.

"Thanks again," he said. "Have a nice evening."

As Eli drove off, the Assassin went back to his own car to consider the role of this newly discovered player . . . and wait.

At 8:00 p.m. another car drove into the area. The passengers looked like an elite corps of the Penitente. Tonight his pawn was getting an honor guard. The big occasion was at hand.

All four of the occupants left the car and proceeded up the hill. That was a break. The Assassin quickly picked the trunk lock and got inside.

Within a few moments, the men were back with Ian. Normally, the latter would have enjoyed this royal treatment. But tonight he wasn't even aware of it.

Ian was back to thinking, but no longer of Meredith. That, he finally felt, was a worn out record. It didn't make sense to him anymore. This afternoon he had unlocked the secret of what Meredith stood for in his life . . . the *possibility* to change, to start over, perhaps find his "true" identity. Tonight he had to find the key to *actually* doing that.

Now he thought of the metamorphosis . . . Fragments of his dream had been coming back to him during dinner. And he felt it was imperative to discover the secret of the metamorphosis as it applied to himself. For the rest of the ride Ian wondered how much agony would be involved.

The drive was less than an hour west and a bit north—a town called Arroyo Hondo. They parked amongst a number of cars, vans and pickups.

As they got out of the car, Ian was given a pair of calf-length, white *calzones* and a robe. He removed his own pants as well as his shirt and shoes, and donned the new wardrobe, anxious to get inside.

The temperature was about 40°, cold enough to keep the light snow that had fallen, though the night wind blew it into small patches. It was the second day of the full moon and the *morada* was illuminated as they climbed to the crest of the hill on which it stood. A larger structure than either of the others, it stood like a surreal portrait. A huge wooden *madero* had been erected in the front yard. And nearby, leaning on their left arms, were two more crosses.

Along the crest on the farther side of the hill and silhouetted against the sky, there were processions of various groups, each with a man dragging a *madero* while his followers flagellated themselves. It made Ian shudder to see it.

Still others came up the hill on their knees. Some lay across the path and were stepped on by those going past. And others, wearing black hoods, disappeared around the side of the building . . . these Ian assumed being the *secretos* who would enter by a special door.

Near the front entrance was the *Hermano Mendicante,* begging for alms. One of the men with Ian took some coins from his pocket and placed them in the bowl. As he passed, Ian noticed the beggar had a band of cactus under his robe. The man struck his breast once for each coin received. And each time he did, the needles of the cactus cut into him.

As each group came to the door, they called out, "*¿Quién en esta casa da luz?*"

From inside came the response, "*Jesús.*"

"*¿Quién la llena de alegría?*"

Again from inside, "*María.*"

"*¿Quién la conserva en la fe?*"

"*José.*"

Ian was handed a sheet of prayers and responses as they came to the door. His honor guard gave the oration and they entered.

The shoes of those who still wore them were taken at the door by an *Ayudan,* or helper.

To Ian's surprise, there was an enormous hooded figure just inside. It was the *Guardia de Concilio* . . . Vincente Cruz. And, there on his knees, was El Conciliador, performing the *Mendatum*—the washing of feet of all who entered . . . a reinactment of the exercise in humility Christ performed at the Last Supper.

From within the folds of his hood, Ian thought he caught a glint of teeth as Mortez looked up while washing his feet.

As the clock struck 9, the doors to the *morada* were closed.

Ian was placed with a group of similarly dressed men, most of whom were much younger than he. The ground where they stood was covered with *arroz*—rice and tiny, sharp stones. As the ceremony started, they were made to kneel, an act painful in itself to Ian's knees . . . but on this ground, it was pure agony. It did not take long for cuts to appear. Then on top of everything else, their robes were taken.

As El Conciliador went up to the altar, Ian noticed the *bultos* in the chamber were finer than he had seen in the other *moradas* . . . more intricately carved. Then his eyes fell upon the altar behind Mortez. Resting upon it were six skulls.

Mortez leaned down and took a beautifully carved box from under the altarcloth. He removed something and placed it in the center of the altar between two single white candles and in front of the candelabrum of thirteen candles, now the only source of light in the hall. As he stepped to one side, raising his arms, Ian's eyes widened. He could now see the object of veneration . . . a skull of pure gold . . . Quetzalcoatl! Alex would have freaked!

The flickering candlelight reflected from the fallen god, glimmering off the markings telling a secret. How near he was to the goal, yet . . .

El Conciliador took a rosary from the altar and began to lead the service. The proceedings moved slowly, too slowly for those who knelt on the *arroz*. The *rosario* took a full hour, during the last quarter of which Ian became numb. Even the beauty of the golden skull waned. He tried to focus on the thoughts he had had before dinner, then his fears.

There were many things in his life that, at first blush, frightened Ian. But once he did something, he could never understand why it had so frightened him beforehand. And he did things well!

Five years ago he would never have entered a slalom; or left his job; or been here . . . Never.

As the rosary ended, the doors to the *morada* were opened. A cold blast of air filled the chamber, extinguishing a few of the candles.

Two young boys marched up to the altar to collect El Conciliador, then turned and began a procession to the out-of-doors, in which everyone was to take part.

Ian had to place his hands on the ground to pry his knees off of it. The others around him had the same problem, but no one betrayed any pain. Ian hoped their robes would be returned, but no dice, nor were their shoes.

The congregation began to sing to the accompaniment of the *Pitero's* flute as everyone filed out into the night. Ian had not been aware of there being women and children in the group until he heard their voices, "*Perdona tu pueblo, Señor . . .*"

Ian had no idea what the words meant, but he liked the chorus.

His group followed out the Brothers wearing the black hoods.

They, too, had removed their robes and wore only *calzones.* As they departed, they were handed *disciplinas* and immediately began to scourge themselves.

At least, Ian thought, it will keep their blood moving. He himself was freezing before he even hit the door.

As the moonlight hit the backs of the flagellants, Ian saw each of the men had from three to six long scars running the length of his back. A chill ran up his own spine as he had a premonition of things to come.

The procession marched around the *campesanto,* or cemetery, behind the *morada* and over to the First Station of the Cross. They knelt, Ian wondering how long this would take. He was thankful that, although stoic, the rest of the novices huddled against each other for warmth . . . all except a few hardcore. Showoffs . . . he thought.

Ian looked at his sheet and gasped as he remembered Sunday night . . . 14 Stations! And, so it had been for 250 years.

There was an *alabado,* or hymn, "*Considere alma perdida . . .*" with a verse for each Station. Then there was a meditation; an "Our Father" . . . the original, without "the Kingdom, the Power and the Glory" part . . . ; a "Hail, Mary"; a "Gloria"; and a short prayer . . . "*Adoremos a este Cristo y benedicenos que por tu santa cruz y pasión y muerte redimiste al mundo y a mi pecador. Amen.*"

Then everyone kissed the ground, rose and walked to the next Station singing another hymn, "*Lloren los corazones de todos los cristianos por la pasión y muerte de nuestro Señor.*"

Along about Station XI, Ian heard the bell strike 11. He was numb again, wishing only the noise would stop so he could think.

Finally, it was over and they were marching back: "*Por las tres horas de tu agonia . . . Perdonale, Señor.*"

As they moved back into their places, there was another hooded and robed "guest" in their midst. The One watched as the *Coadjutores* washed the backs of the flagellants with *romerillo* . . . silver sage tea . . . to alleviate swelling and pain.

Meanwhile, the two candles on either side of the golden skull were extinguished and another *alabado* was sung. After each verse, one more candle in the candelabrum was extinguished. Ian figured correctly twelve of the candles stood for the disciples of Christ; the thirteenth, for Christ himself. It also dawned on him he might have been able to steal the skull while everyone was out. Might.

After the twelfth candle was extinguished, El Conciliador took the thirteenth and placed it behind the altar. Except for its faint glow, the *morada* was now pitch black.

Suddenly there was a clap and it sounded as if the *morada* were caving in. *Matracas* were clacking. Drums were beaten. Flutes played raucously. There was stamping and the flapping of whips against skin.

Ian's goose bumps weren't merely from the cold this time. The noise continued for many minutes, signifying the chaos following the death of Christ when "the curtain of the Temple was torn in two, from top to bottom, and the earth shook and the rocks were split; the tombs were opened, and many bodies of the saints who had fallen asleep were raised . . ." One could have gone mad.

After what seemed an interminable time, the quiet resumed and everyone seemed to be praying. They were remembering their dead relatives and friends. Then the tumult started over again . . . thankfully, for a shorter duration.

Silence followed once more. The pattern repeated a third time, and then the lighted candle was returned to the altar.

The ceremony was over. The women and children, plus a few men, got up and left.

The midnight bells were replaced by *matracas,* since bells are not allowed on *viernes santo,* Good Friday.

VIERNES SANTO

El Conciliador spoke in Spanish, "This is an important time for us and for Holy Mother Church. We have need of great strength to stand against those who would destroy our faith.

"Normally, we would wait until the end of this day before

initiating our new members . . . but these are not normal times. Therefore, unless there are objections, we shall proceed at this moment."

No one objected, although Ian considered it, and the ceremony went on.

One by one, each novice was called forward by name. There was a call for objections to his admission, after which he was given a creed to recite and swore an oath. While he did so, a Brother called the *Sangrador* massaged his bare back with the palms of his hand. Then having sworn, the new Brother had the *sello,* or seal of obligation cut into his back.

The *Rellador* took a sharp piece of obsidian and cut three wounds lengthwise on each side of the spine. The new Brother then asked to be lashed, "For the love of God." There were 55 lashes in all: three for the meditations on the Passion of Jesus; five for the wounds of Christ; seven for his last seven phrases; and forty for the days he spent in the wilderness.

A few of the initiates fainted during the last forty. The survivors were given whips of hemp so they could continue to beat themselves.

Ian thought of balking as his time came. Maybe someone would object, he thought, and he could leave. But there was no such luck, especially with El Conciliador's *Guardia* there.

It was his time. Ian got up, walked to the altar and knelt in front of Brother One. He realized this was no kidding around . . . nor was his life something to be lived in the future. The blade was entering NOW and his blood poured forth. Then the dreaded lashes came, "For the love of God."

Whatever the *Sangrador* had done worked. His back was numb. There was a sting to be sure, but it wasn't excruciating. Instead of being delighted, however, Ian felt somehow cheated. He had wanted to feel the pain.

El Conciliador bent and whispered in his ear, "You have done well, my son. Rest until tomorrow afternoon. We will prepare then for our visitor."

His back was washed with *romerillo* and Ian was soothed.

He had done it! He was a Penitente. He was fulfilling his

obligation to a higher authority . . . Was it his country? No, that was once before, wasn't it? Wasn't it?!

Ian blanked out. He had a vague sense of being carried outside. It had happened before like that . . . with explosions all around. Like now.

But the sounds were of the motorcycle The One had stolen in town during the rosary. He drove back toward Taos with Ian propped in front of him. At one point the latter opened his eyes and saw the road rushing at him. He panicked and almost threw the bike out of control. A chop on the neck quickly put him under again.

Soon they passed near the *morada* where Velenari's body lay hidden. It was, in fact, the sound of the cycle that gave Braden his chance to move.

For Braden it had been a vigil of more than twelve hours. The good news was the *morada* was heavily guarded. The bad news was the "heavily"; too many to take out during daylight.

Braden was hoping there would be a change of guard after nightfall. There had been, and he used the occasion to move in closer, amongst the aspen surrounding the dried out pond in front of the structure. There he waited for the guards to tire.

Things had been quiet since midnight. He was sure at least half of the men would be asleep by now. Then, as he heard the motorcycle coming up the road, he knew the time had come.

The outside guard was distracted by the noise and looked in the cycle's direction. Braden rushed from his hiding place and came up behind the man, quickly drawing a blade across his throat. He heard another coming out of the front entrance and sprang in his direction, somersaulting and completing the motion by jabbing the knife into the man's belly. As the man began to fall, Braden saw a third inside begin to reach for his gun.

Braden stepped back and stooped for some pebbles as he pulled out his own gun. With his silencer leveled, he rose and tossed the pebbles at the window beside the doorway. The guard's attention was drawn to the glass as the CIA chief stepped inside and took him out. Another man rushed into the room and was taken out before he could even react. It had all taken place within ten seconds. Four down and two to go.

The fifth was asleep in the next room. He never awakened.

Then Braden was jumped from behind. His attacker was powerful and had taken him off guard. The two reeled into the *piesa*, the small room off the *capilla* where the whips were kept. The guard clung to Braden, pinning him beneath and using his own head to bash the CIA chief's against the ground.

Braden grabbed for a whip while trying to raise up his back. He managed to get to his knees, then to his feet, but the man held on and slammed him up against the wall. As they recoiled, Braden bent and caught the whip around the guard's left leg. He rose and as they went into the wall again, he looped the whip around a hook and threw himself backwards. They hit the ground and Braden continued a backward somersault which his assailant could not complete. The man's instinct was to loosen his leg and Braden used the instant to loop his throat with a second lash. Both pulled with all their might, but the night was Braden's.

The victor sat back to catch his breath, and then cleaned himself off. Afterwards, his nose led him to Velenari.

They had kept him in the coffin, wrapped in plastic. The cold had detered decomposition somewhat, but not completely. Braden understood why the guards had been burning incense.

The gun was there, too. Braden used a specially treated tape to transfer Ian's print onto the handle . . . just in case. Then he dragged the other bodies into the *piesa,* found and ripped out the bug he was sure would be there and activated the transmitter to let Diana know it was all clear. Exhausted from the assault, he slumped against a wall to wait.

Diana had spent the evening in Talpa at the same *morada* where she had met Ian the night before. She had been worried at first that he might show up again, but Guadalupe assured her the big events would take place elsewhere.

The ceremony she witnessed was much the same as Ian's, only without the flagellants.

It was not until most of the people had departed that Diana finally got to meet Guadalupe's father and some of the others. They had witnessed Ian's actions in the *morada* over the past few nights and had been impressed. But Diana's earnestness persuaded them to go to Arroyo Seco and look.

As they got within a half mile of the *morada,* Diana switched on her receiver and picked up Braden's transmitter. What disturbed her, however, was the fact she also picked up the one she had placed in her car. Whereas Braden's pulsed louder as she got nearer the *morada,* the other never changed. It was moving. They were being followed.

The three pickups arrived and Braden came out to meet them.

The Penitente were given their proof . . . Ian Stone was a killer of both a pope and a cardinal. He had to be dealt with.

The Penitente agreed to call in reinforcements to handle the morning shift of guards. There was no need to let out the fact they knew of Velenari's death until a sound plan was formulated. Diana and Braden had not implicated El Conciliador, but the fact his elite guards were there meant he at least had a lot of explaining to do.

Diana saw the six bodies in the next room and it made her ill. This had been a night of too much Passion and death and she wanted no more of it. She therefore kept quiet about the other signal, though she secretly checked on it the entire way to the Ski Valley. It never changed. Yet there was not even so much as a flicker of a headlight as they came up the mountain. Their shadow was excellent.

Her eyes nearly popped when they arrived and she saw her car still parked in the lot.

"He's played a joke on you," Braden chuckled. "You better get out here."

He had known all along what she was doing. Diana made no response; just left the car.

"Let me know who it is," Braden ordered as he drove off.

In a few moments another car pulled into the lot. The moon was almost down, but there was still enough light to see Eli.

Instead of being relieved, however, Diana was struck with fear. In fact, she had never been so frightened.

* * *

Ian was also frightened . . . not merely by the howl breaking the stillness of the night . . . He had escaped and was being pursued.

In the darkness, the base of the mountain was barely illuminated by the fading moon. Ian was out of breath as he reached it. He stopped at a large rock, panting as he regained his wind. In the distance, a branch snapped and he knew the chase was on.

He started up the slope, grabbing at roots and limbs to help him along. The sounds from behind were now nearer. There was another howl. Was it a coyote . . . or a wolf?

Ian would not look back as he attempted to increase his speed. The cold air rushed down at him, making him shiver. He rubbed his bare shoulders for some warmth and scrambled on, the rocks cutting into his bare feet. He slipped and bruised his knee. He had to clench his teeth so as not to scream.

The higher he rose, the louder and closer were the sounds of his pursuer. Ian's resolve became stronger, however, and his speed increased. But the slope was growing steeper and the pace soon became exhausting. And always the sounds grew nearer.

Ian reached some larger rocks and had to stop to catch his breath again. Had he been here before?

He could now hear breathing!

Ian sprang up on all fours, grabbing at anything that would move him forward. Suddenly, the rocks began to slide and he was moving backwards. He tried to dig in, but it was of no use. His hands, knees and feet were bleeding . . . and he could only move backwards. It seemed all too familiar to him.

He turned, knowing he was about to be bathed in moonlight. He could feel the presence of his pursuer as well as if they were touching. And there was nothing he could do to keep from sliding back . . . right into his lap.

Ian grabbed desperately at a large rock with both hands, arresting his descent. That was typical . . . a timely reversal. Where was the crest? When was the awakening?

But only the pursuer came.

Ian was alarmed. It had never been like this. The dream had always ended in time.

He hoisted a rock and rolled onto his back, preparing to hurl it at his pursuer; preparing to hurl it at . . . himself.

Gazing up at him in the pale moonlight was a teenage boy . . . a callow youth who, quite remarkably, did resemble Meredith . . . Though he had never seen a picture, there was no mistaking . . . it was his teenage self. The pursuer of countless dreams had been himself.

Ian dropped the rock and they both caught their breath. It had been a long run. They stared at each other until the lad started to speak, "I'm . . . "

* * *

A needle entered Ian's arm—his dreaming, not dreamed arm. There, in the room at the Abominable Snowmansion.

"No . . . ," he muttered.

He had already had this dream. But the sodium pentathol was real.

"Who are you? What is your name?" he heard a voice ask.

Ian writhed on the bed. A few moments ago, he had seen himself as if in a mirror floating above him. Now his mind moved through thick liquid. He heard the questions again and someone was responding, "Stone . . . Ian Stone."

The questioner smiled. He had never been sure how much identity his pawn had lost through amnesia or post traumatic stress syndrome and how much was just good old suppression. The drug was still taking effect. Would it bring forth the truth? The One felt it would be a shame to have to sacrifice his surrogate after he had started to feel close to him. But it was inevitable.

"Now, tell me your real name."

Again, "I..Ian Stone."

The Assassin bent and whispered into his ear, "Your name is Michael. Don't you remember Michael Esmund?"

"My. . .M..Mich..Michael. . . ," the drugged man repeated. "I'm Michael Es..mund . . . Michael Esmund."

Bravo, The One thought, "Now, tell me everything you remember, Michael. Everything."

His questions moved on to the events of the last four days.

There was no holding back. The decoy poured forth with all the intelligence he had soaked up, from Dashwood's story of the Aztec treasure to his meeting with El Conciliador. Mumblings about Meredith and Diana were thrown in gratis. Afterwards, the listener sat in the darkness, pondering his options. THE ONE . . . It was hard to believe. He had never heard anything suggesting such a person existed . . . although he had once fantasized the possibility. Like father? . . .

So, what about the CIA? Were they out to trap both THE ONE and El Conciliador? Or did the Agency fit in at all? Surely the entire Company couldn't be under his father's control. Or could it? That wasn't important. It didn't have to go beyond Braden. Even *he* could be being duped. The scenario was simple . . . He was supposed to get information even Velenari was unable to get . . . "Running with the wolves . . ." The Cardinal's transformation now made sense. And Braden was a tool to pass on what information he learned.

But why had his father called upon him now? What was so special about this treasure? Or did the treasure really have anything to do with it? Was this just a test? For what? Was he trying to reveal himself as the God he knew his son was seeking? Was it to be a slow revelation so he could build his faith? Was he coming now to see if his son would accept him?

There was a boundary within himself the Assassin, too, was unwilling to cross . . . at least tonight. He turned instead to the fact he finally had a handle on what was transpiring. Now he could deal; now he could do some manipulating. But first, he would make a final test of the scenario. He would get rid of Braden.

The One continued to sit in the chair staring at the sedated man in the bed. Michael Esmund, indeed.

In a short time, there was no light behind the gaze. The One was asleep.

21

They came not in wagons, but in vans and pickups. Not swiftly, but slowly . . . stealthily. And from every point of the compass. Like birds, they began to congregate at crossroads . . . major, secondary, even trails . . . moving in to a circumference of over 300 miles before holding at the boundaries of Taos County for the rest of the night. Gypsies. An army of them. Ready to do their Master's bidding.

Ian felt as if he were swimming to the surface. Then undersea swells would toss him over and down as he tried to rise.

* * *

A large tube, housing a walking ramp, ran like an umbilical cord from a central complex to the new shop.

Inside, the young man whom Ian had seen a dream ago was stacking the empty shelves with books, while his more darkly-complected partner hung large abstract paintings of asymmetrical shapes.

Then Ian felt he became the young man. Euphoria swelled within his breast. Yet he found himself constantly checking the door as if he sensed some possible danger.

He turned to his partner and said, "No matter what happens, I want you to know I think you've done a great job."

No sooner had he finished speaking than his partner's face began to flush. A black area appeared like a rash and started to spread. A voice in descending tone snarled from his lips, "I don't think you're going to like this."

Young Ian replied, "Don't do it. Please don't do it," and began heading for the door.

He walked outside while continuing to make the Sign of the Cross, "In nomine Patris et Filii et Spiritus Sancti . . . ," *and concentrating on each step . . . taking one . . . and, then, another . . . without listening to the threats or beckoning of "The Dark One."*

Suddenly a crowd rushed past him and he looked back to see everyone congregating around something on the ground. He went back and moved through the group to discover they were looking at The Dark One's dead body.

Ian looked up and spotted one of his friends across the ring of people. The boy was making comical faces as if he might now become possessed and turn into a monster. Ian smiled at him, and then headed back toward the store.

As he got near the front window, he saw a werewolf inside. Ian quickly crouched down under the glass and moved toward another window at the back. He peered through and saw four people, including two women, dressing up in werewolf costumes. One of them spotted Ian and, smiling, waved him inside. Their attention was then drawn to the front of the store where a customer had come in with some children to be titilated by the "monsters."

Young Ian leaned against the side of the building and started laughing . . . laughing at the make-believe danger.

* * *

Startled by the laughter, The One almost went off the road again. Ian, his face covered by the bandage mask, was laughing in his sleep as the motorcycle swept up the mountain in the predawn darkness. The dreamer continued to swoon as his mind rolled under, then tried once again to swim to the conscious surface.

The driver, in the guise of Antonio Troni's nephew, didn't put him out this time. They were almost there and he wanted his pawn on his feet.

There were only a few workers out and about as the first light of dawn silhouetted the mountain. To anyone who noticed, the two men appeared to be buddies home from a bender as the drugged man was led, stumbling, toward the Assassin's room.

It would take the entire morning for The One to set up his plan. By the afternoon, he would be rid of Braden, Diana and, unfortunately, his pawn.

After sedating his decoy once more, The One took out a makeup kit that included collodion, rouge and dried blood. He attached a brush to a hanger and worked with a mirror to spread the collodion in strips on his back. Once the clear substance dried, he attached a razor to another hanger and, painstakingly, slit the hardened rows from top to bottom. Finally, he filled the slits with rouge and dried blood. By the time it was fully light, The One had copied his pawn's back, scar for scar.

He went to the window and looked up into the sky. It would be a cold and overcast morning. In the distance, he could hear explosions as the avalanche areas were being cleared. According to plan.

The One turned to the small coffee table behind him. He took samples of the unconscious man's handwriting from a microfile and sat down to practice. It took awhile, but he finally got it to flow. Unfortunately, a maid's knock at his door broke his concentration and it took another half hour for The One to relax enough to get it back.

The Assassin was surprised at his jumpiness. But the entire plan rested on his doing this right. The letter would have to be short and to the point. It could betray nothing that would make Diana suspicious.

"Dear Diana,
I've learned where the treasure is! Am going to meet my source at 12:30 to see it. Come, if you can . . . West Basin Ridge. But hang back so no one will see us together. You might be watched. Tell Alex, if he's back. We need allies to help get information to the right people.
Love you,
Ian."

The One sat back and wondered if Braden would be smart enough to understand the last phrase was meant for him, that he was signalling compliance.

The CIA chief would be wary. He would be expecting a set up. But hopefully not the one he had prepared.

The One looked again at the trail map. There appeared to be only two ways to get to West Basin Ridge. Sooner or later Braden would be drawn into the open.

It was just past 11:30 when he finished. The Assassin changed into Ian's clothes, then sat down again to write a note to his pawn. He would need Ian's help one last time to pull off his plan.

As The One finished, he spotted Diana heading toward the main lodge for lunch. Eli followed soon after.

The Assassin grabbed Ian's jacket and put it on. As he began to fill the pockets with his own equipment, he removed the herb pouch given by the Cacique and dropped it on the table.

He arranged his note, a trail map, a pair of binoculars and practice samples of the letter to Diana so they could easily be seen; then again put on the mustache, wig and glasses that transformed him into Troni's nephew.

The players were in motion . . . except for his pawn. The One prepared an injection to bring the comotose man out of sedation.

Ian looked exactly as he did at their first meeting. The One had stood then, watching the wounded medic's face being unwrapped. The young man had been given up as lost and the bandages were needed elsewhere. What a startling revelation it had been!

The Assassin took the long way around to the St. Bernard. He went into the men's room behind the bar area and took off his disguise. In a moment, he emerged as Ian Stone.

He called over one of the barmaids, handed her the note for Diana along with a five dollar bill and walked out. Peering through the window next to the door, he watched the note being read. Diana immediately went to the phone by the office.

"Is it his handwriting?" Braden asked.

Diana was staring at the "Love you" and trying to think of where she might have seen a sample of Ian's handwriting. The hotel registry was on the desk near the phone. She quickly paged through to the past Sunday. "Yes," was the answer.

"I'll go up right now," Braden said, "and see if anyone follows. You know, maybe Stone was set up," he baited. "The Jew may be The One. This could be perfect."

The last phrase was said more to himself. Braden saw the possibility of finding the treasure and ridding himself of all the loose ends. If Diana could be kept confused, she would be no threat to him. And keeping her confused should be no problem. Where Eli fit in, he himself didn't know. Braden wasn't sure whether he was another spy for THE ONE or was part of one of those obscure Jewish watchdog groups he had heard of. One of them could be keeping tabs on The Light, he thought. It didn't really matter now; he would have to be eliminated. They all would.

Braden looked over at the bed where the Gypsy lay unconscious. How did such an easy mark get into his Master's service, he wondered. Then he looked back into the mirror. The transformation was almost complete. He was not as expert as his adversary, but the face staring back was more Gypsy than Braden. He was not about to expose himself until he was quite sure of the Assassin's true intentions.

Braden checked his trail map and looked at West Basin Ridge. Would the Assassin lead or follow? If he were signaling his intention to accept the assignment and the treasure *had* been found, The One would be in the lead and would expect him to follow after Diana and the Jew. But Braden could not accept this possibility. There were more likely plots.

Assuming, as he did, a trap, if Stone was an innocent, the Pawn was being lured with the promise of seeing the treasure. In this scenario, The One would already be at the end point or would follow everyone up. If Stone was working with The One, he would still act as the decoy everyone was to follow to his doom. In this case, the Assassin would surely follow, expecting Diana, the Jew and himself to be ahead. Braden needed his own decoy . . . and fast.

The CIA chief looked again at the Gypsy and sprang into action. With the scissors he had used to trim his fake mustache, he quickly and roughly cut off the other man's whiskers. He wrote out a transcription of the note Diana had just read to him and left it on a pile containing the clothes and ski mask he had worn in the Walkyries. Braden hoped, from a distance, the Gypsy would be mistaken for him.

Finally he prepared to give the unconscious man the same type of injection just given Ian.

Ian rose up on an orange mist against a green backdrop. His back was arched and he floated by crimson waves expanding around him. Then, as if reaching an apogee, he started to float back and down. There was an impending heaviness in the air . . . silver, battle green. It came crushing in on him on the backs of his knees, turning his legs into burning rods. His eyes widened with the same scream of pain which tore from his mouth. They saw pieces of the helicopter he had set down on the landmine showering over him along with the blood of the already dead pilot.

"Don't bother with this one," someone was droning like a record at half speed, "but we need the bandages."

Was it him they were talking about? It really didn't matter. He was on his back, feeling comfortable, feeling nothing. Only two weeks until his term was up. Two weeks to go . . . forever.

Suddenly, sharp jabs drilled against his head and back— torrential, driving rain. His guts bounced against the shoulders across which his body was slung. The arms squeezing the back of his knees had brought him to painful semi-consciousness. His groan caused the head to turn. It must be a dream. He thought he was looking at himself.

The sound of incoming shells whistling through the rain caused the face to turn away. There was an explosion nearby which lit the night and pitched him into the air. It was pure flame scorching through him as his legs hit the ground. Then, nothing.

The next sensation was his eyes fluttering. He was surrounded by a web . . . no, a cocoon. His face was mummified.

"You're mighty lucky, Stone. We lost the other captives . . . the whole rescue team," said the full bird colonel. "Think the gooks might have taken one. Bad deal. After two years in that hellhole, I wasn't about to let them lose you now."

He could make out the uniformed figure in the doorway.

"You'll be fine, lad."

But who was Stone? He couldn't remember a thing. Who was he?

* * *

"Mr. Esmund! I'm sorry. I thought you'd left," said the maid, standing in the doorway.

Ian's head lifted off the pillow with difficulty, "What did you say?"

"I said, I'm sorry . . ."

"No, no . . . What did you call me?"

"I just said your name, Mr. Esmund," the girl said, starting to get frightened.

"Oh," he backed off, "I'm sorry, I just woke up."

"I'll come back later," she said, closing the door.

His hands rose to his head. He pulled the mask off his face and stared at it. As if a dam had collapsed, a flood of memories swept over him. Michael Esmund . . . His name was Michael Esmund. He had been a medic. There was a rescue mission. P.O.W.'s. The helicopter pilot was hit. He had to take over. His off-duty lessons had saved his life. He had done it! But the bird sat down on a mine. He was thrown, pieces of blade smashing against his knees.

And the man who had been wearing the bandage mask had switched identities while he lay dying. *He* was Ian Stone. He had to be one of the men rescued from the prison camp on the abortive raid . . . the man who dragged him away from the burning hospital tent.

Why? The answer was apparent; so he could become the world's foremost assassin and be untraceable. Michael was supposed to have died, to be found dead as Ian Stone, while masked in bandages, the real Ian Stone could return as Michael Esmund. "*. . . looking at himself . . .*," he remembered from the dream . . . no, vision from his past. The two of them even looked enough alike, so once the bandages were removed the "ravages of war" might account for any changes; that . . . or plastic surgery . . . Of course . . . why else the bandages?!

Clever. The man was clever. The One even used his survival to advantage. Michael had become the Assassin's man-in-waiting, the perfect setup for this Penitente caper. For how many past capers as well?

Ian-Michael tried to sit up, but felt a sharp pain the length of his back and remembered why it was there. He tried again, more slowly, and let his head clear a moment. He felt like a fool. But all that was over. He got to his feet knowing who he was. Michael Esmund.

As Michael stumbled over to the table, he discovered there already was mail for him:

> "Have you come to realize who you are, Michael? Well, there are still a few surprises. Come and find out what it's really all about. But beware the CIA agent and the Gypsy. You better wear a disguise. And if you keep a proper distance, I'll see no harm comes to Diana."

Michael read the note to Diana and immediately went to the window. He looked at his watch. It was 12:20.

"Oh my God," he muttered.

The One heard him via the bug he had left in the room. It

was his own cue to leave. The Assassin carried his skis down from the terrace and sidestepped up the small hill to the traverse leading toward the lift. Stepping into his bindings, he was off . . . languidly, as if in pain.

Braden had already come up the hill from the main lodge and was putting on his skis, his eyes furtively surveying the area. He took out a pair of binoculars and looked up the lift. Nothing. Heading toward the lift . . . Bingo! It was Stone in the lead. So, it *was* a trap. But he had to be sure.

The skier removed his hat to adjust his goggles. There was no doubt about the face. Braden moved quickly to the lift.

As Michael dressed, he caught a glimpse of his back in the mirror.

"Holy shit!" he exclaimed.

This had gone too far . . . much too far. He glanced at the clock. It was already 12:30. Diana was probably gone. He looked out the windows through the binoculars and tried to survey the lift, but the angle was poor.

Michael was now frantic, not knowing what to put on first, what to do first. He let out a yell to clear his head. Seeing the herb pouch on the table caused him to calm down. He put it in his pocket, and then put on his ski boots, never questioning why they were there. Draping the binoculars around his neck, he stuffed the map and notes into his pocket, picked up his skis and headed out the door.

He had forgotten something. But what? Michael put his hand to his brow and remembered. He stepped back inside the room and walked over to the insidious mask. He looked at it and turned back to the door.

"Damn!"

He again turned and reached to grab it off the bed. Slipping it quickly over his head, he hurried out, still adjusting the mask as he walked down the hall.

Once outside, Michael charged up the beginners' slope to the traverse trail. He pressed his boots into the bindings, dug in his poles and skated off toward the lift line.

He caught a glimpse of Diana. She was on the lift, nearing the third support pole. He wanted to call out to her, but she was too far out of hearing. Michael put the binoculars to his eyes to see who else was around. He noticed Loudmouth Eli about a half dozen chairs behind Diana, but there was no one else he recognized.

Thank God the line wasn't long. Michael took a chair by himself and was off. By the third pole, he realized he was pumping with his legs. By pole #6, he capitulated to the fact his movement wasn't making the lift go any faster and settled back to think.

What was he going to do once he reached Diana? They'd have to make a run for it. But what if the real Ian Stone was armed? Of course he was armed! Michael wondered if he knew what the hell he was doing?

Snapshots of the past clicked off in his mind: his mother, his father . . . he remembered now he was loath to call him that. Bad memory. Michael wished he were on the Riviera . . . more precisely, back at Eden Roc—there, basking in the sun, having lunch on the veranda overlooking the Mediterranean . . . smoked salmon, wild strawberries and champagne. What on earth was he doing here? Michael swore he'd be back there again someday . . . only this time with Diana.

Diana passed over Braden as she prepared to disembark from Lift 1. She did not even realize it was him. He had pulled up the collar of his jacket to cover his fake mustache and was moving out of view of the chairlift so he could see who followed her. He saw Eli and a dozen or so chairs behind him was the disgruntled Gypsy. At close range, the man looked emasculated with the loss of his whiskers. But anger had sharpened his wits and, from afar, he would, hopefully, prove an apt decoy to the Assassin.

Where was he? Which was he?

It was, oddly, the clothing Braden noticed first. The outfit reminded him of a ski commando. He looked at the bandaged face. He saw the binoculars being raised and that's when he was sure he had his man. How simple. How obtrusively unobtrusive.

As soon as the skier got off the lift, he was on his way. It confirmed he was no joy rider.

Braden wasn't the only one who noticed, however. From the overlooking crest of the Zagava run, Theresa took note of the skier and, while speaking into a walkie-talkie, was streaking down in pursuit.

By the time he reached Lift 2, Michael could not see Diana. The lines were light, so she had probably moved fast to get nearer the man she thought was him.

As he rode the second lift, Braden attached a silencer to the uzie under his jacket. It made the muzzle protrude, but now was not the time to worry about such things.

Up ahead, The One had already begun his trek up to the Ridge. It was a good half hour journey, requiring the removal of skis and hiking up a steep grade.

Looking back, he saw Diana remove her skis to begin the ascent herself. Soon, very soon, they would all be in the open. For the time being, he continued to remain in view . . . and out of range.

What the real Ian Stone did not know was he was being viewed through heavy lenses by a man in the booth at the top of Lift 2. The viewer put down the binoculars and made a call. The man did not, therefore, see the skier with the bandaged face getting off the lift. Best laid plans were about to go awry.

Michael had checked the trail map and it appeared he could either climb the ridge from the lift or cut over on a traverse to an expert slope called Spitfire and climb up to the Ridge from there.

Michael spotted the dark-complected man studying a trail map and then looking up at the Ridge. Could he be the CIA agent? Michael took the traverse before the man could spot him.

Braden just caught a glimpse of Michael as he neared the top. He also spotted the Gypsy and became incensed. Why was he still there? He was fouling up everything.

As the Gypsy prepared to head across the traverse, Braden cut him off.

"You can tell the Master I have everything under control He may proceed on schedule. And if you keep out of the way, perhaps I won't tell him what a fool you are," Braden threatened.

The Gypsy bristled at the man who had disgraced him. But he knew who Braden was and that he could not cross him. He turned down the slope as the member of Metamorphosis disappeared from sight.

Less than a minute later, Theresa and two of the Coyote Clan also disembarked. Theresa called out to a ski patroller, asking him if he saw the skier with the bandaged face. He pointed toward the traverse.

Seconds after, four of El Conciliador's men reached the top in snowmobiles. They all had walkie-talkies and had been in contact with the man in the control booth. Splitting into two groups, one sled went straight up to the Ridge, while the other took the traverse. The lift operator signalled the ski patroller to close the crossover trail as soon as they left.

Meanwhile, the Pied Piper of the merry band made his way along the Ridge to an opening just above Spitfire. He was about to plant a charge and drop down to the tree line when he saw Michael below. He put the charge back into his pack and dropped down immediately, knowing his main target would be following the decoy.

From a distance, Braden could see Michael stop. He glided along, ready to pull the uzie from his jacket as soon as the group behind him passed. He heard their laughing and shouting and pulled up, feigning a loose binding. As he turned to view the intruders, he realized one was very close downhill of him. The noise had been from a female farther behind. He sensed a third uphill as well, but there was no time to turn. He pulled the uzie to fire, but was hit from above by an ancient warclub. If he hadn't been wearing a metal head protector under his hat, the blow would probably have killed him. As it was, he was down for the count.

Michael glanced back as the Indians closed in on him. Before he could react, his wrists were grabbed by spinning cords held by each of the forward two and he was headed down Spitfire between them. Theresa swiftly grabbed his poles and followed after. The abduction took place in a matter of seconds.

The One had seen it all. His pawn was out of reach, but he had Braden. The Assassin skied down to the fallen man. He pulled his gun and hesitated. He had never liked killing an unconscious man. This particular man he, especially, wanted awake. The snowmobile on the traverse came into view and he picked up Braden's uzie to take them out.

"*Señor* Stone," one of the men yelled. "El Conciliador . . . he wants you to come."

Up over the Ridge came El Conciliador's chopper. It dropped down just above them. Two more skiers bailed out and a harness was dropped in front of the Assassin.

The One quickly barked orders, "Bring this one and the two on the Ridge . . . blindfolded and gagged."

He took a pair of handcuffs from his pocket and locked Braden's wrists behind him. Then he climbed into the harness as Diana came into view above.

The copter rose as he was hoisted up. It soared to hover right over Diana. She was dumbfounded. There was her Ian, holding a gun on her from above. In a moment, the snowmobiles converged on her from below and behind, the latter prodding Eli, who shuffled along with his arms above his head. Then the chopper ascended, disappearing over the Ridge.

The Assassin swung into the helicopter and warmed himself with some coffee offered by the pilot. The transfer had been effected, albeit not as he had expected. He had taken a knight, rook and queen. Now he was off to the bishop who would lead him to the king. He didn't have to worry about a loose pawn . . . or did he?

22

Michael had never moved so fast . . . not even the other day through the Walkyries. At least he had poles then and wasn't handicapped by a mask that made seeing difficult. The two Indians dragged him down the steep slope as if the devil were on their heels. Michael suspected it was not an unwarranted tack. He just might be.

It wasn't until they hit the easier West Basin trail that Michael recognized one of his abductors as the man who had jumped from the van the other night and later showed at the Pueblo in skins. The other had also been in the van. Weren't they allies? The kidnapped man did not understand why he was being treated so roughly.

The group careened down Lower Stauffenberg and into the trees where they met up with two more Indians seated in snowmobiles. Michael was shocked to find Theresa was behind him. He was just about to say something to her when a gag was slipped over his mouth from behind and his wrists were locked together against his lower back by the cords attached to them.

He was quickly stripped of his skis and shoved into one of the two vehicles. Their equipment was swiftly packed on, and they were all off into the woods with Michael still wondering what the hell was happening.

After a fifteen-minute ride, they arrived on the opposite bank of the river from the garage where Sheriff Redding's body was left. Michael was yanked out of the snowmobile and pushed across a bridge of two logs to the other side.

"You remember this place?" the tall Indian interrogated, as he shoved him along.

Michael shook his head, no, and looked to Theresa for solace.

The Indian took him by the elbow and pushed him toward the garage so forcefully he went down on one knee. One of them opened the door. The police car with Redding's body was still sitting there. Michael could see the bloody head against the glass.

"You remember this, don't you?" his captor shouted.

Michael finally got the picture. Someone had seen the man in the bandaged face with Redding, or perhaps even witnessed his murder. He shook his head again and tried to grunt.

"Take his gag off," Theresa said.

As the Indian did so, he felt the "bandages" shift and tore off the entire mask. Theresa was the most astonished.

"Ian!" she exclaimed.

"It wasn't me, Theresa. I was after the man you want. Let me try to explain," Michael pleaded.

"You said you saw Stone on the Ridge," the gruff Indian barked at Theresa.

The man was full of rage. His nose was flared back and Michael could see the fire burning in the coal black eyes. Redding must have been someone special to him.

Theresa was speechless.

Michael cleared the phlegm from his throat, "You saw someone disguised like me. Check my pockets. You'll understand."

The Indian stuffed his hands forcefully into the jacket and brought out the map, pouch and letters. Theresa and the others came closer to see.

"Michael?" Having read the letter, Theresa looked at him, confused.

"It's a very long story, but you're the one person I don't mind telling," Michael answered.

"Let's go to Puye," she said to the others. "Untie him."

She had exerted the authority the Cacique had given her and the others acquiesced. It *did* appear they had the wrong man.

The garage was reclosed and all but two of them went to a pickup parked across the road. The other pair headed back to the Ski Valley to try and pick up the trail of the "right" man.

Theresa and the Indian who appeared to be the youngest of them rode in the cab. The young man carried his shoulder in an awkward manner and Michael thought he must be the one who was hurt the night he was brought to the Cacique. The tall, gruff one rode in the back with Michael. It appeared he still distrusted him. Why else, Michael wondered, was he forced to lie on the floor with a tarp around him, each bump in the road causing new misery to his back?

For awhile Michael kept his head up and, as they passed through Taos, saw processions of Penitente making the final Stations of the Cross as part of the Good Friday services.

Once they got through town, Michael thought it would be okay to sit up, but the Indian would not let him raise his head at all. Every so often, the others would become very animated, as if they were stereotypical "redmen" out for an afternoon party. Then they would grow still again.

"Okay, you can sit up now," the tall Indian finally said. "I'm sorry I gave you a rough time. Sheriff Redding had always been good to my people. He was my friend."

The Indian put out his hand, "I am called Coyoteman. My brother, Shadow, sits with Theresa. Those are our Indian names, of course . . . but the ones we prefer. The other two you saw are our cousins, Red Fox and Long Claw."

"Why did I have to keep down?" Michael asked curtly.

"Partly, I had to get over my anger," Coyoteman admitted,

"but mostly because of the strangers. Taos has been encircled by them; ten miles to the south, then running through Petaca to the west, Questa in the north and Black Lake in the east. They watch all who come and go."

Indeed, a number of the residents had taken notice. Some had even called the sheriff's office. The deputy was getting frantic. He had not heard from Redding in over a day. Besides, what could he do? Someone had to watch the office. And he didn't want to alert the highway patrol if there was really nothing happening; Redding had a strict rule about Taos taking care of its own business. Probably just some hippies caught in the wrong time warp, he thought.

Meanwhile, the helicopter ride had given the honored passenger the overview he had wanted . . . the Ski Valley, Arroyo Seco, the plains, the roads in and out and to and from. The One committed the map to memory.

The copter came toward the plateau and descended before rising straight up the side, just as was done two afternoons prior. The Assassin understood the reason. He remembered Michael mentioning the installations within the turrets while under the serum. They housed anti-aircraft guns triggered by radar. As they landed, The One wondered if the treasure was nearby.

The craft was met by a guard who rectified his only problem. The boots they had had on board were too tight . . . Michael's size. He had told the pilot he needed a full size larger because his feet had developed a swelling from all the skiing. His request had been called ahead.

The One was met at the door by Vincente. The man seemed even bigger than he had appeared to be in robes the night before—big and naturally strong, though somewhat older than he expected him to be.

The Assassin was ushered to the lower chamber, where he found El Conciliador pacing.

"You gave me a stir, disappearing as you did last night," the old man complained. "And then to be out on the mountain today . . . ," he shook his head.

"I had to flush out those who would thwart our efforts," the Assassin replied in his best imitation of Michael's voice.

"The CIA?" Mortez asked, not noticing any difference in his guest.

"An agent, working in concert with some group within the Church," The One responded.

Mortez was surprised, "The Light?! Velenari's Light. I told him his Guardian was too dedicated."

"I don't know what group, but your men have them all in custody. They should be brought here," The One said.

"Not here, my son," El Conciliador shook his head. "I let no one of ill consequence within these walls. I will not risk discovery. They will be brought to this evening's Passion Play. We will deal with them there. At the moment we have a bigger problem."

Mortez was troubled, nervous. Even more . . . He had that look most clients had, a cross between fear and anger. Fear, because, when it came right down to it, they were hiring him to do something they didn't have guts enough to do themselves. Anger, because he *did* have the guts.

"We are being surrounded," the old man said. "My scouts have seen them in every direction, a ring 25 miles outside of Taos . . . men at every mile. Gypsies . . . over a thousand!"

"What did you expect," the Assassin asked matter-of-factly, " . . . that your mark would walk into a trap? If this guy is who you say he is, he would damn well make sure he was secure before coming in . . . and not because of the paltry ten million."

"Then we must solidify our plans now. The dear brothers must be mobilized," Mortez said disparagingly. "I must have an estimate of how many I may have to sacrifice; how many, in total, I will need."

The old man was starting to play God. It was time to bring him down a few pegs.

"In view of the current situation," said The One, "I think we should first solidify *our* relationship."

Mortez's eyes flared, "I have made you a Penitente . . . one of my *cryptos* . . . my general. We do what we do for the greater honor and glory of God."

"When it comes to killing," stipulated the Assassin, "I do what I do for a lot of money. And it appears I'm going to have to do a lot of killing. So . . . I want 5% of the total take from our mark, with a million in advance."

El Conciliador was stunned. The man was asking for as much as $5,000,000!

"We work . . . ," Mortez started to repeat.

". . . For a fee," The One reiterated.

El Conciliador was boxed in. "I don't keep such sums around . . . but it . . . it is agreed," he waved his hand. "I will have it tomorrow."

"Perhaps not such sums, but objects of value. When I say in advance," clarified the Assassin, "I mean in advance. I want to see what I'm protecting. And I will choose my fee from it."

The old man shot up like a bolt, bringing his fist down on top of the desk. Vincente's presence could immediately be felt behind The One. But he did not flinch and Ramon realized he had no choice. He sat down and smiled, then laughed.

"Tonight, after the ceremony, we will go there and you will choose."

"Then you are well served," the Assassin said, pulling up his chair to the desk. "Now, let's get down to work. I need to know the quality of your men as well as the number you can call on."

Mortez was surprised.

The One smiled, "I know you are a man of your word, so I will go ahead in good faith. Time, my friend, is of the essence."

The Old man smiled again as he realized with whom he was dealing. This was not one of those peons who was subject to him. He could not hope to be a match for his mysterious adversary with a peon. No, he had made a pact with Evil for his deliverance. He could only beat a devil with a devil. He would need The One to conquer THE ONE.

By the time the deal was concluded, the loose pawn was on a dirt road in the wilderness some two hours away. Here the ground was covered with only a smattering of snow and the temperature was considerably warmer. To the west, in fact, it looked as if rainclouds were moving in.

Michael had been sitting up for over an hour, but there hadn't been much to look at. Suddenly, however, there was a sight he had never before seen—the cliff dwellings carved into the side of the plateau rising before him. The ancient dwellings looked like file compartments in some fossilized brain. The mineral content of the aged rock seemed like faded paint on the face of the structures. It was, quite simply, beautiful.

There was no movement, no hint of life amidst the ruins as the truck took a trail circling up to the top of the plateau. But along the way Michael could make out sentinels in the trees. Then as they came over a crest, he saw a parking area with numerous vehicles in thatch-topped stalls. The area, indeed the entire plateau, was alive with Indians. And in the center of the plain a huge tepee was being erected.

Not much notice was paid to them as the truck arrived, but when Michael got out, a buzz seemed to carry from one end of the plateau to the other.

Michael had been dying to flex his sore muscles, but the attempt only ended with more throbbing in his back. He was given no time to relax; Coyoteman led him to the edge of the cliff where a path wound down to the top tier of dwellings.

"Ian?"

As he came down, Michael could hear Dashwood calling from one of the Pueblo structures. He headed over to it and peeked inside.

"Ahh, c..come in," Alex stuttered. "H..Have I got something to show you."

"And I've got a lot to tell you," said Michael, crawling through the small opening to the domed chamber. "First off, the name's Michael."

"M..Michael?!" Alex exclaimed. "How . . . ? Well, as you will," Dashwood had no patience for befuddlement.

There was another man seated in the chamber of some dozen feet in diameter. He had a thin, wizened face and long, straight black hair with streaks of gray.

"Oh, this is Juan Cordobes," said Dashwood. "You didn't get to meet him the other night at the Pueblo."

The man extended his slender, boney hand and Michael shook it.

"Sit . . . sit," said Alex. "I'll talk to you later, Juan."

Cordobes got up, nodded to Michael and left.

"He's quite a nice fellow," Dashwood said, after Juan had gone. "He brought me out here to meet The Bruja. Quite a fascinating woman. You'll never guess what she had passed down to her."

Alex uncovered an ancient metal disc very much like the one he described finding in Mexico. Only this one had different markings than the cloth copies he had shown Michael. It was the other disc Dashwood had guessed existed.

As tired and as sore as he was, Michael could not help but respond, "It's unbelievable!!"

"I..Isn't it, though?" Alex beamed. "According to The Bruja, the Aztecs had a peasant cult of sorcerers. They were the only religious leaders who survived the Spaniards because they left Tenochtitlan before the city was destroyed. Apparently they roamed throughout northern Mexico . . . some even came up as far as this area.

"Anyway, this disc was passed on from age to age through leaders of the fragmented cult until The Bruja ended up with it. None of them, of course, knew its true meaning," Alex explained, "but legend has it the disc was made by their great teacher, Quetzalcoatl, and contains a magnificent mystery.

"I've spent the last two days trying to decipher it. It's a poem of sorts . . . a song about the plants and seasons . . . like the Battle Of The Trees, if you know it," Alex looked up at him for recognition. "But I can't crack it. I'd give anything for the mind of a Robert Graves. It's so frustrating."

"I know what you mean," Michael consoled as he slumped down against the wall, trying not to aggravate his back.

There were a few small mesquite logs burning in the ancient fireplace at one end of the chamber. It made Michael feel cozy and secure, the most secure he had felt in years. An old scholar was mumbling over an ancient tablet, surrounded by an army of Indians . . . What could go wrong? Don't ask, he reconsidered.

Michael felt removed from the anxiety he had had on the way there. He had so many memories he wanted to catch up on . . . yet, so many present considerations that had to be dealt with first; trying to figure out what the Assassin, Ian Stone, meant about there being more surprises and finding out what the underlying story was . . . wondering whether Diana was safe. If only he could rest there for a very long time, he might regain the energy to pursue all the answers.

Dashwood looked up and rubbed his eyes, "I'm sorry, I forgot to ask . . . How are you? And what's this Michael business? Diana met up with you all right the other night, did she?"

"I'm basically okay. I'll tell you about Michael, but how *did* you find me the other night?"

"It was that tracking gizmo of hers," Alex said. "Didn't she tell you?"

"Her what?" Michael asked, confused.

"She told me not to ask," Dashwood related. "I assumed you and she had worked it out in advance. There must have been some sort of homing device in her car."

"Why would? . . ." Michael's voice trailed off.

Why wouldn't? She *was* part of it all . . . whatever the hell *it* all was. And she had made accusations about him!

"She seems rather sad to me in some way," Alex mused. "Lovesick over you, I suspect."

Michael didn't want to talk about it. He decided instead to give Dashwood a short history of Michael Esmund.

"Well, I'm glad you're here, Michael, or Ian," Alex finally said. "The Bruja wants to meet you. Apparently, there've been all kinds of rather strange goings-on such as Brown Bear, the Cacique, alluded to. Like it or not, you're the key to it and they need to know what you've uncovered."

"Wonderful," Michael frowned. "If you find my horoscope in there," Michael said, pointing to the disc, "let me know if I'm supposed to come out of this in one piece."

"Yes . . . yes . . . ," Dashwood's voice trailed off as he turned again to his work.

Michael, too, was lost in thought for awhile. "So, when am I supposed to meet this Bruja?" he finally asked.

"At the peyote ceremony," Alex said matter-of-factly.

"Peyote ceremony!" Michael exclaimed, sitting up.

"By Quetzalcoatl, I think you've struck it!" Dashwood leapt up, almost striking his head on the low ceiling. "Of course . . . of course . . . It's layed out like a chart! I was looking at it backwards and out of order . . . Thank you, my boy. I've got to tell Juan and The Bruja . . . "

Without further ado, Alex picked up the disc and disappeared through the doorhole, leaving Michael bewildered and soon deep in sleep.

* * *

In the next chamber there was a hole in the floor with a ladder leading down to another level. Michael descended and walked along a narrow passage. It was dark, but as he came into the next chamber he found an oil lamp illuminating the room.

On a table in the middle of the chamber was a shrouded body. Michael began to sweat as he approached. By the time he reached it he was visibly shaking.

A thin veil covered the face. Michael had to wipe the perspiration from his eyes so he could see. His hand looked magnified to him as he reached down to pull back the veil.

At first he was frozen in shock. Michael had thought his tears had been exhausted, that all revelations had been given. But now, the sobs swelled up into his throat anew and needed expression. Although his memory was still sketchy, he felt the body was his mother's, her face ashen gray and withered.

As he wept, his tears threw up dust from her cheeks and eyelids. Once more he had to brush the moisture from his eyes . . . and saw hers were now open. Michael was stunned, but her eyes were not threatening. They were supplicating, pleading, begging for an embrace. Michael felt squeamish and yet, somehow willing. He reached down and grabbed the fragile body, pulling it to him. He could feel the bones within. He kissed the parchment cheeks and continued to weep uncontrollably. And through his own cathartic veil, he saw she was smiling.

* * *

Michael opened his eyes and brushed away his tears. Dashwood's hand was on his shoulder.

"My boy, it's time. Are you all right?"

Michael couldn't speak. He just nodded.

Outside, he saw the day had already given in to night. As he tried to rise, a shot of pain ran through his back and quickly brought Michael out of his sleep state.

As they went out into the evening air, Michael asked quietly, "Did you do it?"

"Yes," Alex said excitedly. "It was really so easy after you gave me the clue. All the pieces fell right into place."

"Well, what is it? What does it mean?" Michael wanted to know.

"What it is, my boy," Dashwood beamed, "is a formula. I would venture to say it is a most incredible formula. And it was developed by our very own Quetzalcoatl. Obviously, some sort of hallucinogen. The Bruja is preparing it right now. She seemed to have had all the ingredients, just never put them all together in the right way."

"What does it do?" Michael asked impatiently.

"That she won't say . . . perhaps doesn't know. But there *was* a hidden meaning to the poem. It *was* in poem form," Alex said, looking back at him, "just as I thought. I recognized the old, '*Dechymic pwy yw.*' "

"Alex, what the hell are you talking about?" Michael grew irritated.

" *'Dechymic pwy yw?'* It's the Celtic taunt to, 'Discover what it is.' Well," said Alex, "that I think I did. But I don't understand what it means. Usually these poems would have the name of the tribe's or cult's god hidden in them. The god, and therefore the tribe, would be safe from enemies as long as the mystery was kept. If it became unraveled, however, it was like stealing their power . . . their magic."

Dashwood saw Michael wasn't interested in the background, "This poem didn't hide a name, though. Instead it was a phrase. And it seemed to beg for discovery. Odd. Well, I'm sure it will become clear tonight," Alex shrugged as he began to ascend the ladder to the plateau.

"Can't you at least tell me the phrase?" Michael yelled as he followed.

When he reached the top, Alex was catching his breath. The weather was not any colder than the day, but the winds were gustier. The smell of rain was in the air.

"Of course, my boy," Alex said as Michael reached the summit. "It translates, 'the vision within.' "

There were many Indians amongst the ruins of the ancient village that once stood on the plateau. They were all guests like Michael . . . camping out; now, stretching canvas across the tops of the stone walls in preparation for the expected rain. Michael licked his lips as he saw food being prepared in the old ovens. He wondered how long it had been since he had eaten.

The campfires illuminated the huge tepee that had been completed. Alex and Michael walked toward its east-facing entrance. As they neared, a murmur went through the groups camped around the area. And from inside they could hear a drum being beaten in an irregular rhythm as it was being tuned.

Alex bent his head to enter, and Michael followed after. He walked into another world.

Seated on blankets around the perimeter of the tent were over two dozen men, a few on their knees, praying.

Opposite the entrance, suspended from two support poles, was a large picture of Christ with a bleeding heart. Seated beneath it, toward the center of the structure, was an old woman wrapped in an undyed blanket of dark wool. Though perhaps 80 or more, she had the eyes of a young woman . . . penetrating eyes that delved deeply into his soul, though not threateningly. This, Michael knew, was The Bruja.

On the ground before her lay a white cloth. In front of it was a crescent-shaped mound, the points of which curved toward the entrance. At the mid-point of the mound two sprigs of sage had been placed.

A cedar wood fire burned in the center of the tent, its smoke sweetly permeating the air. Sitting before it was a pot of water, some corn, a piece of meat and, just in front them, another white cloth.

Dashwood took Michael's wrist and moved clockwise to two empty places near the entrance. As they sat, Michael felt sagebrush under the blankets.

A man seated in from the perimeter and to the right of the opening rose and brought over a pot which he placed between the two white men. Michael noted the multi-colored designs painted on the man's face.

As he looked around the tepee, he saw many had such painted faces. Many also wore traditional native dress, including mocassins, buckskins, beading and jewelry.

Michael wondered about the reason for the pot.

A man to the right of The Bruja was shaking a similar, though larger pot across which was stretched buckskin. He beat on it again until he was finally satisfied with the sound. It had a pleasing tone.

Michael's eyes returned to The Bruja again. He was sure hers had never left him. She took something from a pile to her left and leaned forward to place it on top of the sprigs of sage. Although he had never seen it, Michael rightly assumed the gnarled herb was peyote.

A hush fell over the enclosure. The ceremony had begun.

The Bruja took a bag from the ground to her left and removed some tobacco leaf and a corn husk, then passed the bag to the man on her left. As he followed suit, she made a cigarette. And as the bag went clockwise around the tepee, everyone did the same.

The man sitting in from the outer circle got up and put the tip of a long stick into the fire. As soon as it took, he blew on the ignited end until it glowed, then lit The Bruja's cigarette. He passed the stick to the man on her left, who lit his own cigarette and continued to circulate the glowing match.

As they puffed, many of the men waved their smoke with fans of beautifully colored feathers.

Once everyone had lit up, The Bruja spoke. Hers was a very clear, resonating voice.

"Great Spirit, Father Peyote . . . shine with favor on your children who celebrate the death of the Great Sage who fulfilled your promise by returning joy to the land. Grant us the courage to make the stand he did, so joy may continue to prevail."

Her eyes and arms had been raised while she spoke. She now lowered them both and spoke in softer tones. "I wish to welcome all my brothers . . . representatives of the Zuni, Ute, Pima, Hopi, Navajo and most of the Pueblo peoples. You have all put aside your skepticism, your fears of The Bruja," she smiled, "because your own signs have shown you the arts are necessary to stand against the encroaching dangers.

"I speak in English tonight," she continued, "in honor of my *anglo* guests who have restored to us a great medicine lost for centuries."

The Bruja took a puff of her cigarette, "I must begin far back in the time of man, and talk of the things that unite us and the things that separate us.

"The peoples of the earth have always guarded their magic . . . their secrets . . . their powers . . . lest their enemies would use these against them. All claimed special gods . . . fragments of the Great Spirit . . . and these were jealously hidden; their names rarely spoken.

"Knowledge in these beginning times came only from experience . . . from being close to the earth. Understanding was drawn slowly from within," she gestured.

"But the human being is impatient. So what he wished to know, often became his 'revelations.' These revelations, then, became the base of his 'faith,' and the need for understanding became secondary or was met with intolerance."

As she spoke, The Bruja's eyes moved from man to man, "Instead of seeing their role as part of all peoples, tribes fought to make their own faiths, their own gods . . . supreme.

"And the people in tune with the earth migrated to find new lands where they could live in peace . . . as was the case of our ancestors.

"From time to time a *makai,* as the Pima would call him . . . a man of great magic . . . , would come amongst the peoples of the earth and attempt to restore understanding. Such was the *Cristo,*" she said, pointing to the picture behind her.

"Unfortunately, as is sometimes the fate of a *makai,* he was destroyed by those whose revelations, whose wishes demanded a wargod. And soon after his death, his true identity, his true message was deposed and a wargod was substituted in his place . . . yet with his very own name.

"It was not long after the *Cristo's* death the first known white men came amongst our peoples. They were men of peace who searched for understanding. One such was a powerful *makai* . . . a man of great learning, a teacher of healing. He became a god to the people of the south. They called him Quetzalcoatl."

There was a murmuring amongst the assembly as The Bruja continued, "But the *makai* did not wish to be used by those whose revelations demanded a wargod . . . such as the forebearers of our Aztec brothers. And he came north to this very place.

"It was on this journey, as told in legend passed amongst the disciples of Tezcatlipoca, the Lord of Night and patron of *brujas,* that he discovered a great secret . . . a key to restoring the balance between knowledge and understanding.

"A part of that secret was the peyote with which we celebrate tonight. But when other of the earth's fruits are brewed with it, it becomes *the one* potion . . . *the one* giving perfect clarity . . . the true vision . . . the vision within." She gazed at her listeners with eyes aglow.

"This magic was lost to us when the Aztecs brought their treasures to hide in our land, and destroyed the followers and descendants of great Quetzalcoatl.

"But, many centuries ago, in the Region of the Dead where peyote is found, ancestors of my clan found this . . . "

The Bruja lifted the white cloth on the ground in front of her and exposed the ancient disc. Those around the circle rose to their knees to look in awe at the mysterious piece.

"Yet," she went on, "until this day, no one knew its meaning, though the legend of its secret did survive through many of our peoples.

"This," she said, pointing to the disc, "masked under a quest for gold, is what stirred the early *anglo* exploration of our land. It is this that can restore balance to the terrible knowledge man now possesses. And it is this we must protect from those who would seek to destroy or pervert it."

The Bruja re-covered the disc, put out her cigarette and placed it on the west side of the crescent mound in front of her. Each of the others then extinguished his own and rose to put it alongside hers before returning to his place.

Once they all had done so, the man seated next to her got up, took some ground cedar from a bag and sprinkled it on the fire. A white, sweet-smelling smoke arose, its scent filling the tepee.

The Bruja picked up a bag of peyote buttons and a sprig of sagebrush and waved them through the smoke four times in a form of blessing. Then she sat down again and patted her forehead, chest, shoulders, thighs and arms with the sprig before passing it clockwise around the tent.

While the sagebrush was going around, The Bruja took four peyote buttons from the bag and then passed the pouch in the same direction as the sagebrush. Everyone took a piece, and once the circle was completed, each of them began to eat his peyote; some first picking the white hair-like strands off of it, others chewing it all.

Michael did not at all feel threatened. He was more skeptical than anything else. Over the past 15 or so years, he had tried most all of what he, then, considered non-lethal drugs . . . cocaine to LSD to THC . . . just about everything but the feared heroin. And nothing affected him. A mild flush in his cheeks from LSD was about all. He couldn't believe anyone would actually pay for the stuff. People often said he must have some tremendous block. Well, maybe he did, but he still felt his druggie friends were fools to lay out good money.

Michael bit into the peyote. The bitterness immediately made him spit it out into his hands. He looked about him furtively and found that seemed to be an okay thing to do. A number of the others were doing the same, then rolling the pieces into wads which they tossed back into their mouths and quickly swallowed. Michael imitated them and nearly choked. The piece was too big and lodged in his throat. His first thought was not to draw attention to himself and he tried, desperately, to open his throat wider. His eyes began to bulge as his breathing turned to futile gasps. He began punching himself between his stomach and his rib cage until the piece finally dislodged. Michael bit hard, splitting the piece, and then swallowed twice in quick succession. It was an awful way to start a party, he felt.

Once everyone had eaten his peyote, the Cedar Man threw more incense on the fire. The Bruja then blessed a gourd rattle and a staff with twelve feathers on it in the smoke. She took another sprig of sagebrush and held it, together with the staff, in her left hand; in her right was the gourd.

The drummer waved his drumstick in the smoke and began to beat his instrument. The Bruja shook her rattle and began to sing, "*Heyowicinayo* . . ."

As usual with drugs, Michael felt nothing happening. Now he had done peyote. Big deal.

The Bruja seemed to be singing the same song over and over, but he didn't mind. It had a good beat. He gave it an "8." The thought of food crossed his mind.

The sprig, staff and gourd were exchanged for drum and stick, and the drummer began to chant in The Bruja's place . . . again, over and over . . . four times, Michael counted. He thought it had been the same for her, too. Probably for each of the four winds, he correctly surmised.

A good hour had passed by the time the fourth person started his chant and prayers. Michael looked over at Alex. The man appeared ill. Then, he himself felt a cramp. Sweat started oozing out of him and he immediately understood the reason for the pot placed between them. Michael grabbed for it and vomited.

The Bruja observed and took a jar from inside her blanket. She unscrewed the top and poured its contents into a gourd cup. The man near the doorway rose and came over to take it from her. He brought it directly to Michael. The younger man looked up and nodded gratefully, then drank its contents despite the bitterness.

Michael quickly began to feel dizzy and had to put the cup down. Another wave of nausea passed through him. There seemed to follow waves attacking each part of his body . . . from a splitting headache to cramps in his feet. Michael felt as if the whole tepee were collapsing in on him.

The sudden heaviness in his chest began to worry Michael. He truly thought he might be having a heart attack. He wanted to call out, but his need to draw in oxygen prevented him. He looked at The Bruja and she seemed to be zooming away as he was standing still, fading back within himself. He was moving down a tunnel backwards, the exit to the outside world seeming smaller and the light, dimmer.

Soon the light appeared to be above instead of before him. Michael felt he would suffocate and no one would know.

The earth trembled; there had been a cave-in above. Now he was sealed off in darkness.

23

Security around the outdoor amphitheatre was incredibly tight. Guards were stationed among the rocks at intervals of 50 feet. Everyone was checked on entering.

It was a study in contrasts—the steel faces of El Conciliador's Basque guards and the reverent visages of the native Penitente in their worn jackets and jeans . . . many of whom came on their knees, all of whom came with conviction.

The outdoor gallery was nearly filled. There were even more people than there had been the previous Sunday. Well over 2,000 candles burned, held by the congregated *Hermanos Salidos a Luz.*

The *matraqueros* whirled their wooden clackers and the *entradas,* or entrances began; first, the novice *Hermanos de Tinieblas;* then, the *Hermanos Disciplinantes,* whipping themselves as they entered; the *Hermanos de Obscuros* following in their black hoods; and finally the *Hermanos de Cryptos,* including El Conciliador and his new general.

The One did not at all have the same feeling for this type

of ceremony as had his pawn. He did not like being in the open, exposed to so many . . . despite the fact he was shrouded in his hooded robe. To take his mind off it, The One continued to try to figure out what his father had in mind by setting him up, whether he would play along or actually destroy his prodigal parent. The One had prepared plans as if he were dealing with any other mark, including contingency strategies and his escape. They were all works of art. But a lot depended on rallying these pious souls into an army . . . El Conciliador's task for the evening.

In the meantime, they had sent out scouts to watch the gypsy camps. When the gypsies began to move, the Assassin would know his father had arrived.

El Conciliador stood on the small hill near one end of the amphitheatre—the one symbolizing Golgotha, the hill of the Crucifixion. The effect of dampness in the air and the clouds moving in to mask the waning full moon made their Brother One seem all the more mysterious. A sound system had been set up so he could speak and be heard by all.

"*Alabado sean los dulces nombres de Jesús, María y José,*" he began, humbly.

"*Manos, bienvenidos a nuestra junta secret cierta la mas grande de . . .*"

He spoke in Spanish, telling the crowd that their greatest hour was at hand . . . that they had the opportunity to rid the world of a great evil and help the Church to grow to even greater heights. To lead them on, God had sent one of his avenging angels, a descendant of the first Penitente and their newest initiate.

The One stepped forward and removed his robe, exposing the fake scars on his bare back.

A buzz of approval went through the audience, and the two men felt success was theirs. But suddenly, a chant arose, growing in numbers, volume and intensity . . . , "*Cristo . . . Cristo . . . Cristo!*"

The Assassin was confused, but El Conciliador understood. On Sunday, the arrow of the hideous skeleton, *Doña Sebastiana,* had landed at his general's feet. The Penitente always looked for a miracle or a sign to determine the next brother to play the *Cristo.* That incident was a sign. The One was to have the honor.

El Conciliador explained what was going on.

"Don't be apprehensive," he whispered. "They love you. It will not be like Sunday. Just ropes. And then they will follow you anywhere. Besides, anyone who refuses to take up the *madero* is considered unworthy."

The Assassin was swept up in the atmosphere of the moment. He turned his face to the crowd and raised his arms. There arose a deafening cheer that impressed even him. Then the two conspirators walked together to the other end of the amphitheatre to prepare the drama.

"You may choose your Dysmas and Gestas, the two to be crucified with you," Mortez said.

"Really?" responded the Assassin. "How about you, old man?"

El Conciliador did not appreciate his humor.

The One turned to him, "I will go through this indignity, but this will cost you an additional five percent performance fee, and another million in advance. If I'm to make my debut, it will be for a greater price than has ever been paid . . . and I will forget about choosing you for one of the thieves."

"You are more a thief than any two," Mortez said bitterly.

"Done?" The One asked simply.

The old man bit his lip and expelled a sigh, "Agreed."

The One smiled, "Good. I want the two men taken captive on the mountain to be the thieves . . . but bound and gagged all the way. Let the woman play a part as well."

El Conciliador gave the order, and leaving the Assassin to prepare for his performance, returned to the arena for the start of the rosary.

As long as his "scars" didn't split or peel, Ian Stone thought as he oiled himself, he would get through this evening. But now he wished his pawn were there instead.

Outside there was still darkness. Pain was the only sensation. It was as if something were pulling on Michael's navel from the inside and drawing it up through his stomach, then through his chest, and, finally, out through a hole in his cranium. His legs drew up to his gut and seemed to follow after. He was being turned inside out.

But as the incredible force turned his eyes around to the inside, there was light! At first tapestries of blues and reds. Then lattice-like gradations of indigos and ochres rushed at him . . . extraterrestrial stratocruisers. They started to turn over on their backs, then flip up again, over and over until they became cones . . . funnels . . . and, finally, vortexes that overcame and spun around him. Michael seemed to be dropping through them to lower and lower plains. And on each plain the light and the colors seemed even more brilliant.

The pain in Michael's gut had subsided. Instead his belly felt a chill from exposure. Then a tremendous pain shot through his knees. The inverted eyes shut with the shock and, as they reopened, Michael saw himself as the young medic in Cambodia. Silver beads of rain beat upon his body as it bounced off the shoulders of a dark figure. He could hear the whistling of incoming shells.

Why? Why wasn't he allowed to die in peace? Why??? echoed off cavernous walls as he slipped from the plateau he was on and dropped through the vortex into a field of incredibly dazzling light . . . the light of birth.

Colors blew like gusts of wind passing around him. The fascination was matched only by the ache in his gut from having been wrenched from the womb . . . the experience of lack. And other cries seemed to echo his own.

From this nadir his body began to float aloft. Michael saw his mother as a young woman and ran to her. She smiled and ran, also . . . but not for him. There was someone else. He turned, rolling his head through a sea of purples and scarlets. A soldier appeared out of the swirls and took his mother under puffs of crimson.

Pok . . . pok. Fireballs shot up and exploded, cascading showers of chroma about him. Pok . . . pok.

A young boy of four bounced his rubber ball off a wall. Pok . . . pok . . . it spun in yellows and oranges. Suddenly the ball was caught above him by another hand. Bolts of blue and black fell off in shards.

The young boy arched his body to see glints off silver steel blades as they spread apart, then glided side by side, slicing the rubber ball in two as they came together.

A deep male voice reverberated off the tunnel of light around him, "If I find you with another, I'll do it again."

The child mumbled, his soft voice tumbling down a tunnel to Michael's ear, "Then I'll find a secret ball and you won't know about it."

The hand came hard against his cheek and the reverberant male voice echoed, "And if you don't watch out, I'll do it to you, too."

His father didn't have to threaten. He had already done it . . .

Michael felt the same feeling he had touched on the lowest plain . . . separation . . . lack . . . a split from the world around him. But the separation was not just from others, it was also from a part of the self within.

A roll of color began to carry Michael aloft. White shafts rose up in front of him . . . casts of plaster enveloping his legs.

The young man looked up through the all-white cocoon enveloping his face. Someone, also in white, lifted the dog tag around his neck. "Ian Stone," he heard. Ian Stone, he thought as he drifted back into unconsciousness. Which part of him was Ian Stone? Of course . . . there was now a name for his other self . . . the secret half. "Ian Stone" was his "secret ball."

Now, storm clouds of ominous grays began swirling toward him and Michael was tossed end over end.

Fleets of images swooped down at him, disapproving faces of dark purple . . . mother, father, teachers, all the influential authorities.

Suddenly reinforcements arrived . . . a phalanx of unarmed men forming a protective circle around Michael, turning him upright and providing the weapon needed to repel the establishment onslaught . . . the conviction of their conscientious objector status. It wasn't his own burning conviction, but it would keep Michael safe from the fear of becoming like the hated soldier who had turned his mother against him. He would be a helper, not a killer of men.

Then all the images, friend and foe, dispersed to their own realms, leaving him alone.

From below, a child's face rose, growing and growing as it neared. It was his own face. And as it came alongside him, each eye was as big as Michael's head. He found himself staring into one of the crystals mirroring him, seeing both the pleading in the orb and the aloneness of the reflected figure . . . a figure divided in half. The huge head turned and in the other eye was reflected his other half. And Michael felt he did not want the division to continue.

Michael looked down and saw he was standing on a teetering flat surface. He felt as if he had forever been perched upon it, trying to balance himself. But now he could no longer feel any strength in his legs; in fact, he could feel nothing.

It was time to feel something . . . to put away the fear of feeling. With both desperation and terror, Michael leaned his body and fell off the surface into nothingness. And there he stayed; not sinking, not plummeting, but afloat in the sea of transparent shades and hues.

He saw his platform had been half a sphere which he was now able to grasp in one hand. From inside his gut, he drew out what appeared to be a dried, flattened sponge. Exposed to the cosmos, a gamut of color wisps permeated the object as if wetting it . . . and it puffed into another half sphere.

Michael drew his hands together, tears of prismatic color streaming down his face, dripping onto the approaching surfaces to form the glue which, as the halves touched, bound them together. He had merged into his essential identity . . . the "who" he was.

Michael had reconnected.

The rosary had finished and the atmosphere in the amphitheatre was upbeat with anticipation. The singing, "*Perdona tu pueblo . . . Perdonale, Señor,*" sounded more an anthem than the dirge of the previous night.

The *madero* was a heavy load for Ian Stone, but at least the heat he worked up kept him from being cold. The One felt humiliated having to parade with a crown of thorns attached to his head and clothed only in a loincloth. It made him remember the indignities he had suffered in the Cambodian prison camp. It made him remember carrying Michael Esmund from the makeshift field hospital . . . the providential meeting that had given him his new identity.

It wasn't until Station V, when Vincente, in the role of Simon the Cyrene, took most of the weight of the cross, that the Assassin started to feel the chill of the night. Then someone threw a cloak over his back. He was home free.

Up ahead, The One could see Braden and Eli being pushed on toward the "Mount," with their own crosses. Perhaps, he thought, they could use real nails for them.

Station VI. He came to Diana, bound at the wrists, her hands holding the cloth which, as Veronica, she would extend to wipe the face of the *Cristo.* A guard had to prod her into compliance. Stone wiped his face and the image was transferred onto the treated cloth, drawing exclamations of wonder and pleasure from the audience.

As Stone finished, he looked up at Diana. Her eyes had a look of sadness restrained only by a sense of duty. But the look quickly shattered. This was not her Ian. These cold eyes were not those she knew. She would have screamed out, had her gag not prevented it.

The One smiled. This was his night.

By the time Ian Stone reached the hill of the crucifixion, Braden had already been stripped and tied to his cross. As it was being raised and placed into a hole in the ground, Stone noticed the amulet hanging from his adversary's neck. It was the same as Velenari's.

His first thought was he had been right in his suspicion of Braden. "Who didn't his father own?" Not him. But the son-of-a-bitch probably thought he did. He expected to come out of the woodwork after all these years and have him come running. The Assassin felt nothing but hate for his unknown sire. His second thought was, "Why hadn't the amulet been taken?" He didn't understand it was not the way of these people to fool with another man's magic.

Stone decided he would examine the amulet later. It held, he realized, the drug which produced the sensation . . . the memory of Velenari's eyes flashed before him . . . no, it was more than just a sensation of running with the wolves.

Eli was being tied to his cross.

"Take the gag off him," Stone demanded.

The guards complied.

"Tell me, old man," he directed, "How do you fit in?"

Eli was silent. And there was no time to persist.

"Enjoy the view, my friend," the Assassin taunted.

The "soldiers," wearing the red bandanas symbolizing helmets, came for him. The One started to sweat as his hands and feet were tied to the cross. He had never in the last 16 years allowed himself to be in so vulnerable a position. But the possible win . . . as much as $10,000,000 . . . had never been so great. And he had not even begun to deal with dear old dad.

The *madero* was ready to be raised. Then one more "Roman" came into the circle and, from a leather belt, drew out a hammer and three nails.

"Take this, pope-killer . . . ," he cried.

Guadalupe's father put a nail against Stone's wrist and drove it home.

A wave of pain swept through the Assassin. Caught . . . goddamn it . . . caught; with sweat pouring out, neck stiffening, breath choking in his throat, veins pulsing, a sickness sinking into his bowels . . . caught.

In a flash, the man was on his other wrist and a second nail tore through.

Stone grabbed at the man's hand, grasping it for a second before it was pulled away. But a second was all he needed to prick it with his ring.

Guadalupe's father did not even notice the cut. He took his final nail and put it between tendon and bone on Stone's right ankle. Then, as he tried to overlap one foot on the other, he was yanked off the ground by the nape of his neck. Vincente held him, his legs dangling in the air.

The old man yelled in Spanish, "He is a killer of a Pope. He killed Cardinal Velenari . . ." He screamed in El Conciliador's direction, ". . . your friend.

"This man," he bellowed, pointing to Braden, "has the proof. He is with the CIA."

El Conciliador stood at the other end of the amphitheatre, stunned. It was inconceivable; Velenari found, his general accused. Did they know he was responsible for withholding the news?

The enraged "soldiers" around the cross raised the crucifix and put it into a hole so everyone could see the alleged killer writhing in pain.

Stone's eyes flamed with anger and agony as his hands grasped at air.

Mortez started to move across the field to view the damage to his general. His squinting eyes saw the blood from Stone's wrists was not excessive. The main arteries had been missed. But there was no getting around the fact The One might now be a liability. El Conciliador knew he had to confront Braden and the accuser. If they were smart, they would not implicate him.

It was a fair supposition. Hanging from the cross and Vincente, both men were in too vulnerable a position. And they both wanted to live.

"We have the finger . . . ," the old man choked for air and then hung as dead weight in Vincente's grasp. It was not, however, from choking; Stone's ring had done its job.

With the man's last breath, Braden drew in one of relief. He was not sure who was hanging beside him. Either a switch had been pulled or Ian Stone had been an exact double for The One. It was, therefore, a 50/50 proposition to mention the fingerprints. It would take guile, not "proof" to save his ass. Braden knew he only had one long shot.

As his gag was cut, Braden cleared his throat and called out to the crowd, "I've been tracking him for over two years. He *did* kill John Paul I and Cardinal Velenari. I have reason to believe he came here to kill El Conciliador as well."

A murmur went through the assembly. Their *Cristo* had betrayed them. And El Conciliador was satisfied he could escape implication.

But Diana knew it had all been a lie. There were *two* Ian

Stones, and this was not the man with whom she had fallen in love. Braden had used her to find this man . . . and she did not believe it had anything to do with stopping a conspiracy to kill Church officials. It had been for his own gain. This Stone might be guilty of some heinous crimes, but Braden was no better.

She used the distraction to hook her gag on a staff one of the players had stuck into the ground near her. With some effort, it pulled loose.

"Show them the fingerprints you showed me," she shouted to Braden. "Prove he is who you say."

Diana felt she had nothing to lose. El Conciliador wasn't going to be too happy to hear for whom she worked. Her best hope was with Stone.

"Look in the old man's pockets," she directed Vincente.

Those around the dead man went through his pockets and found the prints.

Stone, meanwhile, accepted his new ally and called out with all his strength, "They are not mine. Check them . . . See . . . "

Vincente took a spear from one of the "Roman soldiers." He dipped the paper bearing the prints in Stone's blood, put it on the blade point and touched it to the crucified man's outstretched fingers. As the crowd waited in silence, El Conciliador limped his way quickly over the rest of the distance to see the results for himself. Vincente extended the lowered spear tip to him.

Braden bit his lip in anticipation as El Conciliador compared. There was no match.

Anger ripped through Mortez's stomach. He grabbed the spear away from his bodyguard and jammed it into Braden's side.

"*Anathema!*" he shouted as Braden bellowed like a stuck pig and passed out.

Brother One looked up at his general. What could the Assassin do for him now? He wondered whether he could carry out their plan on his own.

His eyes fell to the bare feet on the cross in front of him and suddenly Mortez realized something was not right. The thought had been festering all day. It had started with the boots. They had a precise size from the other day. Why was it wrong today? The feet did not appear swollen, at least not the one untouched by the nail. These were not the feet he had washed the night before.

"There are two of you," he whispered. "Like Christ."

Mortez had long believed Christ had been two men, doubles, who in concert worked their miracles . . . one of whom was captured and died, one of whom "arose" and "ascended." The god he had come to believe in was a devious deity who played both sides . . . as he did; a god who triumphed no matter if good or evil was victorious. Things temporal were no more than temporal. If the man hanging before him had not killed Velenari, then his double had. If this man could not help him, then his double could.

Those around the cross were perplexed by El Conciliador's trance.

"Shall we take him down, your Excellency?" one of the men asked.

Diana shouted, "If he is a worthy *Cristo,* let him take himself from the cross. Then we shall follow him anywhere."

Mortez turned in fury. Who the hell *was* this woman?

"Silence her," he demanded.

But the crowd had already picked up the chant, "*Cristo,* come down to us. *Cristo*, let yourself down."

It was madness, deafening madness.

Mortez turned to Vincente, "Have her taken to where Velenari lies. She is a heretic and must be dealt with in the proper way. And tell them to dispose of anyone else there. Quickly, I want to leave here."

Mortez turned to Stone, "I'm sorry, my son."

"You crazy fuck, get me down from here," the Assassin screamed.

"You must rise in time to defeat our common enemy," El Conciliador responded. "It is God's will."

The wind had been gusting heavily during the last half hour, making it difficult to keep the candles lit. Now thunder was heard and a bolt of lightning split the sky. On a howling wind, the rains came.

El Conciliador took the microphone, "Go now, my brothers, and be ready to witness the miracle that will give you the strength to vanquish our enemies. The *Cristo* must die to live again."

With the same spear he used on Braden, Mortez pierced the Assassin's side. The One screamed and fell unconscious.

The rains washed out the remaining candles and shorted out the spotlights. There was a thunderclap. Everyone was on the run.

Mortez looked up at Stone. The same thought repeated itself over and over . . . It would happen. It had to! It had to!

Vincente hurried away his master, while Diana fought in vain with her escort. The assembly hurried off to the safety and comfort of the vehicles scattered about the area, everyone confused and bewildered by what had transpired.

Within minutes the amphitheatre was empty; even the body of Guadalupe's father had been carried off. All that was visible amongst the flashes of lightning were the three crucified men . . . a tableau so close to the scene on the original Calvary it was frightening.

Descending through the sudden storm were two helicopters that had come north from Mexico below radar scan. State-of-the-art in attack craft, they had flown completely undetected through the night. In the second was Radu Scotia, the man called THE ONE.

As soon as the mechanical birds touched down, the Gypsy net began to close. El Conciliador's scouts were also on the move. There was no chance to call in their news. All lines into the Taos area had been cut and diverted. The CB channels had been jammed. The region was now isolated.

24

SÁBADO DE GLORIA

A whistle was heard over the winds wracking the tepee.

A second.

A third.

A fourth.

Michael had gradually felt his body reinvert, his eyes twist back toward the outside world, his conscious mind float back to the surface. And then his eyes opened.

The Bruja was staring into his soul just as she had before his eyes first closed. She was pleased.

The tepee smelled of incense. Michael gazed over at Dashwood. The man looked numb, but had a charming smile on his face.

As his sight adjusted, Michael suddenly realized he had an incredible urge to urinate.

A young Indian entered the tepee, bowing as if in apology. He went around the perimeter to whisper something in The Bruja's ear. She shook her head in the affirmative.

Michael now felt as if he was going to burst. He tried to rise, but it felt as if his legs were no longer there.

The Cedar Man came back inside, soaking wet. He was drying off the eagle bone whistle he had just blown to the four winds. Noticing Michael's plight, he and the messenger helped the struggling man to his feet. Then the young brave guided him outside as The Bruja began the Midnight Song.

Michael had no coordination as he was taken out into the rain. He could not at all feel his legs under him. Luckily, he could feel his zipper and was able to undo himself in time.

The rain felt wonderful to him. It was like a baptism. By the time he had finished relieving himself, the Indian was back with a rain poncho and, throwing it over Michael's head, he hurried him toward an awaiting van.

Theresa was at the wheel and drove hard, despite the torrent. Coyoteman, his brother Shadow and their two cousins, Red Fox and Long Claw, made up the rest of the party.

To Michael the ride was fabulous. Lightning exploded into incredible auras of color. The textures of the rolling clouds were a constant wonder.

Then at one point, he was shoved down below the window level and everyone played drunk.

"Hey, come to the party at the Pueblo," Coyoteman shouted out the window.

Michael was let up again as they returned to their more sober demeanor. Looking back, Michael saw the vans in the road behind them, almost as if it were a checkpoint.

The storm began to let up as they bounced along a dirt road a short while later. At one point, the lights of another vehicle blinked in the darkness and theirs were extinguished. They crept along slowly until Coyoteman gave the okay. Afterwards, they moved along by the light of their fog lamps.

By the time they finally stopped, Michael felt much more conscious—his limbs attached. He was invigorated. And in great need to urinate again. He hurriedly climbed out of the vehicle to relieve himself in the darkness.

The rain had nearly stopped. The air was almost warm compared to how it had been all week. Overhead, the clouds moved swiftly, occasional breaks allowing the moon to shine through.

Theresa stayed with the van as the rest of the party departed on foot.

As Michael was led up the road, he realized he had been to this place before. In the flickering moonlight he recognized the outline of the amphitheatre. It seemed so long ago. His equilibrium was still off and walking in the darkness didn't help matters. Michael started to get dizzy. His guides had to steady him as they entered the grounds.

A dark cloud passed over, pitching them into total darkness. Red Fox turned on a flashlight to illuminate their path. They proceeded about a hundred yards with Michael concentrating only on the spot of light. He could make out the gradations of color in the glow. Then as the light was turned up from the ground, they could make out the three crosses in the distance.

As the band continued to move on, the dark cloud passed and the moon penetrated a thinner blanket. By the time they neared the hill of the crucifixion, the veil slipped completely and the moon beamed brightly on the central figure hanging before Michael. Himself. The self he had been for the past 16 years. Ian Stone.

What does one do, Michael wondered . . . how does one act before a replica of oneself? He fell to his knees.

The man on the cross rolled his eyes in Michael's direction and met his stare.

In a feeble, rasping voice he spoke: "If it isn't Mrs. Stone's secret son, Michael. What kept you, little twin brother?"

Time froze. Michael was in shock. What did he mean . . . "secret son" . . . "little twin brother?" How could he look so much like him?

Michael remembered the birth trauma from his vision— *other cries echoing his own . . .*

"Get me down from here," Stone requested. "This is no way for a Buddhist to die."

Michael remained frozen, but the Indians complied, taking

the cross from its hole and laying it gently on the ground.

Michael Stone? He was Michael Esmund. He started to choke. Did this confusion never end?

Coyoteman quickly and carefully removed the nails from Stone's wrists and ankle. The Assassin's cries of pain brought Michael from his stupor. He rose and went to his twin, kneeling beside him.

Stone had lost an enormous amount of blood. The dying man glared up at his bewildered twin. "Look at me, Michael. It should have been you."

Michael reacted with anger. "I did enough for you," he replied hoarsely.

"You owed me," The One hissed, then swallowed and continued, "That jungle hut I dragged you from took a direct hit."

The Assassin started coughing up some blood.

"Get him some water," Michael demanded.

"I've had enough the last three hours," Ian Stone said, his voice weakening. "What I need is blood."

Michael could still not grasp the implications of this revelation. He bent forward and took the dying man's face in his hands.

"Amazing, isn't it?" Stone commented in a whisper. "That lady I came home to after I took your identity . . . that Irene Esmund . . . was some cousin of our mother. I had to force the story out of her. It literally killed her to tell me. Heart failure." The Assassin stared up at Michael, "But then . . . I would have had to do it myself anyway, when I learned you survived."

His look made Michael shudder. He knew the man would not have thought twice about killing his mother. His mother?

"Esmund played the midwife. We were delivered in secret and Cousin Irene took you," the Assassin continued. "She was pregnant herself. But her child was stillborn a month and a half later, so you were given his name; his identity. Very neat of her and mother, I thought.

"Our mother wanted to be sure one of us would survive. You, the second out," his eyes penetrated Michael's soul, "were chosen.

"Did enough for me?" Stone coughed again as he tried to laugh. "This week does not make up for what I endured for you as a child . . . the plastic surgery to make me look different than you. It wasn't just to destroy a memory she hated. I knew it was her way of protecting you, making sure you would survive. You see, I felt sure you existed, but never knew where."

"But why?" Michael wanted to know. "What 'memory she hated?' Survive what?"

The Assassin started to cough again and Michael cradled him in his arms. Stone looked up at him and an almost mischievous smile crossed his lips. He would keep his brother in suspense. Then he was hit with an obvious twinge of pain. As it subsided, however, The One's powerful hand grasped Michael by the wrist, shocking him with its force.

"Listen to me . . . ," Stone commanded. "I am a master of death. Even now, I could kill you with the poison in my ring. It would be fitting for us to die together, don't you think?"

Michael felt a shudder pass through him. He believed the man could and would do what he had threatened.

"But you must be my avenging angel," the Assassin commanded.

Michael began to shrink back, but was pulled even closer to hear the weakened voice, "THE ONE engineered all this. I have been his pawn as you were mine . . . Kill him!"

Stone felt Michael begin to shrink back again and had no strength of muscle to hold him—only words.

"I made her come," he whispered.

Michael looked at him quizzically.

"Your Meredith," taunted Ian Stone. "Then I beat her. And, to her surprise . . . She liked it. That is what frightened her away from you."

Michael's teeth bared as they clenched together. His nostrils flared and his eyes flamed.

"That's it," the Assassin coaxed. "Get angry. Use your anger. The only way you will be able to survive is to become me. Make sure Braden's dead. Waste Mortez and THE ONE. You can do the world some good. Avenge my death. Avenge your life . . . , little twin . . . "

The last was barely audible. The grasp on Michael's wrist loosened. Ian Stone was dead.

For 16 years this man had made no serious mistakes. He had become a legend in the highest and darkest corners of the world of power. Known only to a few. Feared by all these. Assassin of presidents and popes. Dead on a field in New Mexico.

Ian Stone's greed, his effort to take it all in one bite, had failed. He had put himself in too vulnerable a position. He had been beaten by the unforeseen. It was simply the law of averages. The inevitable. The balance.

Michael stared at the dead man. But not really at him . . . at the part of himself lying there. This macabre game was over. He could go home now. He did not want any part of the rest. There was too much to contemplate already . . . an assassin for a brother, a mother he never knew, a father . . . Who was his . . . their . . . father, if not that pig he now remembered hating until the day he died? From whom was the threat to the boys' survival? Their father? To finally remember who he was and now find out he wasn't even that . . .

Had his brother really slept with Meredith?

The Coyote Clan had taken down the other two crosses. Both Braden and Eli were unconscious. Although the wound in his side had not been mortal, Braden, too, had lost a lot of blood. Eli, on the other hand, was suffering from nothing more than exposure. He started to revive as Shadow returned from the van with some blankets. Theresa had followed after, standing off at a distance. As the Indian wrapped a blanket around the old man, Eli coughed and sputtered, and then began to open his eyes.

Braden elicited no pity or care from the Indians. He was left tied to his cross. As Michael went over to him, his eyes opened and showed panic.

"You escaped?" he asked in astonishment. His eyes darted about the area and fell on Stone. "No . . . a double . . . a double."

As his eyes focused on Stone's body, Long Claw had started to lift the Assassin to a sitting position and noticed one of the "scabs" hanging down. He pulled and it came off like a bandage.

"He was good," Braden sputtered. "But he was a ruthless killer. It was my job to stop him." He winced in pain and turned pleadingly to Michael, "Please, release me. Don't let me die like this."

Michael looked up at Red Fox, motionless beside him, "Give me a knife, please."

The Indian hesitated, then extended his blade. Michael cut the cords at Braden's wrists. As he went to cut the leg bindings, Braden grabbed for the amulet hanging around his neck and quickly bit into it. Coyoteman kicked it away, but not before the liquid was half drained. The tall Indian put a few drops on his finger to sniff and taste.

Braden, meanwhile, was already going through some sort of transformation. Color returned to his body and he sat upright and rigid. A flame seemed to ignite behind his pupils.

Coyoteman turned to Michael, "Shapeshifter."

He pulled his knife, but Braden had already sprung up on all fours in a defensive posture. With his free hand, the Indian quickly stripped off his own coat and boots and dropped to the ground. Michael was drawn back by the others and all the flashlights were extinguished.

"Coyoteman will fight him," Shadow whispered.

The clouds drifting swiftly overhead kept cutting off the little light there was. It became like watching an old kinescope. Something was there and then it wasn't. But what Michael *did* see, or thought he saw, was altogether more strange than anything else he had witnessed the entire bizarre week. He was not sure, however, whether it was real or the result of the drugs he had been given.

He recalled seeing, years past, an Ionesco play called "Rhinoceros," in which the main actor transformed from a man into a rhino on stage. He was so good, the audience accepted it was actually happening. But this was different. These bodies did actually seem to emanate another form, even while keeping the original. Michael kept blinking to try and synchronize with the light, as if that would somehow explain the "trick."

There was no question, however, the sounds he heard were quite real. Braden snarled and bayed. And his calls were answered in the distant night.

Although Coyoteman's own "transformation" was thought induced, he kept tossing his head wildly as if there was also a chemical reaction to his taste of the amulet's liquid.

Their circling and sparring done, the two attacked each other savagely. Michael wasn't sure what a camera would have recorded, but he could swear there were two animals ripping at each other. Soon he had no doubt, if Braden had not been weakened, Coyoteman would not have had a chance. The CIA man was frighteningly ferocious, biting the Indian's arms and into the side of his neck. Coyoteman began kicking at the wound in Braden's side, and then went after one eye, gouging . . . clawing . . . until it was finally destroyed.

Only then did Braden recoil in agony, leaving Coyoteman limp, with blood oozing from his neck.

The others advanced on Braden with knives drawn. In the flickering light, he glared at Michael with his one good eye, then raised his head in a howl and took off into the night. Theresa screamed as he shot past her. Michael knew they shouldn't allow him to escape. Yet they could not leave Coyoteman there to die . . . Nor Diana . . . Where, it suddenly dawned on him, was Diana?

The shock of the scene had abated Eli's chills. "I've never seen . . . I've never . . . ," he repeated over and over, shaking his head.

Coyoteman writhed like a wounded animal, at once both knowing and not knowing his friends. The others used one of the blankets to snare and cover him. Then with one cousin at each end, they carried him off toward the van. His brother took Stone's body over his shoulder, picked up the amulet and followed.

"Hurry," he ordered.

Michael and Theresa assisted Eli, who managed to regain some of his poor humor, "Now I know why they held a grudge against my people. It's no fun hanging on one of those things."

Michael didn't even hear him. "Where's Diana?" he wanted to know.

"They took her to wherever Velenari's body is. I'm afraid it was to dispose of her in some ritualistic way," Eli replied soberly.

Michael's teeth clenched again as the rain again returned. The three of them hurried after the others toward the van. Along the way they found a pile of wet clothes, Eli's, Stone's and Braden's. The lot was grabbed into bundles as they ran.

"Who are you?" Michael asked Eli.

"I might ask you the same question," was the retort.

"I'm . . . ," Michael almost started to stutter, "M..Michael . . . Stone, I guess."

"And I'm the Loudmouth, I guess," was the unsatisfying answer.

"But how do you fit in? What are you doing here?" Michael persisted.

"Patience, my boy. Let's get away from this godforsaken place first," Eli beseeched him.

By the time they reached the van, Coyoteman and Stone were being lain in the back. The former had lost consciousness and one of the cousins was working to apply pressure in order to stop the blood loss from his wounds. The brave looked very weak. He would need help quickly.

As soon as they were aboard, Theresa, her eyes glazed as if in a trance, hit the gas.

Michael and Eli were crammed up front so the others could work on their fallen comrade. Michael looked back at them and noticed a pouch, larger, but not too dissimilar from his. From it Red Fox removed herbs to use in treating the wounds.

Michael turned to focus on Eli, who was trying to dry his hair with a blanket. The stare was noticed.

Eli finished and sighed. "Given the rather extraordinary circumstances in which we find ourselves, I will tell you I'm part of an old Kabbalistic Jewish Order called Binah. We are a type of intelligence agency. We follow, we observe, we report on anything and everything felt to be of importance. But unlike your CIA or other intelligence networks, we do not influence. We attempt to sense which way the winds are blowing in the grander scope of things and pass on information which may be to our people's benefit. As my father did before me, I observe the Church . . . in particular The Light, for which Diana Bastian is an agent."

"Velenari's Light?!" Michael was once again thrown for a loop.

Eli corroborated what Mortez had told him . . . how Velenari had brought The Light into existence and what Binah knew of his ties to the Penitente. To Eli, the fact Diana had come to Taos portended something big might be happening. He had followed her to make sure it was not merely a vacation.

A number of gaps were filled in for Michael, so he reciprocated, explaining to Eli where he was both right and wrong—the plots and the coincidences.

"My boy," Eli finally responded, "there are no coincidences. None at all."

Michael felt he was probably right. He recalled the riddle mentioned by the Cacique, "The one who is not the one, yet may be the one." He now understood the first part to mean he, Michael, was "The one who is not The One" . . . Ian Stone, but the rest eluded him.

His thoughts turned to Diana. From what Eli had said, she probably didn't know Velenari was behind her organization. He wanted to believe she was just out to protect the Church.

He decided to be dropped near the *morada* in Arroyo Seco.

The ceremonies had been kept away from there after Velenari's death. Perhaps that was where his body was kept . . .

"Why aren't we going faster?" he said to no one in particular.

But they were. Theresa was doing her best.

Red Fox moved close to them to allow his cousin, Shadow, more room. It was obvious he was nervous and upset over the wounded Indian's condition and he started to talk to keep his mind off it, telling Michael and Eli how special Coyoteman was within his family.

Michael, of course, was curious as to what they had witnessed at the amphitheatre.

The Indian explained they were all shapeshifters . . . part of a clan related to The Bruja. Until the recent events, they had always been shunned, even treated with hostility by the other tribes. And they probably would be again, even if they succeeded in this battle against evil.

Michael wanted to understand shapeshifting, but saw they were getting near Arroyo Seco.

"I want to get off near the *morada,*" he told Theresa.

"Me too," added Eli.

Theresa wanted to get Coyoteman to the Pueblo first and pick up reinforcements before looking for Diana. But Michael insisted.

"Just slow down enough for me to jump out," he pleaded.

"I will go with them," Red Fox told Theresa.

The *morada* was less than a quarter mile off. She reluctantly stopped to let them off.

"Quickly. Make sure nothing happens to them," she ordered Coyoteman's cousin.

To Michael, it felt good to be treated with importance, especially as his real self.

As soon as the three men bailed out, the van screeched off into the darkness.

Red Fox led them swiftly over the prairie in the direction of the *morada.* Michael was impressed with Eli's ability to stick with them. His age belied his energy.

They stopped a few hundred yards off and their guide peered into the darkness as if he had binoculars. The night was frighteningly still.

"It looks quiet," Red Fox finally spoke.

Michael got a sick feeling in his stomach as the Indian moved ahead of them through the brush. They were signaled to follow and, before long, found themselves among the aspen surrounding the pond outside the meeting house.

The Indian crept up to the wall of the structure and moved cautiously toward the entrance. Suddenly there was a bang as he kicked open the wooden portal. They all froze.

Nothing . . . The cousin entered. A minute went by . . . Forever. At last he reappeared and motioned for them to come inside.

The interior still smelled of putrefaction, but there were no dead bodies; not Velenari's, not the guards', not Diana's. Their guide lit a few candles, which allowed them to see the entire chamber. A freshly dug hole in the center of the room looked as if it were made to hold a body vertically.

"I read it was an ancient practice of the Penitente to bury heretics upright," Eli explained.

Footprints surrounded the hole and it looked as if the ruts near the rim were made from a body being dragged from it. As they looked within, a small object seemed to be lying on the bottom. Red Fox reached down and tried to stretch for it. Michael held his legs and helped to lower him, and then pull him up.

They crouched around to see what he had retrieved. It was a bug Diana had placed on herself, hoping they could track her.

Michael bit his lip. There had to be something else, some clue.

They looked in the adjoining rooms, but there was nothing else. Michael felt helpless, vulnerable . . . and dizzy from the smell pervading the *morada.*

He stared at the casket that had held Velenari's body. It now contained the wooden *bulto* of Christ. Michael had to blink. Was he still hallucinating?

In the center of the *Cristo's* forehead was the brand of a wolf's head. Michael remembered Mortez's story of Velenari playing wolfman. He knew Diana was in the hands of THE ONE.

25

Diana had no idea what would happen next. She and the three guards who had taken her to the *morada* lay face down on the floor of a small truck, their arms bound behind them. They were the captives of four Gypsies, two of whom now sat watch over them with Russian-made machine guns as the truck bounced along a dirt road.

One of her Penitente guards was near death, his jaw having been crushed by an incredibly huge man who sat up front with the driver. She had witnessed the extraordinary scene. With one hand, the man had grabbed the guard and "simply" squeezed.

Diana felt she herself was living on borrowed time. Still, she wanted to believe whatever happened next could not be any worse than suffocating underground, her last gasps inhaling the stench of Velenari's corpse . . . the corpse now wrapped in a bodybag attached to the roof rack of the cab.

The driver of the truck she now remembered having seen around the Ski Valley the last few days, although previously sporting a mustache. She was sure he was connected with the man Ian Stone was supposed to kill and assumed he had arrived. She also assumed the visitor was someone far more awesome than Ian had let on. No doubt, she and the others were being taken to him for interrogation.

Diana's thoughts turned to Ian, her Ian. Where was he? Had the real assassin done away with him? Had he been forced to write the note to her, or was it a forgery?

Her only hope lay in the possibility Ian was still alive and would seek her out. But in view of what she had tried to do to him, why should he? It was a million to one shot . . . but a shot . . .

The truck stopped and they were forced into the darkness—the three of them remaining. The fourth had died, choking on his own teeth.

Diana surveyed the scene. They were on a mesa in the midst of an armed camp. In the center of the plain was an attractive *hacienda,* flanked on either side by two large helicopters. A few smaller out-buildings were scattered about the area.

On the roof of the *hacienda* two giant dishes were being set up; one for radar scanning and one for satellite down-linking. There was an uplink facility as well. The visitor came equipped. But, she supposed, if this guy could afford to bid $100 million on Montezuma's treasure, he would be equipped.

The three prisoners were hurried to the main house. At the entrance they were met by an attractive Gypsy woman with coal black eyes and even darker hair. She was dressed in a black leather jump suit with a red scarf at the waist. Her beauty was marred only by the ferocity of her expression, the made-over pug nose flaring back and the thin red lips tight over her brilliant white teeth.

"Strip," she barked as they entered.

Two of the guards behind them grabbed one of El Conciliador's men and tore his jacket and shirt off.

"Without hesitation," the Gypsy woman deadpanned.

They complied, Diana staring hard into the woman's eyes all the while.

As she got to her panties, the woman smirked, "Leave the underwear."

It meant more to the men than it did to Diana.

From the hall, they were led into a den with a beamed stucco ceiling. El Conciliador's men continued to be more embarrassed than Diana in front of the armed guards. She, however, paid no attention to them, focusing instead on the small showcases of jewels about the room.

Diana had spent a few summers during her youth working at a museum in London. She therefore recognized the eras . . . Ottoman; Tsarist, including a few pieces known to have disappeared before the revolution; Egyptian; Greek; Napoleonic. She was in awe.

Suddenly it was as if a cold draft had entered the room. Diana's skin felt like it encountered dry ice. And she began to turn even before he spoke.

"Part of my collection. I get lonely traveling without it," the speaker said.

In the doorway before his huge bodyguard stood the strangest man on whom Diana had ever laid eyes. It would have been no use to cover her bare breasts or anything else. She wondered why, in fact, it had been necessary for them to strip. Diana was sure this man could see through anything.

His slender build, regal stance, thick lips and hair, these were scarcely noticed. Diana's gaze was immediately drawn to the eye with the bloodspot. It made him seem bird-like . . . a bird of prey. The effect made her shiver and become aware she was afraid. And that, she was sure, was the way he wanted it. It was only then she noticed the rest of his appearance and his clothing. Like the Gypsy woman, he was in black . . . a black silk smoking jacket with satin lapels, a red ascot at his throat.

"Radu Scotia," he said commandingly with a slight nod. His voice was thick, accented.

He walked around them, forcing his captives to turn their backs to the door in order to face him.

"So there will be no question about the need for immediate

and complete response . . . ," he said matter-of-factly, snapping his fingers.

The huge bodyguard came up swiftly behind one of the two male captives, took his head between his large palms, and turned it almost 180 degrees. It happened so fast the man felt no more pain than a bullet would have made.

The impact on the other two, however, was most dramatic. The remaining man started to sob. Diana was paralyzed with revulsion.

As the bodyguard removed the corpse from the room, the Gypsy woman entered and closed the door. The look of hate she bore Diana brought the latter back to consciousness.

"Now, I need to know everything you know," Scotia said softly.

Trying to get control of himself, the Penitente guard stood wavering and shaking his head.

"Sit . . . sit," Scotia said warmly. "I know you've had a long day."

Outside there was a commotion. Shouts emanated from the foyer and there was the sound of men running. The door to the hallway was reopened by the giant bodyguard whose gaze was fixed on something at the *hacienda* entrance. The group heard growling and gurgling noises, followed by panting. Diana turned and rose by reflex.

It was Braden. He came crawling into the room like a dying animal. His appearance was demonic, like some crazed beast. The hole in his side no longer dripped blood . . . there was no more. He seemed beyond the moment of death, yet some unhuman force had driven him on.

What was he? Diana wondered. What could have turned him into the human beast she saw?

With his one eye, Braden looked up at Scotia and tried to pull himself to all fours; to draw himself, as it were, to attention for his master.

Diana realized all the intelligence had been for Scotia. It had been Scotia's set up all along.

Her mind raced. Had they all escaped from the cross?

Braden turned his head and saw her. His nostrils flared and his one eye reignited. It looked as if he would try to speak.

Very boldly, Diana stepped to the side of her chair and, before anyone could react, grabbed it by the back brace and swung it in a vicious arc, crashing the leg struts against the bridge of Braden's nose. There was a crack of wood and bone, and Braden lay dead.

As the bodyguard moved toward her, Diana dropped the chair and turned to Scotia, "This man was your enemy."

Scotia liltingly raised his hand for the bodyguard to stop.

"You wanted Ian Stone here," she continued. "You wanted him to be your man inside the Penitente. Braden went against your wishes. He was jealous of Ian and tried to have him killed. We would already know where the treasure is if it hadn't been for him."

"We? . . . Diana of The Light . . ." Scotia inquired.

Sweat oozed from her forehead. He probably knew everything there was to know about her. There was no time for thought, only gut reaction.

"Ian and I were working together," she said. "We're lovers."

Radu smiled and looked at the Gypsy woman whose teeth ground as she gripped the scarf at her waist.

"Get her a new chair," he directed his bodyguard. "One that doesn't lift so easily," he added wryly.

Scotia turned to El Conciliador's dumbfounded henchman, "Do you know where the treasure is?"

The man was not even from the inner circle that would know of its existence. He looked stupified.

"Of course not. Take him out," Scotia ordered his giant.

He turned to the Gypsy woman, "Nadja, give this lady her clothes. And have some port brought in." He smiled at Diana with admiration, "We will talk."

Diana knew her life had been spared . . . for now.

Two goats bleated as they strained the ends of their leashes in the predawn darkness. El Conciliador's head hung low in thought as he led the animals through the tunnel leading to his secret cave. Today, he did not count the steps. There were other things on his mind.

As he came into the open air, he lit a torch that illuminated the area in soft light. He secured the torch in a cleft of rock, and then tied the goats to a stake before entering the cave with the wrapped bundle containing the golden skull.

In a few moments he returned with a golden dagger which he took and lay on the raised stone in the center of the natural atrium. He gazed up into the darkness for a moment and then went to bind the feet of one of the goats. With some difficulty, he lifted the struggling animal and carried it to the stone where he lay the offering, all the while mumbling prayers in Latin.

Mortez started a small fire of dried brush and wood. As the flames crackled, his mumbling got louder. The old man knelt in front of the altar stone and crossed himself as he performed his ritual penitence. Taking the dagger, he made another sign of the cross in the air, then slit the throat of the sacrificial victim.

Hearing the dying gasp, the other goat started bleating again and would not stop. But Mortez paid no attention. He leaned his head against the altar stone and sighed, his mind far away in thought.

Intelligence had been coming in all through the night . . . the helicopters, the closing of the circle. There were Gypsies within ten miles of the cave! Of course they would never find it. This place had eluded the New Mexican authorities for over a century, and who knows what others long before. That wasn't the problem.

Mortez's mind returned to the reality of the present. For what was he sorry? Why was he atoning? Certainly not for his "sins." No, it was for underestimating his adversary . . . for not realizing the man's intentions might be as devious as his own. Perhaps, also, it was for not standing beside his general, the only one who might have been able to get him out of this mess. But most of all, it was for incorrectly assessing his general's ability to get himself off the cross.

His men had gone back a few hours before and found the bodies had disappeared. Likewise at the *morada.* Was The One alive? If so, would he forgive him? Or would he ally himself with his enemy?

Mortez knew his destiny was to rule the Church . . . to make it strong again, more powerful than any state. These trials were but tests of his mettle. They would not have been given if he were not destined for greater things. The old man man did not think to question to what higher power he was attributing these challenges. He was only concerned with the necessity of succeeding.

El Conciliador pulled a log from the fire and cast it on the pyre under the dead goat. The other's bleating finally crashed through to his senses. Putting the dagger into the sash under his cloak, he took the upset animal back through the tunnel.

Just the faintest touches of morning were beginning to backlight the mountains as he exited. Mortez would not risk returning again until after the fateful meeting. The old man turned west and headed toward the plains. He walked over two miles before the sun reached the tips of the mountain range. Unloosening the goat, he doubled the leather leash and whipped its haunches. The animal went scurrying into the wilderness. It was a symbol of expiation. El Conciliador's weaknesses and errors were being remitted to oblivion, never to be seen again. This day would mark a new beginning.

Mortez turned and began to walk southwest to the tunnel that would take him back to the Foundation. It was time to return to the computers.

As sunlight broke over the mountains, a shaft struck a tall stone obelisk almost squarely on, illuminating some strange markings at its summit. On the west side was a carving of a face . . . the Celtic god, Bel. The god's eye was drilled through . . . or perhaps the face had been carved around a natural hole. Too many centuries had passed to know for sure.

The shadow of the obelisk ran down the rocks, across an

open plain just next to the tunnel's entrance. Suddenly a shaft of light shot through Bel's eye and landed to the right of the opening. In another day it would be the keyhole to the hidden door.

"That's it! That's it!" Dashwood was sure he had found the key. "I..It's incredible, Ian!"

The younger man's eyes opened, "The name's Michael, remember?"

"Yes . . . yes," Dashwood fluttered. "I was just seeing if *you* remembered. Look at this!" he said excitedly. "The Ogam on the back of the disc *is* the key to the treasure."

Michael sat upright. So did Eli. Both had been asleep in the inner chamber of the cliff dwelling. As they crawled into the forward chamber where Dashwood was working, they could see the sun was already high in the clear blue sky.

"What time is it?" Michael asked.

"Noon, I think . . . or thereabouts," Alex answered impatiently. "Look, damn it."

They did. Dashwood had translated the newer Ogam markings on the reverse side of the disc. It was a short message which said Quetzalcoatl died 21 days after the vernal equinox and was laid to rest in the secret temple. And the eye of Bel would gaze upon him each year to mark the date.

"Michael . . . Eli . . . ," Alex exclaimed, "tomorrow is 21 days after the vernal equinox! D..Don't you understand? B..Bel is the sun god. At sunrise or sunset . . . and my guess would be the former . . . the cave's entrance will be exposed. So says Gwynne, descendant of Orem, who first met the Quetzalcoatl and brought him to this land.

"Don't you see how interesting this is?" Alex continued. "I now doubt Quetzalcoatl was a Celt. I think Gwynne's ancestor met up with him, probably in the Mexican Region of the Dead and made the disc to celebrate with his friend the finding of the wonder drug."

"And now, all you have to do," Michael said, "is comb a

50 mile radius of Taos in the next 18 hours and hope the Gypsies and the Penitente won't interfere."

"Well, I never said it would be easy," Alex shrugged. "At least now we have something to go on."

"You can forget the 'we,'" Michael corrected. "I'm only interested in finding out if Diana is still alive."

"Before you spout off on what you are or are not interested in doing," Alex lectured, "I think you'd better have a talk with The Bruja. She may have some answers for you. She wanted you to come by as soon as you got up."

Michael tried to rise and stretch, but had to keep his knees bent so as not to touch the ceiling.

"Do they have any food around here?" he asked.

"I'm sure they do," Alex said, "but don't go out without wearing this."

He handed Michael a hooded cloak.

"Why?" Michael wanted to know.

"The Indians are having a powwow with some of the Penitente leaders," Alex responded. "They'd rather not have their guests see the risen *Cristo* quite yet. People get what's called *susto* . . . or witch fright . . . very quickly around here."

"And me?" Eli asked.

"You can leave if you like," Dashwood said, "but I'm sure you'll find it a lot more interesting around here."

"I'm sure you're quite right," Eli agreed. "I meant, should I be under wraps?"

"Probably so," counseled Alex.

Michael donned his cloak, "Which way?"

"The boy outside will take you," Alex said, pointing to a young Indian boy sitting outside in the sun. He sat carving a piece of wood.

"See you," Michael waved as he left.

Eli came over to look at Dashwood's translation, "You know, I studied dead languages when I was in . . . "

As Michael came out, the young Indian turned and grinned. He reached into his pocket and withdrew an apple which he tossed Michael's way. It was immediately and voraciously devoured.

Michael felt unsteady as he was led along the face of the cliff past the ancient dwellings. Aftereffects of the peyote ceremony, he figured. He started wondering what it must have been like there 500 years ago. He realized he hadn't had thoughts like this the past 16 years. Any musings on the past had been bitter reminders he had none.

The two went up a ladder to the plateau and headed away from the ruins into the brush, where Michael paused to relieve himself.

In a short while, they wound their way to a clearing where The Bruja sat in meditation. As the two neared, her eyes opened and Michael felt instantly she probably knew more about him than he did himself.

"Sit here," she invited, motioning to a spot directly in front of her. As he did, the boy left.

"Would you like some tea?" she offered.

"Is it spiked?" Michael inquired with a smile.

For some reason he felt he could jest with her. He was right. She returned his smile and poured a cup which she passed to him. Michael took it down in one gulp and she poured another, the wind dancing wisps of gray around her forehead. Michael liked the way she wore her hair down. It had always bothered him that older women cut their hair or wore it up.

"So, you have seen yourself clearly," she said. "Your Gordian knot has been carefully unraveled and you are reborn. You are among the most fortunate, my son, the most privileged."

"I understand," Michael said humbly, "and I am truly grateful."

"Now you know what the Dark Lord from the east is seeking," she explained, her eyes aglow. Then a heaviness came upon her brow. "I knew he would come. I have felt his presence growing for some time.

"His people have long known the legend of *the one* drug. That which you drank is what many of the conquistadors of old were sent to find . . . by the Dark Lord's ancestors. Mineral treasures were but secondary, as they are now to the Dark Lord. Coronado's gold was supposed to have been a liquid."

Michael swallowed in awe, realizing he was privy to the inner workings of history.

"My people have long known of his legend," The Bruja went on, ". . . the drug of the wolf . . . his attempt to control. The irony is that which he seeks puts an end to his power; for once one has experienced the vision within, one has no further need for his drugs."

"Then, why not give it to him?" Michael asked.

"Because he would destroy it and all who know of it," she explained. "It would be lost forever. And my people have need of it. It will allow us to finally put away our peyote . . . to stop our retreating to the past . . . and bring us into . . . the present."

"But if *he* experienced it, wouldn't he change?" Michael questioned.

The Bruja smiled, "This is no *toloache* or *psilocybe* that grants to all its hallucinations, Michael. The formula only works in conjunction with the drinker's aspects. One must be ripe for the vision . . . as you were."

"How did you know I would be?" Michael wanted to learn.

She smiled again, "I didn't. But I knew you could not make a contribution until you knew yourself. Without self-knowledge we are destiny's pawns instead of its shapers. It was worth the gamble."

Michael felt he should respond, but was at a loss for how.

"When one is reborn," she continued, "it is like being a child again. There is a new period of growth in which it is desirable to languish. But we have no time for such luxury now. Unfortunately, Michael, you must become a man today."

Michael liked the strange pronunciation she gave to his name, putting the accent on the second syllable.

"I am very appreciative of everything," he responded, "but what have I to do with all that is going on here? I was tricked into coming here. I'm here by coincid—"

Michael recalled what Eli had said last night about there being no coincidences. She would probably have repeated it had he continued.

"We all play a part in a grand design," The Bruja explained. "Our lives flow in a direction inherited from destiny. We may fight against it, but that course is bound for doom. That is not what I meant by 'shaping.' Young man, haven't you fought against yourself long enough?"

"Yes," Michael confessed, shaking his head. Then a look of pleading entered his eyes, "But now that I know who I am, I want to enjoy it."

"It is not enough to simply know who you *are,*" The Bruja cautioned, her voice consoling at the same time. "You must be concerned with who you can *become.* And right now you must become a man of action. You must realize your purpose."

"I don't know that I have a purpose," Michael said, moving his hand in circles over the dusty ground.

"You know," she assured him. "But you fight it. It is not easy to become a man of action."

She realized he was not comprehending.

"What is it to the Indian, you may ask, if the Penitente are corrupted by El Conciliador and take over the Roman Church? The answer is . . . we believe the highest good comes from mutual cooperation and sharing. As a *bruja*, I know my knowledge of the arts must be used for the improvement of life.

"You, too, must play your part," she told him. "Today you will learn what has to be done. Tonight . . . tomorrow . . . it must happen. The choice *must* be action, for the Dark Lord is very powerful, and we alone cannot hope to defeat him."

Michael wondered what choice he really *did* have.

"The moon child is alive," she spoke out of the blue. "She is well for now. She awaits you."

Michael felt a chill run up his spine. He was just wondering about Diana. How did she know?

"Thank you," he said, clearing his throat. "But why do you call her that?"

"It's what she is," The Bruja responded dryly.

She leaned forward, and with her finger drew four circles in the dirt; filling in one, half filling another, drawing strange markings within the third and adding emanating rays to the fourth.

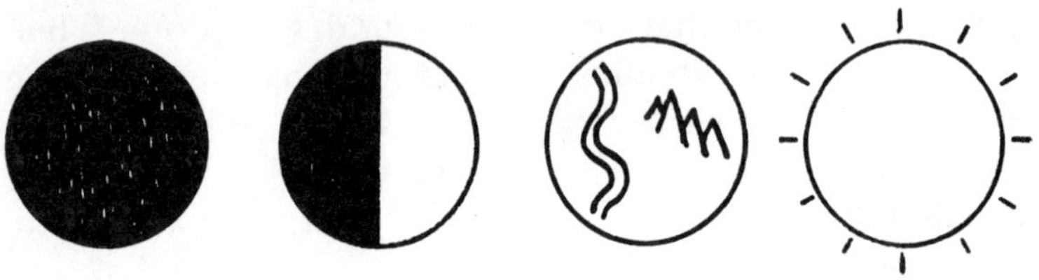

"These represent the major aspects of man," she said. "Each of these aspects is in all of us, but one always dominates . . . one is secondary, and so on.

"This first," she pointed to the filled-in circle, "represents the aspect of Darkness. The Children of Darkness, like the Dark Lord and El Conciliador, are malevolent. Though their numbers are few, their power is enormous. They are causers of death and destruction. They are anti-life, anti-beauty.

"This second," she said, indicating the half-filled circle, "is the Moon aspect. The Children of the Moon are suspended between light and darkness. In and of themselves, they are lifeless, detached. They need the Sun for their light and warmth. Their cold passion, often in the form of melancholy poetry, stirs the hearts of many, but never delivers enough to satisfy."

She leaned back, "I have heard it said the full moon raises the temperature but a few degrees. And so it is with these. In many ways they are the most unfortunate."

She pointed to the two halves of the circle, "Moon Children divide themselves into those of the Dark Side and those of the Light Side. One does the bidding of the Children of Darkness, the other bewitches the Earth and the Sun."

She held up her hand to delay the question about to issue from Michael's lips.

"This aspect," she said of the circle marked with symbols, "is the Earth. The Children of the Earth are the most blessed, for they are in tune with the existence we have been given on this planet. They divide themselves between the Water People and the Land People. The first are very much affected by the Moon Children, the others by the Sun.

"The Children of the Sun," she said, pointing to the last circle, "are our source of light and nourishment. Few in number, like their Dark opposites, they are the indomitable optimists . . . and therefore the least satisfied with things as they are. The world can never measure up to their lofty vision. It is also their misfortune often to be blinded by their own light reflected from the eyes of a Moon Child.

"So, four or six aspects," she said, looking up at him, "depending on how one chooses to look at it. All in each, each in all.

"When the dominant and secondary aspects within a person are adjacent . . . Such as Sun/Land, Land/Water, Water/Light Moon, Light Moon/Dark Moon, Dark Moon/Darkness . . . one's life achieves a stability. But when they are spread about . . . a Sun/Moon person, for example . . . there exists what you call schizophrenia. The personality is split because the life flow is out of sequence, is pulled in opposite directions. Do you understand?" she asked.

Michael nodded, fascinated by the old woman's dissertation.

"The woman Diana, like your other white goddess, is a Moon Child," The Bruja continued. "She was drawn to you for two reasons . . . reasons which confused her. Her Dark Side was attracted by whom you claimed to be . . . Ian Stone, your own Dark Side aspect. But being highly sensitive, she perceived the light and warmth that appealed to her more dominant Light Side. This is because you, Michael, are a Child of the Sun.

"And that is why she appealed to you. She reflected the light you have been hiding from yourself . . . your own light. Doubtless, this has not been rare in your life."

Michael's mind was ready to roam through the characters of his women, but she continued. "El Conciliador and the Dark Lord are both devils—one of the mind, the other of the senses.

It has taken much of my strength and the strength of others like me to balance the evil of the man who has others crucified for him. But if he and the Dark Lord were to join together, the power of their union would be unimaginable; certainly more than my people could hope to contain.

"Few could withstand the strength of these two. You may. Darkness cannot hurt the Sun. It shuns it. It fears the light. And that is why you were brought to us."

Michael looked as if he were about to say something stupid again. This was entirely too much mysticism for him.

"I know you are skeptical," she anticipated, "but these things were put into motion centuries ago. Again, ask not why you, but why we should be involved? We are not of the *anglo* civilization—a civilization that causes so much misery with its basis on the Moon. Ours is a happy civilization, for an Indian strives to be close to the Earth. But here in our little land the balance of all civilizations may now be in jeopardy. So we must interrupt our lives and do our part in this drama, even if it means many of us must die. We cannot allow the golden skull to be found."

Michael's throat was parched, "What am I supposed to do," he heard himself utter, "confront these 'devils'? I'm not a trained killer like my brother." It was the first time he had voiced the word, admitting his kinship to the outside world. He had a brother. *Had* had . . . He sighed deeply.

"You need not be," The Bruja kindly assured him. "All you need to know will be taught to you today."

"Mortez I could probably find, but how about this new character?" Michael wanted to know.

"Coyoteman will lead you there," she said gravely.

"I don't understand," Michael said. "I thought he was . . . I know he was seriously injured."

"He is," she nodded. "But he has agreed to play his part."

Michael was confused, "But how?"

The Bruja reached under her cloak and withdrew the amulet pulled away from Braden, the amulet that had transformed him into something inhuman. Too much mysticism? He had seen it, hadn't he?

"Will it work?" he asked.

"It must," she said, staring through to his soul.

Michael knew taking the drug would mean the Indian's death. It would burn him out. He also knew that with such displays of courage around him, he could not avoid playing his part. Or could he?

"What is my role, exactly?" he wanted to know.

"You must prevent the union of both the Dark Lord and El Conciliador, even the dominance of one over the other. The influence of this Penitente leader has already begun to interrupt the natural flow of the Roman Church . . . the return to its ancient roots before the Christ *makai*, a time when there was balance between the Sun God and the Moon Goddess, a time when poetry was as important as power. You are not educated in these matters, but Mortez and the Dark Lord are both from patriarchal orders. Beyond their other evils, these two men, together, would destroy the Church's happy regression. They would subvert goodness and attain incredible strength, becoming the cancer that would weaken the Roman Church as an important citadel of light and destroy the balance against darkness. This must be prevented at all cost. If this is beyond your comprehension, we will talk on it again later. Right now, the tribal leaders await you. You must be prepared to assume the role of Ian Stone once again. And there must be a plan."

Michael stood up. He turned and walked away. He was thinking about Meredith, his "white goddess." He remembered that she menstruated whenever there was a full moon, liked melancholy poetry and often wore a half moon on a necklace. Case closed.

Had his brother . . . had Ian Stone really fu—? Didn't he remember seeing a bruise on her face during that last awful confrontation. Maybe that's why she called him a "schizoid." She was wrong.

Michael sighed as if a curse had been lifted. He turned and walked back to The Bruja.

"Can people change their aspects?" he asked.

She looked up at him seriously. "With time and with great

pain and work one can change . . . most readily to one's secondary aspect. If you seek happiness, Michael Stone, you must touch the Earth. But it means coming down from the sky . . . a long journey . . . not an easy one to make," she smiled.

"But your question is about the woman, not yourself," The Bruja intuited. "She, also, would have to come down . . . from Moon to Earth. That is possible, but again, it takes much time."

Michael turned and began walking again. A discouraging bit of hope, yet something to hold onto. Tonight, however, he would need every little something.

Michael stopped after a few steps and turned to The Bruja again, "One last thing . . . You say Darkness cannot affect the Sun. Can Sun affect the Darkness?"

"We will see," The Bruja said dourly.

That gave Michael no comfort.

As he departed, The Bruja sighed. She had not told him everything she foresaw . . . her vision of death . . . of what could happen to him. But The Bruja realized her visions were now clouded with concern about the future of her people. She wanted them to have the chance to be a part of the new world, even though it would mean an end to *brujas* and shapeshifters and peyote. Her own wishes and fears had thus become too wrapped up in these events. She was no longer an impartial observer.

Michael's question had been proper. But the time for visions was over. Nothing save real events could give the answers now. The old woman was certain only of her fear for Michael . . . her fear for all of them.

26

The sun was setting in a blaze of blood red glory. For some reason it reminded Diana of the first time she went hunting. She had hired a guide to take her out on a preserve in northern England. The old hunter acted bored and told her to take her rifle, follow a path through the tall grass and fire if she saw something.

Diana had wanted to show him she was worthy of more respect and moved as quietly as possible through the brush until she heard a noise nearby. She saw a fleeting movement and fired impulsively.

The huntress practically leaped over the chest high growth in pursuit of her prey, only to find a young doe sitting silently in a clearing with blood spurting from its neck, each heartbeat oozing its life away. Diana fired again to put the poor animal out of its misery. Then she became very ill.

"Your last sunset," said a voice behind her.

Diana turned to see Nadja, the Gypsy woman, in the doorway. She wore the same black leather jumpsuit as the night before.

Diana smiled with the thought the bitch probably hadn't changed her underwear either.

"I saw your fortune in my tea cup," Nadja continued.

"You should drink herb teas," Diana countered. "They won't cloud your vision."

The Gypsy woman glared at her. Diana couldn't understand why there was so much hate for her in those coal-black eyes. What had she done to her? Unless the woman was somehow jealous of her relationship with Ian . . . She laughed at the thought.

In three strides Nadja crossed the room and slapped her across the face. Diana tried to raise her manacled arms, but of course could not. She would not again be given a chance to pose a threat.

"It's easy when I can't fight back," Diana taunted. "Take these off and then try it."

The woman whirled around and left, slamming the door after her.

Diana turned back to the window. The sun was down. And so were her hopes.

Meanwhile, El Conciliador was in limbo. The *morada* had been contacted. He had been invited to THE ONE's *hacienda* for their meeting. A message had been sent back thanking him, but suggesting the Interspec Foundation would be a more suitable place. No reply had come as yet. Nor had there been any word as to whether his "savior" would return. All Mortez was sure of was his doubt—doubt as to his forces' ability to match those poised around him.

But the reason there had been no reply concerning the meeting site was due to the fact the raven eyes of Radu Scotia were still closed. He was keeping to his Romanian body clock and was not to be disturbed.

Michael's eyes had, however, just opened. He had taken a short nap after his long strategy meeting with the tribal leaders.

No dreams again. Just as well, he thought. He didn't need any additional anxieties. What he quite honestly believed would be his last rest, Michael wanted to be uneventful.

But awake, he began to feel the weight of the responsibility being laid upon him. There were, Michael thought, too many chances for something to go wrong. If it wasn't for his "white knight" compulsion with regard to Diana, he would have been out of there.

Michael rolled over and found Eli sitting beside him.

"I'll be following you tonight," the old tracker said. "You know I can't participate, but I'll be there."

"Sure you can't make an exception?" Michael asked.

"I wish I could," Eli smiled, "but someone has to be sure to survive."

"Thanks," Michael nodded, "I needed that."

Dashwood appeared at the doorway of the adobe hut.

"It's time," he said.

Michael rose and put on his brother's clothing and effects. It was still hard for him to imagine having a brother. How nice it would have been, he thought, to trade clothes, argue, share good times . . . His mother . . . Who was she? What had she been afraid of? Who would harm her children? Or was she afraid they might be taken? By whom? Her husband? Who was his father? Why would he be a threat to her children?

The realization hit him . . . Not only had his own subconscious or some other part of his mind been hiding his identity all these years, so had everyone else. In fact, they started it! Now all Michael had to hold onto was his identity. And he was going to hold onto that for dear life . . . for his dear life.

"Hurry," Alex complained.

They went up to the darkened and silent plateau where a jeep waited for them.

As they drove, Alex turned to Michael, "The Bruja was telling me the Towa Indians have stories of a *sawish,* or witch cult, that used to hold their ceremonies in a secret cave south of Lobo Peak."

"When was that?" Michael was curious.

"In the mid-1800s," Alex replied.

"Terrific. I'm sure there's a hot trail," Michael said sarcastically.

Dashwood paid him no mind. "We've done some research on Mortez, too. Seems he's related to a member of the old Society of Thieves who roamed this area around the turn of the century. Legend has it they also had a secret cave for a hiding place. It's probably the same one."

"Alex, we're supposed to be tracking THE ONE tonight," Michael said impatiently, "not the treasure."

"Quite right . . . quite right . . . ," Dashwood trailed off, mumbling to himself.

They drove for another three quarters of an hour in silence. They had cut off the main road and were staying to the west of Taos and the Gypsy perimeter.

Michael wondered what the chef at the St. Bernard had cooked up for the last night of the ski season. There was no question he would rather have been there, eating.

In the midst of an arroyo they saw a campfire. The air was clear, but a chilly wind began to kick up. Michael was glad he still had a ski parka. Hearing the chattering of night insects, he wondered if they were cold, too.

Some sort of ceremony was being performed. It centered on Coyoteman.

Michael felt another chill run up his spine. It didn't matter the man would have died anyway . . . he was willingly going to a certain death. That took more balls than he had.

As they neared, Michael could see Coyoteman was near the end. He could not believe the Indian would be able to lead them to THE ONE.

Then his blood ran cold. Michael had a conscious realization death was also staring *him* in the face. Even up to that moment it had still been a fantasy, a game . . . an unreal game he felt he could have dropped at any time. But now he was a prime mover.

He was supposed to be a man of action, yet he was very

reluctant to become one. Michael had hoped a few more millenia of training were in order. Couldn't they understand the problem he had in facing all this now that he was just beginning to live? He just wanted to go home.

The Bruja came over to him. Michael was surprised at how nimbly she moved.

"Walk with me," she said, drawing him aside. "I will tell you two short legends from my youth as a final advice. The first concerns a shapeless, ugly, black form called *el basilisco.* The legend says, if it saw you first, you would die; whereas, if you saw it first, *it* would die." Michael thought there was going to be more, but she just nodded her head as if a heavy truth had been imparted.

"The other is a saying, really," The Bruja spoke again. " 'If you meet the devil, look not into his eyes, but stare instead at the spot where his third eye should be,'" she said, tapping the center of her forehead. " 'It will destroy his concentration.' "

The old woman extended her hand and opened it. There was a small gelatin capsule in her palm.

"Take this," she commanded. "I had it made this afternoon. Put it in your mouth. If you are given the drug Coyoteman takes, it may counteract it."

"May? What is it?" Michael asked.

"That which he seeks. The same you had last night," she responded with a gleam in her eye.

Michael laughed as he took the capsule from her. How ironic. He would be carrying the real treasure right into the enemy camp. That afternoon it had never been directly stated he would have to go into the enemy camp or meet THE ONE. But The Bruja's words confirmed what he had assumed might be the eventuality.

Coyoteman's head turned toward them at the sound of the laugh and Michael stopped abruptly. The Indian was ready.

Michael noticed the symbols painted on the man's body. Other than the markings, he wore only the skin of a coyote and a few pieces of jewelry.

Coyoteman raised the amulet to his lips as Michael, unconsciously, put his capsule under his tongue. The metamorphosis commenced.

It was extraordinary, and at the same time the most pitiable sight Michael had ever seen. Suddenly the dying Indian came to life. It was almost as if he were transfigured with an animal-like visage. He rose to all fours, glaring at the assembly around him. It started as a look demanding pity, but it quickly faded into a cold, harsh stare. He growled and snarled at them, then turned and scampered off into the night.

Michael was taken off guard. What were they supposed to do next?

Horses were quickly brought up. Shadow, the cousins and another Indian were already mounted. Michael and Eli took the other two. As he mounted, Michael's mind raced back to the last time he had ridden. It had been years ago. He looked down at The Bruja.

"Keep your wits about you," she warned. "The darkness will try to transcend and destroy your senses . . . what is most dear to you."

Her gaze bore into him. Both knew they would never see each other again.

"Good luck," said Dashwood, as he scurried over.

Michael smiled and then looked to the perimeter of the group where he saw Theresa staring somberly.

"*¡Yamo!*" he shouted to her as they rode off in pursuit.

The Indian camp had been set up between two Gypsy posts and at more than a mile's distance from the perimeter. The scouts had picked the spot as a weak link. Hopefully, they would be able to ride through without detection.

The object was to get word back to the tribal leaders once THE ONE's position was located. Then their plan could be set into motion. It was, Michael felt, a plan with a chance . . . as long as Braden hadn't shown up at his Master's doorstep and informed THE ONE Stone was dead.

And if he did? Then Michael knew he soon would be dead. There would be no chance.

Why did it have to be such a nice night, he wondered as they galloped along? Up ahead of them, Coyoteman was still in sight. Every once in awhile he would stop and howl into the night. For awhile, there had been no response. Now there was. His ears seemed to perk up and he headed in the direction of the sound. Before they knew it, he had disappeared.

"Oh, great!" Michael exclaimed.

"No matter," Eli said. "Here."

Eli handed him a signal receiver, "I put the bug we found at the *morada* in the pelt he's wearing. Stone would have thought of that. You must try to think of everything as he would. Your life depends on it."

Michael knew that, but also knew it would take constant reminding.

The howling of wolves grew louder, filling the night air. Then there was silence . . . even though the tracking device showed Coyoteman was near. Very near.

The terrain had risen to a higher elevation. They were into rocks and the horses had to watch each step. Suddenly, the animals began to spook. One of the Indians drew his knife as eyes appeared . . . all around them. Everyone drew knives. Low growls raised the hairs all over Michael's body. He could count over a dozen pair of watchful orbs.

There was a semi-human growl and one of the wolves yelped and snarled in defense. In the moonlight, Michael could make out Coyoteman bearing down on the creature's neck, ripping at it with his teeth. All eyes turned.

Michael felt a jab in his side. It was a small pistol Eli pushed into his hand, "Take it and get out of here. Go," he implored.

Michael spurred his horse through the pass. Coyoteman ripped himself off the wounded animal and, as Michael rode by, their eyes met for an instant. All Michael could think of was the torture going on within the Indian's brain. And he knew he probably couldn't imagine the half of it.

Coyoteman scampered along the rocks above him and was soon out of sight. Michael had no time to think of the scene behind him. He had to pick the best spots to quickly lead his horse among the rocks.

Michael was soon forced to dismount in order to find a path. He moved along slowly for hours, every few minutes checking the receiver with a small penlight. The signal had gotten very weak, but now it was getting stronger again. Then it was very strong.

Michael looked up and saw the Indian's eyes looking down at him from a ledge above. There was nothing left in them . . . no glow, no life. The low staccato noises of the automatic weapon he now heard were being wasted. The man was already dead.

Michael could hear the footfall of boots and reached for the gun he had been given. He got back on his horse and stood on the saddle to see over the ridge. A single figure could be seen moving in the direction of the body. Michael put one leg forward to find a foothold in the rocks. Just then, the horse decided to move. For an instant, Michael couldn't decide which way to go. By the time he opted for the saddle, it was too late. He fell, pulling his leg out of place as he landed . . . and the gun went tumbling into the rocks.

"Son of a goddamn . . . !"

Michael lay there for a moment, wondering how much damage had been done. He was making too many mistakes to be able to survive. He rolled over onto his side and felt the pain rise up from his hip. Michael ground his teeth in anger, "Son of a goddamn bitch!"

Holding his knife with a vise-like grip, Michael slowly crawled up the slope. By the time he reached the ridge, the guard had already checked over Coyoteman and was just putting a whistle to his lips. Michael rose up behind him on his good leg and stuck the fingers of his left hand into the man's back.

"Don't move," he ordered.

But of course, the man did; easily knocking aside the empty hand. Michael's response was automatic. His other fist plunged forward, burying the knife into the man's stomach.

Even as he acted, Michael's mind flashed back to the fourth grade. He remembered there was a class bully who always bragged how quick he was. Michael had thought of this ploy back then. His right hand had held a water pistol and everyone laughed when the bully's face got squirted.

Memories. How good it was to have them. But Michael knew he couldn't afford them now. And now it wasn't for laughing . . . though Michael did feel a macabre satisfaction along with the horror. He had not been aware the man in the Walkyries had died the other day; so, as far as he was concerned, he had never before killed a man. As awful as that was to the former medic, it was the first thing he had done right tonight. He was thinking like Stone. His brother lived inside him.

The whistle dropped from the man's lips and he slumped to the ground on top of the Indian. Michael was left holding the blade in his hand. Looking up, he saw the lights of a *hacienda* just a few hundred yards away. The goal.

"Holy . . . "

Michael reached down to retrieve the fallen guard's machine gun and felt an excruciating pain in his hip. Using the butt of the weapon for support, he made a slow circle. Each step brought new pain but it was bearable as long as he kept off his heel.

He crouched and drew the dead man's pistol from its holster. It was much nicer than the one he had dropped. Michael decided to slide back down the slope to his horse and hide it under the saddle along with the tracking device. He tied the horse out of sight and crawled back to where the two dead men lay.

Michael rolled the guard off of Coyoteman and removed the gypsy's jacket and hat. Putting them on, he slung the Mauser's strap over his shoulder, retrieved the whistle and limped toward the lights.

It was the longest, loneliest walk of Michael's life. Even though the land rose slightly, he felt as if he were descending into the rings of hell. Chills mixed with the cold sweat on his back. The blood was icing in his veins.

A waist-high wall stood a hundred yards from the *hacienda.* Sentinels were posted all along it. Michael put the whistle to his lips and blew . . . "Colonel Bogey's March." It drew attention . . . . plenty.

As he hobbled toward the armed camp, Michael played a guessing game with himself. How many machine guns were trained on him and how many bullets could strike him before he hit the ground? A lot, he figured. He began to wonder what it would feel like, but decided he could live without it. That made him smile. He went off key.

As he reached the wall, Michael took the Mauser off his shoulder by the strap and extended it to one of the guards, "I guess I have to check this here. But I would like to keep my whistle."

He went through an opening in the wall without breaking his limping stride. The guards, at first, stood dumbfounded. Then a patrol formed around him while a few men dashed into the direction from which he had come to check the flaw in their defenses.

"Take me to your *buli basha,*" Michael directed them.

His mind flashed to Alex. The man even knew Gypsy phrases. Amazing!

More lights went on in the *hacienda* as they neared. Michael noted the helicopters and the uplink facility. He was duly impressed.

Then the giant appeared in the doorway and Michael felt fear flow freely through his entire being. He wasn't sure who was bigger, this guy or Vincente; or who might win if they were pitted against each other. There was no question, however, either would make short work of him. The gorilla made a motion indicating he had to be frisked. Michael noted there was more an element of request than demand in the gesture. It calmed him slightly.

As he raised his arms, his wrists appeared from the jacket arms and a buzz went through the group around him. It had been Eli's idea to copy Stone's technique and create the wrist wounds of the nails. They were wrapped in gauze, but hints of the "wounds" were exposed from the wrapping and were noticed.

As the big man quickly and thoroughly frisked him, Michael quipped, "Easy on the back, please. Thank you."

Satisfied he was without weapons, the giant ushered him into the king wolf's lair.

"You must be thirsty," Nadja stated.

Michael had not anticipated her and was immediately struck by her sensuous beauty. She had a musky scent about her that overwhelmed him. They stared deeply into each other's eyes. Hers, at first, seemed cold, but then embers were stirred and they radiated a bit of warmth.

"A hot buttered rum would be nice," he said with a hint of a smile.

"Take Mr. Stone into the library," she ordered and left.

He was taken to the den where Diana had waited the night before. Michael remembered The Bruja's story of *el basilisco* and swept the room with his eyes. No one was there, only the samples of THE ONE's collection. Michael was impressed but purposely fought getting wrapped up in them. He walked around the showcases so he could be facing the door. Suddenly, the knob turned. Michael's eyes rose from the ruby commanding his attention to the red eye appearing from behind the door. He could swear it was a dead heat. What the hell could that mean?

Michael remembered The Bruja's other anecdote as well and his eyes continued up until he stared at a spot just above the entrant's nose.

"Welcome. Radu Scotia," he stated with a slight bow. He was dressed in charcoal slacks with a black cashmere jacket over a scarlet turtleneck sweater.

Michael's eyes wandered around the man's face before returning to their original point of focus. The man's amiability had taken him off guard; that and the impeccably-spoken English.

"Ian Stone," he replied, almost saying Michael Esmund.

"Most ingenious, your way of tracking me," he said, laying

on the table the amulet one of the guards had retrieved from Coyoteman's neck. "But I had hoped you would have followed poor Braden last night."

"I was a bit hung up last night," Michael said with an ironic smile, "and really wasn't at my best."

Scotia smiled as well, "I see your leg has been injured. We will have it attended to later. Sit. Sit." As he did, Michael was aware the giant had returned to the room. In his peripheral vision he could see the man held an unusual looking pistol. It looked like the kind that held knockout darts. Radu Scotia wanted him alive. It was a comforting thought.

"Had you heard of me?" Scotia asked as he took a seat across from him.

"Myths . . . fantasies. Nothing concrete," Michael shrugged as nonchalantly as he could. "I still know quite little."

"That's the way I wanted it," his host said, sounding pleased with himself. "I say 'wanted,' because now you have earned the right to know all . . . as I know all about you."

"You know nothing about me," Michael blurted without realizing why, thinking afterwards he had just made a great error.

But Scotia only laughed, "Nothing? Let me see . . . How about if I tell you it was one of my people who responded to your very first ad when you let it be known you had entered your new profession. It was I who gave you your first assignment in Paris in '68," he beamed.

Michael had been in Paris in '68. He had gone to Europe to set up his new life after first trying to reconstruct his memory at home. But, after his discharge, he learned his mother had died and found Ian Stone had no relatives or friends. It was too depressing. Paris was the ideal choice. Then it was the center of everything that was happening, as New York was today. He had taken a position in marketing with the international division of a pharmaceutical company, the same that eventually brought him back to New York. Perhaps, by coincidence . . . no . . . design, his brother had picked Paris as the place to go into the assassination business. Perhaps he was his pawn even then. How could he doubt it?

Scotia went on, "It was after that *I* gave you the sobriquet we share.

"Or before Paris . . . ," Scotia bragged. "In Viet Nam . . . Cambodia. I observed you during your tour of duty. At the time, I was solidifying my control of the Golden Triangle. A messy business . . . dealing with Montagnards and all the other riffraff. But I always insist on setting up the major operations myself. 'It's the hands-on touch,' as my grandfather said, 'that keeps one in tune with the realities.'

"Your prowess . . . your recklessness; they were well known. Not just to me; you gained the respect of your enemies.

"But you needed seasoning," Scotia observed, wagging a finger at him. "Prison was good for you."

"You had something to do with my capture?" Michael asked, almost looking him in the eyes.

"You know your comrades were all killed," Radu reminded him. "Rather think of my role as keeping you alive . . . so your mettle could be tested.

"You know, you were very unpopular with your captors," he told the astonished listener. "They finally told my people to take you off their hands or they would get rid of you. I could have brought you to me then, but there was that streak of the evangelist you have," Radu smirked. "It had to be dealt with.

"So, I had your rescue set up . . . at a very costly price, I might add. Very chancy, too, wasn't it? I almost lost my investment. But you survived . . . as you always do . . . A very admirable trait. I've always been amazed at how you can appear to be in several places at once," Scotia said approvingly. "You have done well . . . especially this week."

Michael still could not get over the fact he had had his brother imprisoned. Why?

"You see," Scotia explained, "all this was necessary . . . witnessing the hypocrisies of demagogs and sacrosanct leaders.

It had to be done properly, so you would hear me out before judging . . . "

"Nothing like being master of your own fate," Michael interrupted with mild sarcasm.

Scotia raised his hand from his thigh and gently waved it side to side, "Don't be deluded. In this world there is only one master of his fate . . . only one prime mover . . . and that is me," he said touching his chest.

"I am THE ONE. And that entity is more than my person. It is what I represent. My dynasty.

"Ian," he said, touching Michael's knee, "let me tell you about power . . . real power."

Michael was almost trapped into looking into Scotia's eyes, but held his gaze on point. Scotia felt there was something odd about the young man's look, but couldn't figure it out.

"I get ahead of myself," Scotia said sitting back. "Tell me first, where did you get your information about me?"

"From El Conciliador . . . Ramon Mortez . . . who got it from Velenari," Michael answered tersely.

Scotia nodded, "So, Velenari broke his oath to Metamorphosis. Metamorphosis is what I call my inner circle . . . an interesting collection of iniquity. Betrayal has happened only a few times in the past 500 years. Always the same ilk . . . feeble old men with religious backgrounds. That's why the family had traditionally shied away from religious types and politicos. They cannot be trusted." THE ONE mused, "But in the end, Velenari used his amulet, didn't he?

"So, you heard some things . . . ," Scotia returned to the present, " . . . but had the good sense not to pass them on; except, perhaps, to . . . "

"I don't pass on anything," Michael stated, now daring to look straight into the raven eyes, " . . . as Braden came to realize. Not even to the woman I trust you're keeping for me. I appreciate your liberating her," Michael deferred without breaking his gaze. He now felt a new confidence in his role.

Scotia smiled. "She is 'kept.' But she knows more than you think."

Nadja had come in with a tray of drinks. Her eyes blazed at the allusion to Diana.

"You've met my niece, Nadja?" Radu asked.

Michael stood and nodded to her, "Very lovely."

He noticed her nostrils flare in appreciation.

"Her hospitality might have ceased if we had come to think you were avoiding us," Scotia said with a wink. "But let us drink to our meeting and to our friendship."

Michael wondered what Stone would do? "Poor Braden" had been mentioned, but there was no hint as to his whereabouts or what he might have said or could still say. And what was Scotia's fascination with his brother? Why . . . ?

The hot buttered rum was passed to him. Now was the moment of truth. Michael took a sip. It was hot. This was going to be a very weird evening, he thought, if he started bounding about playing wolfman. Maybe it was time for the capsule.

Where was it?!

Michael felt around his mouth with his tongue, but it was gone. Had he spit it out or swallowed it? When? It had to be during his fall or fight. But either way, it simply wasn't there!

Nadja's hovering told him he was right in assuming the drink was drugged.

"Anyway," Scotia broke the silence, "I will tell you why I wanted you here."

He looked up at his niece, "You may leave us now, Nadja. Tell our guest that her friend has arrived. And remove her bracelets. But tell her to go easy on the furniture."

Nadja left brusquely.

"Your lady put away poor Braden last night," Scotia related. "Said he was a traitor." Radu shook his head. "Not really. He was only jealous of you . . . as Nadja is of your woman. They've figured out my purpose . . . to some degree, at least."

Michael wasn't listening. He was too preoccupied with wondering when he would start to freak out.

"But let's start at the beginning," he heard Scotia say. "No doubt, Velenari told this Mortez of Vlad Tepes. Yes?" He did not wait for a response, "Most thought him a cruel man. But his were cruel times. They don't appreciate the sense of humor he also had.

"Once some Turkish ambassadors came to see him," Radu bubbled, "but would not take off their hats to him. So he sent them back with their hats nailed to their heads."

Scotia roared and Michael smiled, knowing this was all filler. His host was waiting for the drug to take effect.

Scotia went on about Tepes' history and the Gypsy Queen. By the time he got to the secret of shapeshifting, Michael had become more involved in the fascinating story than his worries.

"What you have seen is only a 'speed' version to be used in emergencies. It allows one to die feeling the power of the wolf. But the full experience shared by my inner circle is a new range and intensity of emotions, new mental processes, incredible sensations . . . the power of the beast."

Michael felt a switch go on in his head. His veins began to swell with an orgasmic-like rush. And then, just as suddenly the switch seemed to click off. He felt the wave subside and, literally, flow back. It was like stopping a tidal wave and returning to the quietude of a pond. Had some residual effect of last night's drug helped him?

"Hemlock, belladona, nightshade, clarified baby fat, henbane . . . the old shapeshifting ointment with a special nectar . . . the power of a dynasty," THE ONE gloated.

It was amazing, Michael thought, how the drug paralleled that of Quetzalcoatl . . . but at the opposite end of the spectrum. He wondered why was he being told all this, even if he was Stone? What was the reason for the test through which he had supposedly been put?

Scotia became more animated as he continued, "By this century, we had influence over the majority of the planet's underworld . . . everything of consequence in the civilized nations. But influence . . . not dominion," he gesticulated. "We were like feudal lords, our power centered in the Middle East, Eastern Europe and the Mediterranean.

"My father realized the world was changing. Communications. World marketing . . . your cover field." Radu wagged his finger in imitation of his father, "The future would belong to the world powers, those who spread their control over the entire globe.

"Unfortunately, dear father tried too much too soon. He became too involved with the politics of things. Politics is too volatile, too changing," he observed. "And the politics of zealots . . . ," Scotia shook his head and then pointed a finger at Michael. "Never deal with idealists. They're too unpredictable. Our success has always been based on prediction.

"Better to have hands-off relations such as we had with the Ottomans, now with the Soviets, than to be involved in Ferdinand's assassination . . . Rasputin's. As a consequence of my father's folly, I was set up to deal with lowlifes like Stalin and Hitler."

Radu threw up his hands and looked at the Empire clock on the mantle. "Fortunately, my father died in 1939. I was only 23," Radu gloated proudly, "but I was determined to come out of the new War a superpower . . . but not a political one. I took a lesson from the Swiss . . . adopted a complete laissez faire neutrality . . . so whatever happened, the family would emerge what it now is . . . the drug supplier of the world! I knew if I concentrated on what we knew best, in the long run I would always win.

"And I was right," Scotia boasted. "It has been incredible! Unbelievable! For each of the first 25 years after the War, the family's annual income could easily pay off this country's national debt." He sat back and shook his head, "But since then, world affairs have accelerated even beyond my anticipation. There is incredible chaos here . . . everywhere . . . all of which will bring about a new dimension of change. The family must be ready.

"You see," he leaned forward and was tapping Michael's knee again, "in this Mortez is right. He has found a key to control the 'upper' world and it is beyond the scope of our underworld.

It is the key to the future . . . for ultimately, there will be no more ownership of property and materials, just managers of resources for the vast amounts of humanity. Drugs are just one of those resources.

"And, at that point in time, the pinnacle to the owners of those resources will be the owner of the chief resource . . . men's minds."

The bloodspot in Scotia's eye was like a flame ignited, "But, from what I have been able to learn about him, this Mortez, like Hitler, is another fanatic. He believes his own nonsense."

Scotia segued again, "If I had been ready at the time, I would have used the Nazi machinery. Velenari thought I was just being vulgar when I talked of the Church of the Eternal Joystick. No," he hissed, "I will use my resource along with Mortez's machinery and the faithful will taste of a new Host . . . when I am Pope of the Roman Church."

Michael's eyes widened. This guy was crazier than Mortez . . . and eminently more dangerous.

"I have been preparing, Ian," he confided in hushed tones. "My experience has taught me what it is like to be God. Listen—as something is begun, so it flows. Once something is set in motion, it is subject to the force that put it in motion. If, as they say, an explosion began this world, this dimension, then we must follow the direction of the blast . . . ride with it.

"But perhaps I confuse you," he said, seeing the puzzled look on Michael's face. "The point is simply this . . . We come out of chaos, and yet everyone seeks a unifying principle. Demi-gods spring up proclaiming the answer. It's happened since man's beginnings. But," he was pointing again, "the only real answers *are* in chaos. The human spirit senses this. And my drugs bring people into that realm of chaos for a brief glimpse. It is the closest they ever get to truth . . . to reality; for societies, religions, philosophies are all just built on fantasy.

"A glimpse, however, is all I allow the masses," Radu explained. "They are fools, and fools deserve not an ounce of sympathy . . . only what they can pay for.

"The real experience," he glowered, "is saved for my inner

circle . . . for the ones who are able to break the chains of society and learn to be truly outside the law. The experience is the ultimate release. That is why, in the end, even a Velenari will turn from his Christ to me.

"Men are greedy, my son. They think only in the short term. Their purpose is too narrow." He gestured to himself, "A god is beneficent. He confuses men by offering his grace to all. That, as I started to tell you before, is what real power is all about . . . setting things in motion and letting the players play.

"And so, the masters of evil dance on my strings," Radu smiled, moving his fingers like a puppeteer. "When the Mafia gets too greedy, I bestow my beneficence on the Blacks, the Cubans. When the Turks attempt to flex their muscles, I open the Golden Triangle. Those in Metamorphosis think they are *at* the source. True. But *they* are *not* the source. Remember this," Scotia lectured, "the head never allows the arms to know what it is thinking. It only allows them to act in accordance with how they are set into motion.

"Only I have it all," Scotia said, standing. "Only I own it all. And that is because only I have set it all in motion."

The passion in his voice had swept Michael along. He could feel his breath coming in short bursts. His fingers tingled so much he could not hold his mug.

Scotia looked at the clock again and smiled, "And that is what brings us here tonight . . . my setting you in motion, my sending you out to see the chaos and the weakness of men, even the most high . . . so I could bring you back to me to fulfill your grand purpose. Yes, it is time."

Time seemed to stand still as Scotia came directly in front of him. He took Michael's face in his hands and gazed into his eyes. There was no menace in the bloodspot.

"You have tasted the elixir, and yet it has no effect on you. This has been the case only with the rulers of the family. It has been our proof we are not from the beasts . . . but from the gods.

"Give me your hand," Scotia directed.

He took Michael's open hand and brought it between his

legs where his balls should have hung. Should have . . . there was nothing there.

"Everyone has his little cross to bear, or not to bear as in this case," Scotia smiled. "Now, I am truly the androgynous god. It was a hunting accident some 37 years ago. It would have left me without progeny had I not once been smitten with someone outside the clan . . . Your mother, my son . . ."

If he had not been holding Michael's wrist, the young man might have collapsed. Michael felt the breath evacuate his lungs. His eyes darted light years away in all directions as his brain overloaded. It couldn't be. And yet, it could.

Michael looked at Scotia and saw in him the shape of his own cheekbones . . . the nose.

And Stone had figured it out . . . figured it out, but wouldn't tell him because the Assassin knew he wouldn't have carried out his brother's order to kill their own father.

If Michael had had the strength, he would have laughed. Here he was, a jilted, unemployed runaway from himself in a New Mexican *hacienda,* surrounded by the treasures of fallen monarchies, with his hand in the crotch of a man who claimed to be his father and wanted him to take over as Emperor of the Drug World so the old man could retire as pope. Michael shrugged internally; in this world, why the hell not? And why not go for it? What would his brother . . . the real Ian Stone . . . have done?

"I had let you wander to complete your search," Radu continued, sitting on the coffee table and still holding Michael's hand in his. "You had to realize nothing is sacred, nothing is evil . . . that those terms are only the projections of weaker men.

"And I, too, have had to complete my search . . . so that the new world I envision can be realized. For 500 years our family has searched for *the one* drug that would allow us mastery over all. Some felt it was only legend, but I was sure it existed. And the answer, I am convinced, lies with the Aztec treasure."

Michael laughed to himself and came back to reality. If Scotia only knew . . . what he sought would establish the individuality of every man. There would be no Controller in a world where everyone could experience the vision he had seen. Oh, surely it would be chaotic . . . but in the true sense of chaos as he understood it . . . out-of-controlness . . . each person concentrating on his individual purpose while respecting the purpose of others. Scotia was correct that each would follow the direction according to which all was first put into motion. But he only saw the negative side of the coin. Michael recalled a feeling from his vision. The "big bang" wasn't filling a void in random direction. It had provided the energy by which the universe was molding itself into the orderly "design" of a new dimension. It wasn't reaching toward, but was already at the ends of the universe. And this universe would continue to perfect itself as long as there were no controls or limits put on the channel which linked it to any previous dimensions . . . the channel of choice.

Scotia was wrong. There *was* the "sacred" and the "evil." Michael began to realize evil as being no more than the unknown trying to frighten choice, trying to prevent that which was sacred . . . *possibility*. This man . . . his father . . . was Evil, the embodiment of the Devil, the mirror image, the other half of the brain.

But what could he do about it? Michael knew only that both sides of his brain wanted to leave the room alive. He had to cover.

"I'm supposed to kill you once El Conciliador gets his diamonds," he said.

"Well, of course," his father shrugged. "That's why I wanted you on the inside, to find out if he had what I thought he had as well as what his intentions were."

"He claims he has it . . . what's left of it," Michael managed a smile.

"Velenari told me much of what the Church received was melted into bullion. The thought has caused me no end of agony," Radu confessed. "But I know the best is there."

"If he has any formula for a super drug, he's not aware of it," Michael related.

"Of course he isn't," Scotia flared. "It's the pity of lesser men in high places. I see it all the time. There are so few with any breeding, any class."

Michael knew what was still on Scotia's mind, and that it was his ticket out.

"The 'where' I don't have yet. I will by morning," he said, confidently.

Radu stared at him. There was a visible crack in his usually emotionless face. He felt he had found his son.

Michael outlined El Conciliador's plan as it was learned through the Indians' powwow with the Penitente . . . his brother's plan in actuality. The Penitente women, dressed as men, would parade visibly in Easter procession while the men took out the Gypsy circle and sealed off Scotia from his elite guard during the meeting at the Foundation.

Michael felt a sense of pride in how he had changed his brother's plan. He had remembered that in college, one of his professors had a lecture series called Battle Nights. The strategies of great conflicts were analyzed for their strengths and weaknesses. Michael most enjoyed those involving great deceptions.

It was Michael's idea to have the Indian women in the place of the Penitente men as a false line of attack and have the Indian men come at the Gypsies from outside the circle. The Penitente allies who were already concentrated within the Gypsy ring would, meanwhile, attack both Scotia's and El Conciliador's elite guards.

The plan's only flaw was Michael was to be in charge of the operation against Scotia's elite; a flaw because he was going to clear out as soon as possible.

Scotia said he would agree for now to meet at the Foundation, and then would ask Mortez to come to him once Michael had located the treasure.

They discussed all they needed to discuss. Scotia felt he had a son. Michael felt he had done his part. But he knew he had reached his limit. He was going to lose it if he stayed any longer.

"Now, if you'll have Diana brought down . . . ," Michael concluded.

"Diana? I thought she'd be safer here with us," Radu smiled.

Michael played his last card, "Look, it's been a long day, and my kind of father doesn't make you beg for the family car. . . I need her tonight. And as for safer . . . not with cousin Nadja around."

Radu returned his smile, "She wants you. That's why she's jealous. Your heir must have Gypsy blood. You are exception enough. Although I admit she has impressed me.

"Victor," he turned to his bodyguard, "bring the girl down."

Victor hesitated.

"You two have not been formally introduced. Victor takes good care of me. Go on," he ordered the giant.

Victor left reluctantly. It was just the two of them alone. Michael could kill him and rid the world of . . . what? He was the flesh of his flesh. Michael laughed, "The Devil as my father."

"The Devil *is* the god of this world," Scotia retorted.

What could Michael say to refute that?

Victor returned and his face relaxed as he saw everything was all right.

"Well . . . ," Michael suddenly felt torn. Where, he thought, does one have evenings like this? He had proven he was a great actor. He had actually pulled off his charade. But whoever said, "Always leave them laughing," was a very wise man. It was a life-saving statement.

"I'll see you later, father," Michael said.

"When?" Scotia asked.

"At the right time," he smiled.

Radu laughed. He was relaxed.

"You are The One . . . ," Scotia bellowed.

"THE ONE, Junior . . . ," Michael said as they both laughed.

Diana came into the room. She was not sure which Ian Stone was there or what her fate was to be. Her teeth were clenched. She was tight.

"Look at her scowl," Scotia said, amused, but admiring. "She is a tough one."

Michael looked into her eyes and let her see who he was, "And loyal."

He was sure people outside of Metamorphosis who knew of Scotia were not allowed to live. Letting her leave was a concession. Michael wanted Scotia at ease about it.

"*La revedere . . . Pe miine . . .* Until tomorrow," Scotia saluted. "Ah . . . your leg. I wanted to have it looked at," he remembered as he saw Michael limp again.

"Tomorrow . . . After our work is done," Michael said.

"We will make them pay for last night," Radu scowled. "But now you have what in ancient times they called 'the sacred heel.' Watch out it does not prove your vulnerability."

Michael's coat was waiting for him at the door. He put it on and then bowed his head toward Nadja.

"*La revedere,*" he said, repeating his father's goodbye; and he and Diana walked into the night.

Michael did not look back. He walked in front of Diana toward the direction from which he had entered the compound. He was thankful for every step. The dream floated back into his mind . . . moving away from the dark one, "*In nomine Patris et Filii et Spiritus Sancti.*" He realized his thumb was making little crosses on his forefinger.

They arrived at the wall and a guard offered a flashlight. He turned his head in Diana's direction and she took it. They walked on with her casting a path of light in front of him.

Finally, they reached the spot where Coyoteman had fallen. The bodies had already been removed. There were only bloodstains. Diana helped him down the rocks and they were finally out of sight. Michael could hear the horse. Passage home.

At last, he turned to Diana. The light from the flashlight blinded him.

"Turn it off," he said, starting to shake. "Hold me, please," he pleaded as chills overcame him.

He couldn't be ignored; nor did Diana want to avoid him.

She embraced Michael and felt the tremors rippling through his body.

"Tighter," he begged and she gripped with all her strength.

As soon as Michael started to get on top of his chills, Diana took his face in her hands. As their eyes met by starlight, she herself realized how close to the edge they had been. They began to sob and stood there a good five minutes, first crying, and then kissing desperately.

"Let's get out of here," Michael finally said.

They walked the horse down to less rocky terrain and mounted. Michael had expected Eli and the Indians to pop up at any moment . . . at least, he hoped they would. He didn't want to consider what might have happened to them, or what still might happen to Diana and him.

Not too distant they heard the howl of wolves. Michael checked for the gun he had wedged under the saddle. It was still there. He put it into his belt.

In a short while, Michael could feel Diana was slipping in and out of sleep by how she bobbed against him. He realized it was the horse who was providing their direction. He had no idea where they were heading.

He saw a light . . . headlights. A truck was almost dead ahead, moving at an angle to their left. Michael reined, judging the vehicle would miss them by a good distance. The moon was lower and there were clouds, making them not too visible.

Then he heard the sound of another engine to their right. Diana was awake now and they both saw the truck's lights. They were directly in its path.

Michael wasn't sure what to do, but Diana went into action. She angled the horse left. There was some Utah juniper alongside a small ditch. They descended into the gully and dismounted. Diana made the horse lie down with them. Michael thought she must have been around horses all her life the way she handled it.

The truck passed within 50 feet of them. As the two looked up, it was beginning to change its direction, now angling to the southeast. The first vehicle they had seen was beginning to do the same. The Gypsies were moving in a zigzag pattern. It allowed them to observe their rear and flanks while exposing whatever lay ahead.

Michael realized Scotia didn't trust anyone. With a family history like his, it was understandable. He was, in fact, right to exercise a contingency strategy. It was a good lesson.

Diana brought the horse to its feet and prepared to mount.

"Where are we headed?" she asked.

"I haven't the foggiest," Michael confessed.

"We've been going north. Is that where we're supposed to head?" she asked, unsure of his meaning.

"Look, I just want to get out of here," Michael blurted.

Their eyes met in the remaining moonlight.

"Who are you?" Diana wanted to know.

"Michael Esmund . . . Stone . . . innocent. No, not so innocent," he said, looking down. "Especially after tonight . . . I had to kill one of the guards."

"Michael, do you understand what's going on here?" Diana questioned.

It almost sounded like a reprimand. Diana didn't have all the facts yet. Come to think of it, he didn't have all the facts on her either. It was time for show and tell.

"Two megalomaniacs are trying to corner the religion market; one with Aztec gold and the other with drugs . . . Simple," he said flippantly.

"That's his power?" she asked.

"Whose? Scotia's? He's known as THE ONE," Michael lectured. "His family has owned it all . . . ALL . . . for over 500 years. Right back to the original Dracula, if you can believe that. He set this whole deal up. He sets it *all* up. CIA, KGB, chairmen of international cartels, oil sheiks, Union Corse, Mafia . . . he's got the heavy hitters in all the places it counts paying homage to him. And I, supposedly, am his son."

Diana tried to put the remaining pieces together in her mind. "And the real Ian Stone?"

"My brother . . . supposedly."

"You . . . you didn't know Stone?" she asked, perplexed.

"Met him casually once in Cambodia," he flipped. "We weren't a very close family."

"Don't joke with me. Not now," Diana demanded.

Michael became serious. "I was a medic on a rescue team sent in to liberate a POW camp. The pilot of the copter I was in got hit and I had to bring it down. Unfortunately, I set down on a mine. Ian changed identities with me when he thought I was dying. But somehow I survived and woke up in a hospital as Ian Stone. I couldn't remember anything, so I've been making it up as I go along . . . whatever suited me.

"Stone found out I was his brother when he came back as Michael Esmund, but I don't think he knew who our father was until this week," Michael explained.

"Anyway, now I just want to be me . . . get the hell out of here and get on with my life." He looked directly at her, "I'd like you to come with me."

"Do you know who I am?" she asked him.

"Diana of The Light, Daughter of the Moon, Goddess of my Soul," he said opening his arms to the night.

She could not help but smile, even though she didn't understand his full meaning.

"As one of The Light, you know I can't leave. I'm sworn to protect the Church." It sounded almost rote.

"The Indians and most of the Penitente are working together. I worked out a plan this afternoon and fed Scotia Stone's old plan. They'll handle it. There's nothing more you or I can do," Michael tried to convince her.

"Did he fall for it?" she wondered. "This movement of the Gypsies . . . It could change things. We have to report it. Didn't you see those two attack helicopters? They could destroy a small army. Does anyone know about them? Michael," she said, looking into his eyes, "if we don't stay involved, there's going to be a lot of extra bloodshed. We've got to throw a wrench into Scotia's defenses."

"You want me to go *back?*" he asked in amazement. "I just came out of the jaws of hell! So did you. It was luck. Pure luck. And it took everything I have. Think of the odds of pulling it off again."

"Think of what happens if we don't," she responded. "I have a duty, and as a human, if nothing else, so do you.

"You might have had some shocking revelations . . . might know who you are now . . . And it took courage to do what you did tonight. If it was for me in part, I'm grateful," she said. "But think about this . . . You did it as Ian Stone. You proved you're a great actor. Now do something as Michael."

Michael was a blank. He could not respond.

"You think about it," she said. "I have to act."

"Where? . . . What are you going to do?" he asked, dumbfounded.

"I'm going to try and find El Conciliador. Without him, without the treasure, the whole thing falls through," she explained.

"You're going to kill him?!"

"I'm going to try. Though I haven't had to yet, it was always a possibility my job might require it," Diana said. "I need the horse, the gun in your belt and any help in directions you can give."

Michael never did respond to dares and this definitely was a dare. He handed her the gun.

"The helicopter went north and west of the Ski Valley. If we've been going north, head east. But don't do this," he pleaded. "You don't know the whole story. You don't have a chance."

"I'm tough," she said, looking straight into his eyes. "I'm Ian Stone's woman."

Diana mounted and rode east into the darkness.

It was goddamn ridiculous. What the hell was she trying to prove, Michael agonized? He limped off in the opposite direction, cursing to himself. How was he going to get anywhere on this leg? Moon people . . . Moonies . . . He recalled reading about white goddesses, vestal virgins who sacrificed their males for having made love to them. Cold, lifeless, barren . . . Where the hell was he going? And how does one disappear from a Radu Scotia? Being dead . . .

Man of action . . . The Bruja was right; he wanted a childhood. At least time to relive old memories. It was owed him. But what was owed to Coyoteman?

The world wasn't the way it was supposed to be. It figured . . . He was a Sun Child. But he was still avoiding it. Perhaps it was time . . .

It was also cold. His body heat had dropped. It quickly shot up. Michael had heard the cracking noise in time. His body was turning as the blade glinted above him from behind. Michael threw his weight into the stealthy attacker, knocking his arm away. He found himself rolling on the ground with the faceless body. The man was powerful, more powerful than he. He grasped the armed hand as hard as he could, digging in his nails until the man's other fist came crashing into his jaw. He heard his assailant utter a cry as he pulled from Michael's grasp. Was there help?

Michael blinked the sweat from his eyes and saw the blade poised above him, ready to descend. There was no time to react. It was the moment of death.

But the blade remained poised . . . long enough for his head to clear. He heard his would-be killer struggling for breath. Then the body slumped on top of him.

Bewildered, Michael rolled the man off of him. There was no one else there. He looked at the body and saw a trickle of blood on the hand holding the blade. Michael opened his own palm and observed the exposed pricker on the ring which had been part of his brother's effects. Hadn't he said he could have killed him even as he lay dying? Hadn't he been holding Michael's hand?

Shit, he thought. He could have settled the whole affair by shaking hands with Scotia. My God, he thought, he could have killed himself! Michael pulled the ring off and threw it away. Too soon. There was another sound coming his way.

Michael crawled behind some sagebrush. He heard hooves moving faultingly, as if searching. Closer now.

Michael squinted into the darkness. He felt he had no strength left. Damn. Where was the man's knife?

The sound was very close.

Then Michael laughed. What an ass he was.

And so was the intruder.

27

PASCUA

Ramon Mortez was starting to panic. His "savior" had not materialized. That he was alive, Brother One was sure, but that he would appear was becoming less probable.

El Conciliador had just received the latest reports on the Gypsy movements and, as scenarios were reviewed by the computers, one prospect loomed greater every moment—his general had defected to the other side. The enemy knew their plan. It would have to be changed.

Something was also worrying Radu Scotia. It was the dead Indian. Scotia didn't know much about Indians, merely that they were originally nomadic, like his Gypsies . . . only more passive.

However, this dead Indian had been no pacifist. How many more like him were there, Radu wondered? Where were they? How did they figure in? Answers. He needed answers. Did he have a loyal son or didn't he?

The Bruja, too, was troubled. She perhaps more than anyone understood the delicate human balance between good and evil. This balance was in great danger of being destroyed. But inherent in nature was also the possibility of reestablishing order. Michael Esmund-Stone was the key. But he was just a man, a man with choice. He could decline the task.

There had to be a contingency.

The old woman tried to clear her mind for direction. The answer was there . . . Nature always provided options . . . *had* always provided options. Perhaps this was uncharted territory . . . The cataclysm. The Final Battle.

It was the hour before dawn . . . the Hour of the Wolf.

Michael had had no trouble in re-entering the Gypsy perimeter. His trouble was four hours on the burro he found . . . or did it find him? . . . felt more like four days.

There had been no sign of Diana he could detect. He figured she would be at least an hour ahead of him, assuming he was going in the same direction. Other than hoping he was pointed her way, Michael really had no idea of where he was. He was following the direction of the burro, which seemed to pick its way through the rocks as if it knew where it was headed.

Michael's thoughts had been drifting back to childhood . . . to all the new memories flooding back to him . . . things he might never have a chance to think of again. Behind it all, he was feeling sorry for himself . . . losing his optimism.

In the distance, Michael could hear the howling of wolves. He hoped he wouldn't have to face them again. He hoped Diana wouldn't, either.

It was time to unkink. Michael dismounted. His back was killing him, inside and out. He still could not put his heel down.

There was another howl and the burro bolted. Michael tried to hobble after it. He tripped over a rock and fell. The whole thing struck him as funny and he started laughing.

"Great vacation," he muttered.

He wanted to send postcards; the first to his brother . . . "Wish you were still here . . . "

Michael started to rise. Losing the burro would be the last straw. Then he noticed a hoofprint in the budding twilight. It had to be Diana's horse! But there seemed to be smaller prints as well. They weren't paws, however . . . not wolves'. Michael was savvy enough to know that. But the light was too dim for the "seasoned tracker" to figure out what they really were.

Where the hell was the burro? He scrambled over the rocks and listened. Nothing. Michael crept forward. Then he heard something.

He moved forward and saw a clearing. The burro was there, standing still. Something else was making the noise. Michael crept closer. What the hell was he doing, he wondered? All he had was the dead Gypsy's knife.

Michael decided the sound couldn't be a person. No one else except him would make that much noise. He heard a bleat and stood up, "Baa, yourself."

He was about to laugh again when a hand grasped his mouth and pulled him off balance. He felt the barrel of a gun at his head. Then the click as the safety was reset.

"Damn it, Michael, don't do that," Diana whispered.

He went limp against her, "Jesus Christ! I could have wet my pants."

"Get off me," she demanded, unamused.

"*You* pulled me back," he joked. "Give me a minute."

He turned his head and brushed his cheek against hers, "Did we win yet?"

"You Americans are impossible," she exploded. "So damned naive."

"But gutsy," he retorted, playfully.

"Naive," she insisted.

"Maybe," he gave her. "But I'm here and willing despite myself."

"Quiet," she ordered. "Did you know you were behind me?"

"Not really," Michael confessed. "Why?"

"I've sensed someone," Diana said, worried. "I thought it might be Loudmouth."

"Eli?!" Michael exclaimed. "I only wish. I'm afraid he might not have survived the wolves."

"You found out who he is?" She was surprised.

"I told you there was a lot you didn't know," Michael lectured. "He's part of some Jewish intelligence group called Binah. His beat is making sure everything's kosher in the Church. He's not the enemy."

Diana was silent, trying to compute the new information.

"So what's with the goat?" he inquired. "And where's my horse?"

"I found the goat wandering out here when the horse went lame," Diana told him. "It threw a shoe and split its hoof, I think. I left you the light, remember?"

Michael didn't want to tell her he probably left it in the ditch where they hid.

"Great!" he mused. "We have a gimp-menagerie. Tell you what . . . I'd give you my burro, but I can't walk. Are goats rideable?"

"I don't think I'd get too far," Diana frowned. "Does any of this look familiar to you?"

"Just you," he said. "You wouldn't like to make love, would you?"

Diana smiled, "It's not that I wouldn't . . . we just don't have the time."

"Actually, peyote seems to have dulled my appetite anyway," Michael confessed. "You really think we're going to be able to do something?"

"We're going to try," she assured him.

"What the fuck . . . right?"

"Do you always get blithe when you're scared?" she wanted to know.

"It's when I stop taking myself seriously," he blurted. Michael thought about that. It hadn't happened in a long time.

Faint glimmers of dawn began to backlight the mountains to the east. It was *Pascua.* Easter Sunday.

The goat bleated and started toward the light.

The air was getting warmer. Michael surveyed the appearing horizon as they moved on, he riding and Diana on foot. Something to the south looked a bit familiar, but the perspective he had could not quite bring it home to him.

The goat became their point man, bleating as if for a lost soul. The animal had climbed a rocky slope and stood out against the cloud-spotted sky building in luminescence. It was as if flames were trying to leap over the mountains and get higher with every bound. It reminded Michael of a dream.

Then the goat scampered down out of sight as if it had spotted something. Diana and Michael looked at each other. He dismounted and followed her lead. Both of them felt a bolt of adrenaline. There was something to be seen.

The tips of the high rocks began to glow as they reached the crest. Over they went and then down after the scurrying animal. Its bleating echoed in the little valley below as it headed into what now appeared to be a cul-de-sac.

The sun began to peak above the far horizon, shooting its first rays westward. A needle-like shadow began to run across the valley in pursuit of the goat. They both turned automatically to see its source.

At the top of the rise opposite them was a natural obelisk. As the sun continued its ascent, it stood out as a long needle. Then, suddenly, the needle had an eye.

"Look!" Diana cried.

Michael turned back. The shadow of the needle now stretched down the valley and ended at the cul-de-sac. The eye formed a pinpoint spot of light on the rocks where the goat stood. Then the animal disappeared.

"That's it!" Michael yelled. "Quetzalcoatl's tomb! . . ."

Michael began bounding down the rocks on one leg with Diana in hot pursuit. By the time they reached the bottom and ran the natural gauntlet, the sun had moved and Bel's eye no longer cast its light. If they had not fixed the spot in their minds, it would have been near impossible to find.

A large rock shielded the opening. They had to step up a

few feet and go around it. Then it seemed as if they were staring into another wall of rocks, but these were slightly set back. The opening to the tunnel was behind some brush in the shadows to the right.

The bleating of the goat echoed off the tunnel walls. Their laughter joined the sounds as they hurried along . . . until they reached the end. Then Michael stopped short.

"Give me the gun," he whispered, without looking back.

"Can you use it?" Diana asked.

He looked at her, his lip pursed and his extended hand twitching impatiently, "Just give me the damn gun."

Who the hell did she think she was, he wondered, the Vatican Hit Lady?

"Okay. After you." Michael decided not to demur.

Diana peered out. In the center of the open space, the goat was bleating at the natural stone altar on which its sibling had been sacrificed. Some instinctual bond had brought it back to mourn. Ramon Mortez would have no remission of his sins.

Michael peered over her shoulder. No one seemed to be around. Slowly they emerged from the tunnel and split, each following the circumference of the courtyard's almost perfect circle. But half way around, Michael could no longer control himself. He hobbled to the center where the charred bones of the sacrificial goat lay, and then fixed his gaze at the entrance to the temple tomb. In the rock over the entrance was the sign of the god Bel Alex had shown him. This *was* it!

"Come on," he yelled, and like children they both dashed inside.

They stood stunned in the dim light, looking at each other in wonder. There was nothing except a large wooden table and chairs, a kneeler, a few *bultos,* a painting, a tapestry and a crucifix hanging from the ceiling.

"Perhaps he moved it all to his home," Diana speculated.

But Michael didn't buy it. "Look around," he said, lighting one of the torches lining the near wall. "There must be something."

Diana examined the slightly askew painting.

"Look at this," she laughed, removing a small pistol that had been taped to the back. "It seems our friend is prepared for entertaining guests."

Michael thought for a second.

"Take out the bullets and put it back," he directed. "Let's find if there are any more goodies around."

Michael sat at the head of the table and felt underneath it. There was something . . . were two things, in a hollow. He removed the first.

"Voilà . . ." He exclaimed in wonderment. "What is it?"

Diana came over to look.

"Gas pellet," she explained matter-of-factly. "Cyanide."

He pulled out the other object—a small gas mask.

"Well . . . well . . . well," he mused. "Can this be detonated and put back so you wouldn't know it?" he asked her.

Diana looked it over, "I wouldn't chance it. But I might be able to jam it so it couldn't be triggered."

"Fine," Michael nodded, leaving her to work on it. "Now, what else? What else?"

He went over and knelt on the kneeler in front of the crucifix to view the cave from that perspective. "Look at this," he pointed to the crucifix. "It's Mortez's face!"

Indeed, the *Cristo's* head was a likeness of El Conciliador, a depiction of him as his own suffering god.

Michael rose and approached the cross. It was suspended from the ceiling by a very old chain, yet was also affixed to the wall by another chain that ran through a hole in the bottom of the tapestry.

What a shame to ruin such a nice tapestry, he thought. And why was it necessary? Michael looked behind the cloth and saw cuts into the rock facade. He stepped back and pulled on the bottom of the cross as Diana watched in amazement, "Open *sesamè.*"

A makeshift door of rock-covered wood opened in the wall.

It was about four feet off the ground and perhaps a yard square. A small folding ladder was attached to the inside.

"Grab the torch," he said without looking back. "I think you're going to like this."

Diana quickly grabbed the taper while Michael pulled down the ladder. They climbed together and, as the light illuminated the interior, they were dazzled by what they saw.

"My God!" Michael uttered.

Scattered in front of them was Montezuma's treasure . . . or, rather, what was left of it. Yet it *was* fantastic . . . gold and jade masks, daggers, carvings and artifacts of every kind . . . the best of what had been.

There was a ladder on the other side of the wall as well. They climbed down into the chamber and reveled in the booty, laughing all the while.

And there, on a small gilded table with a jade top, Michael saw the golden skull. He became silent as he went and picked it up. He turned it over and, indeed, there was a skull within. Michael treated the object with reverence as he righted it and looked at the back. A chill went up his spine as he looked at the Ogam markings. This was a part of history . . . a man who became a god.

"Look at this!" he exclaimed in awe, knowing another man who was mistaken for this "god" had caused the death of a race, of an empire.

Michael, now, began to appreciate the events with which he was involved. Diana had been watching him and sensed his understanding.

As he replaced the skull, however, she sensed something else. The goat had stopped its pining. Something had disturbed it.

"Michael . . . ," she interrupted him.

He had noticed the silence also. They quickly climbed through to the outer chamber and looked out into the open arena. The goat had just disappeared into the tunnel and was beginning to bleat again. They had not mourned with it and so it sought others.

"Damn animal," Michael cursed. "Where's that other gun?"

"I already emptied it," Diana replied.

"Great . . . "

Too late. They heard movement in the tunnel and ran across the courtyard, each to opposite sides of the opening. Diana held her gun ready to fire.

"M..M..Michael . . . D..D..Diana . . . It's A..Alex . . . ," came Dashwood's voice.

"Alex?!" Michael was astonished.

In a moment Dashwood emerged with Red Fox and Long Claw.

"This is it, i..isn't it?" he bubbled.

"This is it," Michael admitted. "But how the hell did *you* get here?"

"Quite simple, my boy. Eli bugged your saddle. He gave us one of those tracking gizmos, like Diana's. Once we got to the horse, your other animal friends led us in," Alex related, pleased with himself.

"Then Eli's all right?" Michael asked.

"Thanks to the boys here," Alex deferred to the Indians. "One of the other chaps was badly clawed, but he'll survive.

"There've been a few changes in strategy," Alex went on. "I'm sure this will cause some more. We were using CB radios to relay messages, but there's been jamming since we tracked you to the *hacienda.* It was quite fun. We all have code names. The Bruja's the Bitch, I'm Finder, Eli's Tracker, Diana's the Angel and you're the Ghost."

"I'm glad someone's been having a good time," Michael interrupted sarcastically.

"Well, let's not dawdle," Dashwood said. "Let me see it."

Dashwood was overcome.

"Amazing! . . . Truly amazing," he repeated over and over.

Alex went immediately to the skull. Michael sat by him as Diana and the two Indians looked over the various other pieces. It was like trying to pick a favorite out of an assortment of candies.

"Amazing how they gilt the skull," Dashwood commented. He pulled out a notepad and wrote as he looked over the skull. He started mumbling louder and louder as he continued. The others stopped their activities in anticipation.

"My God!" he finally exclaimed, looking up at them. "There's more!"

"What?!" Michael gulped.

"Remember my telling you of a secret chamber Cortez never knew of?" Alex reminded him, " . . . Montezuma's surprise for him? It says here the 'untouched' works . . . those not profaned by Cortez, I guess . . . 'lay with Quetzalcoatl's body in the inner chamber.'"

"Isn't this the inner chamber?" Diana asked.

"It is 'inner,'" he replied, "but there's no body. And I don't think they'd let it decompose; not if they went through all the trouble to gild the head. Many of these types of temples have more than one inner chamber. I would venture to say there's got to be another."

Alex pointed to the opposite wall. They all went to check for indications of an opening . . . all, except Michael.

"Wait a minute," he interrupted. "Don't we want to get this stuff out of here before Mortez and Scotia show up?"

"That *was* the plan," Alex said, "but now I don't think we have the time. Besides, I've got a better idea."

Just then Red Fox found a loose rock.

"Good man," Alex congratulated him. "Easy. Let's not disturb things too much."

Diana understood, having guessed his plan. "You're going to put all this in there. Right?"

"Correct . . . assuming it fits," Alex shrugged.

They all worked to reopen the cavity sealed for over five centuries. Daylight was now coming into the natural atrium and was spilling into the first chamber. Flecks of light were beginning to dance around the walls of the second chamber as well.

The group worked feverishly to ease the stones out of place without having them all tumble down. Finally, they exposed a wall of dried mud, like the covering of an adobe structure. Alex carefully pierced the layer and air was sucked into the inner vaccuum. All lights were focused inside.

"Good God!" Dashwood exclaimed.

"Holy sh—!" Michael went breathless.

They quickly widened the hole so they could enter.

The chamber was not as large as the first. In that aspect it was like most of the inner chambers of the cliff dwellings. But what it contained was infinitely more breathtaking than the outer chamber.

Only two could enter at a time in order to move around. Alex and Diana were the first team.

"Look at this!" Alex said excitedly as he came to the opening with a sword.

There were rubies set into the hilt and scabbard.

"This had to be Quetzalcoatl's sword," Alex postulated as he examined it. "It's not Aztec, although they might have added some stones. It's not Celtic either," he then observed. "I would venture to say our god-man was actually Phoenician or some such. This is an incredible find!"

"Someday Scotia will be found buried with a hypo," Diana joked.

It was so unlike her, Michael cracked up. Alex smiled, and then turned serious.

"Michael, if we can hide all this treasure, there will be no deal between Scotia and El Conciliador. What's more, even though it was Mortez's money that put people in high places within the Church, Velenari was the front man. With him gone and Mortez's funds reduced to what his banks have on hand, his influence would be severely crippled. He might never recover," the older man reasoned. "What I'm getting at . . ."

". . . is that a lot of people don't have to die today," Michael finished.

"Precisely," said Alex.

Michael crawled past him into the chamber. He looked at the wonders around him. These were things perhaps no other *anglo,* including Quetzalcoatl, had ever seen. There was a golden throne with winged and plumed serpents, one of the manifestations of the god. Michael sat on it and gazed upon the riches at his feet. Any one of them could set a man up for life. But how many more deaths were they worth . . . how many more than the thousands who died in the events leading up to their being there?

"How has the strategy changed?" Michael asked in a low voice.

"The Gypsy ring is vigilant to both the front and rear," Alex explained. "Indian women, dressed as men, are on both sides of them. The attacks are to be directed only at the two strongholds. You know, the Foundation isn't more than a few miles from here."

"It won't work," Michael said. "Scotia has two attack helicopters that could wipe out more men than you could send against him. Even if the Foundation was taken, we'd end up having to defend it against him. Why not just send everyone home and let the two of them battle over nothing?"

"We couldn't be sure the confrontation would be fatal," Diana reasoned. "El Conciliador might fall under Scotia's thumb and, even if they didn't find this chamber, Scotia might decide to finance the corruption of the Church for his own ends."

Michael knew she was mostly right, even without knowing all the facts. Scotia would end up believing Mortez about the existence of the skull. He had it in his mind to believe something would give him the secret he sought. He wouldn't rest until it was found.

"So, what's the answer?" Michael asked, knowing whatever it was would have to involve him.

Diana sat at his feet, looking up at him, and said, "Cause friction. Get them to come here. I'll hide the gun under the table out there . . . ," she hesitated, " . . . and you can kill them both."

Michael looked at her as if she had leprosy. He bolted forward through the opening.

"Screw you. What do you think I am?" He looked back at them, "Screw all of you . . . "

Michael waved his hand as if dismissing the other four and hobbled to the ladder. He hopped up and over, his pulse racing.

"What side of the goddamn table?" he yelled back without turning.

Diana had to hold back a sob welling in her throat, "Opposite end from the gas."

He stopped, "How will you know where I am?"

"Shadow is outside. He'll give you the bug from your horse," Alex said, pulling out his two way radio. "We'll meet later at the Pueblo."

Michael looked at the table and tried to picture the situation he would have to create.

"Middle . . . opposite the entrance," he yelled back to Diana.

Michael limped through the tunnel and out into the cul de sac. On the rise above, Shadow was fixing the shoe of the lame horse. There was just one other horse and Michael realized only Alex rode on their way there. The Indians were shapeshifters like Coyoteman. They probably did their number to fight off the wolves and then led Alex across the terrain in the dark on foot.

As he exited the tunnel, Shadow turned and watched him. Michael wanted not to look at him. He realized he felt guilty for Coyoteman's having to die and did not want to see any incrimination in his brother's eyes. But as he passed under him, Michael did look up and tried to smile. Shadow smiled back and tossed him the bug. Michael looked at his only link to his allies and put the object into his pocket. He went over to the burro that was standing there, patiently waiting for him, and patted the animal. Michael again wondered if he himself was not the biggest ass of all. He swung his leg over with difficulty and the animal started up the slope.

Michael had no idea of what he was going to do . . . Stop men from dying . . . figure out a way to get the two enemies to the cave. He realized there wasn't much time to figure out how to do any of that. For all he knew, he could already be too late. Then what?

He'd go home. Enough was enough.

The burro took him out of the depression and over the rise. Michael now realized what had seemed somewhat familiar to him before was the back side of the plateau on which the Foundation stood. It was logical Mortez would situate himself near his booty. He spurred the burro toward it, sighing as he looked up into the lightly clouded sky.

At least it was a nice day. Yes, it was a good day to die.

28

The bluish pasqueflower waved in the breeze. The blossom was being observed by Theresa Kittinger as she and her Indian sisters, dressed as men, crouched among trees and rocks along the foothills facing the gypsy ring. Her thoughts were of picking the flower and taking it to church, there to lay it before the statue of the Risen Lord.

The sky was the same shade of blue. It was being watched through the narrow, wrinkled eyeslits of an aged Penitente. He did not want to be lying, shotgun in hand, on the slopes leading to Scotia's encampment. And he would rather bend his thoughts to singing in procession than wondering if he was going to die today. Most every man encircling the plateau felt much the same.

Even the Indians and those Penitente who wanted to be in on the attack of the man who they felt perverted their ancient brotherhood began to wonder what they were doing. This was a day for celebrating resurrection, not causing death.

Michael would have liked to have been occupied with such elevated thoughts. Unfortunately, each step along his short journey brought him closer to believing he'd have to be the sacrificial lamb so everyone else might survive. He was, in fact, trying to come to an acceptance of his fate.

The young man tried to reason it out as a way of overcoming his anxiety. Malaise . . . That was a possibility. But it would have been better last week, when he had had no memory of the past.

Duty and obligation . . . the old good-of-the-many-versus-the-individual tack. But unselfishness was not part of his memories.

Death as being the first real thing a person does for himself . . . Again, something that might have worked last week. But now it would no longer be a "first." He *had* done some things for himself.

So, what was he doing here? Duty and obligation out of malaise . . . It was all too confusing. Couldn't he come up with a better way . . . some alternative to dying?

Maybe he didn't have to be so self-rejecting. Perhaps he *could* pull it off. What if there was the possibility he could succeed?

But the problem was, Michael had no idea of what the elements of success were . . . not this new non-dollar oriented success. He wasn't experienced enough with real life. Life . . .

Michael suddenly realized he was being watched.

"*El difunto,*" a hidden Penitente pointed, thinking he was seeing a ghost.

"*Del otro mundo* . . . ," gasped another, also believing it was a being from the other world.

A few, more daring, moved into the open from their concealed positions among the rocks.

The burro stopped and Michael looked at the poorly armed, impoverished souls . . . probably the last vestiges of piety in what he thought of as the big business of religion. He had been touched by them this past week, had become envious of their fervent belief. And the dark night of his soul had touched them as well.

Now they thought he was the crucified *Cristo,* risen and riding amongst them. A miracle.

More of them came from their hiding places and began to descend the rocks. Only a few of the Indian leaders knew of the other "Stone"; so to these, some of whom had also been in the amphitheatre on Good Friday, his appearance was just as miraculous.

One of the men approached and spoke as he started to go down on one knee, "*Mano,* what would you have us do?"

"I would have you never kneel before any man," Michael responded.

The man was confused, "We are simple men. We . . . "

The man's eyes watered. Michael suddenly realized both he and they were all children in need. He had never before let out much of his real thoughts or feelings because he never knew who he was. He had always felt he was living in a dream . . . Well, it *was* a fantasy. But now, faced with the possibility of death, he knew what he wanted to say to them . . . and he found both his voice and a plan. "Today is too nice a day for dying," he said. "Let us go pray. How far is the old *morada* in Arroyo Seco?"

"Maybe nine miles," the man answered.

"You lead the way," Michael directed him. "Send someone ahead for a priest to say mass there."

Michael spurred his burro on while the man raised his rifle in the air, gesturing to those hidden. Then he brought it down, barrel first, into the ground.

A cheer went up from the rocks. Men appeared and began to descend everywhere around them, falling in behind the burro in a procession along the route to Arroyo Seco.

El Conciliador was apprised of the situation immediately. He came up from his underground den and peered through heavy lenses into the valley below. There was his missing general. Yet he was confused. What were all these Penitente and Indians doing there in the first place? Who had turned them against him . . . THE ONE? He was consoled only by the power of his general to lead them away. He would have to get word to him about the changes in his strategy. Mortez's pulse accelerated. The day would yet be his.

"Send the helicopter. Tell Stone we must talk," he ordered.

Michael heard the whirring of the blades as the helicopter lifted off from the plateau above. It quickly moved over them and dropped up the road.

The men in the procession began to ready their weapons, but Michael spoke softly to the lead man. "Tell them to put their guns away."

The signal was given and, the weapons being lowered, the four soldiers from the helicopter approached.

"El Conciliador wishes to see you," one of them said gruffly.

"Tell him," Michael started to say and then wondered what he was going to tell him, " . . . he'll have to meet me at the *morada* in Arroyo Seco. I want to conclude a deal, not start a war."

"And what of the others surrounding us?" the soldier asked indignantly. "What do they want?"

Scotia's men had to be in the area. They, too, were probably trying to figure out what thc hell was going on. Michael realized that, had he not pulled them off, the men in his procession would have served as Scotia's first wave. He also realized his father had gone ahead and deployed his men without waiting for him. Perhaps there was no way to outsmart him.

Michael remembered playing chess with a younger cousin when he was around 14. Was he really his cousin? Michael would set up brilliant strategies, but the boy would always make some stupid, illogical move that would throw his strategy completely off.

Perhaps there was no way to outsmart Scotia. His only chance might be to "outdumb" him; make some stupid, illogical move to throw off his father's game.

Michael turned to the slopes and yelled, "Send down an emissary. I want to get a message to the *hacienda.*"

Nothing.

"No message, no meeting," Michael yelled. "No meeting, no deal."

Nothing. Then, someone stirred . . . a lone figure with a Mauser strapped over his shoulder. Others appeared with weapons ready while the Gypsy descended and came to him.

"I have a message for your *buli basha.* And you listen, too," he told El Conciliador's men. "I want all your men called off. I want all those here and all the Gypsies surrounding the Taos area, plus everyone," he specifically addressed both the Penitente leader and the men from the helicopter, "surrounding our visitor's *hacienda* to come to the *morada* at Arroyo Seco. In addition," he told the Gypsy, "I want one of the Indians to take one of your men and one of the men in the chopper to the Pueblo. I also want a similar trio to go to the Puye Ruins. All the tribes are to be invited, too.

"Puye is normally an hour and a half away," he told the gypsy. "I want it reached in one.

"What time is it now?" Michael asked, turning to one of his men.

"Eight," the man said.

"Then I want everyone there . . . *everyone,*" he emphasized, "by 11:30.

"All weapons are to be unloaded, and both weapons and ammo are to be put into the *morada's* back room. Understand?" Michael asked.

The men nodded, understanding, but mystified.

"Form joint inspection crews and meet everyone at least a half mile out of the town," he directed them, now feeling on a roll as the ideas came to him in random fashion.

He addressed the chopper pilot, "Now this man," he said, referring to the Gypsy, "is going back with you to El Conciliador and is going to be given $50,000. Then both of you are going to go to your *buli basha* for another $50,000," Michael told the stunned henchmen.

He was remembering a scene from "Bananas," his favorite Woody Allen movie. Some Latin American rebels went into a restaurant and ordered take-out for over a thousand. He was about to make real life even more ridiculous.

"Meanwhile," he told them, "I want squads representing all factions sent immediately to start gathering food."

The men looked at each other as if he was crazy. But that was just what Michael wanted.

"I want food Gypsies like, what Indians like and what Penitente like . . . But no alcohol. I want some lamb and pigs roasted . . . a nice dessert . . . enough for, say 10,000," he smiled. "And music . . . I want mingling and dancing.

"You two," he directed the pilot and the Gypsy leader, "will fly into town and pay the money to get everything set up by 11:00. Dinner is at 12:30.

"*Hombres,*" he turned and yelled to the men behind him, "we're going to have a feast!"

The men gave a resounding cheer.

It, Michael thought, would be his coming out party.

He spoke to both Gypsy and Basque, "Tell my two friends that if they want to make a deal, to come to the *morada* at 11:45 precisely. Each can leave whomever they want to protect his stronghold . . . but they'll be missing a great party. Understand, however, no men in the field . . . and I want one of our visitor's choppers disabled. There will be an air inspection on their arrival," he warned. "At noon, each will come with his personal unarmed bodyguard into the *morada* where I will await them. If either is missing," Michael said with a smile, "I will join the party myself and there will be no deal.

"Now, is all this understood?" Michael asked. "Did I leave anything out? Oh, yes . . . The women are invited, too."

Everyone was dumbfounded. All that morning each of them had thought only of death, had tried to steel himself, to prepare for its possibility in his own way. And now, despite lingering apprehensions, they shared a sense of relief. Perhaps it didn't have to happen.

The Gypsy called down a dozen men.

"Are there any trucks nearby?" Michael asked his point man.

The man shook his head in the affirmative.

"Okay," Michael barked, "a driver for the Pueblo, a fast one for Puye and a few for town. Shake them up."

Orders were given. A few Gypsies took the place of two of the copter's passengers and it lifted off. The ground messengers scurried. Michael's off-the-cuff plan was set in motion. And he was as much in wonder as any of them. If he could pull this one off, Michael thought, he could sell them the Brooklyn Bridge to boot.

"What?!" El Conciliador exclaimed. He was . . . He didn't know what he was. He tried to maintain his composure in the presence of the Gypsy and sent someone for the money.

He had to have confidence in his general. After all he *was* pulling the enemy away from his citadel. Mortez felt he could wait to get the upper hand. There was no point in decimating his army until the strategy was clear.

As the copter flew on toward the *hacienda,* the passengers could see the Indian women already moving off from their battle line in the pathway of the Gypsies' closing circle. And as they neared their goal, they could see the Penitente men moving away from their encirclement of the plateau.

The Gypsy radioed in and they were told to land a mile from the *hacienda.* One of Scotia's helicopters went to pick them up.

Scotia laughed and threw in an extra $50,000 to be used on liquor, "Later . . . after the deal is concluded."

When they left, he began to second-guess.

His second copter was being disabled. He didn't like that. And where was the girl? His man had not mentioned her. Nor had the reports from the field. He didn't like not knowing where all the players were.

Scotia had a message transmitted to call off his men and ask for information on the girl. Nadja came in as he was giving his orders.

"You should have killed her," she chided. "Let me go find her."

"You'll go to this *morada* first," he barked back at her, "I want it checked over thoroughly. Then you can do as you please."

She left in a huff and Scotia just shook his head. He wondered why he couldn't trust Stone. But then, how could he ever trust someone like himself?

Scotia wondered also about the treasure. Had his son found it? Was the clue to what he sought there?

As he prepared another dose of his secret elixir, Scotia worked over some contingency plans in his mind. He decided to test his son one more time.

29

By the time Michael arrived at the *morada,* his procession was some 1,200 strong . . . both Penitente and Indian. It was 10:30.

There were more than 1,000 people on the grounds to meet them. Bonfires were ablaze, pits had been dug and the first of the lambs was already spitted. Tables were being set up as quickly as they were unloaded from the trucks. The *Pascua* feast ingredients from hundreds of households were being laid upon them. Gypsies moved freely among Penitente and Indians, everyone elated, yet cautiously wondering what was going to happen.

Mixed patrols had cordoned off the area and searched everyone who entered the boundaries.

Surprisingly, the Gypsies seemed to be enjoying the situation the most. The last few days of being crammed into trucks and vans had gotten to them. They were as hungry as . . . well . . . wolves. Once fed, the prognosis was they would be more docile.

Nadja had finished her inspection of the *morada* and was coming out as Michael dismounted and stretched. She watched as the Penitente approached him in awe. The news had, of course, preceded him. But to actually see him was, for them, an incredible sight. At first they were hesitant, but then rushed to him, cheering.

Michael stood on a low wall extending from the *morada.* He held up his arms and they saw the false wounds on his wrists.

"Rejoice, for He is risen," he exclaimed in a loud voice.

"*¡Aleluya! Aleluya!*" they responded.

Michael was overwhelmed. This was as good as being a rock star. At 36 to be a cult hero. The amazing thing was it seemed natural to him.

Michael climbed down from the wall and went to the entrance where Nadja stood, waiting. They stared into each others eyes.

"Where's the bitch?" she asked caustically.

Michael smiled. He looked over at a dog playing with a stick, then back to her eyes. "In view." He smiled at her again and entered the building.

His coolness grated on Nadja and she stomped off.

The stench of Velenari's body was gone from the *morada.* Michael was glad of that. He watched as the weapons were being loaded into the *piesa.* Although a good size, the room was already more than half full.

The ammunition was being sorted and thrown into barrels of like type. Michael was happy to see some grenades. They were just what he needed.

"I want the windows and doors set so any tampering will explode the arsenal" he ordered. "Only the door to the *capilla* will stay clean."

A few thousand more people were arriving, including the Penitente troops that had surrounded Scotia's compound. In the field to the east, the priest was preparing to say mass.

The Ski Valley was closing today and earlybirds headed back toward Albuquerque had begun taking detours to find out what all the commotion was. The sentries were turning them away, but some complained they had bought tickets from locals in Arroyo Seco. Michael thought that was fabulous.

11:30. Mass was over and the party was getting into full swing. Michael came outside and saw the last Gypsy vans rolling in. Everyone seemed to be there save the "stars."

"Have the guards put their arms inside now," Michael directed. "Then send out vans to block all the main arteries at the closest crossroads. The party is closed."

It was done as he ordered.

11:45. The whirring of helicopter blades. Michael went inside, a big smile on his face.

"Okay. Everybody out," he ordered.

He looked out the window and saw Diana riding up on their horse, followed by Dashwood. They had done it! Now, it was all up to him.

Michael took some line and attached it to a grenade, which he wedged into one of the ammunition barrels. He led the line to the chapel door. Stepping inside the door and using a small clip he had found, Michael attached the line to the latch on the *piesa* side of the door. If anyone pulled it open more than a few inches, the grenade would be detonated.

The copters had touched down and the blades were coming to a stop. Hooded passengers disembarked from each. Somewhere a clock struck noon; time for a meeting.

Michael was amazed at how cool he felt. He had kept himself busy so his mind could not work against him. Action. Perhaps he was becoming a man of action.

El Conciliador came in first with Vincente, who carried a small, wrapped box. Michael gave him a disconcerting wink. He thought it was a silly idea, but his was a strategy of whatever popped into his head and it seemed right. It was like the time he had gone into a client meeting having just learned they had fired another firm for the very proposal he was about to make. He had had to wing it in the same way. And as it was, the gesture had put Mortez at ease. Come to think of it, Michael himself had never been more at ease.

Scotia entered with Victor, who carried a suitcase.

Michael sized up the two giants. Vincente was actually a bit taller and broader, but Victor was younger and seemed meaner, if that were possible. All in all, they looked a pretty even match . . . if it came to that.

Each bodyguard searched the other, and then each other's boss. Finally, they both searched Michael. The suitcase and the small box were placed on the table. The Summit of Evil had begun.

"Well, gentlemen," Michael said, animatedly, "if everyone's satisfied . . . Happy Easter. Now why don't we remove our hoods and get down to business. Radu Scotia . . . Ramon Mortez. Victor . . . Vincente. Sit down, please. I love parties, don't you?"

Scotia played along, but Mortez was not amused as the two, now unmasked, stared at each other. Michael noted El Conciliador was hooked by the bloodspot. Scotia did, too.

"You neglected to mention the diamonds, but I came prepared," THE ONE said, indicating the suitcase.

"My apologies," Michael offered. "These last minute parties are murder to prepare and I completely forgot the favors. I hope we can conclude matters quickly so we, too, can join the festivities."

"That would be fine with me," Scotia agreed.

"And me," Mortez responded, breaking away from his gaze.

"Good," Michael smiled. "I was getting the feeling things were becoming strained even before we had a chance to meet. That's why I wanted to remove all the tension, not to mention the bullets . . . and bullshit.

"First of all, I think we're all here under false pretenses," Michael said disarmingly. "El Conciliador here thinks I wanted to join the Penitente to help him make the Church his own pre-eminent domain to stand against whatever he considers evil. So, Mr. Scotia, once you turned over your diamonds, he wanted me to kill you."

Mortez crimsoned and Vincente stood up.

"Relax . . . relax, Ramon," Michael said calmly. "You see, Mr. Scotia here actually engineered my coming so he could get inside knowledge of the scope and authenticity of your wealth because what he really wants is a secret drug, the formula to which may be found marked on some item of your purported treasure. This formula would be used to subjugate all of Christendom while *he* sat as pope, presumably with you as one of his cardinals."

Scotia sat stone-faced as Michael continued, "Both of you have offered sizable payments for my services; so, in a sense, I stand to do very well whatever the outcome."

THE ONE spoke, "You are, of course, renowned for your incorrigibility. Now that you have embarrassed us, let's do business."

"Another reason for the party," Michael said. "I didn't want this to be a wasted trip. You see, I've found the cave where the Aztec treasure is supposed to be . . . the one with the tunnel leading to the natural atrium in front of the ancient temple . . . "

Mortez gasped.

"You should have studied your history, Ramon," Michael chided. "There is a key to its location, you know."

While Mortez tried to regain his composure, Michael continued. "Now, I didn't get to spend much time there, but then, there really was no need. The cupboard was bare. I mean, the paintings and the tapestry were hardly worth the trip. Did you think you could con a man like Radu Scotia, Ramon? Although, to be fair," he smiled, "who knows much about Radu Scotia?"

Mortez could contain himself no longer, "You fool. Did you think I would have it laying in the open? The treasure is there. Priceless items, like this . . . "

He picked up the small box and slammed it down. Michael calmly unwrapped and opened the package.

"What have we here?" he mused as he drew out a golden dagger inset with jade.

"As I say," Michael repeated, " I wasn't there long, but I

was thorough. Ahh . . . very nice. I assume this is a gift for you, Mr. Scotia."

Mortez grabbed the dagger away from Michael and offered it to Scotia. "The treasure's there. One simply has to know how to get to it."

Scotia took the dagger and examined it, "I'd like to verify that for myself."

The two old men glared at each other again. At that moment El Conciliador felt he understood what was going on. Stone was drawing Scotia into a trap. He either knew of the weapons he had hidden there or, at least, wanted to get them to a place where they could take the advantage. He held Scotia's stare without regard to the red eye.

"Be my guest," El Conciliador offered, smiling with confidence.

"Perhaps I might have overlooked something," Michael acknowledged, "but I wanted to set up the game rules. You see, if there's nothing there, I wanted to explore Mr. Scotia's financing the Church's takeover anyway. With Mortez's contacts, your money and my help, it could be done.

"So there was no reason for anyone to act in anger or spill a lot of blood," Michael concluded. "This, after all, is business. Agreed?" he asked, looking at the attentive faces around the table. "Good. Now, let's negotiate.

"Normally, I would ask for a ten percent finder's fee from both sides. However, I have not fulfilled our agreement, Ramon. So if I am mistaken about the treasure, I will take no fee from you."

Michael turned to Scotia, "Our arrangement, on the other hand, has been fulfilled. So from you, I expect ten percent of those diamonds if there is no treasure or ten percent on top of what you pay for it, if there is one.

"And if you two decide to work together, I want five percent of your joint holdings for my permanent services.

"But whatever happens," he looked from one to the other, ". . . no reprisals. Agreed?"

Michael sat back. He wanted to release a sigh, but he had to hold his pose. This, after all, was a business deal and even though the stakes had never been this high, he had been through hundreds.

"Agreed," Mortez hissed.

Scotia was more enthusiastic. "Let's drink to it."

Victor stood and opened the satchel containing the diamonds. He removed a bottle of vintage wine and, although it was sealed, Michael was sure he knew what it included.

"Let's hold off on that," Michael said. "I'm going to fly the helicopter to where we are going, and it's been awhile since I handled one. We'll take it with us."

Scotia was not sure why his son wouldn't let him take control of Mortez now. But this was the young man's show and so far, he had to admit it was brilliant. As for the treasure, either his son couldn't find it and had goaded the volatile old man to lead them to it . . . or it didn't exist and there was no "magic" formula. Until now, Scotia had never really considered the latter. Perhaps it *had* been exhausted. In that case, would he be willing to finance a takeover of the papacy with his own money? He'd have to think about it.

The group emerged from the *morada* to cheers from all factions. The hooded men waved back.

"Which chopper?" Michael asked.

"Mine is more comfortable," Scotia responded.

"Which can you fly?" Mortez asked.

"Good point. I think Ramon is more sensible on this," Michael said to Scotia. "Have yours disabled. We don't want to be followed by any zealots."

Scotia reluctantly gave the order. He sensed he had somehow blown an opportunity by speaking too quickly. Was his son, perhaps, smarter than he?

They boarded the aircraft. Michael saw Diana watching and froze. He suddenly had the feeling he would never see her again.

He nervously reached for the controls and tried to focus.

Things had been moving smoothly, but he didn't know what would happen now. Funny, he hadn't thought of what his brother would do all morning. And he had done all right by himself to this point. Hadn't he?

But what now?

Goddamn it, why did he get these thoughts? Michael took a deep breath and tried to regain his composure. He was wrong. He *would* see Diana again.

30

They were in the air five minutes before Michael realized he must have subconsciously studied the pilot on his previous trip to the Foundation. He found it easy . . . far easier than what he had been used to in Cambodia. Right now, it didn't seem so long ago.

Michael remembered his oath never to kill anyone. He had made it with some other medics with Conscientious Objector status. Until this week, he had kept that oath, memory or not. Now he wondered if it had a release date?

It looked to Michael as if Scotia was enjoying himself. Michael thought he probably spent most of his time cooped up in Transylvania. He smiled. That's really where Scotia lived. What was funnier was Radu wanted *him* to live there. The family business.

The great thing about helicopters, Michael thought, was the noise. It precluded conversation. It allowed him to be alone with his thoughts.

How the hell was he going to be able to kill them? He could

take the whole chopper down. But Michael wasn't ready for that level of commitment. In fact, he was back to not being sure of any level.

It was a relief to see the landmarks. He didn't have to think anymore.

As they climbed over the rocks and down into the cul-de-sac, Michael related the Aztec history without references to Dashwood or the disc. He presented it more as supposition and legend.

The two old men listened intently while the bodyguards kept their vigil for anything amiss.

Michael pointed out the key . . . Bel's eye . . . and they entered the tunnel with pulses beating rapidly . . . all for different reasons.

For Michael, it was not at all like earlier that morning. Each step, he now felt, was bringing him closer to death. He couldn't, therefore, believe the tour spiel coming out of his mouth. What crap, he thought. Who the hell was this guy doing all the talking? He was dying of fear and some idiot was using his mouth to carry on about ancient Aztecs and Celts. If only he could have sorted himself out like this long ago.

El Conciliador's refuge was being invaded and it was obvious he did not at all like it.

"Welcome," he said, but it was a sufferance.

They entered the temple . . . the tomb. For Michael, it took all the strength of his will to cross the threshold. He wanted to run, for he felt it would become his tomb as well.

"What did I say?" he asked, gesturing to the empty cavern. "Nothing."

"Of course not," Mortez bellowed, feeling on top of things again. "I will show it to you, Mr. Scotia, but first I would like to see the diamonds."

Scotia snapped his fingers and Victor brought the suitcase across the chamber to Vincente. The latter took hold of the case while Victor unsnapped and opened it.

What was inside was not as amazing as what happened next. As attention was focused on the $10 million in stones, Victor grabbed hold of Vincente's chin and the back of his head. With a powerful twist, he turned the man's head almost 130 degrees. A loud crack was heard as the neck bones snapped. Vincente and all the stones tumbled to the ground.

"Don't be alarmed," Scotia assured. "It's just a demonstration, my friends, of the fact I don't like to be earmarked for assassination.

"There is only one who leads; and that ONE is me. Now," he said, turning to Michael, "I pledged there would be no reprisal on my host and I will abide by it. I'm here to deal . . . Let's deal."

There was an edge to his voice not there last evening. It was the edge of certain power.

As the two old men glared at each other, Michael realized The Bruja was right; the Devil had two faces. In a cave in New Mexico they had come together . . . the evil of the mind and the evil of the senses. *This* was the union The Bruja feared in the abstract . . . the one that could tip the world's balance toward malevolence and enslave millions.

Mortez showed no fear, but Scotia bettered him by showing no emotion whatsoever. "Children of Darkness," The Bruja had said.

In Scotia's void there was no right or wrong . . . nor belief. There was only pragmatic action.

Mortez, on the other hand, was imbedded with belief . . . a warped belief he could irradicate free will by imprisoning men's minds . . . for the greater glory of himself, who had replaced the God he didn't accept.

The air was heavy with their polluted vibrations. Michael knew he was trembling. He was afraid. And he thought his fear was of them.

"That will cost you," Mortez finally hissed.

"What?" Scotia taunted. "A new bodyguard? I'll give you a good one. Let's see the merchandise . . . please."

El Conciliador did not know whether he was now totally on his own, whether Stone was allied with Scotia or everyone was simply out for himself. However, he had no choice but to show them the treasure. For the moment, he was at their mercy.

Scotia knew Mortez realized this. It was the realization he had wanted.

"I don't steal . . . I deal," he assured Mortez.

El Conciliador went toward the crucifix. Michael's heart started pounding so loudly, he was sure it could be heard across the chamber. Scotia's bodyguard was brutal. There would be little opportunity to try to retrieve the gun under the table.

He broke into a cold sweat. Which side? He had forgotten on which side of the table he had told Diana to place the gun.

Michael was unable to think. Perspiration dripped into his eyes. He couldn't even see.

As attention focused on Mortez, Michael backed up against the table and sat against it, trying to feel underneath with his fingertips. The sweat on his fingers made them slide along the wood.

He could feel nothing near the edge and it became awkward to reach back any farther. Michael wondered how he could possibly hold anything anyway.

The door to the chamber opened as the tapestry swung away. There was a look of glee on Mortez's face—a look that slowly shattered into a million pieces as he peered within.

There was nothing except for a few gold masks hanging on the inside of the door. They looked as if they were laughing at him.

"*You* . . . ," he growled, turning to Michael.

It sounded like a voice from the pit. If Michael had not been propped up against the table, it would have made his legs give way.

"*You* did this . . . ," Mortez accused.

Michael froze. Not answering was the right thing to do, but he did not because he could not.

El Conciliador moved toward him, speaking in a strange, almost unnatural voice, "Where . . . ? Where is it?"

"If there were a few coins," Michael said softly, " . . . or small pieces, I might have put them in my pockets. But there was nothing when I found it . . . except those masks. What are they worth . . . half a million? Not even enough for me."

Victor went over and looked inside. Michael used the movement as his opportunity to push away from the table and walk to the other side.

"Face it, old man," he said caustically, "you set up this meeting because you exhausted it all."

Mortez moved back toward the head of the table. His teeth were clenched and his arms flailed about, "No . . . no . . . It was there."

Scotia moved to where Michael had been standing, "Let's put our cards on the table . . ."

Mortez reached under the table and drew forth the cyanide pellet and mask. He clasped the mask to his face and tried to trigger the pellet. But nothing happened. He looked ludicrous.

Michael's fingers trembled. His knees were caving in and his breath was coming in spurts. It had to be NOW.

Still, he hesitated. Why not let them fight it out . . . become a son or general? But how could he live up to it? That's the question that plagued him. He couldn't even act now.

There had to be a time when play-acting ended and Michael Esmund-Stone-Scotia began. He reached under the table. The gun was there. It was in his grasp. He pulled it loose as Victor moved toward the astonished old man. Michael raised the firearm automatically. It seemed so very heavy and time slowed to a crawl. Victor looked at him and broke stride. There was a flash. Michael could see . . . actually see . . . the bullet fly past Mortez and strike the giant in the upper part of his right shoulder. The impact moved the shoulder back slightly, but the big man continued to move forward.

There were another few flashes as Michael saw Scotia's face turn in his direction. The bullets struck Victor in the chest area, but seemed to have little impact. Three more in his belly merely made the giant break stride momentarily.

Michael could barely hear the shots above the pounding of his heart. Where was this guy vulnerable? He wondered if he were wearing a protector? Oh, God!! . . . He raised the barrel. Another few flashes. Impact in the left side of the man's neck.

Blood oozed. The next two shots were fired at a distance of five feet. Both struck the inner corner of Victor's left eye. The head snapped back and the huge man fell back against the table. Michael fired twice more into the man's head. He felt his arm beginning to shake, and lowered the gun.

Scotia's eyes were ablaze with anger and powerlessness.

There was a pause while time returned to its normal pace. Then, Michael spoke in a hoarse voice, "This was supposed to be a truce. I don't like anyone . . . ANYONE . . . changing my rules," he said with intensity.

The thumping in his chest was subsiding. Michael thought of the number of bullets he fired. He had never had a chance to count how many were in the clip. How many did a gun like this hold, he wondered? The Lone Ranger only had six. He had already fired twelve. Michael tried to think back. Clips had either thirteen or sixteen . . . or did it depend on the gun?

If it was a full clip to begin with, he could only count for sure on there being one left. One bullet to kill two devils. At best, he could rid the world of half its evil. Which half was the question.

A smile slipped across Michael's face. It gave him time to think, to postpone.

He had just felled an attacking giant, but could he kill in cold blood? The juices were flowing, but Michael didn't think he could do it.

He turned to Mortez. "Put it down, amateur. I may need that mask to get away from your stench."

Michael tipped up one side of the table so Victor's massive corpse slid off at Mortez's feet.

"Sit down . . . both of you," he demanded as he put the gun on the table.

Michael wanted desperately to clear his throat, but he did not want to betray his fear.

"Put the dagger on the table," he said to Scotia.

Radu smiled and took the dagger from his coat. He placed it on the table and pushed it toward Michael hilt first.

"I don't think you two can be trusted," he lectured.

"I don't think any of us can be trusted," Radu retorted.

"Me?" Michael shrugged. "I'm just a referee. I don't play by the rules . . . I *am* the rules."

Michael noticed Scotia's lip quiver as he forced a smile. The man had never been in such a situation. He obviously didn't like it. But Michael did . . . immeasurably.

"Kill him," Mortez yelled, his face contorted in rage.

"I assume you no longer want to deal," Michael said calmly. "Then I'll kill one of you and deal with the other.

"What do you have to offer me?" he asked Mortez.

"He is a menace to all mankind with his drugs," El Conciliador screamed. "You can't side with him . . . You are a Penitente."

"Yes," Michael agreed. "*I* am a Penitente. I am a brother in a society you have corrupted for your own ends . . . "

"No," argued Mortez. "For the power of The Holy Church . . . so the world could be rid of vermin like this. There would be no more drugs . . . no more Scotias."

"And I am to become your general," Michael iterated. "The Scourge for God."

The old man shook his head, "After me, *you* will be El Conciliador. Kill him now and we will share these diamonds to strengthen our cause."

"Then there is no treasure, is there?" Michael tried to force the words into Mortez's mouth.

The old man could not understand. Hadn't he been the one who stole it? What was the motive in his question? Or could it have possibly been someone else? If that was the case, then why should this assassin know of it. He was demanding enough for his services.

"No . . . just those remain," he acquiesced.

"And the bullion in your bank," Michael clarified.

Would he ask a share of that, too, Mortez wondered.

"*Some* bullion in the bank," the old man said with false humility.

"But he offers me so much more," Michael retorted. "The

chance to be his heir . . . To deal with the scum surrounding him. To be a lord over pimps and pushers and lowlife of every imaginable type. To be their patriarch; to decide when they should live and when they should die. Five million is just pocket money . . . my allowance . . . Right, father?"

His father? Mortez was shocked by this new information.

And "Father" Scotia did not like the tone of the his son's voice. Where was he leading? Radu was beginning to feel like the high priest at Nemi being stalked by his successor. He could barely force a smile.

Mortez rose and moved toward the wall. "I can't believe you would go against your own beliefs."

He turned back to Michael, "The men you have assassinated . . . they were men like him. Take all the diamonds, but rid the world of him."

Mortez turned and took the painting of Christ off the wall, "Look at Him and see the truth of what you must do."

Even though Michael knew exactly what Mortez was doing, the old man had done it so well he made no response. The painting slipped to the ground and Mortez held the small gun concealed behind it.

"Look at this and see the truth of what I must do," Mortez beamed, "for undoubtedly you have forgotten our discussion. Or perhaps . . . "

A light seemed to go on in El Conciliador's mind. Michael guessed what it was. Mortez realized he may have had the conversation with the twin. Too bad, Michael thought; he had just come to the decision it wasn't his duty to rid the world of its evil. His only duty was to himself. And now the old man was forcing him to defend that duty . . . the duty to protect his identity. Self-preservation.

Michael reached for the gun on the table. The small pistol in Mortez's hand clicked in futility as Michael raised his and fired a single shot into El Conciliador's temple. The body flew against the wall and slipped to the ground.

"Or perhaps you were too gullible," Michael finished the

dead man's sentence. "I told him I checked thoroughly," he said, looking at Scotia.

There was one thing Michael hoped he would never do in life . . . murder. This week it was forced upon him. No, two things actually. Neither on a conscious or subconscious level had he ever wanted to accept an identity. He had done that, too.

All his adult life he had been trying to survive rather than find something to which he could commit himself. Now he knew discovering his past and accepting himself would not necessarily change this reality. There was more to this lack of commitment. He had thought his failure to metamorphosize into some higher self was due to a fear he was not of the same stuff as those supposed greater "others," i.e., fathers, heros, authorities, Mortezes, Scotias . . . But it had really been more a fear of removing all internal boundaries, of looking at the other side of himself . . . the unknown. And the only real payoff for overcoming that kind of fear was clearer vision . . . seeing fear is groundless and realizing one can achieve the "sacred" . . . the possible. There was, also, the realization all those outside others were no different than he was. Even THE ONE . . . especially THE ONE . . . was no more than a shitting, pissing, fucking human being. Check that. Could he even copulate anymore?

The Bruja had been right; knowing oneself wasn't enough. To really be a part of life, one had to become a man of action.

But had he acted correctly? Had he shot the right man? Had he just acted to selfishly protect his own identity? Michael really didn't know. Yet he supposed he could as easily have shot Scotia if that was the case.

Beyond his knee problem, Michael had suffered migraines and back spasms in his life. At times they all had made him feel he wanted to die. But the headaches were the worst. Perhaps, likewise, the evil of the mind was worse than the evil of the body. There would always be the Dionysians . . . the Scotias . . . who would sell the joystick to those who wanted it. It was a tradition of evil that would exist as long as mankind. It was a going overboard on the things sensual, the things of this world . . . the Darkness that went into the balance with the glories of life. It was the part of himself he would never before yet could, now, learn to confront. But the Hitlers and the Mortezes were the fanatics who could pollute the minds of entire peoples. Their Darkness robbed men's souls of all hope of balance. He had acted correctly. If you only have one shot, go for the head. Besides, he really wasn't into patricide. At least, not today.

Michael looked over at Scotia. Was it wishful thinking or did he notice some other common features? And what was his real mother like? Better than . . . too good for his father.

"He was out of his depth," Scotia shrugged. "Now, where is it?"

"Where is what?" Michael asked.

"The treasure," Radu demanded impatiently.

"There is nothing," Michael said with casual emphasis. "Certainly not if it was supposed to be here."

"Then it was a hustle?" Scotia asked incredulously. "For a lousy ten million dollars?!"

"As you said, he was out of his depth. How about you?" Michael asked.

Scotia tightened, "I'm beginning not to like you."

"Fine," was Michael's reaction. "I've decided I work better alone. I don't need a father."

Scotia started to panic, fearing the worst. "You think I walk into a place without a backup? If my men are not contacted at the stroke of every hour, your party will be over . . . There will be much bloodshed. Your woman will be killed. And you will be hunted by every member of Metamorphosis. You are not the only one considered to replace me. THE ONE will survive and make a terrible example of you."

"Calm down and act like a man," Michael reprimanded.

Scotia's teeth clenched as tightly as his fists.

"You didn't listen," Michael clarified. "I told you I would kill one and deal with the other. Here's my deal . . . Live and let live. I don't want to be your son. I don't want your diamonds. I didn't want anything from him, either. What I want is . . . me.

"So, you go back to Transylvania and beat off playing devil-god. Can you beat off, Scotia?" he taunted.

THE ONE was speechless.

"Your life has never been in danger here," Michael assured him. "Would you believe it? I had more to fear from him. Besides, I don't think I'd want you dead anyway. You I can handle. It's the unknown that causes problems. Anyway . . . I don't hurt women . . . and that's what I consider anyone without balls."

Michael limped out of the cave and through the atrium. The sun was high in the sky. It was warming.

Scotia came to the mouth of the cave and yelled after him. "No one walks away from me. No one outside of Metamorphosis can know of me and live. I'll come after you."

Michael turned, "Oh, you can try. But I advise you to forget it. Face it, Scotia," he smirked, "you're just dealing with the wrong man."

Michael tossed the gun and the jeweled dagger to the ground and walked through the tunnel and up the slope to the helicopter, wondering if Scotia would ever figure out the irony in his last phrase.

It wasn't until he heard the whir of the blades that Scotia noticed the gun lying near the sacrificial altar. As the helicopter rose and came into sight for a brief second, he fired the remaining three shots.

Michael heard the reports and laughed, while below Scotia hurled the empty gun at the altar and vowed revenge.

Meanwhile, Michael could hardly concentrate on the flying he was so excited. He had done it! And he had escaped! If only Diana had gotten to the Pueblo . . .

He circled to the northeast so as not to be seen from the *morada.*

The clock on the control panel showed one o'clock. Suddenly the copter reverberated from the shock waves of a terrible explosion.

31

"He did it!" Diana shouted from the van as she passed the binoculars to Dashwood.

"Shall we go back?" Alex questioned.

"No," she said, "Let's get this over with. Shadow will meet him."

Alex reached over Red Fox's shoulder and started honking the horn.

Michael's attention was drawn to the column of smoke to the south and he did not notice the van as it went up the road to the Ski Valley.

In a few minutes, he touched down inside the Pueblo compound. His heart was thumping again. He knew Scotia's people would be on his tail. He hoped Diana and Alex had come up with a good disappearing act for him.

As he got out of the cockpit, Michael noticed a leak in the fuel tank. One of Scotia's bullets had hit it.

Coyoteman's brother ran out to meet him.

"Where is she?" Michael demanded.

"You're to wait here," Shadow told him. "They will be back soon."

"You don't understand," Michael pleaded. "They're in danger. I've got to get to them."

Shadow was stoic.

"Look," argued Michael, "you don't want to lose your cousins, too, do you?"

That was the last thing the young man wanted.

"They took Stone's body up to the Ski Valley. They will have him found as you."

Michael climbed back into the copter.

"Wait. I'll go with you," the young Indian said.

The barriers in front of the Pueblo entrance were moved to allow a number of speeding vehicles entrance. A jeep zoomed over to them and screeched to a halt.

The young Indian driver got out, shouting. "You should have seen it . . . It was incredible! Some Gypsies tried to get into the *piesa.* Oh, man, the *morada* is totally blown away. About a dozen Gypsies got killed. Lots of them got hurt. But now it's a standoff. No one has any guns. Most are leaving, but a lot are still partyin'. It's bizarre, man," he laughed.

"About five squad cars from Santa Fe showed up as we left. Everyone's running every which way and they don't know what to make of it. It's real funny, man."

Michael was relieved to hear there was no bloodbath going on. He wanted to prevent another.

They took off with him worrying about the fuel leak. He wondered whether they could make it.

"Go straight east," Shadow recommended.

The wind was blustering as they neared the mountains.

"What's happened to my brother's body?" the young Indian asked.

"I don't know for sure," Michael answered. "I think the Gypsies brought it to their compound. We'll go there when Scotia leaves."

"*We* will go there," Shadow said with an inflection excluding Michael. "You must disappear now. And the treasure must remain hidden until The Bruja decides it is safe. Then, you will get your share."

"No thanks," Michael said, looking at him. "No gifts, no tokens, no souvenirs . . . Just memories. That's all I want."

Good ones, he still hoped.

They had made it above the lower peaks leading to the Ski Valley. Michael was pushing as hard as he could, but the fuel gauge was falling toward empty.

"Come on, baby," he pleaded while his mind raced over the possibilities. What other contingencies had Scotia made? How much time would they have? His mind stopped on a dime . . .

Nadja . . .

She stood there with an Astra automatic pointed at them.

"Come in. Come in," Nadja beckoned. "I've been waiting for you."

The two Indians had not noticed her in the loft as they carried Stone's body through the door of Michael's room. Diana and Alex were also across the threshold before they were aware of the machine gun. Diana cursed under her breath. Why hadn't her intuition signaled Nadja's presence?

"What have we here?" the Gypsy woman continued. "Close the door and let's have a peek."

They unwrapped Stone's body on the floor.

"Well, well," she exclaimed as she descended the ladder, ". . . that explains a lot. My uncle will be amused. Step forward, bitch," she ordered Diana.

There was a silence cut only by the now audible whirring sound of helicopter blades. Nadja pointed the weapon directly at Diana and started to squeeze the trigger.

"Diana!" Michael shouted from outside.

Michael was running up the bank behind the chalet. His shout distracted Nadja for an instant and Diana used the opportunity to dive at her. Bullets riddled the ceiling as they wrestled for the gun.

Michael had rounded the building and was taking the steps by twos.

Coyoteman's cousins joined the struggle and the group toppled over the booby-trapped bed.

Suddenly Michael felt himself flying from the balcony and tumbling in mid air. His mind flashed back to Cambodia and somewhere a voice was calling, "No . . . not again . . . "

His body slammed into the snow bank. Fiery pieces of debris began to shower him. He looked at the inferno above as he slipped into unconsciousness.

* * *

A squad of naked men was moving in unison. Michael wasn't observing them; he was, in succession, each one of them observing the others. And they all looked the same. Each held a spray can which shot out fine fibers. One after another they used these to wrap themselves in warm, shell-like enclosures.

* * *

A shot of pain brought Michael to consciousness. He felt it through the entire lower half of his body. But it wasn't the only sensation. There were also walls closing in about his head.

Michael opened his eyes and realized his face was enveloped by the bandage mask. Eli and Shadow were standing over him. They had just set his leg back into place. His head, back . . . everything throbbed.

"That's a good fellow," Eli said. "It's time to go."

Michael saw he was in his brother's room, stripped of his own clothes and half dressed in his twin's.

"I'm afraid they're all dead," Eli told him, soberly. "Braden must have booby-trapped your room . . . he or Stone. Anyway, it's Stone's remains they'll find with the others."

Michael felt as if a huge hole had been punched through his stomach. Diana . . .

"No one saw us bring you here," said Shadow. "Only we know you're alive."

Michael sat up with difficulty even though he felt numb.

"I'm sorry about your cousins," he offered.

The Indian lowered his head, "The Great Spirit had his reasons."

What were His reasons for robbing him of his friends, his love? Michael wondered.

"Finish dressing," Eli said. "You've got a bus to catch in ten minutes.

"Here's a little cash," the old tracker said. "And this is from Dashwood."

Eli handed Michael a golden medallion.

"Alex was blown clear of the fire," Eli related. "Before he died, he told me to give it to you in payment for making his findings known someday. It's not Aztec, but Middle Eastern . . . So it won't be linked. I have the name of someone in New York who will pay dearly for it. It will give you a start."

"What about you?" Michael asked.

"Who me . . . 'White Shadow?' I'll be around," Eli winked.

Vehicles passed along the Ski Valley road: a bus heading south, a firetruck and Gypsy vans heading north. The shadow of a helicopter also crossed the bus's path.

"When do you get them off?" the child next to Michael asked, referring to the bandages.

Michael was startled. He had felt as if he had been holding his breath the last half hour, not wishing to breathe freely until he was truly out of danger. Or would that ever be the case?

"As soon as I get home," Michael finally answered.

He lay back his head. Where was home?

Michael thought back to the hospital in Saigon. His head had been bandaged then, too. Taking off this mask would be like emerging from a similar cocoon . . . except this time he would have changed back into who he really was. Completely. From here on there would be no more masks.

He thought of Diana and Alex. He loved them both. What's more, they were also family. The closest thing to a family he had ever had. And he grieved.

There was a traffc jam from Arroyo Seco all the way through to the south end of Taos. The party was over and everyone was going home. But Michael took no notice. He was overwhelmed with sadness.

Sometime later they passed a church at Tesuque. A sensation ran through the scars on Michael's back as he broke from his mourning trance to look out the window.

The One True Church . . . The One assassin . . . *the one* drug . . . Brother One . . . THE ONE . . . They were not bigger than, only parts of a process by which he had come to recognize himself.

"The one who is not The One, but may be THE ONE."

Well, that he had become . . . though, thankfully, not in the way his father may have wanted. His identity was his ONEness. And action . . . his saving of many innocent lives . . . had made this ONEness part of the whole. The riddle had been answered. Michael leaned back in his seat, proud of himself at last.

The bus slipped by Santa Fe.

He wondered what Meredith was doing.

Epilogue

In the months following the events in Taos, the Vatican was rife with financial scandal. Mortez's Milan bank folded and confusion abounded. It was some time before any semblance of stability could be reestablished.

The Light's investigation put together many of the pieces of the Velenari/Mortez conspiracy and, with the Pope's blessing, many of their men were uncovered and removed from office. Father Vittorio became exhausted almost to the point of illness trying to root out the long chain of corruption.

Fortunately, the Guardian had some unseen angel who fed him information whenever he thought he was at a dead end. It was just as well the angel was unseen . . . or at least, unheard. The cleric might not have appreciated his boisterous humor.

There were attempts at retaliation against the Pontiff, including an assassination plot, but fortunately those commissioned were rank amateurs compared to The One. They only succeeded in revealing more of the Church's cancer to the indefatigable Guardian.

Meanwhile, in a county of some 6,000 households, neither the CIA nor the FBI could find one person who had been at the largest party in Taos's history—this, despite their best efforts to infiltrate. The intelligence community was able to conclude not much more than, in what was probably a drug-related incident, they had lost three agents.

In the fall, a young Indian enrolled at Berkeley to major in anthropology. Long letters from his aged aunt kept up his spirits as he adjusted to his new lifestyle. After awhile Shadow felt quite comfortable . . . except, of course, when the moon was full.

Theresa Kittinger continued her painting in earnest and the following winter she won her first art contest. Oddly enough, it was for a work entitled Balance.

The only official outside of a small northwestern Connecticut town who took note of Michael Esmund was an IRS agent the following year. The reason was due to the sharp decline in income reported on his tax form. Most likely, the agent thought, Mr. Esmund was another victim of the recession.

And until the patient had recovered enough to be moved to the Aslan Institute in Bucharest for plastic surgery, the records at the burn clinic of a renowned Zurich hospital showed monthly visits for over a year by a Romanian gentleman who went by the name of Herr Scott.

He had lost a niece and a son, but Radu Scotia believed fate had left an open trap door for a reason. He would, therefore, stop at no expense to rehabilitate the only known survivor of his visit to America . . . the young woman he had come to admire, his "adopted daughter," Diana.

Brian Porzak lives in northwestern Connecticut where he is at work on his next novel, PRESIDENTIAL IMPERATIVE.